How hard is the fortune of all womankind,
Forever subjected, forever confined,
The parent controls us until we are wives,
The husband enslaves us the rest of our lives.

('The Ladies' Case', *trad*. C18th English song)

The Misbegotten

Katherine Webb

An Orion paperback

First published in Great Britain in 2013
by Orion
This paperback edition published in 2013
by Orion Books,
an imprint of The Orion Publishing Group Ltd,
Orion House, 5 Upper St Martin's Lane,
London WC2H 9EA

An Hachette UK company

1 3 5 7 9 10 8 6 4 2

Copyright © Katherine Webb 2013

A CIP catalogue record for this book
is available from the British Library.
ISBN 978-1-4091-3590-6

Printed and bound in Great Britain by
Clays Ltd, St Ives plc

The Orion Publishing Group's policy is to use papers that
are natural, renewable and recyclable products and
made from wood grown in sustainable forests. The logging
and manufacturing processes are expected to conform to
the environmental regulations of the country of origin.

www.orionbooks.co.uk

Thy heart is bound to another,
Wound tight, like a lovers' tree;
Both may fall, but not one, or the other;
In between finds no place for me.
So let me, then, like a briar rose be —
And grow myself around both of thee.

1803

The day the child walked in from the marsh was one of deadening cold. A north wind had blown steadily all day, making ears and chests and bones ache; the child's bare feet crackled through a crust of ice on the watery ground. She came slowly towards the farmhouse from the west, with the swollen river sliding silently beside her and the sun hanging low over her shoulder, baleful and milky as a blind eye. A young woman quit the farmhouse and crossed the yard towards the chicken coop. She didn't see the child at first, as she wrapped her shawl tightly around her shoulders and turned her face to the sky, to watch a vast murmuration of starlings that was coming to roost in the horse chestnut tree. The birds chattered and squealed to one another, shifting in flight like a single amorphous being, like smoke, before they vanished as one into the naked branches.

The child kept walking, right through the gate and into the yard. She faltered when the young woman did notice her and call out – not hearing the words, just the sound, which startled her. She stopped, and swayed on her feet. The farmhouse was large, built of pale stone. Smoke scattered from its chimneys, and through the windows of the lower floor a warm yellow light shone out onto the muddy ground. That light pulled irresistibly at the child, as it would a moth. It spoke of heat, of shelter; the possibility of food. With jagged little steps she continued towards it. The yard ran slightly uphill towards the house and the effort of the climb caused her to zigzag, stumbling left and right. She was so close, so nearly able to put out her hand and soak it in that golden glow. But then she fell, and did not rise again. She heard the young woman cry out in alarm, and felt herself handled, gathered up. Then she felt nothing more for a time.

The child woke later because of the pain in her hands and feet. The unfamiliar warmth of her blood caused them to itch and throb and tingle unbearably. She tried to fidget, but was held too tightly. She opened her eyes. The young woman from the yard now held her on her lap, wrapped in a blanket. Beside them, a fire roared in a cavernous fireplace. The heat and light were staggering. There was a beamed ceiling over her head, and lambent candles on a nearby shelf, and it seemed like another world.

'You cannot mean to put her out – not with it so cold!' said the young woman. Her voice was soft, but passionate. The child looked up at her and saw a face of such loveliness that she thought it might be an angel that held her. The angel's hair was very, very pale, the colour of fresh cream. Her eyes were huge and soft, and very blue, fringed with long lashes like tiny golden feathers; she had high cheek-bones, an angular jaw, and a pointed chin gentled by the hint of a dimple in it.

'She's a vagabond, make no mistake about it.' This was an older voice, grim in tone.

'What does that matter? She's a child, and she'll surely die if she spends another night without shelter, and food. Look – look at her! Nothing but bones, like some poor chick cast out of the nest.' The young woman looked down, saw that the child was awake, and smiled.

'She'll be unlatching the door for her people in the night – you mark my words. She'll let them in and they'll carry off everything we have, including your virtue!'

'Oh, Bridget! Don't be so frightened, always! You're a

slave to your suspicions. She will do no such thing – she's just a child! An innocent.'

'There's none so innocent in this house as you, Miss Alice,' Bridget muttered. 'I speak from prudence, not from fear. Which way did she come?'

'I don't know. One moment she was not there, the next, she was.' The young woman pulled a feather from the child's hair with her fingertips. 'It was like the starlings brought her.'

'That's naught but fancy. She'll be crawling with lice and vermin – don't hold her so close to you! Can't you smell the rot on her?'

'How can you speak like that about a child, Bridget? Have you no heart?' Alice cradled the child closer to her, protectively. The child pressed her ear to Alice's chest, and heard the way her heart raced, even though she seemed calm. It raced and it faltered and it stumbled over itself. She felt the rapid rise and fall of breath beneath her saviour's ribs. 'To put her out would be tantamount to murder. Infanticide! I will not do it. And neither will you.'

For a moment, the two women glared at one another. Then Bridget got up from her chair and folded her scrawny arms.

'So be it, and on your head the consequences, miss,' she said.

'Good. Thank you, Bridget. Will you kindly fetch her some soup? She must be hungry.' Only once the older woman had left the room did Alice relax a little, and press her spare hand to her chest. She looked down at the child and smiled again. 'Arguing with Bridget always sets my heart stammering,' she said breathlessly. 'What's your name, little one?' But the child could not reply. Her tongue felt frozen in her mouth, and her mind was too crowded with the sensations of heat and tingling. 'You need have no fear now. You will be safe and warm here, and you will have food. Oh, look

– here's another!' Alice said, teasing a second feather from the child's hair. 'We shall call you Starling for now.' Starling gazed at this angel and in that instant forgot everything – where she had been, who she belonged to, her name before, and the hunger raking at her insides. She forgot everything but that she loved Alice, and would stay with her always, and do everything to please her. Then she slept.

1821

The day of the wedding was one of signs and portents. Rachel tried not to see them, since the higher half of her mind knew better than to believe in them, but still they kept coming. She could well imagine her mother scolding such frailty of thought, but with a smile to soften the words. *Nerves, my dear. 'Tis nothing but a touch of nerves.* Nevertheless, Rachel kept seeing them, and the signs seemed like warnings, one and all. A solitary magpie, strutting on the lawn; a mistle thrush singing on the gatepost. She stepped on her petticoat as she put it on, and tore it along the waistband; as she unwound the rags from her hair, every curl fell flat immediately. But it was the first dry day in over a week – that was surely a good sign. Early September, and the weather had turned stormy during the last days of August, with heavy rain and strong winds that tore down the still-green leaves. Rachel had hoped it would still be summer when she wed, but it was definitely autumn. Another sign. Arms aching, she gave up on her hair and went to the window. There was sunshine, but it was low and brittle – the kind of sun that got into your eyes and was blinding instead of warming. *This will be the last time I stand at a window of Hartford Hall, wishing I was somewhere else*, she reminded herself, and this thought trumped all the warning signs. In the morning she would wake up to a new life, in a new home, as a new person. A wife; no longer a spinster, a nobody.

Rachel's mother would have brushed away these supposed signs, for sure, and reassured her daughter that the match was a fair one, given the circumstances. Anne Crofton had been a practical woman; kind and affectionate but wholly pragmatic. She hadn't married Rachel's father for love, but out of good sense; though love later grew between them. She would have approved of the cautious way in which Rachel had considered Richard Weekes's proposal before accepting. He was lower than her in birth, to be sure, but his prospects were good, his business flourishing. His income was more than enough to keep a wife in modest comfort. His manners were a little coarse but there was no doubting his charm; and with innate charm, Rachel could work to shape the rest. A rough diamond, to which she could bring a shine. And however more rarefied her birth had been, the fact remained that her current status was lowly. All these things she could hear her mother say, when she shut her eyes at night and missed her parents with a feeling like a terrible ache in her bones. And in her father's voice . . . well, he would have said less. Instead, she would have seen the misgiving in his eyes, because John Crofton had married for love, and always said it had made him the happiest man alive.

But Rachel had an argument ready for him, as well: she knew that Richard Weekes loved her. Thus she entered into the match on much the same footing as her parents had, and hoped to be as happy as they had been. Rachel hadn't believed in love at first sight – not until she'd met Richard for the first time in June, and watched it hit him like a thunderbolt. He'd come to Hartford Hall with a selection of Bordeaux wines for Sir Arthur Trevelyan to sample, and was waiting for the gentleman in the small parlour when Rachel came into the room to find a deck of cards. Outside a summer storm gathered, brought on by a week of torpid heat; the sky had gone dark and odd flickers of lightning came and went like fireflies. Trapped indoors, her two younger charges were restless and bad tempered, and she'd hoped to distract them with whist. She hadn't known that anybody was in the room so she entered with unladylike haste, and frowning. Richard leapt up from the chair and tugged his coat straight, and Rachel halted abruptly. They faced each other for a suspended, silent moment, and in the next second Rachel saw it happen.

Richard's eyes widened, and words that had formed in his mouth were never spoken. He went rather pale at first, and then coloured a deep red. He stared at her with an intensity that seemed to border on awe. For her part, Rachel was too taken aback to say anything, and her murmured apology at intruding also died on her lips. Even in the wan light from outside, which made his burning face look a little sickly, Richard was arrestingly handsome. Tall and broad at the shoulder, even if he did not stand up as straight as he should. He had light brown hair the colour of umber, blue eyes and a square jaw. In spite of herself, in the face of such scrutiny, Rachel blushed. She knew she wasn't beautiful enough to have caused such upset with her face or figure alone – she was too tall, her body too flat and narrow. Her hair was the palest of blonds, but it was fine and wouldn't curl; her eyes were large, heavy-lidded, but her mouth was too small. So what else could it have been but realisation? The realisation that here was the person he'd been looking for, without even knowing it; here was his soul's counterpoint, the one who would bring harmony.

There was a mist of sweat on Richard's top lip when at last Sir Arthur's footsteps were heard, and they were released from the spell. Rachel dipped him a graceless curtsy and turned to leave, without the deck of cards, and Richard called out:

'Miss . . . forgive me,' as she walked away. His voice was deep, and smooth, and it intrigued her. She went back upstairs to the children's rooms feeling oddly breathless and distracted. Eliza, the eldest daughter of the house, was curled up in a window seat reading a book. She looked up and scowled.

'What's the matter with you?' she said, loading the question with scorn. It was lucky for Eliza that she was dark and delicate and pretty. A plainer girl would not have got away with such a waspish personality, but at fifteen Eliza already had a great many admirers.

'Nothing at all to concern you,' Rachel replied coolly. There had been times during the six years that Rachel had been governess at Hartford Hall, more times than there ought to have been, when her fingers had itched to close Eliza's mouth with the flat of her hand.

For a few weeks after that, Richard Weekes appeared here and there, unexpectedly, claiming to be on business in the area. Outside church; near the grocer's shop in the village; on the green on a Sunday afternoon, where people gathered to gossip and plot. He came to Hartford a number of times, ostensibly to ask after the latest wines he'd delivered, and how they were drinking. He came so often that Sir Arthur grew irritable, and dealt with him brusquely. But still Richard Weekes came, and he lingered, and when he caught sight of Rachel he always found a way to speak to her. And then he asked for her permission to write to her, and Rachel's stomach gave a peculiar little jolt, because there could be no mistaking his intentions from that moment on. He wrote in a crabbed hand, each character stubbornly refusing to join up with the next. The prose was coloured by quirks in spelling and grammar, but the messages within it were sweet and ardent.

She'd had only one proposal of marriage before, even though, in the days before their disgrace, her family had been wealthy and well respected. Rachel was never beautiful, but attractive and well spoken enough to arouse interest in more than one young gentleman. But she never gave them any cause to hope, or encouraged them at all, so only one ever plucked up the courage to ask for her hand – James Beale, the son of a close neighbour, on his way up to Oxford to read philosophy. She'd turned him down as kindly as she could, feeling that she ought to wait – wait for what, she couldn't say. There was loss in her family already, by then, but it was not grief that stopped her; only the want of something she could hardly put her finger on – a degree of conviction, perhaps. She was not romantic by nature; she did not expect her soul to take flight when she met the man she would marry. But she did hope to feel *something*; something more. Some sense of completion, and certainty.

Richard Weekes fumbled his proposal when he came to it, tripping over the words with his cheeks flaming; and it might have been that sudden show of vulnerability that convinced Rachel, in the moment, to accept. They'd been out walking, with the children to chaperone them, on a warm afternoon in late July. The countryside around Hartford Hall, near the village of Marshfield to the north of Bath, was more golden than green, drowsy with warmth and light. It had been a hot year, the wheat ripening early and the hay fields rife with wild flowers – poppies and cornflowers and tufted vetch. They came to the top corner of a sloping cattle field, where the air was scented with earth and fresh dung, and stopped in the shade of a beech tree while the children ran ahead through the long grass, like little ships on a waterless sea – all but Eliza, who seated herself on the low stone wall some distance away, opened a book and turned her back to them conspicuously.

'This is a beautiful spot, is it not?' said Richard, standing beside her with his hands linked behind his back. He had stripped off his coat and rolled up the sleeves of his shirt, and Rachel noticed the solid build of his arms, the scuffed and weathered look of his hands. A working man's hands, not those of a gentleman. He wore long, well-worn leather boots over snuff-coloured breeches, and a blue waistcoat just slightly too big for him. *Bought second-hand and never altered. That does not make the man any less worthy*, Rachel thought.

'This is one of my favourite views,' Rachel agreed. Beyond a line of birches and willow pollards at the bottom of the slope, the land rose again, sweeping up, chequered with fields. High above them a young buzzard was calling to its parent across the cloudless sky, its voice still whistling and babyish, though it soared half a thousand feet over their heads. The skin felt tight over Rachel's nose, and she hoped it wasn't sunburned. Her straw hat was making her forehead itch.

'You must never want to leave Hartford,' said Richard.

'There are plenty of places, I am sure, that I might come to love as much. And places left may always be visited again,' said Rachel.

'Yes. You might always return to visit.' After this, Richard Weekes seemed to sense that he had assumed too much. He looked down at his feet, shifting them slightly. 'You grew up near here, you said?'

'Yes. My family lived in the By Brook valley, not six miles from here. And I spent three seasons in Bath before . . . before my mother was taken from us.' *Before everything fell into pieces*, she did not say.

'Forgive me, I had no wish to summon sad memories.'

'No, you did not – they are happy memories, Mr Weekes.'

After a pause, Richard cleared his throat quietly and continued.

'I imagine you have some acquaintances then, in Bath and around? People you met during your seasons there?'

'Some, I suppose,' said Rachel awkwardly. He didn't seem to understand that all such society had ceased with her father's disgrace; she found that she had no particular wish to enlighten him. She had spoken of losing her parents, and he'd seemed to accept that as reason enough for her to have taken a post as governess, without any connotations of shame or penury. 'But it has been a good many years since I was there.'

'Oh, you will not have been forgotten, Miss Crofton. I am entirely convinced of that. It would not be possible to forget you,' he said hurriedly.

'A good many people come and go from the city,' she demurred. 'Did you grow up there yourself?'

'No, indeed. I grew up out in the villages, as you did. My father was an ostler. But life in the city fits me far better. Bath suits me very well – I would not want to live anywhere else. Though there is sin and hardship there, of course, same as anywhere, and it's more visible, perhaps, where so many people live in close quarters.'

'Life can be cruel,' Rachel murmured, unsure why he would mention such things.

'Life, but also men. I once saw a man beating a small child – a starving, ragged boy no more than six years old. When I forestalled the man he told me that an apple had fallen from his cart, and that the child had filched it from the gutter. And for this he would beat the wretch with his stick.' Richard shook his head, and gazed out into the sunshine, and Rachel waited. 'In the end it came to blows. I fear I may have broken his jaw.' He turned to look at her again. 'Does that shock you? Are you appalled, Miss Crofton?'

'Does what shock me? That a cruel man might beat a child over an apple, or that you might step in and punish him?' she said severely. *He tries so hard to make me know he is brave, and just, and sensible.* Richard looked anxious, so she smiled. 'The cruelty to the child was by far the worse evil, Mr Weekes.'

Richard took her hand then, and suddenly Rachel was all too

aware of Eliza's rigid back and listening ears, and the distant laughter of the other children. A breeze trembled through the beech leaves and fluttered a strand of hair against her cheek. *Now it comes.*

'I have already told you how much I . . . admire you, Miss Crofton. How much I love you, as I have never loved another. You *must* marry me.' Richard's voice was so tense that this proposal came out as a clipped command, and his cheeks blazed with colour. He looked at his feet again, though he kept hold of her hand. It was almost like a bow, like supplication. 'It would be an advantageous match, I do believe, for both of us. Your gentility and your manners are . . . so admirable, Miss Crofton. Your acquaintances in Bath . . . our combined resources, I mean . . . can only . . . can only lead to a shared future of far greater – I mean to say, please marry me, I beg of you.' He coughed, regrouped. 'If you would do me the great honour of being my wife, then I swear that I will devote my life to your every comfort and care.' He was breathing deeply, looking up as if he hardly dared to. *Two proposals, near a decade apart; this one somewhat the less graceful, but doubtless will be the last.* Rachel did not feel certain, but the sky was the most brilliant blue, and his hand was as warm as his flushed cheeks, and his eyes were frantic as he waited for her answer to his clumsy words. The sun glanced from the sloping lines of his cheekbones and jaw. *A beautiful face, and all coloured up for the love of me.* She felt her heart swell, then, and crack open just a little bit; a glimmer of feeling that was unexpected, long absent, and brought tears to her eyes.

'Yes. I will marry you, Mr Weekes,' she said.

Rachel and Richard were to marry in the chapel next to Hartford Hall and then travel at once to Bath, to Richard's house, where they would live.

'What street is the house upon?' Eliza pounced, when she heard of this plan.

'I forget. Kingsgate, perhaps?' said Rachel, inventing the name evasively. The house was in fact in Abbeygate Street, and her heart had sunk when she'd told this to the head nurse, Mina Cooper, and watched that kind woman trying to find something good to say about the address. *I dare say it is much improved since I was there last.*

'Kingsgate? There is no Kingsgate that I know of. It can't be near any of the better streets, if I haven't heard of it at all.'

'It is possible that there are things in this world that you don't yet know of, Eliza.' There were things, for example, that Rachel now knew about Richard that few others did. That in spite of his youthful looks, he was already past thirty. That his favourite thing to eat was bread dipped in the hot butter where mushrooms had been sautéed. That he was afraid to ride, having been thrown badly as a child. That though his father had been a lowly ostler, Richard had raised himself up through hard work and good taste and self-education, to become one of Bath's most successful wine and spirits merchants.

All these things he told her, without her asking him; like a man laying himself bare – letting her know the good and the bad at once, so that she might know him completely, and it made her trust him. He didn't seem to notice that he'd asked her little in return, or that she'd volunteered scant information about herself. And for each thing he told her, a dozen further questions were asked in a distant recess of her mind. This curious observer was subtle as a shadow; it was like the echo of a voice, coming up from a deep place; a part of herself she had somehow become separated from, in the years of loss and grief that had followed her happy childhood. But it was a voice she cherished; which, when heard, gave her a pang of loss that went deeper than flesh, and of joy at hearing it again, however softly. On the subject of Richard Weekes it was almost childlike, full of fascination, shy pleasure, and fleeting doubt.

Sir Arthur and Lady Trevelyan dutifully declared that they would miss Rachel, when she told them she would be leaving. She suspected that what they most regretted was having to advertise for a new governess. Only Frederick, the youngest child, seemed to genuinely grieve at the thought of losing her. When he threw his arms around her waist and buried his face in her skirt to hide his tears, Rachel was stabbed with regret.

'You're a good boy, Freddie, and I will miss you a great deal. I hope we will visit each other often,' she told him.

'I doubt that,' Eliza chipped in. 'Bath is so dull and . . . reduced, these days. We shall be travelling more often to Lyme from now on, I should think. And even if we did come to Bath, I dare say we would move in somewhat different circles.' In her increased unkindness, Rachel read a touch of sorrow in Eliza, too. She feared that Eliza was one of those people who would only ever be able to express themselves through anger, so she found it in herself to cross over to the girl and kiss her cheek.

'Be happy, Eliza. And try to be kind,' she said. Eliza scowled furiously, pulling her face away. She stared resolutely out of the window, looking as though she would love nothing more than to throw open the casement and fly away through it, into the world beyond, far from her home with all its walls and doors, its straight lines and straighter rules.

A knock at the door made Rachel turn from the window. Her wedding gown – in truth her only good gown, of pale fawn cotton, short-sleeved and gathered beneath the bust – shifted around her ankles. She felt the failed curls of her hair brush her neck, and wondered if it was too late to do anything about them. It was Eliza who came into the room, not waiting for her knock to be answered.

'If you're ready to wed the shopkeeper, Father has brought the barouche to the front for you. I said it was fifty paces to the chapel and easy to walk, but he insists that a carriage is in order for a wedding,' she said, sounding bored. She was wearing a beautiful dress of cream satin, edged with intricate embroidery, finer than anything Rachel possessed. Rachel thought this a final act of tactlessness from her former charge.

'Thank you, Eliza. I am ready.'

'But . . . your hair . . .'

'My hair will have to do. It's windy out, anyway. And besides, Mr Weekes will not mind.'

'He might not, but perhaps you ought. Here, sit down a moment.' Eliza picked up some discarded pins from the dressing table and set about fixing up some of the stray tresses. 'You should have had Bessie come and help you,' she muttered.

'As you have so often reminded me, Bessie has enough to do without dressing my hair for me.'

'It's your *wedding* day, Miss Crofton. And why you refuse to wear a false front of proper curls, I'll never know. Miss Crofton, Miss Crofton – I thought you might like to hear it a few last times, before you become Mrs *Weekes*.'

'It's good of you to attend a wedding you so disapprove of,' said Rachel, amused.

'I never said I disapproved. Mr Weekes is . . . well. Right enough for you, I suppose.' Eliza shrugged.

'A good and honest man, and one who loves me. Yes, I would call that right enough,' said Rachel, and in the mirror she saw Eliza blush slightly, her lips thinning as they pressed together. A thought occurred to her then – that Eliza might somehow envy her. She'd caught the girl out, more than once, spying on Richard Weekes from a window. He cut a romantic figure, and he was handsome – more than handsome enough to enchant a fifteen-year-old girl. Rachel knew she shouldn't let this please her, because Eliza was really just a child; but still, when she rose from the table at last it was with a good deal more resolve.

Down the wide staircase with its sweeping balustrade, along the rich Turkey carpet in the hallway, towards the tall front doors. Rachel's reflection accompanied her, flitting from one vast mirror to the next like a companionable ghost, and there was something profoundly comforting in this duality. The temptation to see her reflection as a separate person was strong. She didn't dare turn her head to look, because she knew what she would see – only herself; no companion at her side after all. She would likely never step inside such a grand house again, but Hartford Hall was also cold, and unyielding. There had been little laughter, in spite of the children, and few guests. Rachel had always found it a sad and quiet place, after the warmth and jollity of her childhood home and the constant girlish chatter at boarding school. She pictured the way her father and little brother, Christopher, had wrestled – rolling on the hearthrug, digging at each other's ribs until laughter rendered them helpless; she tried to picture Sir Arthur behaving that way with Freddie, and couldn't imagine it. But perhaps she'd brought some of the quietness with her to Hartford, in mourning the loss of her parents; because some measure of herself had died along with them, or so it felt.

Her mother went first, from a seizure; her father three years later, when grief had led him into ruin, and scandal, and the house and all their furniture had been sold to set against bad debt. The doctors had been mystified as to what actually caused his death, but Rachel, who'd seen the look on his face as she kissed him goodnight for the final time, was quite sure her kind and gentle father had died of shame. The thought was too painful, so she tried not to think it. There was the magpie, perched on the gatepost as the carriage rolled her away from the front doors. *One for sorrow.* Rachel raised two fingers to salute him, in spite of all better sense.

Nerves. Nothing more. Life was about to change for ever, after all. She could be forgiven for feeling anxious, especially since she was alone in all her decisions, with no recourse to advice from a parent or older sibling. *Perhaps I am only in want of a second opinion.* She had come to know and trust Richard, but their courtship had been swift. Sometimes when he smiled it seemed that other, more serious thoughts hovered behind his eyes; and sometimes when he was serious, his eyes danced in silent merriment. Sometimes she looked up to find him watching her with an expression that she didn't recognise and couldn't decipher. *Such things are learnt in time. I will learn to read him, and he will learn to read me.* But he told her that he loved her, over and over again, and swore his devotion to her. And she'd *seen* the effect she'd had on him, when they first met. Still, her heart was thumping as she made her solitary walk down the aisle to join him in front of the altar. She had no male relative to accompany her – long before her mother died, her brother Christopher had been carried off by a fever, at the age of nine; Sir Arthur drew the line at taking on this familial duty himself. The bride's side of the chapel was populated almost exclusively with absent people, but she pictured them there as she made her way past, and she pictured them glad, and approving of her choice. She held herself straight, and walked with measured steps.

Richard was wearing his best blue coat and a crisp white neck tie, with his hair combed back and his jaw clean-shaven. He was strikingly lovely; his eyes were clear and apprehensive as he watched her approach. He stood close enough to her for their arms to press together as the parson gave the welcome. There seemed a promise in the touch – that soon there would be nothing, not even cloth, between their two skins. Rachel felt anxious at the thought. The sunlight through the chapel window was warm. She could smell Richard's shaving soap, a slight aroma of camphor from his coat, and the vital, masculine smell of new sweat. She cast her eyes sideways as the clergyman spoke on, and saw Richard staring fixedly at the effigy of Christ on the cross that hung above the altar. Small knots were working at the corners of his jaw, but when he was called upon to speak, and make his vows, he turned towards her and couldn't keep from smiling. Try as she might to be calm as she spoke her part, Rachel's voice was so quiet and strangled that the parson struggled to hear it. When it was done, Richard raised her hand to his lips and shut his eyes, bowing before her.

'Mrs Weekes. You have made me the happiest man alive,' he whispered, and then laughed delightedly, as though he couldn't keep it in.

* * *

Starling blew angrily at a lock of her reddish hair that kept falling into her eyes. Her hands were sticky with onion juice, so she didn't want to brush it back; the smell of food and cookery lingered on her long enough as it was. In spite of the chunk of stale bread impaled on the point of her knife – a safeguard that Bridget had sworn by – her eyes were stinging from the fumes, and just then her nose began to itch as well, so her teeth were already clenched in irritation before Dorcas came sidling up to her. Dorcas smoothed her apron repeatedly with the flats of her hands, and smiled a quick, thin smile. She hovered there, in the corner of Starling's eye, like some insect looking for a place to land. Starling took a deep breath, put down the knife and raised her eyebrows. Dorcas's smile became a scowl, and Starling could see how much she loathed asking a favour of a lowly kitchen maid.

The sun had only just set and the lamps not yet been lit, so the fire sent shadows capering up the walls like devils.

'Will you do it today, Starling? You know how bad he was yesterday,' Dorcas burst out. The skinny housemaid, with her horse's teeth and her narrow, lashless eyes, was sweating, though whether that was from discomfort or the heat of the cook fires, Starling couldn't tell.

'Is that anyway to talk about the master?' Starling was too cross to make it easy for Dorcas. *Let her beg me*, she thought.

'Don't play me the high and mighty, Starling. You know what I'm talking about,' said Dorcas. Starling studied her, and saw real fear in the girl's eyes. She hardened her heart against it.

'What I *don't* know is why you expect me to do your work for you, Dorcas Winthrop. I don't see you down here chopping endless onions for the soup.' Dorcas's nostrils flared in distaste.

'I'm upper housemaid. I don't do kitchen work.'

'You're the *only* housemaid, so go do your own work and leave me be.' Starling turned back to the onions, feeling the other girl's impotent rage as she backed away.

The kitchen of the house on Lansdown Crescent, in Bath, had a vaulted ceiling and tall windows to compensate for being below street level. The windows looked out onto a narrow, shadowed courtyard, and let in little light. It was a space nestled amongst the foundations of the building, carved into the ground, supporting the house above in more ways than one. Starling sometimes thought of it as like an animal den, a warren through which the servants moved, day in, day out, with grime under their nails and dried sweat in their clothes, blinking at the light of day. The cook, Sol Bradbury, chuckled as Dorcas finally slunk reluctantly up the stairs.

'You're wicked, you are, Starling. It'll end with you going up, and you know that.'

'Perhaps. But she nips at me like a flea, that one. I can't find the will to make it easy on her,' Starling replied.

The gentleman of the house, Mr Jonathan Alleyn, had indeed been worse than usual in the past few days, for which Starling felt gratified. It was her doing, after all. He was ruled by his moods and dreams and the pains in his head; the disarray in his dark and cluttered rooms reflected the disorder in his mind. Starling had many ways to goad him. Earlier in the week she'd learnt, from an old soldier drinking in the Moor's Head, the exact tattoo of French marching drums. She'd beat out this rhythm on the hearth as she swept it, ostensibly to knock the ashes from the shovel and brush. When she'd finished, Jonathan Alleyn had been sitting with his eyes tight shut and his nostrils white, his whole body wrought hard with stress, so tightly that it shook. *No more than you deserve*, Starling had thought, pleased at this result, and that he went downhill the rest of the week. Yesterday, Dorcas had been pale and goggle-eyed when she finished in his rooms. Starling curled her lip at the memory. The girl was as gutless as a rabbit. She tucked the offending strands of hair more firmly under her cap and went back to the onions. Sol beat the batter for a plum cake, quietly singing a bawdy song.

In minutes Dorcas was back, tears streaking through smudges of soot on her cheeks.

'He's gone mad! This time he's gone quite mad!' she cried, all shrill and staccato. Starling couldn't help but chuckle. 'Don't you dare laugh at me, Starling! No decent person should have to go into those rooms! It's worse than anything the devil could devise! And he's like a demon himself . . . I think his soul must be black as tar! As black as tar!' Dorcas clamoured.

'What is all this now?' It was Mrs Hatton who spoke – the housekeeper; a small, brisk woman with iron-grey hair and a careworn face. The three women in the kitchen stood up straighter, and buttoned their lips. 'Well? Out with it, one of you.'

'It's Mr Alleyn, ma'am. He . . . he . . . I went to set up the room for the night and he . . .' Dorcas dissolved into tears again, stretching her mouth into a wide, upturned crescent.

'Saints preserve us. There now, Dorcas! I'm sure he didn't mean you any harm.' The housekeeper fetched out her handkerchief and handed it to the housemaid.

'But I'm sure he did, ma'am! I think he has gone mad this time! He snatched up the smuts bucket and *threw* it at me! If I hadn't ha' dodged it might ha' knocked all my teeth out . . .'

'Perhaps no bad thing,' Starling muttered. Dorcas shot her a look of pure venom.

'Starling, nobody asked you to speak,' said Mrs Hatton, exasperated. Dorcas wept on.

'And . . . and he called me such *names*! I shouldn't have to hear such things. And I did nothing to deserve it!'

'That's enough. Now, calm down. You have work to do, and—'

'No! I won't go up there again! Not now and not tomorrow neither! It's not *natural*, what he gets up to! *He's* not natural, and no decent person should be expected to . . . to . . . have to see him, or serve him! And I won't, even if it means I'm dismissed!' With this Dorcas ran from the kitchen. Sol Bradbury and Starling exchanged a look, and Starling fought hard not to smile.

'Lord, not another one running out,' Mrs Hatton muttered; for a second, her shoulders sagged in exhaustion. 'Starling, stop smirking. Go up to Mr Alleyn, if you please, and make his rooms for him. You'll need to bank the fire well, there's a nip in the air tonight. He'll ask for wine but I have it from the mistress that he's not to have any – the pains in his head have been bad this week, poor soul. Any one of us would be as volatile, had we to live with such suffering. Now, please, Starling – I don't want to hear any argument.' She raised one finger in warning, and then walked out in pursuit of Dorcas.

Starling smiled at her retreating back. It served her well to let Mrs Hatton believe that she was reluctant to go into Jonathan Alleyn's rooms. It would have caused suspicion, after all, if she seemed keen to go in, though keen she was. A strange kind of keen, because her pulse always raced and her breathing came faster, and on some level she knew she was afraid of him. Not afraid of the look of him, or the contents of his rooms, or of his rages, like the other girls; she was afraid of what she might do, and what he might. Because she had known Jonathan Alleyn since she was a little girl, and she knew things about him that the other servants didn't. Things nobody else knew.

She found the supper tray that Dorcas had abandoned on a table in the hallway outside his rooms. He had two adjoining chambers on the second storey of the house, on its west side, sharing a wall with the next house along the crescent. The room where he slept was towards the back of the house, plainly furnished but dominated by an enormous canopied tester bed, its wooden posts all gilded, its drapes of heavy crimson damask. Linked to this via double doors, the room at the front of the house was supposedly his study, and had an enormous bay window arching over the street, giving a far-reaching view of the city and the hills around it. A view almost always hidden by closed shutters. This room had filled a succession of housemaids with horror. Starling paused and strained her ears for the sound of Mrs Hatton's footsteps, or anyone else who might be near, before adding a bottle of wine to the supper tray. A bottle she'd got especially, from Richard Weekes; dosed in secret with extra spirits to make it stronger. Mr Alleyn would drink it, she knew, even if he realised it was doctored. He didn't seem to be able to stop himself. Perhaps – she almost smiled to herself at the idea – perhaps he even thought she did it to please him.

Starling listened hard for a moment. She steadied herself. There was silence from within; no sound of movement, or speech, or violence. He would be waiting in the dark, but Starling was not afraid of the dark. Jonathan Alleyn never lit his own lamps; he liked to sit as the gloom gathered around him. She'd once heard him say that the shadows soothed him. Well, she would banish them. Why should he be soothed? Behind her, the lamp on the wall made a soft tearing sound as it guttered in a draught. That same draught brushed the back of Starling's neck, and made the skin there tingle. *That's all it is*, she assured herself. *Just a cold zephyr where a door has been left open*. It was not fear. She refused to be afraid of Jonathan Alleyn, even though the worst and biggest thing she knew about him, which nobody else knew, was that he was a murderer.

He would be waiting within, nothing to betray his whereabouts but the ruddy gleam of the fire reflecting in his eyes. *For you, Alice*, she pledged silently, as she knocked smartly at the door, and went in.

* * *

Sir Arthur's generosity extended to loaning the barouche to Rachel and her new husband for the drive into Bath for the wedding breakfast. As soon as they'd climbed down outside the Moor's Head inn, the carriage pulled away, and her connection with Hartford ended to the sound of iron-shod hooves clattering on cobblestones. The wind funnelling down Walcot Street was brisk. Richard tipped two strong lads to carry Rachel's trunk south to the house on Abbeygate Street, then he held out his hand to her.

'Come, my dear. Come in out of this breeze,' he said, wrapping her hand around the crook of his elbow. Just then, the abbey bells began to strike the hour, and Rachel paused.

'Wait,' she said. 'It's been many years since I heard those bells.' She looked down the street into the thick of the city, where pale stone buildings clustered in all around, and the cobbled streets ran with carts and carriages, donkey traps, servants hurrying on their masters' business. There were dowdy maids with laundry bundles, scuffing their feet along in the wooden pattens that kept their shoes out of the muck. There were housekeepers and cooks with baskets full of fresh meat and vegetables; sweating bearers carrying the wealthy uphill in smart sedan chairs; street hawkers and urchins and fashionable ladies with their pelisses buttoned tight against the weather. Rachel took a deep breath and smelled the dankness of the river; the sweet reek of rubbish in the gutter; freshly baked bread and roasting meat; a cloud of beery fumes and tobacco smoke from the inn. A mixture of smells she'd grown unused to, living in the sterile calm of Hartford Hall. 'Not since I came here with my parents in the season. My little brother too, before we lost him.' It was a fond memory, but Richard mistook her, and thought her sad.

'Forget all that, Mrs Weekes.' He squeezed her hand, pulling her towards the door of the inn. 'I'm your family now, and this is a new beginning. For sure, Bath is much changed since you were last here – new buildings are finished all the time; and new folk come in. Fine people too, the right sort,' Richard said, and Rachel smiled at him, not caring to explain herself.

The Moor's Head had low ceilings heavy with beams and a red brick floor worn smooth from long years of use. There was a racket of voices and laughter already, in spite of it being just five in the afternoon, and cheering broke out when Richard appeared. He grinned and clasped hands with several men who were already well soused, judging by their red cheeks and heavy eyes. Rachel smiled uncomfortably as they toasted her with tankards of ale and shook her hand more roughly than she was used to. The smoke made her eyes sting, so she blinked frequently. Richard wore a grin from ear to ear until he glanced at Rachel and saw her discomfort. His smile faltered.

'Sadie, is our table ready?' he called out to the girl behind the bar, who was moon-faced, with deep brown curls, abundant bosom and apples in her cheeks.

'Aye, Mr Weekes, just as you asked. Go on up as it please you,' said Sadie. Just then a man came to stand in front of them; portly, with a lined face and a filthy grey wig that had slipped down over one ear. He patted Rachel's hand clumsily.

'Well, young sir, I declare you have done mighty well for yourself. You told us she was a beauty, but we none of us expected you could ensnare such a fine creature as this, hmm?' said the man, slurring slightly. His breath was sour with brandy but his face was kindly, and Rachel inclined her head graciously at the compliment. Her new husband scowled.

'Of course she is fine. Finer than me, certainly. But I hope to raise myself up, and to deserve her,' he said stiffly.

'You are too kind to me, and do yourself a disservice, Mr Weekes,' Rachel told him.

'Well, I never saw a bride so radiant. No, indeed. You are the loveliest thing to grace this poor place in as long as I can recall,' the man continued. 'Let me—'

'That you could even recall the time of year would come as a surprise to me. Come, my dear. This way.' Richard led Rachel away, as the elderly man was drawing breath to introduce himself. He looked crestfallen as they departed, and Rachel turned to smile in farewell.

'Who was that man?' she said, as Richard led her to the foot of a crooked wooden stair.

'That? Oh, nobody. His name is Duncan Weekes. He's my father, if truth be told,' Richard muttered, keeping his hand in the small of her back to urge her onwards.

'Your father?' Rachel was shocked. Richard led her into a cosy room on the upper storey, where the wooden floor rolled and undulated, and the leaded windows were hazy with city grime. But the table that had been laid for them was well scrubbed, and laid with china plates and wine glasses. Rachel took her seat, and noticed that the china was chipped in places, the cutlery stained. She was proud to find herself not as disheartened by such things as she might have expected. 'I understood you had little contact with your father?'

'As little as I may, truth be told,' said Richard.

'And yet . . . you must have invited him here today, for the wedding feast?'

'Invited him? No, I did not. But . . . we have some of the same acquaintances, perhaps. He must have heard we would be coming here.'

'You come here often, I divine. You seem to have many friends here.'

'Friends, some. Clients others, and some acquaintances that perhaps I once enjoyed, and now can't quite be rid of. But never mind them – today is about us. Here, try the wine. It's Constantia, shipped all the way from the Dutch colony on the Cape of Good Hope. A rare treasure, and I have been keeping this bottle for my bride for some years now. I can't tell you how happy I am to finally be able to raise a glass of it in a toast to you, my love.' He filled two glasses, handed one to her and entwined their wrists.

'Happy to have found your bride, or to be able to try the wine at last?' Rachel teased.

'Both.' Richard smiled. 'But you are undoubtedly the greater pleasure. To you, Mrs Rachel Weekes.'

The wine sank hotly into Rachel's empty stomach.

'It's delicious,' she said, and tried not to dwell on the fact that her new name made her a stranger to her own ears. Since childhood she'd envisaged her wedding feast as a rather different affair. She'd imagined her parents with her, and other family, and a white embroidered tablecloth beneath a feast set out on silver platters and fine porcelain; herself far younger, not past her bloom at twenty-nine as she now found herself, and having endured years of the pitying looks aimed at an old maid. But she could never have hoped for a more handsome groom, nor one so devoted to her. 'Mr Weekes, shouldn't we ask your father to join us? Whatever has passed between you, it doesn't seem right that he should be so near at hand, and yet excluded from our celebration,' she said. Richard didn't answer at once. He took a long swig of the wine and then turned the glass by its stem on the table top.

'I would rather have you all to myself,' he said at last, looking at her with a smile that did not quite tally with the look in his eye.

'I fear that you are ashamed of him, and don't want me to know him. Please, I assure you, you need not worry. Duncan Weekes is now my father too, after all, and I should very much like to come to know him . . .'

'You only say so because you don't know what he's like.'

'Perhaps. But a wedding is a time for family, don't you think? He seemed kindly . . . a touch disordered, perhaps, but—'

'No,' said Richard, and there was such a note of finality in his voice that Rachel didn't dare press the matter, for fear of souring the mood.

So they feasted alone, and once the Constantia was finished more wine was brought in by the serving girl, Sadie, along with a huge platter of roast lamb cutlets, a whole trout in butter and parsley sauce and a dish of curried root vegetables. Richard emptied his glass thrice for each time Rachel emptied hers, and soon his cheeks were flushed and his eyes were bright, and his voice as he spoke grew blurry. He told her about his business, and how he hoped to grow it; how soon it would be before they were able to move to better accommodation; how their son would join him in the wine and spirits trade, and their daughter would marry a baronet.

'I fear that you may find our rooms somewhat . . . less than you are used to,' he said at one point. 'I hope you will not be disappointed.'

'What right have I to be disappointed?' said Rachel. 'I who have near nothing, save the clothes I stand up in? Hartford Hall was not my home, and my family home was lost to me years ago. All that you have you have worked for, and got for yourself, and that is far more than I can claim. And you would share it all with me . . . I shall not be disappointed.'

'And yet, in truth, you are accustomed to fine surroundings, fine food and the company of well-mannered people . . .'

'I am accustomed to the company of bad-tempered children,' she said, taking his hand and squeezing it. 'That was not the life I wanted. This is.' She smiled. *Love*, whispered the echo in her head. *Love is what's needed, and what you should become accustomed to. So love him.*

Richard kissed her hand, all pleased and relieved, and Rachel wondered at a strange feeling of detachment that grew in her as the evening progressed.

She felt slightly as though she was watching a scene in which she had no part; watching things that were happening to another person altogether. Some important part of her had slipped away, and gone in search of other things. It was the same odd numbness that had begun with the first death in her family and grown through each one that came after, and she had hoped that the way Richard had touched her heart when he proposed had marked the beginning of its end. At length

Rachel pushed her glass away from her, and held her hand over it when the girl came to fill it. A few drops of wine splashed from the jug onto her fingers, and she looked up to remonstrate with Sadie only to find that it wasn't the dark-haired girl who poured it, but a red-head. A pretty girl with elongated, broad-set eyes that looked clever and too know-ing. She had a short nose, tilted up at its tip; brown eyes and a wide mouth shaped by a lazy curve. Her hair was a coppery colour, like autumn leaves, and long strands of it hung down from her cap. She had halted in the act of pouring the wine, and stood quite still, staring most peculiarly; her gaze seemed to pass right through Rachel, and settle on some other place or time entirely.

'What's the matter?' said Rachel, her own tongue loosened by the wine she'd drunk. The serving girl blinked; shut her mouth with an audible click of her teeth.

'Beg pardon, ma'am,' she said, in a low voice.

'Your cloth, please, to dry my hand.' Rachel held out her hand for the dish rag hanging over the girl's shoulder.

'I'll take some more.' Richard pushed his glass towards the girl, and looked up. He too seemed to notice that this was not their normal server, but he said nothing. He only watched the girl guardedly, and for a moment all three were locked in mute immobility.

'Your cloth, if you please,' Rachel said again.

'Beg pardon,' the girl repeated. She set down the jug with a thump, turned abruptly and left the room.

'Well! What on earth got into her, I wonder?' said Rachel, but Richard didn't answer her. He picked up his glass to drink, found it empty, and put it back down irritably.

'Sadie!' he bellowed towards the open doorway, and mo-ments later Sadie reappeared to take up the wine jug. Rachel kept an eye out, but the curious red-haired girl did not return.

The house on Abbeygate Street was all in darkness when they entered. Richard lit a single candle to guide them up the stairs to the bedchamber, so Rachel could form no impression of her new home other than of a clinging coldness on the lower floor; narrow, creaking wooden stairs and a spacious but low-ceilinged upper room with a rumpled tester bed at its centre. The air smelled as though the windows had been a long time shut; the bed as though the sheets had been much slept upon. *All of which is only the lack of a woman's touch*, Rachel assured herself. Richard put the candle down on the nightstand and came to stand opposite her at the foot of the bed. He laced their fingers together, swaying slightly on his feet; in the candle's glow his face was soft and smiling. Rachel's smile was more uncertain, and she wished then that she'd drunk more wine at dinner. She'd wanted to be fully aware of this night, of this crucial moment in her life. There were only her and Richard to remember it, after all, but now it came to it she was afraid and didn't know what to do, and wished to be less aware than she was. Richard kissed her gently, opening her mouth with his, and Rachel waited to feel something other than the urge to recoil from the wine gone sour on his breath, and the taste of lamb grease on his lips. *Mother did not love Father at first. And Father was a good man.* Richard's kisses grew harder, and more insistent, and soon he was pulling at her clothes.

'Rachel, my sweet wife,' he murmured, kissing her neck. Unsure how to behave, Rachel reached up and began to un-pin her hair, as she normally would before bed. The pins pattered onto the floor as Richard swept her from her feet, and crumpled onto the bed on top of her.

She would have liked more time to become acquainted with his body. The differences with her own intrigued her – the heft of it, the breadth of his shoulders, the fairness of his skin across which, she could just make out in the candlelight, freckles were scattered. He was so solid, so warm. She sank her fingers into the flesh of his upper arms, and pictured bones as thick and smooth as the mahogany arms of a chair. The weight of him pressed on her chest and made it hard to breathe. She would have liked to see the thing between his legs, to know how it behaved, to feel it with her fingers before it touched her elsewhere, but she had no chance to. Breathless and still muttering disjointed endearments, Richard pushed his way into her, remembering only too late to be gentle. He groaned as he moved, to and fro, and Rachel clasped his shoulders tightly, screwing her eyes tight shut at the discomfort and the strangeness of it. *He is my husband. This is proper.* She studied the sensation, which by the end was merely uncomfortable, and tried to feel satisfied that this was a duty done, a milestone reached. A pact sealed, irrevocably. *I am his now*, she thought, and only then realised how strange and limited a kind of freedom marriage might be.

1803

When the sun was well risen on the second day, Starling was fed a breakfast of milk porridge sweetened with honey. She ate until her stomach was full to bursting. Outside, a weak and chilly sun lit the world. The starlings had flown from the horse chestnut tree, and a small flock of spotted white hens were scuffing their feet in the yard. They ate breakfast in the kitchen, where a fresh fire snapped in the hearth; sitting at a scrubbed and pitted oak table on benches that wobbled on the uneven floor. Alice was wearing a blue dress with a wide lace collar, a little frayed at the cuffs but still finer than anything Starling had ever seen up close before. The older woman, Bridget, wore brown wool, and an apron. Starling could not quite make out the bond between the two. They seemed to be young mistress and older servant, but then, they did not always speak to one another that way.

'How old are you, Starling?' Alice asked her. Starling stared at her, wide-eyed. She didn't know the answer, so she stayed silent.

'She won't know. How should she know? Where she's from they don't celebrate birthdays. Most likely her mother dropped her in the field she was working, and made no particular note of day or month. Or year,' said Bridget.

'So her people are farm workers, now? Well, Starling – be happy. You have come up in the world overnight. Yesterday you were a vagrant and a thief, now you are a farm labourer's child,' said Alice, smiling. She had plaited her fair hair to either side of a central parting, and coiled the plaits into a knot at the back of her head. Starling thought her impossibly lovely. Bridget grunted gracelessly.

'Mock all you want. This new cosset of yours could be a faery's changeling for all you know.'

'A faery! Would you like that?' Alice said to Starling, laughing. 'When I was a little girl, I should have loved to be a faery!'

'Well, then. I see I shall get nothing sensible from you until the novelty of this new pet has worn off,' said Bridget. Starling stayed silent, but she listened, and she watched Bridget cautiously. While the women's attention was elsewhere, she reached out for the honey spoon and put it, drizzling honey, into her mouth. The taste exploded on her tongue, sweet and heavy and fragrant.

'Oi! Filthy little beast!' Bridget cried, reaching for it. The wooden ridges rattled against Starling's teeth as Bridget pulled the spoon away.

'Oh, let her have it, Bridget! Can't you see she's starving?' said Alice.

'If she's to stay she must learn to be useful, and she must learn some manners, and she'll not learn them by being indulged in all things by you, miss,' Bridget declared. 'I raised you up well enough, did I not? And you've *never* been allowed to suck the honey spoon, Miss Alice. Not in my kitchen.'

'I was never half starved, nor neglected as she has been. But very well, Bridget.' Her voice took on a tone of calm propriety. 'Starling, you are to put the honey into your bowl, if you would like more.' Starling poked out her sticky tongue and licked at the slick of honey on her chin, and Alice dissolved into laughter once more.

The two women set a tin tub in front of the fire and filled it half with water from the pump, and half with hot water from a huge copper kettle. Starling watched them curiously, and had no idea of the purpose of the tub until Alice rolled up her sleeves and held out her arms to her. Starling went to her obediently, and only resisted slightly as Alice began to unfasten her filthy, rotting clothes. She made her arms rigid, to show her displeasure as the cool air of the kitchen reached her skin.

'Oh, I know this seems strange, little one. But it is most necessary, and you will feel much better without all that grime on your skin. I saw at once that there were three things you needed – sleep, kitchen physic, and a bath. Well, we have had one and two, so now comes three,' she said. Starling squirmed, and twisted away. Nothing good had ever happened to her that began with her clothes being taken from her. 'Stop,' Alice said gently. She put her hands on either side of Starling's face and looked her in the eye. 'It will not hurt, and no harm will come to you. Do you trust me?' Starling thought for a moment, then nodded. 'Good girl,' said Alice.

Alice stripped away each filthy garment. Bridget brought in a cake of soap and a comb, linen cloths and a scrubbing brush with mean-looking bristles. Starling eyed the brush suspiciously. Her clothes consisted of a long-sleeved dress which had been stitched together from mixed scraps of fabric and tied around the middle with a length of twine, then two layers of coarse wool undergarments – leggings that came to the knee, and baggy vests. All were filthy and stinking, and so stained that their original colour had been quite forgotten. Lice crawled in all the seams and Alice pinched a flea that had landed on her arm, crushing it with her thumbnail. The discarded clothes were thrown into the fire, and the two women stared mutely at Starling's naked body for a minute.

'Saints preserve us,' Bridget muttered, and for the first time Starling saw pity in the older woman's eyes. They were looking at the scars and bruises all over her body. Alice put out soft fingers and traced the length of one wound, which had left an angry red welt from Starling's bony left shoulder to the bottom of her hollow ribs. Frowning, Alice turned her. Her back bore the diagonal slashes of having been beaten with a cane or thong. Old scars beneath newer ones, criss-crossing; a cobweb of injury that would haunt the skin for ever. The backs of her thighs had marks that looked like splodges, raised and shiny. 'These are burns, for certain,' said Bridget, and Starling felt the woman's rough fingers examining her. The touch made her shiver, and goose pimples scattered over her damaged skin.

After a while, Alice turned her to face them again; there were tears in her eyes, but she smiled. Bridget wore a thunderous scowl, and Starling shied away from her.

'Well,' said Alice breathlessly. 'You are quite safe from whoever treated you this way here, Starling. Whoever your people were, we are your people now. Isn't that right, Bridget?' Bridget chewed at her bottom lip as if reluctant to answer, but then she said:

'There was never a child so wicked that it deserved such punishment. I've a balm of rosehips and apple that will help soothe those scars. Once she's clean.' She went out of the kitchen towards the still room, and Alice smiled at Starling, wiping her eyes with the back of her hand.

'See, there – Bridget has a sharp tongue and a hard way about her, but underneath it all her heart is like butter, and quite easy to melt. In you get.'

The water in the tub was soon dark with dirt. Alice soaped her all over and rubbed her with the cloths, ignoring the stiff brush, much to Starling's relief. Her hair took the longest time. It was snarled up in knots and rat tails, caked with mud and filth. There were burrs caught up in it, and twigs and pieces of hay. Alice worked through it with her fingers, soaped it, combed it out as gently as she could, until eventually it was clean. Great clumps of it came loose and floated around in the soapy water like spiders. The winter sun shone in through the window, and when Bridget came back into the kitchen she paused.

'Such a colour! Who'd think it, under all that grime?'

'What colour is it?' Alice asked, tipping her head this way and that as though to see better.

'Much the same as that copper kettle, and the fire it's sitting over.'

'Oh, how lovely! Alas, to my eyes it is only brown,' said Alice. Starling tipped her head curiously at Alice.

'Well, she looks far more like a little girl now, and a bit less like a muckworm,' said Bridget, nodding in approval.

As it dried, Starling's hair sprang up into loose curls which seemed to delight Alice all the more. They sat in the parlour, a grander room than Starling had ever seen, though the furniture was plain and faded, and the floor of bare stone. Starling was clothed in an old dress of Alice's, which was too big and trailed on the floor behind her. The woollen stockings were too big as well, and crept down to rumple around her ankles. Her feet were stuffed into leather slippers, tied on with string.

'And now she's a scarecrow again,' said Bridget, and Alice chuckled.

'Only for a little while. Only until we can get her some clothes of her own. We'll go to market on Thursday, and find some cloth. Bridget can stitch you some dresses, and when you're bigger, you'll fit into my old things just fine.'

'Your outgrown dresses might fit her in time, but they're too fine for a servant. She'll have to have others.'

'A servant? Starling isn't a servant. She's my family, now. I always wanted a little sister,' said Alice, tucking Starling's red curls behind her shoulders, and smoothing them down.

'Your sister? Now, Alice . . .' Bridget began, but she saw the look on Alice's face, and seemed to lose heart for the argument. 'She must learn to be useful. It is essential. You may not always be able to keep her.'

'She will be useful! Of course she will. I will teach her to read and write, and be a lady . . .'

'And I will teach her to cook and clean, and have a livelihood.' Bridget's voice was laced with dry humour, and Alice smiled.

'Very well, then.'

'If she is mute, things will be harder,' said Bridget.

'No, she is not mute,' Alice said. She cupped Starling's chin, and gazed at her. 'Fear has chased her voice away, that's all. It will return, when she's ready.'

'There is another problem, of course. Perhaps the biggest of all, which you haven't yet considered.' Starling's heart sank. She wanted to stay. She longed to stay. Alice glanced anxiously at Bridget, as if fearing what she would say next. 'Your benefactor. He comes this Saturday. And who knows how happy he'll be to find he has another mouth to feed? And an urchin mouth at that.' Alice took a deep breath, and Starling felt a tremor pass through her. 'You must prepare yourself to do as he says,' said Bridget, more gently than usual. Alice suddenly looked so sad that Starling felt a pang of desperation. She opened her mouth, but a whistle of empty air was all that came forth. She swallowed, and coughed a little, and tried again.

'I'll be good,' she said, and Alice cried out in delight.

1821

It was easy enough to leave the house on Lansdown Crescent after hours. Starling's room was little more than a cubbyhole adjoining the cook's room, along a shadowy corridor from the kitchen. She had a narrow wooden bed and a rickety nightstand for the pot; no windows, but a rag rug on the floor to keep the chill off her feet. If Sol Bradbury was already in bed then she slept like a dead woman, snoring softly with her chin nestled into the pillowy flesh of her neck. If she was awake, then as long as Starling was reasonably discreet, the woman said nothing. They had an understanding – Sol Bradbury didn't see Starling going out when she should have stayed in, nor did she comment when odd small items of food and leftovers went missing from the pantry; and Starling didn't see Sol Bradbury drinking brandy in the mornings, or tipping the grocer's boy coppers that weren't hers for gossip about her friends and neighbours. The housekeeper, Mrs Hatton, kept herself above stairs once Mrs Alleyn had retired for the night; she and Dorcas had their rooms on the top floor.

Starling made her way to the Moor's Head, to see her friend Sadie and to keep a tryst with Dick Weekes. She would need more of his doctored wine before long, but she was eager to see him anyway, however jealously she guarded all evidence of her favour. It would not do for Dick to know that she liked him overly well. He was devilishly easy on the eye, and never short of followers; dopey-eyed girls without a thought to share between them, who giggled and pouted at him wherever he went, all too keen to part their lips for whatever he cared to put into their mouths. But Dick Weekes was the type that needed something sharp to temper the sweet; that needed something off-kilter to keep his attention. *And I am just the right amount of sharp and off-kilter*, Starling thought, with a smile. The inn was crowded with drinkers and players, travellers and doxies. The heat and stink and press of bodies always cheered Starling after a humdrum day of work, and she smiled a crooked smile at Sadie as she reached the barrels and taps.

'All the usuals to keep you busy,' she said to her friend, as Sadie poured her a cup of frothy beer.

'And some unusuals too – see that man there, the tall one with only one eye? You ever seen him before?' She pointed out an ill-favoured man with a gaunt, sour face and a leather patch over his missing eye. His greasy hair was salt and pepper, and hadn't been combed in a while.

'No, I never saw him. He's wearing a fine enough pair of boots, though. Why do you point him out?'

'He says he's loved me a long time, and watched me from afar. He says if I meet him in the yard afterwards, he'll make me an offer I can't refuse.' Sadie chuckled, and Starling rolled her eyes.

'He'll make you his whore, and thrash you if you refuse.'

'Aye, most likely. Perhaps I'll meet him though.' The plump girl shrugged. 'He might be as good as his word. Those are fine boots . . . maybe he's rich, and soft-hearted, and will marry me and give me a life of idleness.'

'Maybe. And maybe I shall marry King George next Wednesday at noon. If you meet with him have Jonah watch you, for heaven's sake. And keep your wits about you.' Jonah was the stable boy at the Moor's Head, a hulking lad of sixteen years, quite in love with Sadie. 'Is Dick about?'

'Dick Weekes? Not yet. Stay and talk a while, till he gets here.'

Richard Weekes came in not long afterwards, looking as

dandy as he ever did, all loose hair and smiles. Sadie nudged Starling and nodded towards him, and Starling took her leave, planting a kiss on Sadie's fat cheek. She waited until Richard had shrugged off his coat in the heat of the inn, then pressed a brimming tankard into his right hand as she clasped his left and pressed it to her chest. She smiled a wicked smile at him, the way he liked.

'How do you do, Mr Weekes?' she said.

'Dying of thirst, but otherwise well. Leave off a moment, then, and let me drink.' He smiled.

'Leave off, he says! Why, you will break my heart, talking that way,' she said mockingly.

'Your heart?' Richard laughed. 'A thousand men with a thousand cudgels couldn't break your heart, Starling no-name.' Starling leaned closer to his ear, standing on her toes.

'Not a thousand but just one, and just one cudgel too.' She let her hand brush over his crotch, and felt his prick stir in response.

'You're eager tonight, aren't you?'

'I can't stay out for long. Dorcas has taken to getting up after midnight to drink milk. She says she has nightmares – comes clattering around the pantry like a blind heifer. She'd love to find me out, and run to tell Mrs Hatton. How my dissipation would scandalise.' Starling shook her head in irritation. 'So, come, Mr Weekes. Take me somewhere quieter, if you please.'

'It would be my pleasure. Just let me drink this at least. I meant it when I said I was dying of thirst.'

'Can't we go to your rooms?' Starling suggested. Dick had brought her out through the back door, to the yard behind the pub, and was trying to usher her up the ladder into the hay loft above the stables.

'No. Not any more.' Dick put his arm around her

shoulders, and squeezed her left breast too hard. Starling twisted away and slapped his cheek. 'Tease,' he scolded her.

'Clumsy joskins,' she retorted. 'That hurt. What do you mean, not any more?'

'In two days' time I shall be married. I can hardly bring my new bride to a bed that's ripe with your stink, can I?' he said lightly.

'I'm surprised to hear you'd take a wife so squeamish,' said Starling. She swallowed against a sudden tightness in her throat. Somehow, she'd thought all Dick's talk of marriage would come to nothing this time, as it had several times before. He usually backed away in the end, finding some fault in the girl; tiring of her, or declaring that he could do better. 'Don't you think she might smell me elsewhere – on your flesh, perhaps?'

'Rachel Crofton is sweet, and innocent. She suspects nothing of the kind.'

'Not yet, perhaps . . .'

'Not ever. And if she discovers anything from you, I will have your teeth out. Do you hear me?' Dick's voice was hard; he took her upper arm in a bruising grip. Starling grinned in the half-light.

'You mean to say, she believes you to be sweet and innocent, too?' she said. Dick released his grip and gently rubbed away his fingermarks.

'Yes, just so. Apologies, Starling. I am on edge. I want . . . I want everything to go well. With the wedding, and for my new wife. She is a fine creature, clever, and accomplished . . . with her by my side, my fortune and position can only improve,' he said. *Not clever enough to spot Dick Weekes for the tomcat he is*, Starling thought, contemptuously.

'My soul is consumed with jealous rage, sir. For it does

sound as though you love this sweet and innocent and clever and educated Miss Rachel.'

'Aye.' He smiled, somewhat foolishly. 'I believe I do.' Starling stared at him, and for a minute found nothing to say. He was a dark shape, his face outlined by second-hand light from the pub. Starling stepped back into the deep shadows in case her dismay was plain.

'Then perhaps, after she is home, you won't come to meet me any more?' She tried to say it lightly, as if she barely cared. Dick hesitated, as though the thought hadn't occurred to him.

'Perhaps not, Starling. Perhaps not.' His words, so careless, stabbed at Starling. She had a sensation like falling, like things being taken from her control. She smiled, as she always did to conceal such feelings.

'We'll see. Perhaps this milk-white angel of yours will keep the hunger sated for a while, but variety is the spice of life, as Sol Bradbury likes to say. Come then, let me give you something to remember me by.'

She led him up the ladder into the hayloft, and there teased and coaxed and mocked him until his face was ruddy and his teeth clenched in a seizure of utter lust and frustration, and then she straddled him and rode him hard, feeling her own pleasure spread up her spine like a warm tide rising. Afterwards, she laced her small breasts back into her bodice and watched Dick angrily as he caught his breath. Her senses always seemed heightened at such times, and suddenly she could smell the reek of horse piss from the stables, and the cloying scent of Dick's sweat and seed. She wrinkled her nose, and wiped herself with a switch of hay. Dick ground his fingertips into his eyes, where dust from the hay was irritating them, then blinked at her and grinned.

'Oh, I shall miss you, Starling,' he said.

'We'll see,' she replied, shortly.

'What do you mean?'

'What I say. Now, I ask a privilege of you, since we are to part.'

'What?' He was instantly suspicious. 'I already said I will not lace the wine any stronger. If Mr Alleyn should keel over dead . . .'

'Nothing to do with him. I want to meet your new bride. I want to meet Mrs Rachel Weekes, and understand why I am so suddenly set aside.' *And perhaps I will spill some blood-red wine on her pure white gown while I'm at it.*

'You can't,' he said at once. 'I wish to . . . draw a line. Between this old life, and the new one starting.'

'Don't be ridiculous!' said Starling, annoyed. 'A new wife cannot make you a new man. You'll still be Dick Weekes, son of Duncan Weekes . . . nothing will change that.'

'Shut your mouth, Starling. I mean to start anew, and you won't stop me. I won't let you stop me.' He caught her wrist and held it tightly, not letting go when she struggled.

'Leave off!'

'Not until you swear to be discreet.'

'If you let me meet her, I will swear it.' They struggled a few seconds more, then Dick released her arm.

'Very well. Two nights hence, I shall bring her here for our wedding feast. You can play the serving wench for a time, or something. Or merely watch from a quiet place. But you will not speak to her. Understand?'

'A wedding feast at the Moor's Head? Ah, lucky Miss Rachel. Truly, she is bringing you up in the world . . .'

'*Understand?*' he pressed.

'I won't give you away. You have my word.' *You will do that yourself,* she thought, defiantly, *when you come running back to me.*

* * *

To Rachel's relief, there was more to the house on Abbeygate Street than she'd first realised. Steps led down from street level to the main area of the shop, which had its own door, and a sign painted onto the wall above it: *Richard Weekes & Co. Fine Wine & Spirits Merchants*. The room on this lower level was cool and clammy, the brick floor slightly damp. Barrels were stacked in wooden racks from floor to shadowed ceiling, and glass bottles of all shapes and sizes filled shelves against one wall. It was a dark and crowded space, and the air had a ripe tang to it, a pungent mix of wood and fruit, mould and alcohol. Through a door in the rear wall Richard had his tiny office, containing a desk with a simple stool pulled up to it, and a shelf laden with ledgers and receipt books. The desk was scatted with pen shavings, spent candle stubs and spots of ink.

Behind the house was a small yard, closed in by high walls furred with moss and slime. The yard had a stone sink built against one wall, the necessary house against another, and a shallow gully that ran into the sewer. It was poorly ventilated, and smelled accordingly rank. Rachel peered around it, and her heart sank. When Richard had told her there was a courtyard, she'd pictured a small garden where she might plant some herbs or flowers, and sit to read in either the morning sun or the evening, depending on which way the house faced. This yard was more like the damp inside of a cave. Within moments Rachel felt the walls begin to loom over her, and she stepped hurriedly back indoors, keen to conceal her dismay.

'I have always sent the laundry out, and it's probably best you continue to do so, rather than trying to dry it out here,' said Richard, apologetically.

Upstairs, at raised ground level, was a kitchen-cum-parlour, a good sized and better-lit room divided into two halves – one half of simple utility: the stove, a work table, shelves holding a few pieces of pewter plate, candlesticks and cooking pots. The other half was more formal, with an upholstered armchair, settle and ottoman that had finely turned – if battered – legs. They'd been positioned with their backs to the kitchen, as if not wishing to be associated with it.

'The parlour furniture came from Admiral Stanton's widow, when she was forced to sell up. I had it at a very fair price at auction,' Richard told her proudly. 'Do you approve?' He ran his hand along the back of the settle. Rachel nodded, feeling a pull of sympathy towards the faceless Widow Stanton, for her sad decline in life. She knew exactly how it felt to see people perusing and haggling over the things you owned and loved. Richard was watching her, expectantly.

'They will do very well, Mr Weekes,' she assured him.

'In a similar manner, I mean to gradually work towards furnishing the place in a better fashion for you, my dear.' He took her hand, and kissed her fingers.

The room had two large windows, one overlooking the yard, the other facing north onto the parade of shops, inns and accommodation on the opposite side of Abbeygate Street. By looking north-east from this one, Rachel could see the roof of the abbey. On the top floor of the house was the bedchamber where, the night before, Rachel had ceased to be a maid. Its beamed ceiling sloped to either side of the bed, and its window was smaller, tucked into the eaves of the roof. Rachel realised that the body of the house was hundreds of years older than its updated façade hoped to suggest. She ignored the smell of damp plaster, and turned to smile at her husband.

'I shall be very comfortable here. And I'll help make it even more cosy for us,' she said.

Past the jumbled rooftops and chimney pots of their near neighbours, the sweeping curves of Bath's smarter streets and crescents were visible, on the hills to the north. Rachel could make out the elegant march of Camden Crescent, high above the rest of the city; its tall façades uniform, pale, and immaculate. There, when she was fifteen, she'd spent three months one autumn and winter season with her parents and her little brother, Christopher. Her memories of it were a blur of tea invitations, card parties, outings and dances in the assembly rooms. Now Rachel wished she'd paid more attention, and cemented such happiness more firmly in her mind – as if she could have fashioned it into something she could keep for ever. But she remembered standing at one of the front windows in their apartment and looking down on the tangle of older, poorer streets around the abbey and wharves, and wondering about all the many lives that went on there, of which she would have no knowledge, and take no part. She smiled at the thought, with an odd mixture of wistful irony, and determination.

'What is it? What makes you smile?' Richard asked her, brushing a lock of her hair away from her face.

'I am beginning to feel at home already,' she said, deciding to make it true. She felt Richard's arms encircle her, and in truth the sensation was already less peculiar, less alarming.

There was no food in the house, so Richard fetched fresh bread, cheese and a slice of ham pie for their breakfast. Then he took her on a tour of the street, introducing her to the neighbours she needed to know – Mrs Digweed, who took in the laundry, a woman vastly fat and startlingly ugly, with hands like a man's and a broad smile for the world; Thomas Snook, who owned the stables around the corner, on Amery Lane, and hired out his horse and cart to Richard for deliveries. The horse was a squat, piebald thing, with feathery feet and sleepy eyes; Rachel remembered it from the times Richard had delivered barrels to Hartford Hall. Richard rubbed the horse's forehead cheerfully, and said: 'This is

Trooper, and never was a horse less aptly named. "Dawdler" would be more like it, but he's a serviceable chap. In a year or so I hope to be able to buy a smarter cart than Tom's, one with my sign painted along the side, rather than carried with me on a board. And for that cart I shall need a smarter animal, I fear, Trooper. Something with less hair, and more spirit.' He patted the animal's sturdy neck, and Trooper sighed, as only a bored horse can sigh.

There was a small cobbled square called Abbey Green, just along from Abbeygate Street, and the lone plane tree growing there had crisp bronze edges to its leaves. The sky was overcast, and Rachel suddenly wished it was spring, not autumn. Spring would have made everything feel more promising, more like a new beginning. Later, once Richard had gone about his business, Rachel stood for a while in her new home, and wondered what to do. She knew Richard had a housekeeper, Mrs Linton, who visited on certain days, but the woman had yet to put in an appearance. She glanced around at the cobwebs high up in the stairwell, and the ground-in dirt on the floorboards, and thought that Richard had lived too long alone, and that Mrs Linton was either unfit, or had been left too much to her own devices, and grown idle. In the sudden quiet, Rachel took a steadying breath. She had never minded an empty room before, but suddenly the emptiness seemed to ring; it seemed to mirror and amplify the odd, empty feeling inside her. She shut her eyes, and tried to summon thoughts to fill it, to quell the strange and sudden panic she felt. Just then, she would even have wished Eliza Trevelyan back into her life, with all of her arrogance and scorn.

Rachel went upstairs and set about making herself a dressing table of sorts, on top of the small chest of drawers where Richard's clothes and sundries were kept. She opened each drawer in turn, hoping to find an empty one that she could use, but all contained oddments of dress and accoutrements — worn-out gloves and stockings, boot buckles and tobacco boxes and combs with broken teeth. In the end she moved everything in the top drawer to one side, and put in a few of her own possessions. She did not have much — handkerchiefs and gloves, her sewing box, hairpins and what few beauty compounds she used: a small pot of rouge with a tiny, shell-handled brush to apply it; some heavy cream, scented with roses, for her hands; a pot of Lady Molyneux's Liquid Bloom, which had been a present from Eliza at Christmas last. *For you sometimes appear so pale at breakfast, it's like you've died in the night and not realised.* But the gift, meant as a criticism of sorts, had rather backfired on Eliza, because a few drops of the stuff rubbed into her cheeks did in fact make Rachel look lovely. She laid an old handkerchief on top of the chest and set out her hair brushes on it, and then unpacked her most treasured possession — a musical silver trinket box.

Her parents had given it to her on her sixteenth birthday, before any stain of scandal or hardship had touched the family, and the grief of losing Christopher had softened somewhat from the dagger strike of his sudden death. It had been her mother's and her grandmother's before it was hers; an item only as big as one of her hands, standing on little lion's feet. The top was patterned with vines and flowers, forming a vignette around a brightly enamelled peacock; when the lid was lifted, providing the screw underneath was wound tight, it played a lullaby. The inside of the box was lined with deep blue velvet, and a lock of her mother's tawny hair, tied with a ribbon, was pinned carefully to one side. Rachel touched it gently with her fingertips. The hair was straight, and smooth, and cold. She shut her eyes and tried to recall Anne Crofton's face in every detail, even though she knew it was a cruel thing to do to herself, and only reiterated her mother's absence.

Also in the music box was the only other precious thing she owned, which had also been her mother's — a pair of pearl drop earrings with tiny diamonds on the studs. She'd hidden them in her bodice as the bailiffs had taken everything out to their wagon, past her father on the front steps, sitting with his boots unlaced and his face gone slack in shock. The bailiffs would have taken his boots too, if Rachel had not come out to stand over him, fierce as a lioness, shaming them into a retreat. She wanted to keep the box on display, but she hesitated. It seemed somehow boastful, like a deliberate attempt to show up the plainness of the room. Reluctantly, she wrapped it in its linen cloth and put it back in the drawer. Then she rose, and went to stand by the bed to watch out of the window. There was a small, foxed mirror on the wall; she positioned herself so that her reflection hovered in the corner of her eye, and at once felt a little less alone.

Richard was away from the house or ensconced amongst the barrels in the basement for much of the day, but for the first two weeks of their marriage they ate supper together every night, at the small table in the kitchen, with their food and faces lit by the yellow warmth of an oil lamp, discussing the housekeeping, the business, their hopes for the future. One evening, when Rachel had been talking about her parents, she looked up to find Richard watching her with a compassionate expression.

'You miss them a great deal, don't you?' he said.

'Yes. In truth, I do. My mother has been a good many years with God, but still I feel her absence, and the lack of her advice, her . . . good sense and her kindness. And that of my father, of course. But I can do nothing but try to accept, and not rail against the loss. I can remember the happy times we had together, when Christopher was still with us, and I was very young.' *Young and full of feeling, not numb and quiet, as now*, said the shadow inside her head; but such observations were not for sharing.

'Rachel.' Richard covered her hand with his, and smiled. 'I want so much for you to be happy again. For us to be a family,' he said.

'I am happy,' said Rachel, and again she felt something stir inside her, the warmth of gratitude towards him. *He does truly wish to make me happy*. But there was also a fleeting barb of doubt, of deceit, when she spoke. *I will be happy soon*, she amended, silently. *When he grows to fill my heart*.

'We are alike, you and I. In our experiences . . . we have both lost our families, the people who raised us and loved us. I . . . it is hard, not to dwell in the past. The temptation to do so is very strong.' He squeezed her fingers, and in his eyes was some desperation she didn't yet understand. 'But we all need somebody to share life with. To understand us, and carve a future with us. I am so happy to have found you, Rachel.'

'And I you. But . . . your father . . .'

'My father is lost to me,' said Richard, curtly.

'I'm sorry for it, Mr Weekes.'

As a wedding gift, Richard had presented Rachel with a new book by John Keats, since he knew her love of reading. One evening she asked him to read it to her, and he took the book with a look of distaste and anxiety. He did his best, but it was clear that he did not enjoy the experience. The lines of the poems were stilted, the rhythm lost; the meaning hard to follow when read as he did – as words on a page, not as the deepest thoughts of a man, rendered beautiful with language. For as long as she could, Rachel listened to 'The Eve of Saint Agnes' made blunt and bewildering, but Richard's rendition was like listening to a melody played on an ill-tuned piano, and she found after a while that her jaw was clenched tight, and her eyes too, and she longed for the noise to stop. When silence fell she looked up to find Richard watching her, his expression one of defeat.

'I fear I am not a very good reader,' he said quietly. Rachel coloured up with guilt.

'Oh, no! You did fine, Richard. It's only a certain way of speaking, and comes easily with practice,' she said.

'Well.' He closed the book and put it into her hands. 'It's hard to change the way one speaks.'

'Oh, I didn't mean . . . I meant only that reading poetry is rather more like . . . acting in a play, than reading straight, as from a periodical,' she said, trying to undo any slight he might have felt.

'A skill I've never had call to acquire,' he said, a touch crossly.

'No more have you that call now, if you do not wish it. Shall I read to you for a while, instead?'

'As you wish, Rachel. I'm very tired.' So Rachel opened the book and immersed herself for some minutes in the wonderful images, the strange beauty of it. She concentrated, and shaped each line as best she could, seeking to delight her husband, to prove her love of poetry well founded. But when she finished his chin had sunk onto his chest in slumber. She wondered whether to wake him and lead him up to bed, but it still seemed too forward a thing to do. So she sat in silence for a long time, with only the sifting sound of ash settling in the grate for company.

Strange and conspicuous though it made her feel, Rachel took to walking the streets of Bath alone, without an escort. But whether it was a symptom of her age, her faded looks, or the unfashionable nature of her dress, she soon began to notice looks of disapproval, appraisal, and even amusement, aimed at her as she marched along Milsom Street. She wondered if she was mistaken for a servant out on some errand for her mistress. Milsom Street was wide and airy, a parade of shops and businesses running south to north through the middle of the city, its paving stones swept cleaner than the rest. Carriages and carts and people hurried to and fro, causing a constant clatter of hooves and wheels and chatter; barrow boys and hawkers shouted their wares above it all in voices gone ragged. Some of the shops Rachel remembered from years earlier were still in business – like the milliner where her mother had bought her a new hat, trimmed with silk roses and a green velvet ribbon. One afternoon she stopped in the abbey square. Of course the vast abbey and assembly rooms and hot baths were just as she remembered them, and it struck her hard that though they had not changed, she had. She did not belong to them in the way she once had.

Her family had never been rich, but were better off than most. Her father, John Crofton, was the squire of a small estate of four farms, and had owned several hundred acres of rolling countryside where sheep and cattle grazed. The manor house where Rachel had grown up was long and low – built in the reign of Queen Elizabeth – with thick stone walls, mullioned windows and a roof that sagged between its rafters. An ancient wisteria snaked across the entire façade, producing a throng of hanging purple flowers each May and June. It was a comfortable home, well worn-in by centuries of habitation. In Rachel's room the wooden floor sloped so pronouncedly that she and Christopher often used it in games – setting their marbles to roll across it towards a particular target. It was a house in which the children's laughter was encouraged to ring out, and come echoing down the twisted wooden stair, never hushed or reprimanded.

John Crofton was entirely happy in the midstream where

he swam. He did not fret about cozening his superiors, or waste time trying to ingratiate himself with those who held themselves lofty and aloof. Instead, John and Anne socialised with friends they were genuinely fond of, so that supper parties and teas and music evenings were merry, jovial affairs. On one occasion they were invited to dine with Sir Paul Methuen at the impossibly grand Corsham Court, which seemed the sort of place from which Rachel's parents might emerge for ever altered, chastened or mesmerised in some way. But the Croftons returned from their evening laughing about how dull Sir Paul had been, and how preposterous the other guests had made themselves, in seeking his favour. They were not invited back again, and cared not one jot.

The two years that Rachel was away at a boarding school for young ladies, she pined for the manor house, and visited her family as often as was permitted. The three seasons that the Croftons spent in Bath introduced Rachel to a greater scale of society, and to the different fashions and foibles of city life, but the same Crofton rules applied – there was no attempt at social gain, only the pursuit of enjoyment and diversion with like-minded people. If Rachel or her parents happened to meet a young man who might be a suitable match for her, then he would be judged on his temperament, his interests and his inclination to industry, not by his name alone. She never did meet anybody there that she admired in that way, however. Handsome faces almost always turned out to be attached to vain and foolish boys. She preferred walking with her mother and friends, shopping for oddments with which they could improve a dress or a pair of shoes, or could send out as gifts; and seeing Christopher, who hated to be left behind, come bounding down the stairs upon their return.

As Rachel left the abbey square and resumed her walking, Christopher's face came so clearly before her eyes that her steps faltered. A thin, avid face beneath a thatch of sandy blond hair, so much darker than her own. He'd had honey-brown eyes and a sharp, straight nose that the summer sun scattered with freckles. The fever that took him was brutally quick. He complained of feeling dizzy at bedtime on Monday, and was dead by sunset on Wednesday. He'd been so vibrant, so full of life and mischief, none of them could believe it had happened. They sat with his small corpse for hours, all three of them, simply staring and trying to make sense of what they saw.

With a gasp, Rachel stopped abruptly in the street, suddenly unable to breathe. People parted around her, jostling, but none stopped to offer her any assistance. She heard a tut of disapproval, and looked up at an elegant elderly lady, who turned her face aside at once, gazing loftily away. *Who are these people?* Rachel turned off Milsom Street then, and did not return to it.

Her route led her past the Moor's Head, where gulls wheeled above in a rare flood of sunshine, calling out their mocking cacophony. The pavement was crowded with people and tangled with their voices, but then Rachel realised with a start that one voice was calling her name – a name she was still unaccustomed to.

'Mrs Weekes! Won't you pause a moment?' Rachel turned to see Duncan Weekes, now her father-in-law, crossing the street towards her on none too steady feet. She almost turned away and pretended not to see him, remembering Richard's curt statement that his father was lost to him. *But should I blank the old man in the street, then, when he is now also my family as well?* And after two hours of walking, she couldn't help but feel relieved to see a face she knew. Duncan Weekes's brown coat might once have been decent, but it had worn through at the elbows, lost three buttons and had grease stains on the cuffs. His wig was as crooked as it had been the first time she saw him, and his face was ruddy, the nose a pitted ruin of broken blood vessels, knotty and purple.

'Mr Weekes, how do you do?' she said. A smile crowded his eyes with folds of pouched skin.

'Mrs Weekes! I am all the better for seeing your lovely face, my dear. How do you do? And how fares my son?'

'We are both very well, sir, thank you. I was just out walking . . .'

'Very good, very good. I'm happy to see you again. And how are you finding our fair city of Bath? Is it to your liking?' As he spoke, Duncan Weekes swayed, just a little. He peered at her closely, his eyes roving her face with a kind of meandering but relentless scrutiny that Rachel found almost intrusive. His breath was sour, and he spoke with a strong West Country accent.

'Oh, very much, sir,' she said. 'I'd been here before, several times, with my family. It's wonderful to become reacquainted with it.'

'And where are your family now, my dear?'

'They have . . . passed, I regret to tell,' she said. Duncan Weekes's face fell, and he nodded.

'A sad thing, as well I know. You have my sympathies, my dear. Richard's mother, my own dear Susanne, was taken far too soon, when Dick was still just a lad.'

'Yes, he told me he scarcely knew his mother.'

'Oh, he knew her well, and loved her better. But he was just eight years old when she died, so perhaps his memories of her grow dim,' said the old man, sadly.

'What was she like?'

'Well, the handsome face my son inherits did not come from me, I dare say you can divine.' He smiled. 'To me she was as lovely as a summer's day, though she had a temper that could scare the birds into flight five miles away, and a voice to match. So perhaps not a lady as refined as you, my dear, but a lady as dear to me as my own breath.'

'I am not so very refined,' Rachel demurred.

'Oh, nonsense. Nonsense.' The old man paused, and his eyes explored Rachel's face again, full of that strange scrutiny. 'Tell me . . . where did he find you?'

'He . . . we . . .' Rachel stammered, given pause by his odd turn of phrase. 'I was governess to a client of his, outside Bath. It was there that we met.'

'Outside Bath, you say? Well, well.'

Duncan Weekes paused, nodding in thought. 'I could not be happier for my son, to have taken one such as you to wife. I have seen him strive to rise above the lowly situation of his birth . . . And he has done it, for certain. For how else would he win such a lady, if he had not made himself worthy?' Duncan smiled again, but his eyes were full of questions. Rachel reflected for a moment, and thought of the long and lonely path that had led her to accept Richard's proposal. *Would that it were as simple and true a matter as his fair face, his self-improvement, and my admiration of both.*

'I have wanted to apologise to you for . . . for the abrupt way in which my husband dealt with you at our wedding feast. I should have liked for you to join us, since we are family,' she said, a touch awkwardly. Duncan Weekes hesitated before replying, and his tired eyes blurred a little.

'Ah, but you are a kind girl, as well as a fine one. My son harbours a staunch grudge against me, and has these many years. He is angry with me. Aye, still angry.' He shook his head.

'But whatever for?'

'Matters long past. The list is a long one, and there are doubtless things upon it that I do not even remember . . .' Duncan trailed into silence, and looked away as if not wishing to meet her eye. Rachel was sure that she was not being told the whole truth.

'Forgive me – it's no business of mine what has passed between you. But I can see that it saddens you, and I'm sorry for it. Perhaps if I speak to my husband, sir . . . I might be able to persuade him to let bygones be bygones?' she suggested.

'Do not risk his displeasure on my behalf, Mrs Weekes,' he said. Rachel considered for a moment, then took his hand and held it in hers. His fingers were thick, the knuckles ridged with old scars and arthritis. He seemed so tired, so sadly disordered; but his hand in hers soon felt conspicuous, and she was made uncomfortable by her own gesture.

'I can make no promise of success, sir,' she said. 'But I understand the importance of family; I hate to see such a valuable thing cast aside, so I will try.'

Duncan Weekes suddenly looked uneasy. He cleared his throat, and his next words sounded wary.

'Have a care, my dear; wiser not to speak of me to my son. Old wounds are not easily healed, and he has some of his mother's temper, as well as her looks.'

'I have never seen him show a temper,' said Rachel, releasing his hand. She suppressed the urge to brush her fingers on her skirt.

'Indeed?' Duncan frowned, but then his expression softened. 'And indeed, who could show a temper to someone as sweet and kind as you, my dear. Perhaps you might come and visit with me sometime? I should be honoured to have you . . . we might take a brandy together, to toast your marriage, since I was absent from the feast.'

'I will have to ask my husband, of course, but I should like—'

'If you ask him, he will refuse it,' Duncan interrupted, anxious again. 'He would be wroth with you and I both, my dear, if you ask him outright. He might even seek me out to offer a reprimand.'

'I'm sure he would not, sir . . . and I must ask him – of course I must.'

'Then that is a great pity, for I had hoped you might indeed come.' Duncan Weekes tucked his fingers into his waistcoat pockets and looked away along the street, his face losing all animation. Rachel wasn't sure what reply to make to him. The old man was shivering slightly.

'You must carry on, sir, and not stand about to get chilled here in the street. But do give me your calling card, so that I will know where to go,' she said.

'My card? My card . . .' he muttered, patting his pockets absently. 'My card. Yes. I fear I have none, my dear. But I will tell you the place, if you can remember it?' Rachel committed it to memory, and as she took her leave Duncan Weekes caught her hand again. 'But do have a care, sweet girl,' he said earnestly. 'Do have a care.'

That night she lay close to Richard, after they had made love. She'd tried, as she did each time, to find the physical pleasure that her mother had hinted at, on the few occasions when they'd spoken of marriage and what Rachel could expect. But while there was no longer any pain, there was no real pleasure either. Nothing other than a faint ache that she was curious to explore; a feeling that might be satisfying to pursue, like the pressing of a bruise. But Richard had always come to his climax, gasping for breath in the crook of her neck, before she'd had a chance to examine the feeling properly. She told herself that she was happy to give satisfaction, without needing to take any for herself, but at the same time couldn't help but feel mildly disappointed.

But the warmth of Richard's body, lying tangled with hers, was comforting. He felt solid, and real; something like an anchor when she had started to feel oddly cut adrift. She clasped her fingers tightly into the dense flesh of his shoulders, and pressed her cheek into the top of his head.

'Are you all right, Rachel?' he whispered.

'Yes, my love,' she said. She felt him smile.

'That's the first time you've called me that. Called me your love,' he said.

'Do you like me to?'

'Very much so. I like it . . . very much.' Richard's voice was muffled, but she could hear that he was moved. She kissed his hair, and shut her eyes tight, suddenly afraid that she would start crying. She could not have said what the tears were for. 'Are you . . . are you happy, here? With me? You have no regrets?' he asked. Rachel did not answer at once, and Richard pulled back, rising onto his elbows above her so that she could just make out the shape of his face in the weak light from the street outside. 'Rachel?' he said anxiously. She put up her hand, cupped it around his chin.

'I have no regrets,' she said, hoping that this answer, to only part of his question, would be enough. Richard smiled again, and kissed her hand.

'You are an angel, my love,' he said, his voice thickening with somnolence. He returned his head to her shoulder, his chin digging into her collarbone, and was asleep within moments.

Rachel lay awake a long while. She could smell the faint grease of Richard's hair, and the bitter tang of the coal smuts in the grate. *When he plants a child within me, my love for him will grow along with it. Then we will truly be a family, and all will be well.* Through the walls came sounds of movement and words; the bass rumbling of a man's voice, raised in anger. The wooden skeleton of the building creaked with footsteps. A cold draught seeped in around the window frame, and touched Rachel's face with a promise of the winter that was coming. When she slept, it was to dream of a sparkling river, fast running and lively with sunlight. She both loved and feared this river, in her dream, with a foreboding like gathering thunderclouds. She seemed to hover above the water's surface, suspended somehow; she heard a shout of fear, and it wasn't her voice. There was a smell of green summer all around, and the notion that the pretty river wanted something from her.

The next morning, Rachel waited until Richard had had something to eat and drink before she raised the subject of his father. He was often sullen and unhappy first thing after waking, and she had quickly learnt not to talk too much, or too loudly, until he had breakfasted. She fetched him slices of bread spread with honey, and some boiled eggs, putting them down around him as he stared at the table top and swigged from a tankard of ale.

'You won't guess who I chanced upon yesterday,' she said, lightly, when the moment seemed right.

'Oh?' The word was spoken low, and barely interested.

'Your father, Duncan Weekes.' Rachel sat down opposite Richard, and her smile faltered in the face of his bleak expression. 'We happened upon one another in the street, and . . .' She trailed off. 'He asked after you. Asked how you were,' she said instead.

'It is no business of his how I am, and you've no business talking to him. About me, or about anything else for that matter.' Richard's voice was low, but his words shocked Rachel.

'But, my dear, he is your *father*! And since I have none, he is my father now too—'

'No, Rachel! He is *not* your father! Not one whit!'

'Haven't we spoken of the pain of losing family, Mr Weekes? Haven't we spoken of how important such people are, and how we wish to be a family to one another?'

'I have disowned that man. He is no longer my father! Do you understand?' Richard thumped the table top with his hand, making the cutlery and his wife jump. Rachel's heart hammered, but she persevered; she was sure she had the right of it, that she could persuade him. *Have a care.* She remembered Duncan Weekes's words, but rejected them.

'No, I do not understand. What can he possibly have done to turn you away from him like this? And . . . even if you feel yourself aggrieved . . . he is but an old man, and clearly poor and in need of our charity . . .'

'*If I feel myself aggrieved?* Do you doubt me, then? Do you think I would turn away from my father on a *whim?*' Richard's voice was rough with anger; he jabbed a finger at her as he spoke. 'How dare you? That man would not be half so poor if he did not drink his every wage within a day of being paid it! He is a sot, and a fool, and he has blighted my life in ways you can't possibly imagine! He killed my mother – did he tell you that? So do not seek to lecture me on how I should or should not treat him! You will have nothing to do with him, or by God I will hear about it!'

Rachel flinched away from him, from his raised voice and his pointing finger, and the anger stringing his body as tight as piano wire. She was robbed of speech by the shock of it; she had never been spoken to that way before, had never even heard such anger before. Richard glared at her, then picked up his mug to take another swig of ale, as Rachel simply sat and stared, her cheeks flaming and her mouth and mind empty of words. She was still trying in vain to find something to say when Richard stood and drained his drink. 'I must be gone,' he said, calmly but coldly. 'Let us hear no more about this.' He strode from the room with a scowl on his face, and Rachel sat in his wake feeling as though she'd been stripped naked in public – outraged and ashamed. It took a long time for her heartbeat to return to normal, and for her fingers to stop shaking.

* * *

Nine nights since Dick Weekes's wedding and still Starling could not sleep. She lay on her narrow bed in the flawless dark of her room, and listened to Sol Bradbury huffing and mumbling in her sleep. There was a stale smell, sharp and feral, rising from her own body, and she realised she'd forgotten to wash. She clenched her fists tight, angry with herself. She'd been sleepwalking through the days since she set eyes on Dick's new wife – on that face – with only a small portion of her mind tuned to any task and the remainder caught up in what she had seen, and what it might mean. One day she hadn't noticed that the spit jack was jammed, and a shoulder of pork had been charred to cinders on one side. She'd ruined three gallons of ginger beer by adding too much yeast, so that those bottles that hadn't exploded tasted vile. Even cheerful Sol had started to tut and sigh at her vacant expression and distracted frown.

When Starling pictured Dick Weekes's bride, her breathing quickened involuntarily. She pictured large, heavy-lidded blue eyes, high cheekbones and a pointed chin with just the hint of dimple in it, a small, neat mouth, a stony pallor on smooth skin, and pale hair the colour of fresh cream. It could not be a coincidence. There had to be some meaning to this woman's sudden appearance in Bath, and there certainly had to be some way in which Starling could use her. This was the chance she'd been waiting for, the chance she'd been longing for. She was not yet sure what would happen but the first step, she decided as the solid black of night began to pale, was that Dick Weekes must introduce his wife to Mrs Josephine Alleyn, mistress of the house on Lansdown Crescent. There was no other way that this new Mrs Weekes could be brought into the house, no way Jonathan Alleyn could be confronted with her alarming face, than by her first being seen by his mother, Josephine.

The next day, Starling was still mulling over how she would bring this about when a serendipitous opportunity presented itself. Dorcas still refused to go anywhere near Jonathan Alleyn, so Starling continued to see to his rooms. The day had dawned overcast, and drizzly. Viewed from the upper storey of the house, the city and the river valley were cloaked in mist and murk. Still, Starling saw Jonathan flinch as she threw open his shutters. He was tall and lean; long cheek-bones in a fox-like face with a pointed nose and an angular jaw; long fingers, furrows across his forehead. He had dark brows above dark, watchful eyes, and his hair, greasy and knotted, grew in unkempt waves down to his shoulders. He had slept in his chair again, fully clothed, and he hadn't shaved for days. There was a letter in his hand. One of Alice's, Starling guessed at once. Her heart gave a funny little jump in her chest. The paper was old and rumpled, torn at the edges. He'd been sleeping with it clasped to his chest, as if for comfort. *Beg her all you want*, Starling thought. *It's too late. She can't forgive you now, and neither will I.* Jonathan stared at her for a minute in apparent confusion, and she braced herself, but then his head fell back against the chair, and his eyes slid away, fixing on the window glass.

'Get out. Leave me be,' he murmured.

'Your breakfast is on the table behind you,' said Starling, knowing he would not touch it. He rarely ate anything before noon, sometimes nothing until dark fell. Sometimes nothing at all, all day.

'Leave me be, I said.' His voice was cracked and hollow.

Starling drifted away from him to the fireplace. She swept out the cold ashes, laid in kindling and fresh coals, and relit it. There was a smashed glass on the floor by his desk, and she swept that up too, and only realised, as she was ready to leave the room, how quiet and kind to him she was being. *It's the letter*, she thought at once. When he took Alice's letters out of whatever secret place he kept them, it was like some trace of her came into the room; some ghost of her came into Starling's heart, laid soft fingers on the hurt and the anger, and gentled her. *No. I will not be gentled.* She ground her teeth together and called to mind the reason why Alice was not there herself, to make everyone more gentle: the fact that Alice was gone. The thought cut her, and reopened the wound from which her bitterness flowed. She turned and looked at the top of Jonathan's head, just visible over the back of his chair. His arm had flopped to the side now; Alice's letter dangled precariously from his fingertips. *If he lets it drop, like something of no import, then I will kill him here and now.* But Jonathan did not let the letter fall.

Starling took several slow steps towards him. She could tell from his breathing that he was drowsing again, and she listened for a while because there was something pleasing in the sound its simple rhythm, its vulnerability. He murmured in his sleep, his voice deep and indistinct at first, then rising to sound pitiful, frightened, almost childlike. Cautiously, Starling moved to his side. His head had lolled forwards, chin to his chest. She knelt down to look into his face, and saw his eyeballs switching to and fro beneath the lids. There was a crease between his brows and his breathing was faster now, less even. *He dreams. He dreams in fear.* She found herself leaning closer and closer to his face, fascinated. His lips moved, not quite giving shape to the sounds in his throat. *What do you see, Mr Alleyn? What do you see that frightens you so?* He gave a low moan then, and his hands jerked up, clenching into fists. Alice's letter was crumpled between his fingers, and Starling stared at it, wondering if she could prise it free without him realising. She reached for it, pinched it and pulled gently, but Jonathan held it fast. Holding her breath she pulled harder, but the paper would not come free.

'No!' Jonathan cried out, and Starling was on her feet and backing away from him in an instant. But he was sleeping still. 'No,' he said again, in that high, plaintive voice. 'No, no, no . . . I never meant to. I have . . . I have . . .' His eyes had flickered open a fraction, showing a ghastly sliver of white. His mouth moved constantly. 'There is blood! There is blood . . .' he muttered, and then moaned again, a sound of intense anguish.

'Yes,' Starling whispered, suddenly cold right through to her bones. 'Yes, I know. There is blood on your hands.' At the sound of her voice Jonathan flinched, and shifted in his chair. His eyes stilled, and he said nothing more. *Sleep easy while you can, for I will find a way to prove your guilt.*

It wasn't the first time she'd heard Jonathan talk that way. Sometimes, when he'd been drinking or had one of his headaches, he seemed to fall into a kind of waking trance, and would speak to people who were not in the room, as though he heard questions in the empty air. A lot of what he said – most of it – made no sense at all. But sometimes he would say something chilling, something that reeked of guilt and violence; and when he did Starling was reminded of the moment her suspicions became certainty, after Jonathan came back from the war for the final time, in 1812. That was three years after Alice's disappearance, and no one in the house at Box was allowed to say her name. Jonathan lay in bed for several weeks with his leg all bandaged and stinking, and would see nobody.

Starling was a servant in that house, nothing more; she had to adjust herself – her feelings and her behaviour. She could not just speak to Jonathan, as once she might. When she thought of the smooth, bright face she'd glimpsed when first she saw him, she could hardly believe that this ravaged, hollow-cheeked creature was the same man. Eventually she found a way into his room, and she was incautious, and hadn't yet learnt to be wary of his rages. She rushed right up to him, took his hand unguardedly and begged to know if he'd had word from Alice, or planned to search for her now his leg was healed. Jonathan pulled his hand away and dealt her a blow across her face that laid her flat out on her back, dazed and stupid. He was calm as he did it, all empty-eyed and absent. From then on she knew she would have to be more subtle if she wanted to glean anything from him; she knew he was not the same man she had known, and she began to fear what he was capable of.

And then, one day not long after that, she took a jug of warm spiced milk to his room and found him panting and sweating at the pains in his head, pacing the room, gripping his skull with both hands and muttering a steady stream of nonsense. And she heard him say it. She heard it for the first time, and she turned as cold and unfeeling as ice, all over. The crash of the milk jug as it hit the floor brought another servant running, and brought Jonathan wheeling towards her, teeth bared in the incoherent fury of his suffering, and all dissolved into chaos and strife for a while. But she had heard it, clear as day. She had heard him say it. *She is dead. Oh God, she is dead.* Starling did not sleep that night – did not even close her eyes. The long, empty hours distilled all her fears and confusion into a cold, hard conviction. She knew that Jonathan Alleyn was her enemy.

From then on, she tormented him in any way she could. She found a thousand little ways in which to make him suffer, to madden him, to prevent his rest. For why should he rest, when she could not? Why should he rest, when Alice was stolen and gone? She worked to make him betray himself; she worked to make him confess, and unmask himself to the world. And when he did neither of these things she worked on, ever on, driving and provoking him. Years later, when he attempted to take his own life, she had the chance to let him die. She could have made an end to it, but when the moment came she saved him. She stopped him. Death would be a relief, after all – it would bring rest. And she would not let him rest.

In the hallway outside Jonathan's rooms on Lansdown Crescent, as he still slept with Alice's letter clasped in his hand, Starling found Mrs Alleyn waiting for her, tall and serene. Jonathan's mother was past fifty years of age, but still very lovely. In her day, it was said, she had been one of the most celebrated beauties in the West Country. Starling had first met her when she was forty, in the first awful weeks after Alice disappeared, and indeed she had been beautiful then. Now her cornflower-blue eyes sat surrounded by fine lines, and there were deep creases bracketing her mouth, which had begun to lose the curve in its upper lip. But her cheekbones were still high and smooth, her brows still delicately arched, and her jaw still firm. Her hair had once been a deep, dark brown, the colour of molasses; now it was iron grey, swept back against her skull but for some precise ringlets to frame her face. Many women half her age were not half so handsome. Starling curtsied at once.

'Starling! How is it you are upstairs? Don't tell me my son has seen off another housemaid?'

'I don't think she has quite run away yet. Mrs Hatton hopes to persuade her to stay.'

'But she will not go into my son's rooms?'

'No, madam. She will not.'

'Foolish creature.' Josephine Alleyn sighed. 'He is heart-sick, and unwell. He is not a danger to anybody.' Starling said nothing to this, and Mrs Alleyn studied her closely. 'What is it, girl? You look as though you have something you would say?'

'No, madam,' said Starling.

'You do not mind, then – helping my son when others will not?'

'No, madam. Only . . .'

'Speak.'

'It makes it rather hard, to do all my work downstairs, when I have duties upstairs as well.'

'I see. What do you suggest? That I raise you to house-maid, and employ a new kitchen maid in your place?'

'If it please you, madam. There might not be another girl better fitted to serve Mr Alleyn than I am.'

'Ah, but the very reason he does not shock you is the very reason that keeps you below stairs, Starling.' Mrs Alleyn smiled, not unkindly. 'I fear you are better suited to the kitchen and still room.' Starling heard the unspoken implication of this quite clearly: *You are a hedge rat. And you belonged to Alice.* 'But perhaps, if you are to continue with this extra work upstairs from time to time, it ought to be reflected in your salary. I shall speak to Mrs Hatton about it.'

'Thank you, madam.'

'Well. Now tell me, how is Jonathan this morning?'

'He is quiet, madam. He does not eat, and his bed had not been slept in,' said Starling. Mrs Alleyn took a breath; her eyes reflected a deep anxiety.

'He . . . does he shake? Do you think it is the pains in his head again?'

'I think not, madam. He seems only tired today.'

'Well then, I shall visit him now.' The older lady drew herself up, full of resolve. 'Be about your work, Starling.' *She half fears him herself*, Starling thought. She turned to go, but after a few steps she paused, glancing back. *Now is your chance.* Mrs Alleyn's hand had frozen halfway towards knocking at her son's door. 'What is it?' she said.

'I saw Mr Weekes, the wine man, just the other day. He asked to be remembered to you. He is lately wed, and begs leave to present his new bride to you, if it please you, madam.'

'Young Richard Weekes, married at last?' Mrs Alleyn smiled slightly.

'Yes, madam.'

'And is his bride quite fit to be met?'

'By all accounts, she is most refined. Perhaps . . . a deal more refined than Mr Weekes himself. She struck me as a somewhat . . . singular lady.'

'Indeed? In what way?'

'Perhaps you might be the better judge yourself, madam.'

'Well, then, I should be interested to meet her. Curious that he did not call to make this request himself. But you may pass on a message for him to call on Thursday, at four, if he pleases.'

'As you say, Mrs Alleyn.' Starling curtsied and turned away, her heart thumping.

She knew that Mrs Alleyn would wait until she was out of earshot before going in to her son, but she still heard the shouts when she did enter, and the thud of something thrown across the room. Starling carried on to the lowest floor, checked that the coast was clear, then took a jar of pickled eggs from the pantry and added it to the bag of such items she kept pushed far back beneath her bed. *Thursday, at four.* She must make sure she could watch, if possible, the exact moment that Josephine Alleyn set eyes on Rachel Weekes.

At the thought, some restless uncertainty gripped her, and

made it impossible to keep still. She suddenly realised that she had no idea how Mrs Alleyn would react to a person who looked so like Alice, the girl she blamed for her son's illness and decline. And she realised that she herself longed to see the new Mrs Weekes again – however painful it had been the first time, feeling that wild surge of joy, dashed in the next instant when she realised that this was not Alice returned. Still, the novelty of such an uncanny likeness was fascinating. Starling longed to look again, and to compare – to verify her first impression that this woman's face was the mirror image of that which haunted her memories. *And if Josephine Alleyn is incensed at the sight of her, throws her out and refuses to have her back . . . then it is all over before it has begun.* She paced the cramped floor of the bedchamber, turning so many times it made her dizzy. But the thing was set in motion now, and could not be stopped.

1803

The day that Alice's benefactor was to visit was one of driving rain. It fell in stair rods, straight down from a leaden sky, pocking the ground outside and slithering down the chimneys to fizzle in the fireplaces. Alice ran repeatedly to the kitchen window to look for his arrival, all nervous excitement, seeming far younger than her seventeen years. Starling noticed that Bridget had dressed in her best clothes, and wore a spanking clean apron, and that Alice had taken particular care with her pale hair that morning. The wan light of the day glanced from its ringlets. Bridget had run up a plain, long-sleeved dress of grey wool for Starling; she loved the feel of it brushing her ankles, and the warmth of it. They'd also bought her some second-hand shoes from a pedlar who came to the door, and though they were a good fit they seemed intolerably constricting to Starling, and she kicked them off whenever Alice's attention was elsewhere.

'Be still, Miss Alice! Don't excite yourself so,' Bridget admonished her. Alice sighed, and sat back down again. But when the rattle of the gate was heard she was back at the window at once. Her eyes went wide and she clapped a hand to her mouth.

'He is come . . . and . . . and Jonathan Alleyn is with him!' she gasped through her fingers. Bridget was all business. She took off her apron and folded it quickly into a drawer, and tucked some stray hairs more neatly into her cap.

'Alice, to the parlour. Pick up your sewing and do not stir until I bring them in. Starling, child, go upstairs and do not come down until I fetch you. Do you understand me?'

'Yes, Bridget,' said Starling. Her voice was still a small thing, a piping sound so quiet it was almost lost in the roar of the rain outside.

Starling almost did as she was told, but not quite. She stopped at the top of the stairs, where the wooden rails turned, and crouched there with her skinny knees tucked under her chin. She was in shadow; nobody would see her unless they looked right up at her. It was the perfect place to eavesdrop, and to see whoever came into the hallway; she saw two gentlemen, one old and one young. They were dressed as finely as lords, though their coats were sodden and dripping from the hems, and their boots were spattered with mud. The older man was stout and florid, though not un-handsome. He had great hands the width of dinner plates, and wore a curled grey wig under his black hat. When he smiled his cheeks rode up to near swamp his eyes. He greeted Bridget very cheerfully, and far more courteously than a servant might expect, with a wide smile and a *how do you do?* But Starling saw that Bridget's reply, and her curtsy, were stiff and reserved. The gentleman did not seem to notice or to mind.

'And where is my young ward?' he said, his voice start-lingly loud and deep. It boomed up the stairs to where Starling hid, and she flinched. She could not have said where or when she had learnt to fear raised male voices.

'I will take you to her, sir,' said Bridget, and led the pair of them to the parlour.

The younger man, who Starling had yet to examine properly, seemed only just grown, perhaps even slightly younger than Alice. He glanced up as he passed the foot of the stairs, looking straight at her as if he'd known she would be there, and when their eyes met he blinked once but showed no other surprise. Starling held her breath, but he neither paused nor gave her away as he followed the older man out of sight. She was left with the impression of a tall, thin figure, angular and yet graceful; vivid brown eyes in a long, fox-like face; pronounced cheekbones and dark waves of hair. It had seemed that he'd smiled, just a little, as he looked away.

The parlour door opened and Starling heard Alice speak.

'Lord Faukes! How wonderful to see you! How kind of you to come. And you too, Mr Alleyn . . .' She trailed off, unable to keep her favour from sounding in her voice. 'How do you do? Please do come and sit down. Bridget, would you be so kind as to make us some tea? Or perhaps you would prefer hot toddy after your gruelling ride in this weather?'

'That would be most welcome, Miss Beckwith,' said the younger man, Jonathan. Then the parlour door closed, and Bridget returned to the kitchen, and Starling heard no more. She shut her eyes, and waited to discover her fate. *Beckwith.* It was the first time she'd heard Alice's full name, and it made her anxious and jealous at once. Two days before, she'd eavesdropped when Bridget and Alice had thought she was asleep. Bridget had warned that this man, these men, might take her away and give her to the poor house, and even though Alice had declared she would not let them, a tremor in her voice had said that they might, and that Alice would not be able to stop them. *No, no, no,* Starling silently prayed.

Her wait at the top of the stairs seemed to last for ever. Cold, slippery dread made her insides roil; her legs stiffened up from crouching. When at last Bridget came to fetch her, the older woman held out a hand to her and led her down the stairs without saying a word. Starling trembled from head to foot. At the parlour door, she fought the urge to run. A memory came to her then, of a man's hands holding her, of pain and fear, of biting and scratching and fighting to be free. She remembered what to do, if these men tried to grab her.

The three of them turned to look at her when they entered the room, but only Alice smiled.

'Starling,' said Alice, beckoning. Starling went to her obediently, took her hand and gripped it tightly. 'This is Lord Faukes, my guardian and benefactor. And this is his grandson, Jonathan Alleyn. What do you say?'

'How do you do, sirs,' Starling whispered, and curtsied. Jonathan Alleyn smiled; it lit up a face that otherwise had a quite serious caste. His eyes were dark and yet sparkling, and they studied her with a kind of calm confidence that made Starling squirm and want to hide behind Alice's skirt. But she didn't. She faced them squarely, though it took every ounce of her will. 'Please do not take me away from here,' she added, and Alice shushed her hastily, smiling.

There was a pause, then Lord Faukes gave a sudden *har* of laughter that made her jump.

'How old are you, child?' he asked.

'We think I might be seven, sir,' Starling replied, which made the man chuckle again.

'Poor, rootless creature. No wonder you like it here, and want to stay, if you've been living out of doors, and beaten, until now. The question is, have you any *right* to stay? Hmm?' He leaned forward in his chair, and Starling was fascinated and horrified by the way his belly bulged out behind his shirt and waistcoat, and rolled down over his trousers.

'Lord Faukes, Starling is—' Alice began, but the old man cut her off.

'Now, now, Alice. You have said your piece.'

'I am learning to cook and clean, and to read and write,' Starling piped up in desperation.

'Is that so?'

'The child is clearly no idiot, for all her low birth. She certainly seems bright enough to acquire the skills she might need . . .' said Jonathan, but his grandfather waved him to silence. The young man cast an apologetic glance at Alice, whose eyes were huge. There was another pause as the old man seemed to think. His gaze never once left Starling; she did not blink, or look away. After a while, he grunted.

'She's bold enough, I'll give her that. But this is not one of your orphaned chicks or broken-legged rabbits, Alice. She is a child, and will grow to be a woman. What then? Will you take responsibility for her, for all those years until she is grown? Think, before you answer.'

'Yes, sir,' Alice said at once, placing her hands on Starling's shoulders. The old man gave an exasperated shake of his head.

'And you, Bridget? You can usually be relied upon to think more with your head, and less with your heart. What say you?' Bridget was still standing by the door, her hands clasped in front of her. All eyes turned to her, and she shifted uncomfortably.

'Bridget?' said Alice, quietly imploring.

'I think . . . I think the girl could do well. If she were allowed to stay on. She's quick to learn, and does as she's told, for the most part.'

'Which gives no answer one way or the other; but I can hear what you would rather say.' Lord Faukes leaned back in the chair, and drummed his fingers on its carved wooden arms for a moment. 'Very well, then,' he said, with a nod. Alice gasped.

'She can stay?'

'She can stay. But—' He was cut off as Alice flew across the room and threw her arms around him exuberantly.

'Oh, thank you! Thank you, kindest and best of men! Thank you, sir!' she cried, covering his face in kisses until he had no choice but to laugh, and pat her shoulders.

'There, there. A little more decorum, Alice! She can stay

but she is to be a servant in this house, not a sister.' He raised a warning finger. 'A thing that is born wild, stays wild, and can never be entirely trusted. She can be a helper to Bridget, until she is ready to go abroad and find her own position. You shall have a little more money for her upkeep, which will be all the salary she shall have. You will make no effort to turn her into a lady, for she will never be one. Do I make myself clear?'

'Yes, sir,' said Alice. She had come to rest on her knees beside him, with her head pressed to his thighs and her arms clasped around him. In the pause that followed, Lord Faukes looked down at her with an expression that was helplessly fond, and affectionate. A deeper flush of colour crept into his cheeks, and when Starling glanced at Bridget, she saw that the older woman wore a hung, guarded expression, and hovered on her toes as if fighting the urge to step forward and pull Alice away.

During the time it had taken to decide the course of Starling's life, the rain had stopped.

'Shall we go out for a while, before we dine? We could walk into Bathampton, or just to the bridge,' said Alice, as the two men rose from their seats.

'Alas, we cannot stop to eat with you today. We have other business to attend to. Besides, your dress and shoes would be ruined, my dear! The ground is like hasty pudding between here and the lane,' said Lord Faukes. Jonathan looked from his grandfather to Alice with an air of slight desperation.

'A ride, perhaps? We could ride along the river a ways?' he said.

'Oh, yes! Let's,' Alice agreed at once. 'It's always so long between your visits. Must we cut this one short so soon?'

'There simply isn't the time, child.' Alice and Jonathan

were visibly crestfallen at this news. 'Come, Jonathan, we must be back to Box for suppertime.'

'But, at least I might show you our new sow? I will not spoil my shoes – I can borrow Bridget's pattens. Come and see her – she is the fattest creature you ever laid eyes upon!' Alice urged.

'Come and see the sow? Why on earth—'

'I should like to see her,' Jonathan interrupted his grandfather. His eyes were on Alice, and they shone. 'Very much. I mean, if she truly is as fat as you say,' he added, lamely.

'Oh, very well.' Lord Faukes sighed. 'Alice, please take my grandson to see the pig. I hope her corpulence does not detain you both for very long. I shall stay here, in the warm, and have another piece of Bridget's excellent shortbread.' The old man shook his head and sat back down again, lacing his hands across his middle.

Bridget handed the plate of shortbread to Starling to take through to Lord Faukes, but Starling wasn't paying attention. She was watching as Jonathan helped Alice into her cloak; watching how Alice steadied herself with a hand placed lightly on his shoulder as she slid her feet into the pattens, even though Starling had seen her perform the same action without aid a dozen times or more. They did not look at her, or ask her to come with them to the pigsty. They went out into the yard side by side, deep in conversation, walking so close together that from time to time their sleeves brushed. There seemed to be a circle around them, a wall that nothing else might scale or penetrate; and outside that circle the world suddenly felt a little colder.

'Like a pair of moonstruck calves,' Bridget muttered, puckering her lips as she closed the door behind them. 'Run along with that plate, child. Don't keep Lord Faukes waiting. He is your master, now.' Starling did as she was told, then ran to the upstairs window from which the pigsty was visible, behind the house. There stood Jonathan and Alice, paying no heed to the saddleback sow which had come to the rail to see if there was food. All of their attention was on each other. Starling watched them steadily, never blinking, trying to decide if she would love or hate this Jonathan Alleyn for the way he held Alice spellbound.

1821

After their argument over Duncan Weekes, Rachel felt strange and constrained around her husband. She had begun to understand just how much bad blood lay between them, but if Duncan Weekes had been responsible for Richard's mother's death, surely he would have been punished by law? She pictured the old man, with his fumbling steps and almost desperately kind compliments, and the fathomless sadness in his eyes. Could it possibly be true? She longed to know. Here was something she and her husband shared, after all – the loss of a beloved mother. She knew very well how that pain could linger. She wanted him to know that she understood his suffering, that sharing it might ease it. That he should lose his father at the same time seemed too hard, but had she any right to attempt to reconcile them, if blame truly lay with the old man?

So Rachel could almost understand why Richard had been so angry with her for talking to Duncan Weekes. Almost, but not quite, since she couldn't have known his grievance. *He has his mother's temper, the father said. Do such tempers not burn out as quickly as they flare?* But with his eyes snapping and his face tensed up in fury, she'd hardly recognised him; the thought of it made her bite her tongue when her instinct was to raise the subject and talk it through calmly, as husband and wife. Richard seemed to sense her thoughts, and was wary, watchful; tensed as if ready to berate her again. This as much as anything kept her silent. But then when he'd come home on Tuesday with an invitation for them both, and a delighted expression on his face, all memory of the trouble between them seemed forgotten. Rachel had felt knots of worry in her stomach relax. *You have your whole life to come to understand his grief. You need not rush him.*

After their midday meal on Thursday, they made ready.

'Do hurry, Rachel. We are to be there at four o'clock, and we dare not be late.' Richard was agitated as he tugged his cravat into a more voluminous shape, and brushed crisply at traces of sawdust on his coat sleeves.

'My dear, it's not yet ten past three, and a matter of twenty minutes' walk from here to there . . .'

'Do you intend to gallop there? You can't arrive glowing and gasping for breath, with your hair all loose like some blowsabella, Rachel!'

'I have no intention of galloping, I assure you,' she said coolly. Sensing her tone, Richard stopped correcting his outfit and came over to her. He put his hands on her arms, and squeezed gently. His expression was sweet, almost boyish. An excited flush suffused his face.

'Of course you don't. I am only trying to impress upon you the . . . importance of this acquaintance. Mrs Alleyn is a very great lady, much esteemed in the highest circles of Bath society. She has been something of a patroness to me; a loyal client of exquisite taste, since the very early days of my business . . .'

'Yes, all this you have already said, and I am delighted to be invited to meet her.'

'I'm delighted too. I had not heard from her in some time . . . not from her personally, though the household continues to buy its port and wine only through me. It's you, Rachel.' He gave her a little shake, breaking into a smile. 'You have occasioned this invitation. And now we are invited as guests into as fine a house as you will ever have seen . . . Well,' he corrected himself, perhaps remembering her upbringing and her employment at Hartford Hall. 'As fine a house in Bath, anyway. I do hope she approves.'

'Of me?'

'Indeed,' said Richard, returning to the mirror and recommencing with his tie.

'As do I,' Rachel murmured, suddenly more nervous than she had been. *And if she does not, what then?* asked the echo in her head, mischievously. Rachel hushed it.

However excited her husband seemed, she, who knew a little more of higher society and its workings, had no doubt that their invitation was some form of continued patronage. They were like as not invited as vassals, rather than as esteemed guests, but she decided then to make as good an impression as she could. *He hopes to impress this Mrs Alleyn with me, so let me play my part as best I can.* She put on her fawn cotton dress again, though it was too lightweight for the weather, and draped a tasselled shawl – soft grey, patterned with sprigged roses – around her shoulders. She took her mother's pearl earrings from her trinket box and screwed them securely to her ears.

'Do you think she might not approve, then?' Rachel couldn't help asking, as they left the house at last. To her chagrin, Richard seemed to consider the question for a moment. Seeing her expression, he smiled.

'Please don't worry, my dear. It's only that . . . the lady has had great difficulties to suffer, in spite of her grand station in life. She can be somewhat . . . hesitant, to warm to people. But I am sure she will warm to you, dear Mrs Weekes.'

'What difficulties has she suffered?' Rachel asked. She saw a tiny flicker of impatience cross Richard's face, but then he took a deep breath.

'Rumours abound, so perhaps it will be better that I tell you the full truth, as I understand it. Some ten or twelve years back, I forget the exact time, it emerged that her son – her only child – had been engaged in secret to a most inappropriate girl, even though he was intended for another from birth . . .'

'Oh, poor children . . .' said Rachel.

'Not so – Jonathan Alleyn was a man grown by that time, and ought to have known better than to bring such scandal upon his family.'

'What made the girl so inappropriate? Hadn't he fortune enough for both of them, if she was poor?'

'It wasn't her lack of dowry so much as her lack of breeding and manners, as I understand it. But I don't know for certain – I never saw the creature. I only know what the servants have tattled: that the family objected to the match in the strongest possible way.'

'And so he wed her? This inappropriate girl?'

'Not a bit. She showed her true colours before it came to that – she abandoned him, and eloped with another man, and thus proved herself as fine as any cow turd stuck with primroses. Her low nature won out, in the end. She made an utter fool of the man, and left him broken-hearted.'

'Feckless girl!' Rachel breathed, somewhat taken aback by Richard's language.

'Quite so. She was not heard of after she fled, which ought to have been the end of the matter.'

'Was it not?'

'Alas, no. Her betrayal seemed to lead to a kind of . . . collapse, in Mr Alleyn. A madness of some type, from which he never recovered. His wild behaviour meant that many of Mrs Alleyn's old acquaintances cut all ties with her. These days he keeps largely to his rooms, which is a mercy, perhaps. But the damage is done. His affliction weighs heavy upon the lady, constantly.'

'You mean he has not improved, in all this time?'

'It's hard to say.' Richard shrugged. 'No one has seen him, not for years. So I cannot say. But the whole experience wounded Mrs Alleyn very deeply. She is . . . somewhat fragile, now; she does not trust easily.'

'Indeed, poor lady.' They walked in silence for a while. Rachel lifted her skirts carefully over the puddles on the pavement, not all of which were water. *Poor son*, the echo in her head whispered, softly and sad. 'The poor man's heart must have been in tatters, for the girl's betrayal to cause such lasting damage,' she mused aloud.

'Perhaps, but I think his mind must have been frail to begin with, don't you? To be so undone?' Rachel considered this, but said nothing. After a minute, Richard added: 'Say nothing of what I have told you to Mrs Alleyn.'

'Of course, I wouldn't,' Rachel assured him.

They made their way slowly across the city, climbing the steep hill of Lansdown Road at a pace that bordered upon not moving at all, such was Richard's fear of arriving dishevelled. Rachel looked up at her husband's handsome face as they neared the top, smiling apprehensively, tightening her hand around his arm. Richard's answering smile was distracted, and he loosened her fingers absently.

'You will crease the sleeve, my dear,' he said.

Number one, Lansdown Crescent, sat at the eastern end of the curved street. The house reared up four storeys above street level, and gazed imperiously to the south-east. The rain that morning had left dark, sorrowful water marks on the stone, as though the windows had been weeping. The house had a bay front, to match its opposite number at the far end of the row, and was fenced in by iron railings painted Prussian blue. There was an elegant filigree lamp-post on the corner of the pavement outside, and the main door opened through the side of the house, from an alleyway leading to the rear of the crescent. The door was sheltered by a columned portico, and reached by a fan of stone steps. To the left of this a set of steeper, narrower steps led down through the railings, to a lower level courtyard at the front of the building, and the servants' entrance. In front of the crescent the ground dropped away steeply, so that even the trees at the bottom of the slope would not hinder the residents' southerly views. Behind and beyond the crescent the high common stretched away, a sweep of pasture dotted with sheep, bordering the edge of the city. They were high above the river and the air was noticeably clearer and less humid. There was a faint tang of chimney smoke on the breeze but also a freshness, a purity which suggested that the lower reaches of the city sat huddled in a pall of their own stink.

As they paused to take in the house's grand situation, a curricle drawn by two smart grey horses turned into the crescent, and Richard stepped forwards hurriedly.

'Come, my dear. We must not be seen to stare like a pair of simple come-latelys,' he said, and automatically began to descend the small stairs to the tradesman's entrance. Rachel pulled his arm to stop him. With a pang of sympathy, she saw that he felt as unused to his surroundings, as conspicuous in them, as she had first felt in Abbeygate Street.

'Mr Weekes, if we are invited here as guests, surely we ought use the main door?' she said quietly. Richard blinked, and a slow blush crept into his cheeks.

'Yes. Of course,' he muttered, sheepishly. He cleared his throat as they climbed the front steps, cleaned his boots as best he could on the scraper, and tugged at the hem of his jacket as he rang the bell.

The door was answered by a liveried manservant, tall and monolithic, who allowed them ingress in spite of his obvious disdain. From the inner hallway rose a wide stone staircase, turning around on itself to the top of the house. A rich carpet, the colour of blood, was laid down on it, and the edge of every riser had been scrubbed as smooth as skin. The air smelled of beeswax and flowers; and oranges, from a bowlful of spiced pomanders on a side table. The ceiling, far above their heads, was patterned with elaborate plasterwork and lit by a sparkling glass chandelier. The walls were hung with painted paper, showing an intricate design of long-tailed birds and oriental blossoms in gold, teal and crimson. Two enormous mirrors faced each other on either side of the hall, so that ranks of Richards and Rachels stood shoulder to shoulder in both, stretching back into infinity. *Here's an army of us, now, ready to conquer Mrs Alleyn*, said the voice in Rachel's head, and she smiled inwardly.

The butler led them to a huge doorway on the left of the hall. Rachel's heels tapped quietly on the stone floor, and she felt the strongest sensation of being watched. The hairs on the back of her neck prickled, and she glanced over her shoulder, seeing nothing and nobody behind her. And yet there was something unexpected, and somewhat uneasy about the house. It was too quiet, she decided. There was no music, there were no voices. No footsteps on the stairs or in the servants' passageways behind the panelling; no muffled sounds of industry from below stairs, no guttering of flames in hearths. Even the sounds of the street receded to nothing as soon as the door was shut behind them. Rachel swallowed, and fought off a sudden, inexplicable impulse to flee the place. It seemed as though time had halted, as though the house slept, or perhaps held its breath. Her chest burned, and she realised that she was doing the same. Richard's face was stiff with nerves; his fingers twitched, his eyes were restless.

'Mr and Mrs Weekes, madam,' the butler announced, bowing to the room's occupant as Richard and Rachel walked past him.

'Thank you, Falmouth.' The lady who spoke was wearing

an old-fashioned gown of green silk brocade, ruched and over-embellished with bows and ribbons. She was standing on the far side of the room, by the window, feeding seeds to a canary through the delicate bars of its gilded cage. If she had been there for two minutes or more, she would have seen Richard begin to descend the servants' stair, Rachel realised. She hoped that Richard wouldn't think of it. The room was choked with drapes and furniture, the walls dark with large paintings, their gilded frames gleaming dully. The canary cheeped, and its voice came loud through the still air. With the light behind her, it was hard to make out the lady's features distinctly. 'How do you do, Mr Weekes? It has been some months since I saw you,' she said, brushing fragments of seed from her fingers.

'Mrs Alleyn.' Richard bowed deeply, so deeply that Rachel glanced at him in surprise. He'd shut his eyes, and seemed to gather himself. *What does he fear?* 'Please allow me the honour of presenting my wife, Mrs Rachel Weekes,' he said, as he straightened up at last. Mrs Alleyn came a few steps closer to them, smiling graciously. At once, Rachel noticed her great beauty, and was about to curtsy when the older woman halted, and her smile faltered.

'Good heavens,' she murmured indistinctly, pressing the back of one hand to her lips. Her eyes grew very wide.

'Madam, are you unwell?' Richard asked, stepping forward to offer his arm. Mrs Alleyn waved him away.

'I am quite well.' She stared at Rachel for a few seconds more, silent, until Rachel, bewildered, made her postponed curtsy and said:

'It is an honour to meet you, Mrs Alleyn.' *Do I shock her, somehow? Does she think she knows me?*

'Well,' said the older lady. 'Well. A pleasure, Mrs Weekes. Please accept my blessings on your recent marriage.'

'You are most kind, Mrs Alleyn.'

'Do come and sit down,' said Mrs Alleyn, and with each moment that passed she regained more composure, until Rachel grew unsure of her first intuition – that it was something about her own appearance that had given the lady pause.

The conversation moved politely from the change in the weather to Richard's business, and who was coming to Bath for the season. Mrs Alleyn gave all the names and addresses she could think of, providing Richard with a list of potential clients.

'I shall mention you to them, when I write,' she said.

'You have my thanks, as ever, Mrs Alleyn. I have a shipment recently arrived into Bristol of a very fine Bordeaux wine, one of the best I have ever tasted.'

'Ah! How wonderful. Jonathan will not be pleased, but I cannot change my tastes in this: it is the finest-flavoured wine to be had.'

'Jonathan must be your son, Mrs Alleyn? Does he not care for Bordeaux wine?' said Rachel. There was a tiny pause, and Richard gave her a look of mute appeal that told her she had erred in some way.

'My son fought the French in Spain and Portugal, Mrs Weekes. And though he accepts that the war is now over, he cannot be reconciled to the old enemy. He would prefer that I buy wine from Spain, or Germany.'

'And the King would agree with him, for the crown tariffs on French wine still greatly limit our imports.'

'I can't see what is to be gained in bearing such grudges,' Mrs Alleyn said with a sigh. 'But I am in the minority, I am well aware. An acquaintance recently wrote to chastise me for tactlessness! But I fail to see why we should have to drink unspeakable rotgut from Spain, and allow the French to keep all of the Bordeaux for themselves! It seems a curiously backward way to punish them, in my opinion.'

'You are quite right, Mrs Alleyn,' Richard agreed, readily. 'And it grieves me also.'

'But it keeps the prices high,' she said, smiling knowingly. Richard shifted uncomfortably. 'Oh, I understand how business works, you need not look shamefaced. And I trust you not to charge an overly inflated price. To me, in any case; though I must buy in small amounts, and hide it from Jonathan.' She smiled again, but this time the expression was colder.

'Does your son live here with you, then, Mrs Alleyn? I had not realised,' said Rachel. Again came a pause, a significant look from Richard. 'It must be a comfort to you, to . . . have him so near to you,' she stumbled on.

'Indeed,' said Mrs Alleyn, tersely. 'I quit our house in Box after my father died. It was far too large for a woman alone, and I thought that the city would offer more opportunities for society and company. When he had recuperated from the war my son joined me here.' The words came in such a frigid tone that Rachel found no way to reply. The silence stretched on, and Mrs Alleyn watched her without blinking. When Rachel tried to find something light and innocuous to say, she found her mind entirely blank.

Eventually, Mrs Alleyn turned her unsettling gaze to Richard, and asked after his progress with an introduction she had made. Rachel breathed more easily, and decided not to speak again, however many times Richard turned, and smiled, and urged some comment from her. She held her tongue, and smiled politely, and tried not to notice the way Mrs Alleyn kept glancing at her, almost reluctantly, as if she couldn't help herself. Rachel saw an inexplicable mixture of calculation and curiosity in her eyes, and it increased the feeling she already had of the house being watchful. She was glad when, after forty minutes or so, Mrs Alleyn dismissed them with exquisite good manners. As they crossed the hallway once again, a flash of movement and colour caught Rachel's eye. Through a narrow door behind the main stair-case, where the back stairs led down to the cellars, a servant was watching them — a red-haired girl with long eyes and a keen expression. With a start, Rachel recognised her as the girl who'd served them, just the once, at their wedding feast. The girl who'd also paused and stared at her peculiarly, just as Mrs Alleyn had.

'I did advise you not to ask about her son, did I not?' said Richard, as they walked away down Lansdown Road.

'No. You did not,' said Rachel. 'You said only to mention nothing of the misfortune that befell him with the girl he was engaged to . . . I thought Mrs Alleyn might like to speak of him, since I gathered she has little opportunity to.'

'The whole subject of her son is one she feels most acutely. Perhaps too acutely to discuss with a new acquaintance.'

'Well, how could I know if you didn't warn me?' said Rachel, rattled. She felt uneasy in a way she couldn't explain. *The lady thought she knew this face.* Something about that realisation gave her a peculiar, expectant thrill. 'Mr Weekes — I think I just saw the serving girl from the Moor's Head, working there as a servant.'

'Sadie?' He shook his head. 'I'm sure not.'

'No, the other one. The one who served the wine one time, and spilled it on my hand. You must remember — the red-haired girl?'

'No. There's only Sadie working there at the inn, and why would she be at the Alleyns' house on Lansdown Crescent?'

'I do not say that I saw Sadie, I say that I saw the other girl . . . I'm sure of it,' Rachel insisted.

'Well. I'm sure you must be mistaken. I saw nobody. You

did well, though, my dear. I'm sure Mrs Alleyn approved of you.'

'I am not so sure. She watched me most peculiarly, and you must have noticed when you introduced me – how startled she seemed. Do you think she thought she recognised me from somewhere?'

'How could she recognise you, my dear? I did tell you that she is not always the easiest company. I'm sure she wasn't watching you with anything other than the curiosity of making a new acquaintance . . .'

'It startled me to learn that her son was there above us all the time, hidden away.'

'Yes – forgive me. I thought you'd understood. His infirmity goes beyond a mere darkening of the spirits – he was injured in the war as well. One leg is all but useless, and he suffers terrible headaches, I am told. Pains that last for days, and obliterate all thought.'

'Poor man,' Rachel murmured.

'As I said, I have seen him but once or twice in all the years since his downfall. He is a strange and difficult man, impossible to know.'

'Such suffering might make any one of us strange or difficult.'

'You have such a kind heart, my dear,' Richard said, squeezing her hand where it rested on his arm. He seemed to have relaxed in the short distance that they'd walked from the Alleyns' house, his nerves dissipating to leave him buoyant, almost jubilant. 'She is a fine lady, is she not?' he said, smiling. 'And beautiful, though none so lovely as you.'

Rachel smiled at the compliment, but she still wondered about Mrs Alleyn's strange exclamation, and repeated glances; and she wondered about the red-haired serving girl she'd glimpsed at the top of the stairs. And while she could not have said what any of it meant, or if it was significant, it only added to her unusual suspicion that she had been watched, and that much had gone unsaid.

From the hill where Lansdown Crescent sat, aloof, the rest of the city was a tangled mess. As they descended into it there seemed to be less light from the sky, even; the air thickened with the stink of human endeavour. Rachel stepped around piles of horse muck and oily puddles, but could not keep her shoes from getting spattered. *Pattens*, she made the mental note. *I must acquire a pair of pattens*. Richard left her near the abbey, to meet with a man on business, and Rachel walked a convoluted route back towards the house above the shop. She was starting to enjoy the noise and bustle of the narrow cobbled streets, which in places were scarcely wide enough to allow two people to pass without their shoulders bumping. What had once seemed like crowding had come to feel more like community.

Since her retreat from Milsom Street, she had taken to exploring the narrower streets behind and between, where the backs of buildings piled on top of one another as they marched up and down the city's steep hills. Everywhere were tangled gutters and gables and rough cobble walls; chimney pots like rows of broken teeth, stable doors and sink holes, outdoor stairs and crooked sheds; all making a mockery of the strict and serene façades that faced the front. Here Rachel was not noticed, she was not remarkable. She drifted through the hotchpotch, learning its hidden paths and places; the steep, mossy steps that carved unexpectedly beneath a terrace of houses; the butcher's shop built into the arches beneath a road, where cooks and housekeepers queued for the best cuts in Bath. Here there were no confectioners selling fudge or candied fruits, no glovers with wares in silk or kid leather. Here there were coopers selling barrels and baskets, and cobblers hammering new soles onto men's work boots. There were rag shops and haberdashers, and communal bake ovens for those too poor to have their own. Rachel had begun to feel that she knew the city better now than she ever had before.

Buying a paper cone of hot chestnuts from a barrow boy, she checked over her shoulder a couple of times, to be sure Richard was nowhere around, before turning into the street that led to Duncan Weekes's lodging house. She hadn't been sure that she would visit him until that exact moment, but curiosity convinced her to. It had been several days since she'd spoken to her father-in-law outside the Moor's Head, and she now understood that Richard would never consent to her calling on him. *Just as the old man foresaw. He warned me not to ask, but he lied about the bad blood between them, and the cause of it,* she thought, uneasily. *How could he refer to his wife's death as 'matters long past'?* Richard had said such damning things about his father that Rachel was having trouble reconciling his portrait with the sad old man she had met, who had praised her kindness and gentility. *Underneath the blame and anger there must be love. Is there not always love between parent and child?* She thought of Mrs Alleyn, whose life had been so blighted by her son's misadventures and persistent affliction. *But she does not abandon him, and I should not abandon Duncan Weekes so very easily. Not until I have his version of these events.*

She had the worrying feeling that she might come to regret her decision, but she needed to know; because if what Richard had told her was true, then perhaps any love between him and his father had indeed died, and the reconciliation Rachel hoped for would be impossible. It was disquieting, that she should feel too nervous of her own husband to ask him what exactly had befallen his mother. *Keep that curiosity secret*, urged the soft voice in her mind. Still, the sadness in Duncan's eyes fretted at her memory, and he had praised Richard with unmistakable pride. *He loves his son, that much is clear. And he seems to have precious little else left to him.* Duncan Weekes was the only kind of father that remained to her, but as she made her way to him, Rachel prepared herself to sever all connection with him should Richard's condemnation prove well founded.

The building she came to was tall and narrow, cramped awkwardly between warehouses and workshops in the south-western reaches of the city, near the riverside with all its mud and stink. The walls were streaked with soot, the windows opaque. Washing lines were strung from the upper storeys, and threadbare clothes hung limp in the still air. On the front steps sat a little girl no more than three years old, dressed in a canvas pinafore and a tattered cap. She gave off a strange, unwholesome smell, like fish and milk. Rachel bent down with a smile.

'Hello, little one. Do you live here? What's your name?' she said. Shining wet trails ran either side of the child's mouth, from her nose to her chin. She regarded Rachel with steady, wide eyes, and said nothing. Rachel took out her handkerchief and tried to wipe the girl's face, but she shied away, got up and ran down the steps. Just then the door opened, and a woman with a pinched face came out carrying a basket on her hip. She squinted suspiciously at Rachel as she slipped in through the open door.

Inside it was cold and damp. A gloomy hallway with bare floorboards, where the sounds of footsteps and voices and children crying came creeping through the walls. There was a stink of tallow and ammonia. Duncan Weekes's lodging was on the lowest floor of the house, so Rachel went to the stairs at the far end of the hallway, and down into stagnant darkness. Small as it was, the basement was divided into two rooms, and Rachel turned to the one on the right, as instructed. Her hand was shaking slightly as she raised it to knock. She thought of the rooms on Abbeygate Street, and how poor she'd thought them at first. Now the place where her father-in-law lived put a knot of shame and disgust in her stomach, and she fought hard to smile as she heard the bolts slide back within. Duncan Weekes looked almost frightened as he peered out, eyes all rheumy and bloodshot. His wig was off, revealing the scanty grey shreds of his own remaining hair, and without it he seemed smaller, denuded. He smiled and gave her a slight bow, and all the while radiated a kind of anxious shame.

'My dear Mrs Weekes – it is so kind of you to call, so kind . . . I had not thought you would. I fear the condition of my lodgings must disgust you . . .'

'Nonsense, Mr Weekes,' Rachel murmured, but could not make herself convincing. She smiled to belie herself, and handed him the cone of chestnuts as she came inside. 'Here – they're still warm.'

'Thank you. Too kind. Come now – come and sit by the fire.' Duncan Weekes bustled clumsily, clearing a cup and a half-empty bottle of wine from the mantelpiece, and the fallen pages of a newspaper from the single armchair by the hearth. He had but one room, and that was cramped and dark. A narrow bed was against the back wall, with a trunk at its foot; beneath the only window, which was high in the wall and let in little light, stood a plain desk and a bentwood chair, and next to the door was a chest of drawers. The fireplace was mean – just a small grate for coals, a sooty hotplate for a kettle, and nothing more. It cast a meagre circle of light and warmth. Duncan Weekes fetched the bentwood chair and sat down opposite her, awkwardly, with his hands on his knees.

'And how are you, my dear? How is my son?' he said keenly. There was wine on his breath, and she saw his glance drift to the bottle he'd removed from the mantel. He snatched his eyes back guiltily, his face wearing a constant apology.

He is ashamed. Of himself, as much as his poverty. And so eager to befriend me. Rachel felt a renewed resolve – that if she was wrong to disobey her husband, still it had not been wrong to come to these poor lodgings, to take this first step.

'I am well, as is Richard, thank you, sir. I . . . I did speak to him about you, but . . .'

'He would not hear it?' said the old man, sadly.

'Not yet. His . . . pain over the rift between you is yet strong, and persuasive. Perhaps, with time . . .'

'A great deal of time has passed already, my dear, and none of it has dulled his anger. He spoke sharply to you, when you mentioned me?' Duncan Weekes's watery eyes fixed on her, full of concern.

'I . . . a . . . a little, yes. I am sure he did not mean . . .'

'Poor girl. You are too kind and good, to be reprimanded over the likes of me. I am but a ruin of what I once was. 'Tis scant wonder my boy wants nothing to do with me.'

Butterflies took flight in Rachel's stomach. She swallowed before she spoke again, and found her throat dry.

'Forgive me, sir, but I must have it from you. My husband . . . my husband told me that you killed his mother. Does he speak the truth?' Her voice shook audibly; there was a long and deafening silence afterwards. Duncan Weekes stared at her, his eyes gone wide and empty. Rachel suddenly realised that she had no idea how he would react to her terrible question. *Fool! To come here, and be alone with him, and say such a thing!* Rachel started up to her feet and made for the door.

'Wait! Don't go yet, I beg you!' Duncan called after her. Rachel paused, and glanced back. The old man's eyes were no longer empty, or alarming. His whole body had collapsed in misery, shrinking in on itself as though she'd kicked him. 'Forgive my silence, only . . . only you did shock me so. It did shock me, to hear you say it,' he said.

'Then . . . it is not true?' Rachel whispered.

'I . . . I cannot say it is wholly untrue. Alas, I cannot say so.' He wiped at his eyes with a juddering hand. 'But you must believe me, please, when I say that I never had any intention of harming my Susanne. I loved her more than any man ever loved a wife, and never laid a finger upon her in anger . . . For all she did upbraid me often, and point up my many failings.' A fragment of a desolate smile crossed his face. 'I loved her truly, and meant her no harm.' Rachel stayed where she was for a moment longer, then took a step back towards the chair. Duncan Weekes's sorrow was like a physical thing, like something she could touch.

'Do you . . . do you *swear* this to me, sir?'

'I swear it upon my very soul, Mrs Weekes.'

Tentatively, Rachel sat back down. She found she had little trouble believing him; her every instinct told her that he was not a violent man.

'Can you . . . can you tell me what harm befell her?' she said. The old man shook his head. A single tear was flung from his cheek, splashing onto the hearth with a tiny sizzle.

'If you must hear it, then I must tell it. But I beseech you – do not make me. It is my constant shame; it is like a wound that runs right through me, and to speak of it turns the blade in that wound. It is unbearable, my dear girl. It is unbearable.'

'Then speak it not, sir,' said Rachel, decisively. 'It matters only that her death was . . . accidental. And that you are sorry for it.'

'A sorrier creature would be hard to find,' said Duncan, so quietly. Rachel thought for a moment.

'And . . . afterwards, you raised Richard yourself? From when he was eight years of age? And . . . this rift lay between you all that long while?'

'No, not all that while. I . . . I compounded my sin, you

see – I lied to him. Lies of omission, perhaps, but lies all the same. He was a young man by the time he found out what fate befell her, from what source I cannot say. And his grievance was made all the worse for knowing that I had kept the truth from him.'

'You were an ostler then, I think?'

'That's right, Mrs Weekes. And a coachman, too. I was all my life in some such employ – I've a gift with horses, you see . . . I can gentle them, and coax them on. They only want soft handling, you see; they only want a little reassurance, and a little tenderness. But after I lost Susanne, I . . . I drank all the more, to forget my sorrow. I am the architect of my own decline, and I deserve none of your pity.'

'Does our faith not teach us to forgive, sir, upon the repentance of wrongdoing? I believe that includes . . . forgiving oneself.'

'How may a person forgive themselves such a thing? How do I forgive myself, when I have blighted my boy's life so terribly? I have much time to think, now, in these twilight years, and my thoughts are bitter ones, of regret for all the wrong choices I made and all the ways in which I have fallen short.'

'You are hard on yourself, Mr Weekes. You seem to me to be a . . . kind man. I'm sure you have tried to do right – and any one of us may fall short. God can expect nothing more of any man than that he perceives his own faults, laments them and strives to improve upon them . . .'

Rachel thought of her own father, of the shame that had eaten away at him; wasted him, like a canker. She reached out and took Duncan's gnarled hand. It was dark with grime, some unknown dirt worn into the creases and the bed of each nail. 'Such thoughts will prey upon you, sir,' she said gently. 'There must be some joy in life, must there not? You must allow some happiness, or 'tis all for naught. I was sad for many years after I lost my own family. But now I have Richard, and a new life with him, and I feel that the time has come to be joyful again.'

'There ought to be happiness for those that deserve it, aye. For those good of heart and deed such as you,' said Mr Weekes. 'For an old fool like me, the chance has come and gone.' He cleared his throat, and his treacherous gaze wandered to the bottle again before he could wrest it back. 'But that you came to visit me – and stayed to hear me . . . that gives me much happiness.'

'I fear I have brought you no joy this day,' said Rachel. 'I had better leave now – the evenings draw in, and I should be home before my husband.' She stood, smoothing her skirt with both hands.

'But you will come again, my dear?' Duncan Weekes's expression was so full of hope that it pained her.

'I . . . I am not sure, sir. I would have to conceal any such visit from my husband, and it . . . troubles me a good deal to do so. To lie is a terrible thing.'

'But you have it in your power to do what I have longed to these many years, my dear.' He stood up and clasped her hand in both of his, finding a tremulous smile. 'You have it in you to make my boy think kindly of me once more. Or at least to bring me word of him, and how he fares.'

'I . . .' Rachel hesitated, shaking her head.

'Please! Please, dear girl. Do call again. You cannot know the good you would do.'

For a moment Rachel stared into his eyes, all couched as they were in lines of age and desperation. *Will you make an old man beg you?*

'Perhaps the greater sin would be to let a family member languish, all unnoticed . . .' She stopped herself short of saying *in poverty*. 'To let bad blood and misunderstanding continue, when perhaps I could make it right . . .'

'Bless you, Mrs Weekes. And thank you.' Duncan let go of her hand, walking unsteadily to the door to see her out.

'Can I bring you aught, next time? A little food perhaps?' she asked. Duncan shook his head.

'Only your good self, and word of my boy. But . . . you must be *careful*, dear girl. You must be careful not to . . . not to make any difficulty for yourself on my account,' he said, anxious again. Rachel tried to brush off the warning, but it came too soon after the shock of Richard's anger, and as she left the building it was with a trapped feeling like the beginnings of fear. *No. I do not fear my husband, who loves me.*

The sun was setting earlier every day, and as dusk fell countless lamps and torches were lit in windows and over doors, flooding the streets with an uneven yellow light that glanced from the filthy water in the gutters and almost made it pretty. Rachel took a deep breath of the chilly air to rid her lungs of the dankness of Duncan Weekes's room. She walked briskly until she was on better streets, and stopped off to buy a pie for supper, and once she was home she stoked up the stove to warm the kitchen-cum-parlour, and looked around with new appreciation of her home. She thumped the pillows on the bed to raise them, shook the spiders out of the drapes, scoured the pot and brewed tea, suddenly needing to be busy, and to have no time to stop and think about Duncan Weekes. Because if she thought too much about his sad eyes and the filth he lived in she might speak again, unbidden; and try as she might to be calm and courageous, the thought of another confrontation filled her with dread. She was so conscious of guarding her words that she said precious little when Richard did arrive home, only smiling and fetching him the things he wanted. But he was tired, and smelled of the inn, and did not seem to mind her silence.

The next day a card was delivered to the house, and Rachel found that while she should have been surprised, she was not surprised at all. It was an invitation to number one, Lansdown Crescent, that afternoon; an invitation addressed to her alone. Rachel ran her fingers along the crisp edge of the card, and wondered what it could mean. The parlour suddenly seemed every bit as still and watchful as the house on Lansdown Crescent, and her skin prickled. She waited for her husband to return, and practised what she would say when he did. She was almost sure that Richard would be happy to hear about it, but then, his own exclusion from the invitation might temper that. In the end, she was asleep before he came home. He woke her as he came to bed, clumsy and befuddled in the darkness, and she feigned sleep, until his hands, which had roved her body, went still, and he started to snore. Carefully, Rachel pushed his hands away from her and shifted to one side, so that no part of them touched.

* * *

'You asked for me, madam?' said Starling. Mrs Alleyn looked up from the silk divan she was seated on, and raised her eyebrows. Her eyes glittered.

'You are well aware of the reason.'

'Madam?' said Starling.

'Enough!' Mrs Alleyn burst out, rising abruptly to pace the carpet. Starling's stomach lurched, but she cleared her face of expression, and waited. 'You yourself said she was a singular woman – the new Mrs Weekes. You *herded* me into meeting her with no warning of how greatly she resembled that wretched girl! You must have known what my shock would be.' Mrs Alleyn glared at her kitchen maid. Though Starling bridled at the words *that wretched girl*, and the tone of bitter disgust with which they were spoken, she knew better than to argue. 'Well? What say you?'

'I only thought that you would be interested in meeting her, madam.'

'Indeed. Have a care, Starling – you were *her* servant, before you were mine, I know, but you have been mine these twelve years since. I should have no cause to question where your loyalties lie.'

'My loyalty is to you, madam. Always,' Starling lied.

'I should hope so. She abandoned you as callously as she abandoned my son, let us not forget. Your place in this household is a boon that can be withdrawn, let us also not forget. Few others would have taken you on, given the circumstances.'

'I am grateful to you, madam.'

'Well.' Josephine Alleyn grew calmer. She sat back down on the divan. 'The resemblance is truly uncanny. Upon first glance,' she said.

That was true enough, Starling thought. She had watched from the stairs as Mrs Weekes was leaving, and this time she'd been able to pick out a few subtle ways in which the woman did not resemble Alice. It had not been quite the same as that first startling moment, when it had seemed as though the dead walked. 'It is a strange world, when two people can be born so alike and yet be wholly unconnected to one another,' said Mrs Alleyn.

'Not wholly unconnected, madam. For now they have you in common,' said Starling, carefully. This was the crucial time, the crucial moment, for if she could not convince her mistress that Mrs Weekes was of use to them, then any chance of using the woman to goad Jonathan, and make him betray himself, would vanish. Behind her shoulder, Starling could feel the painted eyes of Lord Faukes, Josephine Alleyn's father, staring down at her from a large canvas above the fireplace. She felt her skin crawl. Starling didn't like to look at his portrait; didn't like to see the heavy paunch of a stomach, or the big blunt hands, or the way his smile crinkled his eyes in that kindly, treacherous way. Mrs Alleyn was looking at Starling strangely, and a flutter of nerves made her speak again, ill-advisedly. 'It was my thinking that it could benefit your son, madam, to meet this woman who looks so like Alice—'

'I will not hear that name!' The words lashed out, sharp as a whip crack, and Starling cursed herself inwardly for forgetting.

'I beg pardon, madam,' she said hurriedly.

She waited in silence. Mrs Alleyn turned her head to gaze out of the window and did not speak again for some moments. In the wan light of the afternoon she was pale and lovely; eyes haunted by sadness, face haunted by beauty.

'How do you think it could benefit my son to set eyes upon this creature who, though it be no fault of her own, is the very image of the one person at the root of his distress? The one person I should most like him to forget?' She spoke without looking at Starling.

He'll never forget her. I won't let him. Starling fought to keep her tone neutral.

'Well, madam . . . it seems to me that Mr Alleyn would benefit from company. You have said so yourself, time and again, that it would do him good to be out in society more, and to allow visitors to call on him . . .'

'He will not hear of it, as you know. I have tried every argument.' Mrs Alleyn bowed her head, and suddenly wore her despair quite openly. She drew in a long breath, and when she raised her face again it was marked by pain. 'Upon occasion, he will not even see me. His own mother.'

'Yes, madam. I had thought that . . . perhaps her familiar face might convince him to tolerate her,' said Starling. Mrs Alleyn frowned, so she hurried on. 'Al— the girl he once knew was most dear to him. At one time. And I know he thinks of her still . . .'

'How do you know?'

'He . . .' Starling hesitated. If Mrs Alleyn knew of Alice's letters, she would turn Jonathan's rooms upside down to find and destroy them. 'He mentions her sometimes, when I am in hearing.'

'Go on.'

'She was dear to him, and there is a chance, is there not, that he might permit Mrs Weekes to visit him, for that reason? She seems a gentle and godly sort. Might she not somehow draw him back to himself? It . . . it cannot have escaped your notice that Mr Alleyn has been declining of late. In his spirits, I mean.' *I must tread carefully.* 'Declining as he did at the time of the . . . accident.' It was no accident that had opened Jonathan Alleyn's veins with the broken neck of a glass bottle, five years earlier. They both knew what he had intended. Josephine paled.

'You think he is *that* unwell again? You think he would . . . he might . . . do some harm to himself again?' The fear was loud behind her words.

'His descent has been rapid of late, madam, and it continues.'

'But . . . I want him to *forget* her! That is the only way . . . She *poisoned* him! I have banished every trace of her from this house, and yet, and yet . . . *still* he mentions her? After the way she betrayed him? And all the years that have passed?' There were tears in the older woman's eyes; they sparkled, unshed, full of desperate disbelief.

'He does, madam.'

'Well, *I* cannot tolerate it – I cannot tolerate *her*. I have no wish to see that woman's face again – it is not her fault, but the fact remains: she is a walking reminder of that blight on our lives, and I will not see her.' The older woman's voice shook just slightly. Starling felt desperation getting hold of her tongue again.

'But only think what he might do, if he should decline any further, madam . . . Surely if it might raise his spirits, just a little, to see her . . .'

'Do not press me, girl! You forget yourself! You may have known my son since you were a child, but you remain a servant in this house and I have no need of your counsel! Do you think yourself irreplaceable, because you do not fear to serve him?'

'No, madam.' Staring knew when to be meek.

The two women faced each in silence. Starling kept her eyes on her feet, where her scuffed leather shoes looked so out of place against the glorious patterns of the carpet, all purple and green and gold.

'Is this some mischief of yours?' Mrs Alleyn asked eventually. Her anger had gone; she sounded small, and afraid. Tears still glimmered in her eyes.

'No, madam. I only want what's best.'

'And . . . you truly think it could help him to see her? To be reminded?'

'Since time and . . . obliteration have not worked, madam, then perhaps Mrs Weekes . . . that is, perhaps a small taste of what was lost might give him ease instead.' Mrs Alleyn's tears never fell. She blinked them away, and gathered herself.

'If you are wrong . . . if he is made worse by her . . .'

'I am sure he will not be, madam,' Starling lied again without a second's hesitation. She gazed at her mistress, her face a perfect facsimile of sincerity. Mrs Alleyn thought for a second longer.

'Very well, then. Perhaps it cannot hurt to try. I will invite her,' she said, and Starling's heart soared. *Oh, but it can. It can hurt to try.*

Starling shut the drawing room door quietly, her fingers fumbling with the handle. They were shaking. Her whole body was shaking; her pulse thumped loudly in her temples. She swallowed, and felt the dry skin of her throat pull tight. *She poisoned him!* The words rang in her ears. As if anybody who had ever known Alice could truly believe that. It baffled her that a lady like Mrs Alleyn could be so deceived. In the silence of the hallway she watched her hands as they juddered, fingertips and broken nails all blurred with movement. Then Alice's hand took hers, and held it tightly. Starling shut her eyes and saw the palest golden hair lit up with sunlight, and smiling blue eyes with lashes like tiny feathers. *Find me some poppies, my chuck, and I'll make you a scarlet crown.*

Alice could not see the red petals against the green grasses that grew along the river's wide shoulders. Hand in hand, the two girls ran along, walked to catch their breath, then ran again. The ground was waterlogged, and seemed to bounce beneath their feet. There were cowpats here and there, bejewelled with amber dung flies. They shrieked and leapt and dodged them. *Here! Here are some poppies!* Starling heard her own voice, heard Alice laughing as they sat down abruptly, breathing in the warm smells of damp earth and trampled grass. The poppy stems were tough and hairy; she picked them and passed them to Alice, who plaited them into a garland. *I shall have a crown of flowers like this when Jonathan marries me*, said Alice. *And so shall you. Whichever flowers you wish for, you shall have; and you shall carry my train for me all the way to the church.*

'*Starling!*' An angry whisper startled her. Starling opened her eyes to the dim light of the hallway; golden hair and sunlit eyes faded away like spectres. Dorcas was glaring at her from the servants' door. 'Don't tarry there! What's in your head?' she hissed. Starling didn't stay to answer.

Mrs Alleyn would surely invite Mrs Weekes again soon. She didn't have much time to make ready; to make Jonathan Alleyn ready. She meant for him to be at his darkest when he first set eyes on the woman who was not Alice. She meant for him to be ready to break, and she meant to be there when he did.

* * *

Rachel felt the weightiness of things unsaid, hovering between herself and Mrs Alleyn. She wasn't sure how long she could go on ignoring it. It was stormy outside, and her shoulders were damp with rain from her walk to Lansdown Crescent. When the wind blew it made the flames in the grate flutter; a draught curled in under the door, cold around their ankles. She tried not to shiver, sipping her tea. The pauses between their stilted exchanges were growing longer and longer every time. Mrs Alleyn cleared her throat delicately.

'Tell me, what social engagements have you planned, Mrs Weekes?' she said.

'There is . . . nothing of note upcoming, I confess,' said Rachel.

'But you will be going to the assembly rooms, surely?'

'I . . . do not know, Mrs Alleyn. Mr Weekes has made no mention of any such plans . . .'

'Well, of course he hasn't, my dear Mrs Weekes. He is a man, and men who are married have little need for dancing. But a woman must have such things to look forward to, and to dress for. Must she not? He must take you, tell him I said so,' she declared. Rachel smiled politely.

'I shall indeed tell him, Mrs Alleyn. Do you care for dancing, yourself?'

'Yes, I . . . well. I used to, many years ago.' Mrs Alleyn's lovely face fell. 'It has been a very long time since I danced. My husband loved to, even after we were married. He was such a happy soul, so full of merriment.' She looked away across the room, and sighed slowly. 'The last time I danced was with Jonathan, shortly before he went away to the war.'

'And never since?' said Rachel, guessing it to be well over ten years since that dance. Mrs Alleyn swallowed, and looked back at Rachel.

'And never since,' she said flatly.

There was another uneasy silence. Mrs Alleyn arranged and rearranged her hands in her lap, and moved to pour tea from the pot when their cups were already full.

'And this fine gentleman here,' Rachel gestured at the large portrait in oils that hung above the hearth. 'Pray tell me, who is he?'

'That is my father, Sir Benjamin Faukes. He was a great man . . . a very great man. He had a most distinguished career in the navy. I returned to live with him when my husband died, when Jonathan was still very young. He . . . he was a kind and very loving man.' Mrs Alleyn paused. 'I think he'd hoped I would marry again one day, and be happy, but it was not to be.' Rachel studied the painting, which showed a corpulent but dignified man, jovial eyes couched deep above crimson cheeks.

'He cuts a most handsome figure,' she murmured. 'I was also blessed with a kind and gentle father. He was a gentleman . . . master of a small estate to the north of the city. I grew up there, and my little brother too. For a time.'

'You have lost him?' Mrs Alleyn leant forwards slightly, her eyes keen.

'When he was but a child, still. Such a dear boy. It was . . . very difficult for my mother and father.'

'And for you, I dare say?'

'Yes. And for me,' said Rachel, quietly. Mrs Alleyn nodded in sympathy.

'The world can seem cruel to inflict such losses, can it not?'

'I am sure God has a plan for us all, Mrs Alleyn.'

'Are you, indeed? Well spoken, Mrs Weekes,' Mrs Alleyn murmured, in a tone that was hard to decipher.

Silence fell again; outside, the wind played a mournful note. 'You must be wondering why I asked you to call again,' Mrs Alleyn said at last. 'So soon after our first meeting, I mean,' she added, hurriedly. Rachel smiled at the unintentional slight.

'I'm sure I was simply pleased to be invited,' she demurred, and Mrs Alleyn gave her a knowing glance, tinged with apology.

'Forgive me. In truth . . .' She hesitated, turning her porcelain cup in its saucer. 'In truth, I wish to introduce you to my son.'

'I see,' said Rachel, uneasily. She sensed that Mrs Alleyn was trying to find a way to broach the subject of her son's condition. 'My husband has told me that your son suffers from . . . an illness, brought on by the war,' she said, to ease the way. The older lady drew in a long breath.

'Mrs Weekes, I must be honest with you. My son is considered by many people to be . . . unfit for polite society. The headaches, and the nightmares he endures . . . they can cause him black moods. He has . . . some strange obsessions, since he returned from the fighting. He speaks the contents of his mind too freely. And the things he says can be . . . he is not always . . .' She broke off, and her eyes gleamed.

'Mrs Alleyn,' Rachel said softly. 'Forgive me, but I am left to wonder why you wish to introduce me, in particular, to your son?'

'Well might you wonder.' Mrs Alleyn sighed, and turned to gaze out at the sky for a moment. 'He has few friends left. He has no visitors. I know he is . . . partly to blame for that.

But oughtn't a true friend . . . make allowances?' She shook her head. 'But one by one they have all stopped calling, and writing. I can see that you have married beneath yourself. Forgive my candour, and I mean no slight to your husband. I have known Richard Weekes for a good many years, and I know he will try his best for you. But you have finer manners than his, and a more godly heart. It is plain.'

Rachel blushed. What she knew to be true she was not yet prepared to hear from another's lips. She said nothing, feeling heat bloom over her skin.

'Well,' she said stiffly, and could not think what to add. 'Well,' she said again.

'I have offended you. I am sorry for it. Perhaps I, too, am becoming unfit for polite society. I have no stomach left for the cant and hypocrisy of English manners.' Mrs Alleyn pressed her lips together and waited, and Rachel felt as though she was being tested. She found that she wanted to please this strange and beautiful woman, and not only because Richard esteemed her so highly.

'You merely surprised me, Mrs Alleyn,' she said.

'Good. There is strength in you, Mrs Weekes. I cannot quite put my finger on it, but . . . it is the kind of strength my son needs.' *Or that I will need, in meeting him?* Rachel wondered.

'Will he be joining us today?'

'Yes. That is . . . I had hoped—' She broke off, as at that moment a soft knock announced a servant at the door. Rachel looked up quickly, but it was not the red-haired girl. This one had small eyes and a thin, ferrety face.

'Beg pardon, madam. The master says he won't come down today. He is . . . indisposed,' said the girl, bobbing at them.

'Thank you, Dorcas.' Mrs Alleyn sounded weary, and disappointed. Silence fell again, and Rachel wondered what nature of thing was covered by the handy term *indisposed*. The atmosphere in the room was becoming unbearable. Rachel shifted in her chair.

'Well, another time, perhaps . . .' she murmured.

'Will you go up to him?' Mrs Alleyn said suddenly. Rachel sat shocked for a moment, but the urgent appeal on the older lady's face prompted her.

'If you wish it,' she said.

Jonathan Alleyn's rooms were on the second floor of the house. The two women went up the sweeping staircase in silence; Mrs Alleyn wore a tense, pinched expression. At his door they paused, and the older lady smoothed her hands down the length of her bodice. Rachel was suddenly afraid of what might lie within – what could cause the man's own mother such distress.

'Please . . .' said Mrs Alleyn. 'Please try not to . . .' But she didn't go on. She closed her mouth sadly, knocked at the door and opened it without waiting for a response. 'Jonathan,' she said, somewhat stridently, as she swept into the room. Rachel followed close on her heels, like an anxious child. 'There is somebody I'd like to—'

'Mother,' a man's voice cut her off. 'I told you I did not wish to meet any more of your pointless quacks.' Mrs Alleyn stopped so abruptly that Rachel almost ran into her. 'I told you I didn't want to see *you*. Not today,' he added.

'This is Mrs Weekes. I thought you—'

'You thought of yourself, I don't doubt. As you generally do. Leave me be. I'm warning you.' Mrs Alleyn tensed visibly. Rachel struggled to see where the man's voice was coming from. The shutters were closed, and no lamps were lit. In the dull glow of the coals, she caught the outline of a figure, slumped in a chair behind a vast and cluttered desk.

She suddenly felt an odd foreboding, a feeling of entrapment. Her breath was caught behind her ribs like a bubble.

'Perhaps another time,' she said again, weakly, and turned to go. Mrs Alleyn caught her arm.

'I said get *out*!' Jonathan Alleyn suddenly bellowed, and only his mother's hand gripping her arm prevented Rachel from obeying. The man sounded deranged. Mrs Alleyn turned, and leaned close to Rachel's ear.

'Please,' she whispered. 'Please try.' And then she was gone, closing the door behind her.

For a moment, Rachel didn't dare to move. She didn't dare to make a sound, in case the man realised she was still there. *What is this? Why am I here?* She cast her eyes around, and could see a little more as her eyes grew accustomed to the darkness, and her unease increased the more she saw. The room was set up as a study, with a great many shelves and cupboards, each laden with books and strange objects she couldn't identify. Some appeared to be scientific instruments, with glass lenses and adjustable wheels, notched cogs and ebony boxes to hold who knew what. Others looked like toys. Like children's toys. There were star charts pinned to the walls, and a painted globe showing a map of the world. On the shelf nearest her shoulder, she recoiled from the dead eyes and snarling mouth of a fox, stuffed and mounted in a pose of extreme aggression. On the desk were scattered papers and pens, more strange instruments and three large glass jars, each filled with liquid and greyish, bulbous things that Rachel decided not to look too closely at. There was a strange smell like rotting meat, faint but revolting. It made sweat break out along her brow. On the wall above the fire hung a painting of a scene from hell – human figures being torn limb from limb and consumed by gleeful demons, their faces stretched in unimaginable horror.

'Do you like the painting?' the man asked. His voice was hoarse now, and quiet. Startled, Rachel glanced back at him.

'No,' she said, truthfully, and he gave a hollow chuckle.

'It's by a man called Bosch. A man who dreamed similar dreams to me. Did you think you were invisible, standing there, quiet as a mouse? My eyes see a good deal better than yours in this light. I am used to it.'

'We would both see a good deal better if the shutters were opened,' said Rachel, in the same brisk tone she would have used with Eliza. She turned slightly as if to cross to the window, but stopped when he spoke again.

'Do not touch the shutters.' His voice was cold, and hard. He was no child in a temper. 'Who are you? Why is my mother so keen for me to meet you?'

'I . . . in truth, I am not certain,' said Rachel. Faced with all the strangeness of the man, of his room, of her situation, her mind abandoned decorum and produced only truth. 'Your mother suggested I might do you some good, by my company.'

'Why? Are you a healer?'

'No.'

'Are you a . . . nun? A saint, perhaps? Or a whore?' he asked. Rachel's tongue froze in shock, so she could not reply. 'One of those three, then. I wonder which?' His tone was mocking. 'Nun, saint, or whore.'

'None of those,' she managed at last.

'A pity. I could have used a whore's company. She will not have them in the house, though. My mother. A great irony, given that all women are whores; be it for coin, status or safety that they sell themselves. Come closer, into the light. I can't see your face properly.'

Rachel moved woodenly, feeling as though she'd stumbled into a strange and unsettling dream. She had never been in so alien a situation, not even when she'd stood over her father as all their possessions were taken out into the street. She went around to the far side of the desk and stood in front of Jonathan Alleyn's chair. She felt the meagre warmth of the coals on her face, and when she looked at him she almost recoiled. He was gaunt and deathly pale, with hollows beneath his cheekbones. She made out lines across his brow and at the corners of his eyes, and streaks of grey in his unkempt hair. He was tall but too thin, his shoulders jutting out beneath his shirt, legs long and lean. A hand, curled into a fist and held against his mouth, was ridged with tendons, and his eyes were unsettlingly bright. He drew breath to speak again, but when Rachel met his gaze his voice trailed away, even as his lips still moved. His hand dropped down, and his mouth hung slightly open. This was it, Rachel realised. This was why she had been sent. '*Alice?*' he whispered, and in his voice was a broken heart, an ocean of hope and pain and loss. Rachel swallowed, and didn't dare to speak. *So it is Alice that they see, when they look at me. This man and his mother. The girl who left him, it must surely be?* Tears ran from the corners of Jonathan's eyes, shining with the firelight. His face flooded with such hurt, such misery that for a second Rachel wanted to reach out and wipe his tears away. Her hands rose and strayed towards him, and he snatched at them roughly, pulling her down to kneel in front of him. She tried to pull away but he held her fast, his grip unbreakable. 'Why?' he whispered. His breath stank sharply of spirits. 'Oh, why did you do it? Why did you leave me?'

Rachel stared into his ravaged eyes, transfixed. She could hardly think straight; her heart was jumping in her throat.

'Mr Alleyn,' she gasped, at last. 'I . . .' At the sound of her voice he blinked, and his face hardened. The look of pain and hope in his eyes faded away, and anger replaced it. One hand clasped her chin, and turned her face towards the fire's orange light.

'What trick is this? You are not her. Answer me!' he rasped.

'I am Rachel Weekes, and—'

'Who? *Who?*' He shook her, and she tried again to twist out of his grip. In an instant he released her chin, and his hand locked around her neck instead. 'Answer me, or by God I will choke the life from you! I swear it!' He brought his other hand to reinforce the first, and Rachel scrabbled at them, trying to prise her fingers beneath his, to no avail. Panic surged through her, making her clumsy.

'I am Rachel Weekes! I know no Alice! I . . . I was invited by your mother!' she cried. 'Let go of me!'

'My mother? So this is some game of hers, is it? I should have suspected as much. But how *dare* you, madam? How *dare* you come to me and pretend to be what you are not?'

'I did no such thing—' She tried to argue, but could not get enough air. His hands around her neck were like iron, and bright spots began to swirl in the corners of her eyes. He was all she could see; his face grim and terrible, rearing over her, teeth clenched in murderous fury. Behind him, the room swirled in darkness. She batted at his hands, his arms and face, as though such feeble blows might make him loosen his grip; where her windpipe was crushed there was a deep, stabbing pain. She felt insubstantial, weak; her every effort futile. *He will kill me*, came the realisation in the back of her mind, oddly calm, even as her heart pounded in terror and her lungs burned for air.

'Let her go!' a woman shouted. Rachel felt other hands tugging at Jonathan's fingers. 'Leave off, I say!' There was a flurry of movement, a struggle, and Rachel looked up in time to see the hearth brush strike her assailant's head with a ringing percussion. Soot showered him and he reeled backwards, coughing. Released from his grip, Rachel fell to the floor, gasping for breath. She tried to see who had saved her, but the woman had darted out of reach of Jonathan Alleyn's rage, into the shadows. He stood, rubbing at his eyes, snarling in fury.

'Starling, you treacherous bitch!' he shouted. Rachel struggled to her feet, and fled. She bolted down the stairs, past Mrs Alleyn who waited for her at the bottom.

'Mrs Weekes? Are you well?' she called out in consternation, as Rachel raced by. Rachel didn't stop to speak, or collect her cloak. She rushed out into the rarefied air of the crescent, heedless of anything but the need to escape.

* * *

Starling dissected their meeting, over and over – Jonathan Alleyn and Rachel Weekes. She ran it by her mind's eye as she boiled a ham, as she scraped the scales from a sole, as she scalded the distilling jars and peeled apples for a pie. As the bustle of dinner being prepared and sent up went on around her; the steady exchange of hot plates for cold ones, returning from Mrs Alleyn's table all but untouched. The lady of the house dined alone most nights, with a place set for her son, ever empty, by her side. Starling felt as though she'd stepped aside from it all, like there was a wall around her, muffling everything. She thought about what had happened, and wondered why she felt no satisfaction. Not quite *no* satisfaction, perhaps. Hadn't she wanted him to reveal himself? To show that he was a murderer? And hadn't he obliged her, by near strangling Dick's new wife? But she'd known there was violence in him, that was nothing new. *Was that how he did it, then? With his bare hands around her neck?*

Alice's narrow neck, fragile as a bird's; soft skin and downy hair, catching the light. Jonathan's strong hands with their long, elegant fingers. Once he had sat Starling on his knee in front of the old piano at the farmhouse in Bathampton, and though it was tuneless from the damp, he'd tried to teach her a song to play. She'd watched his hands closely. His nails were so clean, and perfectly shaped; the knuckles and joints stood proud along his fingers. As he'd played she been mesmerised by the movement of tendons beneath his skin, so she hadn't paid any attention to the notes he was playing. When he'd said *your turn*, and she hadn't known where to start, the look of disappointment on his face had stung her somewhat. To distract him she'd grabbed his hand in both of hers and nipped one of the fingers, laughing when he gasped, and then darted away to find Alice. *Your little termagant bit me*, he said, when they found her in the yard, but he was smiling as he said it.

And yet. And yet. *Why did you leave me?* That was what he'd asked her. Starling paused near the top of the servants' stair and leaned against the wall, turning her face to the small window to look up at the night sky. The moon was bright, the stars clear and stark. She could feel the chill coming through the glass, drifting down to settle on her face. It had been a cold autumn so far, and promised a cold winter. The air smelled gritty and old. Starling shut her eyes, furious with herself. *What did you expect? For him to cry: It cannot be! I murdered thee! Idiot.* She had prepared him as well as she could in the short time available to her. She'd taken him more of the strengthened wine, and made as many sharp noises as she could as she straightened his rooms. She'd tipped the food meant for him into a sack to dispose of later, so that his stomach had nothing in it but the spirits. The dead rat she'd left under his desk three days earlier was really beginning to stink, filling the air with the smell of its decay. She hoped it made him feel as though death itself was stalking him.

Why did you leave me? It was that phrase that bothered her. That was not what a murderer would ask of his victim, surely? That made it sound as though he really did believe the lies that were told about Alice having another lover, about her absconding with him, and leaving them all behind. Unless . . . unless that was the reason Jonathan had killed her? His motive had long puzzled Starling. She knew more of men now than she had known then, a good deal more, but still she was sure that he'd loved Alice. He'd loved her for years. He and Alice had grown up side by side, though they'd spent more time apart than they had together. But if Jonathan had thought, for some reason, that Alice *planned* to leave him . . . that could well have been enough to make him harm her. Not the Jonathan from before the war, but the Jonathan from afterwards. The Jonathan who came back from Spain, so very different from the boy who'd set off to fight all full of ideas about honour and glory. But Alice would never have left him. Alice loved him more than air. Starling let her head fall back against the stone wall with a thump.

There was no way she could rest. She finished up her work, threw her shawl around her shoulders and let herself quietly out of the house. Her boot heels rang against the swept stones of the pavement. Beyond the light of the guttering streetlamps was the black swathe of steep pasture in front of the crescent, and beyond that, to the south and east, the rest of the city – a shadowed labyrinth in the darkness. The pinprick sparkle of lanterns looked like a feeble echo of the stars above. Alice would have sighed at the beauty of it, but knowing that only gave Starling a sour taste in her mouth, and she turned her eyes away, refusing to be beguiled. She walked so briskly to the Moor's Head that she was breathless when she arrived, and damp beneath her clothes. It was stifling as ever inside the inn, ripe with the stink of people, of sweat and dissolution. Dick Weekes was there with some of the old crowd, and Starling was happier to see him than she would ever admit. She got a drink from Sadie and sauntered over to his table.

He was laughing at some joke, but fell serious when he

looked up and saw her. He was all russet brown and handsome; lips curved into a subtle pout. Starling hated the feeling that seeing him gave her – a pang of some deep longing or other. The touch of his hands, perhaps, or his desire for her. The way he would let her talk, on and on, propped on one elbow above him after their love play.

'It didn't take you long to find your way back in here,' she said loudly, above the din. 'I'm surprised the missus let you out, tonight of all nights.'

'What's special about tonight?' said Dick, frowning.

'Oh, nothing. Only I imagined she'd be somewhat rattled, after her visit to the Alleyns today.'

'Bring your arse to anchor, wench,' said old Peter Hawkes, who as ever could not tear his eyes from her red hair and tight bodice. Starling shrugged and pushed herself a space on the bench beside Dick. The other men at the table turned away, uninterested, and Dick only looked blank.

'You mean, you didn't know?' said Starling. 'She never told you she was going? Or had been?' She shook her head slowly, arching her brows. 'Such secrets, so early in a marriage.' Dick's nostrils flared. How he hated to be teased.

'I've not seen my wife yet this evening. But I'm sure she will tell me herself, when I do,' he said curtly.

'Perhaps. Perhaps I shouldn't have let her secret out. But then, I'm more allied to you than to her, I suppose.' Starling let her hand rest on his thigh, and leaned closer to speak into his ear. 'I'll need some more strong wine. As strong as you can make it.'

'You'll not have it. Not from me.' Dick took a long drink, then stared down into his cup as if to close himself off from her. 'Let it rest, Starling. Let the poor bugger rest, won't you? What's he ever done to you, anyway? What has all your scheming brought about? Nothing at all, that's what.'

'He's a murderer. He killed his betrothed, my sister . . .'

'Who says so, apart from you? Who in the whole country of England says so, apart from *you*?' His words were hard, and they stung her. 'Who even thinks Alice Beckwith is dead, apart from you? She's probably living in some northern county, happy as a lark with husband and bairns, and all the while you stew away like some witch at her cauldron, plotting to avenge a murder that never took place!' He pointed an angry finger at her. A tiny worm of doubt twisted in Starling's gut, just for a second.

'Alice would *never* have left just like that . . . I know the truth of the matter,' she said.

'So you say. But it wouldn't be the first time a woman was wrong, now would it? You think you were a sister to her, but you weren't. You're some vagabond's brat, taken in as a hobby. Of course she'd leave you, if she saw fit. Do you know how ridiculous you sound, going on and on about her? Do yourself a favour, and give it up. It's not just him you hurt, you know. I was there myself the other day. Mrs Alleyn . . . she sickens alongside her son. Because of you.'

'It's his own guilt that sickens him – I've heard him confess, so I have! I only want the truth to be known.'

'No, you don't. You don't want to hear the truth, that's your problem. Alice Beckwith got hot for another man, and ran off rather than face up to her benefactor. Will you spend your whole life trying to pretend it was otherwise?'

Starling was shocked into angry silence for a moment.

'You're wrong,' she said at last, but Richard ignored her. 'I'd have known if she had another lover.' She took a long swallow of her beer, though her stomach was clenched tight and she found it hard to swallow. Still Richard kept his eyes in front of him, and Starling could only look at the side of his face. She suddenly felt frightened, and couldn't say why. A curl of brown hair hung in front of his ear, and before she knew it she had reached out and tucked it back for him. Dick twisted about, and knocked her hand away.

'I meant what I said, Starling,' he said coldly. 'There'll be no more of that, between you and me.' She stared at him, her mouth falling open. 'Take Mr Hawkes here out the back, if you must rut. He's always wanted to dance the blanket hornpipe with you, haven't you, Hawkes?' Peter Hawkes leered at her, and dipped his grizzled chin in assent.

'You're a devilish good piece. I'd like to see if you've the ginger hackles down below, as well as up top,' he said.

'My thanks for the offer, sir.' Starling rose from the bench. 'But I'd rather couple the old horse in the stable than have you touch me.' She walked away with her head up high, so that Dick wouldn't see the knife he'd stuck into her, wedged between her ribs. She felt the wound of it go deep; it made her breathless.

'Aye, wench, but only take a look and you'll find I'm hung just like that horse that's caught your eye!' Peter Hawkes called after her, and the men dissolved into laughter.

She chose a soldier, little more than a boy, already drunk and half slumped in a bench with his comrades. The brass buttons on his jacket were brightly polished, but his breeches were stained here and there with spilt wine. He had soft blond hair, like a baby's, and gentle brown eyes all befuddled from drink. His voice wavered between a boyish squeak and a man's tenor. She drank with him and his friends, and draped herself over him, ever closer, until in the end she was sitting in his lap. She let his tentative, uncertain hands quest upwards from her hips to the narrow span of her waist, and then even further. When she judged him quite far gone enough she whispered in his ear, and helped him to stand. As she led him towards the back door she looked over at Dick and saw him watching her, scowling, his eyes dark and angry. Just as she'd hoped. She shot him a spiteful smile as she lifted the lad's arm and placed it around her shoulders.

In the yard Starling kissed the boy quickly, all over his face, turning him this way and that until he pulled away suddenly, his eyes sliding out of focus. She stepped neatly to one side as he threw up into the gutter; a watery stream of curdled wine. As he was doubled over, coughing and spitting, she dipped her fingers into each of his pockets and relieved him of the last of his coins. The stink of his vomit made her recoil, and she swayed, suddenly weak right through her body.

'Let this be a lesson to you, sweet boy,' she told him, not unkindly. 'Come tomorrow you will have lost your money, your dignity and your good health, and yet will have kept the maidenhead you're so keen to lose. You will not awake a successful man. Never drink more than you can hold.' He groaned piteously, and she patted him on the shoulder, quite sure he had no idea who she was, or where he was, or why. 'There, there. Your friends will soon come out to find you.' With that she left him and slipped out of the yard into the dark streets of Bath, with tears she hadn't been aware of shedding cold on her cheeks.

* * *

For a long time after she ran from Lansdown Crescent, Rachel couldn't keep still. Her hands shook, and her legs trembled, and she felt the ridiculous urge to burst into tears even though the threat of danger was long gone. She warmed herself some spiced wine but could not drink it, and made a cold supper that she could not eat. She wanted Richard to come home so that she could be comforted, but darkness gathered in the narrow street outside until she could no longer see to watch for him. When it was late and he was still not home, she took a candle up the narrow stairs and fetched the twist of her mother's hair from her trinket box. She pressed the cold, slippery lock to her lips and breathed in, trying to find some scent of Anne Crofton still on it. There was none, but it comforted her nonetheless, and the shuddering inside her that threatened to become sobs eased off. *Soft hair, soft hands. Everything soft and gentle about her, even when she scolded*, the voice whispered, in memory. Rachel lay down on the bed to wait. Her neck was sore, the muscles stiffening from the strain of trying to break away from Jonathan Alleyn. When she shut her eyes she saw his face, the flood of misery and hope that had filled it, followed by that gleam of fury, so terrible, like nothing she had seen in a person's eyes before today.

She was drifting, her eyes still wide and stinging dry, when the door finally banged below, and she heard Richard's footsteps on the stairs. She sat up, her head aching, and attempted to pat her hair into better shape. The candle had burned down to a nub. Richard was scowling when he came in, and his steps were heavy, clumsy; boots scuffing on the floor, catching on the corners of the furniture.

'Richard! I'm so glad you're come home. The most . . . unsettling thing happened to me today—'

'You went to see Mrs Alleyn again.' Richard cut her off, standing over the bed with his face half lit, half hidden in darkness.

'Yes . . . how did you know?'

'Not from you, that's clear enough. Not from my wife, who ought not to keep things from me!' His voice rose, and Rachel blinked. Sweat shone on his top lip and brow, and she could smell the stink of the inn on him.

'I . . . I was going to. But it was so late when you got home last night, and you seemed so distracted, I didn't want to . . . bother you with it.'

'And this morning, before I went out?' he said. Rachel hesitated.

'I thought it of little consequence,' she said quietly. In truth she couldn't say for sure why she'd kept the invitation from him, only that there had remained a nagging doubt over his reaction to the news.

'You thought it of little consequence,' Richard echoed, sarcastically.

'I meant to tell you, of course I did. And I am trying to tell you now. Oh, Richard – it was terrible! Mrs Alleyn did insist upon me meeting her son, even to the extent that I had to go up to his rooms, for he would not come down to us. And then . . . and then . . . he flew at me! I don't know the reason why, for certain – only that he seemed to mistake me for somebody else . . . He flew at me and half killed me, Richard! I was so afraid . . . I think he's quite mad!'

She stopped to catch her breath, and steady herself. She waited for him to reach out for her, and soothe her, but instead he sat down heavily on the edge of the bed, and kept his back turned.

'Richard? Didn't you hear me?' said Rachel, putting a hand on his shoulder. He jumped as if he'd forgotten she was there.

'What nonsense is this?' he muttered. 'Of course he's not mad, only . . . troubled. Of course he didn't attack you.'

'But . . . he did! I swear it!' Rachel cried. 'Look! Look here at my neck, if you doubt me. See the marks his fingers left!' She pulled her shawl aside and turned her neck to the light, where deep red fingerprints still marked the skin. 'Look!' Reluctantly, Richard glanced briefly at her neck, and his frown grew even deeper. He stayed silent. 'But . . . have you no words of comfort for me? Doesn't it move you, that I was attacked?' she said, bewildered.

'Of course it does. Of course . . . I am sure he did not intend to harm you. He is a gentleman. His mother is—'

'His mother left me alone in his rooms! She left me alone for him to do as he pleased! And what kind of gentleman would deal out violence to a . . . a blameless person who had come to call? I tell you, they are gentlefolk neither one of them!' Rachel began to sob, as much from exhaustion and disappointment as from her former fear.

'I will not hear you speak ill of the Alleyns. Were it not for Mrs Alleyn's kindness, and her patronage, I would be nowhere. I would be a lowlife, serving others for a living, instead of a business man of good repute, rising all the while . . .'

'I don't understand you, Richard. Are . . . are we to be so grateful to her for your advancement that her son may strangle me and go unreproached?'

'I say only that . . . allowances must be made. Jonathan Alleyn is not a well man . . . it is unfortunate that he . . . reacted badly to you. But you should not have been in his rooms!'

'Unfortunate? And if that serving girl hadn't been there to make him stop, and he had killed me, would that be unfortunate too? Or would that be merely regrettable?'

'What serving girl?'

'The red-headed one. The one I told you about before, that I thought I saw—'

'Enough about this now. You're home, safe and well. No harm has been done . . .' Richard turned to her now, and put out a hand to take one of hers. Rachel stared at him in astonishment. 'It was a fine thing that Mrs Alleyn asked you to see her again. Perhaps next time it will be a card party, or tea? Let us hope so, for she truly must be taking a shine to you, hmm?' He squeezed her hand and smiled, but his eyes stayed troubled, almost afraid.

'Next time? Richard . . . I can't go back there. I won't! You don't understand what it was like . . .'

'Enough, now. You've had a fright, and you're not talking sense. Of course you will go back, if you are invited. We must hope that you are.' His grip on her hand had grown tighter, and almost hurt.

'Richard, I—'

'You will go back.' He said each word slowly, clearly, and in his hand hers was a small, weak thing that could not free itself.

Rachel said nothing. She did not understand Richard's loyalty to the Alleyns, so profound that her own well-being could be brushed so easily aside. She did not understand his insistence that she go back, even if she didn't want to. She did not understand why he offered her no gentle embrace, but only began to unbutton his breeches as he laid her back on the bed. She did not understand why, when she told him she was too tired and upset to make love, he carried on and did it anyway.

Jonathan and Alice wrote to each other constantly, each letter begun as soon as the one before had been received and devoured, so that missives passed between them like a lungful of air, breathed in and then out, tirelessly. Whenever the letter carrier called with something, Alice rushed to be the first person whose fingers touched the envelope; as if some vital essence of Jonathan might linger on it, and pass to her through her skin. Then she stole away to find some private place in which to read – in her room, or tucked into the window seat in the back parlour, or in the barn – with perfect concentration on her face, and a smile tugging at the corners of her mouth, ebbing and flowing according to the contents of the letter. Each letter was read twice, three times, even four. Then Alice would place it carefully in a polished rosewood box, and sit down with paper and pen to begin her reply.

More than once, Starling opened the rosewood box and tried to read one of the letters. She knew she shouldn't, but that didn't make the temptation any easier to resist. Her reading was coming along, under Alice's tuition, but still she could only make out one or two words of Jonathan's impossible writing, with its curls and flourishes and slanting loops. It was as though he'd designed it deliberately so that none but Alice could read it. And of course she never saw what Alice wrote to him in response. When she asked, Alice would say something like: *I'm telling him about how well you are doing in your lessons, and how much of a help you are to Bridget. And about the owls nesting in the old tree, and to ask when he and his grandfather will next visit us.* Then she'd give a nod and a smile, as if to say *there, be satisfied*. Starling chafed to know what else she wrote. The scant words she could pick from Jonathan's script were usually dull things like *clement*, *mother*, *city* and *season*; only occasionally did she see more exciting things, like *cherish*, *captive*, and *adore*.

Starling always knew when Alice was keeping secrets – it wasn't difficult to tell, because Alice wasn't very good at keeping them. Not that she divulged them, unless they were silly and minor, and hers to divulge: a cake they were to have for tea, or some small present she'd bought for Starling, which was meant to be saved for the day they'd chosen as her birthday but would always be handed over sooner. When she had a secret that was not hers, or was important, she kept it, but the strain of doing so wrote itself all over her face. A tiny line appeared between her brows, and a distracted look in her eyes, as though what she could not tell ran constantly before them. Her lower lip stayed open, away from the upper; ever ready to speak. So she was for five days after one letter from Jonathan came, and Starling ached to know what she knew. Then, on a cool and breezy day, Alice wandered into the kitchen with studied calm, carrying a cloth-bound book of poems and her shawl. She went to stand by the window, and Starling, who was helping Bridget rub salt into a joint of bacon, noticed how high and tense her shoulders were. Eventually, Alice turned to them with an air of tremendous nonchalance.

'I think I might take Starling on a walk into Bathampton today. The weather seems set fair,' she said.

Bridget looked out at the skirling clouds and wind-bent trees, and pursed her lips doubtfully.

'If it's fresh air you want, you could go and see if there are any goosegogs ready for picking yet,' she said.

'Oh, there aren't. I checked them earlier,' Alice replied

hurriedly. 'You'd like a trip into the village, wouldn't you, Starling?' She was slightly breathless, her voice a little high.

'Oh, yes. Can I, Bridget?'

'What about this bacon, then?'

'It's almost done . . . leave it and I'll be sure to finish it later. Please?'

'Go on then, the pair of you. Never mind leaving me with all the work,' said Bridget. Starling jumped down from the stool she was standing on, and untied her apron.

'Run and get your hat, my chuck.' Alice's smile was irrepressible.

The farmhouse sat on the wide strip of land that lay between the river and the newly made canal that linked the River Kennet in the east to the River Avon at Bath. The Avon, wide and fast-flowing, passed to the north of the house; and to the south, a path led to a hump-backed bridge across the canal and then straight on to the high street. But that day, Alice stepped onto the gravelled towpath beside the canal instead.

'Let's go this way today,' she said brightly. Turning west would have taken them the two miles into Bath; turning east led them along the southern edge of Bathampton. The wind bowled along the canal's flat surface, pulling and puckering it; it made their skirts and the ribbons on their hats flutter. As they dodged piles of dung left by the barge horses, Starling was still fascinated to see water in the canal. For a long time it had been a muddied trench where teams of navvies had hacked and worked to shore up the earth, reinforcing the scar they cut so that it would not heal again in their wake. Now boats and barges were free to travel along it, moving cargos with far greater ease and economy than by road. The water had been glassy and clear for a month after the canal was filled. Now it was as green and cloudy as watercress soup, and it had a dank, clammy smell, like rain and rotting leaves.

A third of a mile or so along the towpath, a large inn called the George sat beside the canal, and another bridge crossed the water, linking Bathampton to a lane that went to Batheaston, on the north bank of the river. Alice stopped at the foot of this second bridge, and looked around.

'Shan't we go on into the village?' said Starling, confused.

'In a while. Or perhaps we could go into the inn, today? And have something to eat?' Starling was always hungry and nodded at once, but Alice was looking along the lane towards Batheaston, her face lively with expectation. The hand that held Starling's held it tightly. For a while nothing happened, and Starling watched a barge approach and slide by, its cargo hidden under sheets of canvas. The bargeman clucked his tongue at the horse when it baulked at the shadows beneath the bridge. He was weather-beaten and lean, and had a pipe clamped between teeth the colour of mahogany.

'Where are you going?' Starling called to him, shy but fascinated. He squinted his eyes at her and took his pipe into his hand.

'I'm for Newbury, bantling,' he said.

'How long will it take you?' Starling disengaged her hand from Alice's to trot along the towpath behind the horse.

'Four days, maybe somewhat less – don't run up the rear of that horse or he'll kick you skywards. Depends on the number already waiting at Foxhangers.'

'Where's that? Why should people wait?'

'You've a good many questions, chickabiddy. There's a great big hill, this side o' Devizes. They've not yet fathomed how to make the canal climb it. We've to unload everything and take it up by rail wagon before we can go on along the water once more.' By this time Starling had followed the barge a goodly way from the bridge, so she stopped, and he soon drew ahead.

'How should water climb a hill?' she called after him, but the bargeman just gave her a wave, and turned his back.

She picked a few handfuls of forget-me-nots as she walked back to Alice, who hadn't seemed to notice her absence. A moment later, her arm shot out and grabbed at Starling for support.

'Oh! Look!' Alice gasped, staring along the lane. 'Look, Starling – Mr Alleyn has come!' Starling followed her gaze, and saw, far off, a gentleman who might have been Mr Alleyn, on a grey horse.

'Is it him? He isn't due to visit,' she said, puzzled. She took hold of Alice's arm where it grasped at her. Through the skin of her wrist, Starling felt the older girl's pulse racing and stumbling along. Alarmed, she tugged to get Alice's attention. 'Be calm, Alice. Please, be calm,' she murmured. Alice smiled down at her, and took a deep breath.

'I'm quite well, dearest.' But Starling had seen what happened sometimes, when Alice's heart stuttered like that – had seen her turn pale as milk, and sway on her feet; had seen her faint dead away on three occasions, fits which left her weak and dizzy for days afterwards, and confined her to bed. *Miss Alice's heart is a fragile thing*, Bridget told Starling, in serious tones. *Do all you can to keep it easy*. 'Look – see! It *is* Mr Alleyn.' Starling looked again, and as the figure drew nearer she could clearly recognise Jonathan Alleyn, riding alone.

When Jonathan saw them waiting he urged his horse into a trot, and dismounted in a graceless rush to stand so close to Alice that if either one had moved they would have touched. Neither spoke, and Starling watched in astonishment until Jonathan finally seemed to recover himself, took a step backwards and brought Alice's fingers to his lips. There was colour high on his slanting cheekbones, and he smiled as though he couldn't prevent it.

'Miss Beckwith, how fortunate to chance across you like this.' Starling wondered who the performance was for, since she knew at once that this meeting was the secret Alice had been keeping. 'And Starling – how tall you are growing! Why, you're near to Miss Beckwith's shoulder now.'

'Bridget says I'll be as tall as her within a year, at this rate,' Starling told him proudly. 'How came you here, Mr Alleyn? Were you coming to call at the farmhouse?'

'Well . . . I had some business in Batheaston, so I happened to be passing and I thought I would call in . . . but now I find you here, perhaps we could go into the inn for a while?' he said, as if only then thinking of it. Starling smiled. One did not pass Bathampton on the road from Box to Bathcaston.

'By chance, we had just decided the same thing,' she said.

'Come then,' said Jonathan. Alice was still breathless, and Starling kept tight hold of her hand as they went towards the door.

The George Inn occupied an ancient stone building, huddled and hoary, with tiny leaded windows and cracked chimney pots. It had many chambers inside, all with flagged stone floors worn into sagging curves, and soot-stained walls under low, oppressive ceilings. Jonathan led them to a bench away from any windows, near a hearth that had been swept clean for the coming summer. The other customers in the place were gentleman farmers talking business, travellers on their way into Bath and a few bargemen, who were rougher and poorly dressed. Loud, bawdy laughter broke out nearby, and Jonathan frowned.

'I wonder if this is indeed the right place for you, Miss Beckwith,' he said, but she only laughed.

'I'm not as sensitive as you think me, Mr Alleyn. I like it here. Starling and I have come here before now, and with Bridget sometimes, on holidays.'

'I ate devilled kidneys here last time, but I didn't like them at all,' Starling added.

'Well, then. We shall be quite comfortable here for a time.' Jonathan smiled. They ordered some beer, and a plate of lamb chops to share, and Starling sat, a little bored, as the two of them talked.

They talked of Jonathan's family, and of his home, which was a grand manor house at Box, further to the west. He lived with his mother and his grandfather, since his own father had died when he was very young. They talked of his schooling, and his desire to buy an officer's commission into the army, which made Alice's eyes glow with fearful admiration, that he might put himself in harm's way. 'My mother is not enamoured with the idea. She would rather I went into the navy, where there are better prospects for promotion and wealth . . .'

'But you do not wish it?' said Alice.

'I . . . I am quite ashamed to say it, but the sea makes me terribly ill. The few times I have gone aboard a boat have made me quite sure I never wish to again, if I can help it. Much less commit myself to a career upon it!'

'But you would follow in the very footsteps of Lord Nelson – he also suffers, I have read. And I've heard that such illnesses can pass, once a person becomes accustomed.'

'So they tell me. But if they are wrong, and I am doomed to feel that wretched every time we set sail – oh, Alice, the very thought makes me quail!' he said, with a rueful laugh. Starling goggled at him in outrage, but neither one of them seemed to notice that he'd used Alice's Christian name in a public place. 'I mean to enrol at Le Marchant's college at Marlow, and become a cavalry officer.'

'Marlow? But . . . it is so far away . . .' Alice said quietly.

'I shall visit home very often, I promise. Very often.' He spoke earnestly, and for a long moment their eyes stayed locked together, and some unspoken message passed between them that Starling could not read. 'I mean to . . . I mean to visit Miss Fallonbrooke, before I go,' Jonathan said softly. Alice's eyes grew wide.

'Who's Miss Fallonbrooke?' asked Starling, but they both ignored her. She folded her arms crossly and kicked at the table leg, but they ignored that too.

'Oh?' said Alice, and it was more of a breath than a word. 'I wrote to her . . .'

'You wrote to her?' Alice's face fell.

'Only to ask for a meeting, Alice. Only for that. And I made it plain that . . . that is, in my tone, I sought to convey . . .' He broke off, frustrated. 'I mean to speak to her . . . of freeing ourselves from the intentions our parents have imposed upon us. I have reason to believe that she finds them as . . . onerous as I do.'

'What reasons, Mr Alleyn?' Alice looked as though she was suffering under some tension she could hardly stand.

'I had word that . . . she, too, loves another,' said Jonathan, gazing at Alice in supplication. For a second, Alice radiated a simple, uncomplicated joy. But then her face clouded again.

'I shall be nineteen at my next birthday,' she murmured, sounding inexplicably sad. 'I pray that the visit . . . is a success. I pray that what you heard is right, for only she can release you. Only that way can you conduct yourself as a gentleman should.' Jonathan looked distraught, so Starling fidgeted, kicking her legs some more, and chipped in:

'How old are you, Mr Alleyn?'

'I am not quite eighteen, Miss Starling. But I will be soon,' he said, turning to her, looking relieved at the interruption.

'I shall be nine very soon. We think.'

'Nine! No wonder you're as tall as an elm. And far too big to be frightened of ghosts, I am sure.'

'Ghosts? What ghosts?'

'This building was a monastery, in ancient times. Before old King Henry ordered them to disband. I have heard tell that the ghosts of the monks who once lived here still walk the halls and passageways.'

'In truth, Mr Alleyn?' Starling was agog.

'In truth. In fact, I believe I saw one not a minute ago, peering over your shoulder to see if you'd left a lamb chop for him.' Jonathan smiled, and Starling gasped, craning her head about to check for spectral monks.

'You mustn't tease her so!' Alice admonished, laughing.

'If a ghost monk sneaks up on me, Alice, can I throw something at him?'

'Indeed you may, dearest. Be on your guard,' said Alice, fondly.

When they parted, an hour or so later, Alice waited by the bridge until Mr Alleyn had ridden right out of sight. She watched forlornly, with her arms folded; and when at last he vanished, she sighed.

'Come then, Starling. Let's go back and see how Bridget is getting on.'

'Aren't we going into Bathampton at all, then?' Starling was disappointed.

'Well, we've been gone a good long while already . . . perhaps she might wonder where we are.'

'And how surprised she'll be when we tell her Mr Alleyn came riding and found us!' said Starling. She said it deliberately, to find out what she should and should not say to Bridget, who was somehow both Alice's servant and her mistress. Part of her knew that she had only been invited along to make it decent for Jonathan and Alice to have lunch together. She was at once proud of this important role, and also had the nagging feeling that something might be owing to her for it. Alice paused.

'Perhaps she would not like to hear it. Perhaps she would be cross that we did not bring him to the farmhouse, where she could see him too,' she said. Starling thought for a moment.

'If we walked back along the high street instead of the canal, we might find something to take her, so she won't feel so left out. And so she'll know we've been busy, all this time,' she suggested. Alice gave her a look that was half disapproving, half grateful.

'A small present for her, to make up for us leaving her alone today,' Alice agreed.

So they crossed the bridge and walked the length of Bathampton, and bought a handkerchief stitched with poppies and wheat sheaves from a huckster, which seemed to please Bridget well enough. And while Alice was too bright and nervy, and flew her anxiety like a pennant for the first few hours they were back, Starling found she had no such trouble with keeping a secret. She turned the memory of their visit from Jonathan over and over, like a precious stone in her pocket, and found that not telling Bridget was almost as much fun as the visit itself had been.

'Who is Miss Fallonbrooke?' she asked again, as Alice tucked her into her blankets that night.

'Beatrice Fallonbrooke is just a girl who has never done anything to harm anybody.' Alice sighed, and looked away. 'She is the daughter of a very wealthy man, and she is intended for Jonathan.'

'But . . . *you're* going to marry Jonathan!' At this, Alice smiled.

'Yes, I am, dearest. But the course of true love never did run smooth. It is no fault of Miss Fallonbrooke's that she presents an obstacle.' She smiled again, though her eyes were sad. 'You must not mention her, Starling. It is a secret that Jonathan shared with me, and now I have shared it with you. We must keep it secret. Can you do that?'

'Yes, Alice.'

'Good girl.' Alice sealed the promise with a kiss, pressed to her forehead, and Starling slept soundly, well fed on secrets that were now hers to keep.

1821

My Dear Mrs Weekes,

I do hope this note finds you well and quite recovered from any distress you might have felt upon recently meeting my son, Mr Jonathan Alleyn. I am more grateful than you can know that you agreed to speak with him, in what must have seemed very peculiar circumstances. I can only apologise if his behaviour towards you seemed in any way uncouth. He suffers a great deal, and has been so long out of polite company that I fear he forgets himself and his good manners upon occasion. I pray that you will find it within you to forgive this, and see only the troubled soul that plagues him.

I can quite understand that the meeting was not a pleasant one for you, but it has given me cause to hope. My relationship with my son has been much strained both by past events and by his current malaise, and I regret to impart that he rarely confides in me. It causes me great distress. Forgive the candour of this letter — I thought it best to speak plainly: Jonathan has asked to see you again. It has been far too many years since he made any such request of any visitor, and it fills my heart with joy that he makes it now. So I must ask, though I have little right to: will you call here again at your earliest convenience? Whatever passed between you and my son upon your last visit, it must have had some beneficial effect, and so I have much to thank you for already. But I beg you now, please call again.

Yours &c
Mrs Josephine Alleyn

For several days, Rachel carried Josephine Alleyn's note around in her pocket, and spoke of it to no one. She took it out and reread it often, and thought about throwing it into the grate and forgetting she had ever seen it. Surely if she did, she wouldn't be invited to Lansdown Crescent again, and that would be the end of it. She would never have to see them again – the man who had attempted to throttle her, and his beautiful, unreadable mother, so highly regarded by Richard. When she thought of the house, and of Jonathan Alleyn, waiting in his darkened rooms like some ghoul, she shivered. Even his mother, who was gentility itself, and so graceful, had a lost and mournful air. She put Rachel in mind of a porcelain doll – lovely but frozen, and liable to shatter. But then, when Rachel thought what life must be like for Josephine, trapped with a mad and invalid son who scared all callers from the house, she felt a stab of pity, and of guilt. So she kept the letter, and never quite managed to throw it into the fire, however sure she was that she would not see Jonathan Alleyn again, even if attacking her had indeed been beneficial to him.

Though Richard Weekes chafed at the cost of the extra housekeeping Rachel had arranged, he chafed even more about widening their social circle, and about obeying Josephine Alleyn, and so was persuaded to fund them an evening at a public ball in the Upper Assembly Rooms. Rachel wore her new gown, recently back from the seamstress – plainly cut, wide across her shoulders and low at the neck, but of a wonderfully soft, heavyweight satin, silvery in colour, with long sleeves and a sheer muslin overlay. In spite of it, and the coat she wore over it, she felt the cold as they walked out of Abbeygate Street in search of a pair of chairs to carry them – since even Richard Weekes's sense of thrift would not allow for arriving at a dance on foot. It was early October, and in the mornings the cold glass of the bedroom window was misted over with their night-time breathing. The air had a bite, even on sunny days; the leaves of the plane tree in Abbey Green had turned leathery brown and yellow, and made a clattering sound when the wind shook them. Rachel wrapped her arm tightly around Richard's, and felt the breeze teasing her hair loose from its pins.

They arrived at around seven o'clock to a mêlée of carriages and sedan chairs; horses and people alike throwing their heads and stamping their feet. The scene was lit by oil lamps high up on the portico above the entrance, and by the glow from the tall windows, and Rachel felt a flicker of excitement. The place and the racket of footsteps and hooves and voices had not changed at all since her last assembly, when she'd been sixteen years old; only the fashions and everything about her own life were different. She glanced at Richard, in his best coat and cravat, who looked as tense as a schoolboy called up before the master. He was worried that they would have no acquaintances within, and would drift about all evening making no impression – which was entirely probable, Rachel knew, since the assemblies were always so crowded that even if you knew twenty people in the room, you might not manage to find any of them. But that evening she felt no urge to reassure Richard, so she merely gave him a thin, incomplete smile, and said nothing as they went inside.

A wave of heat poured out through the doors, and after the cold of the evening it felt smothering. From the cloak-room they moved through to the main ballroom, where the cacophony was almost too loud for conversation, and the press of bodies made it hard to move. Above it all, on a central balcony, the orchestra was playing a lively tune, and the floor had already filled with dancing pairs, who added the pounding of feet and the rustle of cloth to the swelling din. The room was a sea of faces, either flushed and happy or scowling and harried; the smell of sweat, perfume and powder was everywhere. Five vast glass chandeliers hung from the distant ceiling, glittering with hundreds of candle flames, banishing shadows from the elaborate plasterwork and columns of the walls. Rachel knew better than to stand directly below one of the lights. Once before, when she'd attended as a girl, the heat from the revellers had caused the candles to soften and droop, dripping hot wax into carefully coiffed hair and propped décolletages. Rachel felt a flush creep into her cheeks, and her underarms prickled with perspiration. Her dress was unfashionably plain, but at least the vogue for wearing few ornaments suited her situation.

The air of merriment was infectious. Rachel relaxed and began to glance around at their fellow guests. She could feel Richard's expectation.

'Well? Do you see any acquaintances here, Mrs Weekes? I understood you had some, in Bath?' he asked, impatiently.

'Had, at one time, indeed. But I see none yet. Shall we take a turn on the floor for the next dance, Mr Weekes?' she said, raising her voice to be heard. Richard looked hot and unhappy, and answered her question with a shake of his head.

'I shall need something to drink first of all.'

'Very well. Can you see no acquaintances of your own, Mr Weekes? Some of your clients, perhaps?'

'I'm looking, I'm looking,' he muttered, and they resumed their slow procession around the room. Then, against all expectation, Rachel did see some faces she knew. An elderly couple, a Mr and Mrs Brommel, who had been her neighbours the year her family had taken the apartment in Camden Crescent. Mr Brommel wore a heavily powdered wig, and Mrs Brommel a gown of burgundy velvet cut after the fashion of twenty years past. She had been quite deaf when Rachel knew her before, and her condition had not improved with the passage of thirteen years. It took a great deal of prompting for her to know who Rachel was, and when she finally exclaimed:

'Rachel Crofton, yes of course, I remember your family now,' still Rachel suspected that she did not. Rachel thought Richard would be pleased, as the introductions were made, but he didn't seem so. Perhaps the Brommels were too old, their garb too dated, their conversation too slow.

They moved on, into the Octagon room, where men and women played cards and gambled in a cluttered maze of tables and chairs. The roar of voices was lower, and underneath it was the soft slap and scrape of cards, the rattle of coins and dice and occasional exclamations of delight, or muttered displeasure. A steady stream of revellers made their way across the Octagon from the hallway and the ballroom to the tea room, and vice versa, and were scowled at by the players for the distraction they caused. At the far side of the room was the doorway to an additional card room, quieter and more private, where the stakes were higher and the mood more sombre. Richard and Rachel paused by the hall doors to enjoy a breath of cooler air, and then Richard stood up straighter, and smiled.

'There! Captain Sutton!' he cried, and was off at once towards a wiry-haired man in military dress. 'Captain Sutton, what a great pleasure to find you here,' he said, smiling as he gave a short bow. 'And Mrs Sutton, you are looking extremely well.' This was spoken to a tiny woman with mousy hair and lively blue eyes. She and her husband both appeared to be past forty, with touches of grey in their hair; they had an air of open happiness and vitality that immediately put Rachel at her ease.

'Mr Weekes! Well met, sir; and who is this charming young lady?'

'Captain Sutton, may I present my wife, Mrs Rachel

Weekes? Mrs Weekes, this is Captain Sutton, a valued client and acquaintance of mine, and his wife Mrs Harriet Sutton.'

'How do you do?' Rachel said, as she curtsied.

'How do you do. And may I offer you my congratulations on your recent marriage,' said Harriet Sutton; a soft and gentle voice, perfectly matched with her appearance. Captain Sutton towered over his wife, though he was not of excessive height. Mrs Sutton stood only as high as his shoulder, and her narrow frame and tiny hands were childlike. The captain was not a handsome man – his nose was too large and too bent, and his ears stood proud of his skull – but like his wife's, his voice and expression were so genial it was impossible not to warm to him.

With the introductions made and a polite conversation about health, family and recent events exchanged, the men drifted away towards a game of pontoon while the ladies found seats against the wall. Mrs Sutton had a painted fan which she used constantly, and angled so that Rachel might also feel the benefit.

'Do you often come to the assemblies, Mrs Weekes?' she asked.

'This is the first time as a married woman, and the first time in thirteen years, truth be told,' said Rachel. 'I came as a girl, with my family. But then we left Bath and I had not been back since, until I wed Mr Weekes.'

'Ah! So you are no stranger to our lovely city.' Mrs Sutton smiled. 'I have heard people say that Bath is out of fashion now – the haunt of invalids, widows and spinsters! Let such nay-sayers stay away, I say. It has been our home these past twenty years, and I would live nowhere else. My daughter has known no other home.'

'And how old is your daughter?'

'She is nine years old now. Her name is Cassandra, and she is a source of constant delight to her father and me.' Mrs

Sutton laughed at her own effusiveness, and Rachel hid her surprise that the girl was not older, since Mrs Sutton herself was no longer young.

'That is a very beautiful name.'

'She is a very beautiful girl. Thankfully, she has inherited only a measure of my stature, and nothing whatsoever of my husband's beauty.' She smiled. 'You have the joy of motherhood all before you yet, Mrs Weekes, and I envy you.'

'Well, yes.' Rachel fumbled for something to say. 'I do look forward to the condition, of course.' She shouldn't say that she couldn't envisage raising a child in the small, dark lodgings in Abbeygate Street, where he or she would always have no choice but to share the one bedchamber with them; yet something about Mrs Sutton encouraged confidence. 'Mr Weekes's business increases all the time. Before long we hope to move to more spacious lodgings, so our family will have more room to grow.'

'Ah, it can be hard, in the early days of a marriage. When I first wed Captain Sutton, we had just one room to live in, at a boarding house near his regiment. We slept on a bed of our own clothes, since the mattress was so thin! My family were none too pleased with my choice, I can confess. I did not marry for fortune! Thankfully, things have improved since then. We have an apartment on Guinea Lane now. And you must come to call! Do you know where that is?'

'I think I do – near the Paragon Buildings?'

'Just so. So, have you remade any old acquaintances in Bath since your return?'

'No, I . . . I was just a girl when I was here, and not a great deal out in society. I met Mr and Mrs Brommel just now,' she said, but Mrs Sutton didn't know them. 'I have made just one other acquaintance of late. A client and patroness of my husband, a Mrs Alleyn, who has a very fine house on Lansdown Crescent.'

Mrs Sutton put one hand to her mouth in surprise.

'Oh! But I know Mrs Alleyn, of course,' she said. 'My husband fought alongside Jonathan Alleyn against Napoleon's French.' As she spoke, a new gravity came into her tone, and Rachel understood that she knew of Jonathan Alleyn's decline. 'His mother was once one of the most celebrated beauties in Bath. I understand she is beautiful still, though I have not seen her in a good few years.'

'Does she never come out into society?'

'I daresay she does, but only rarely. And never to a public ball any more. I think she prefers quieter gatherings, of close friends.'

'I have met her on two occasions now.'

'So . . . you understand that she is greatly troubled,' Mrs Sutton said carefully.

'This last time, I also met her son, Mr Jonathan Alleyn,' said Rachel. At this Mrs Sutton's eyes opened wide, and she grasped Rachel's hand.

'In truth? You saw him? How was he?'

'He was . . . clearly most unwell,' she said. To her surprise, Mrs Sutton's eyes glittered with tears, and she blotted them with her gloved fingertips before giving herself a little shake.

'Forgive me. I cry at the slightest thing – ask anybody. It's only that . . . a more tragic tale would be hard to imagine.'

'Do you understand what ails him, then?' asked Rachel, curious in spite of herself.

'Indeed. Thanks to my husband's close association with him during the war . . . Perhaps I ought not to say. It is not really my place to, and perhaps Mrs Alleyn would not thank me, if you are to be further acquainted with her.'

'It is my feeling that his current condition cannot solely be ascribed to the treatment he received from Alice,' said

Rachel, tentatively. In the back of her mind, her shadow companion stood up, and called for her attention.

'But, then you know some of it already? You know about Alice Beckwith?'

'I know a little. Only what my husband has told me, and then Mr Alleyn . . . mentioned it. He loved Miss Beckwith a great deal, I think.'

'Truly. As much as any man ever loved a woman. There was some impediment to their being wed, I know not what it was. Yet they were betrothed, and determined to marry. Jonathan went into the army, and went with my husband to fight the French in Portugal and Spain, in the year 1808. Early in 1809 they returned to England, and were billeted in Brighton when he got word from Miss Beckwith that she was breaking off their engagement. Captain Sutton has told me . . . he has told me just how grievously Mr Alleyn took this news. He took leave of his regiment and rushed home immediately, only to find that she had already taken off with a new suitor, and presumably wed him forthwith. Mr Alleyn never saw her again, and had no word from her since that last letter she sent him in Brighton.'

'But . . . where did she go? What became of her?'

'Nobody knows. She and her new companion made good their escape. Alice Beckwith was the legal ward of Mr Alleyn's grandfather, you understand – of Mrs Alleyn's father. So her disgrace was a disgrace to them all.'

'And so it is this alone that has driven Mr Alleyn to . . . that has left his health so ruined?'

'In part. It is at the root of it, to be sure. He waited for word from Miss Beckwith for as long as he could, but to no avail. Then he returned to the war, and did not set foot on English soil until after the siege of the fortress of Badajoz, in 1812. He was injured in the battle, and fought no more after that. And upon his return he . . . he was most altered. Those of us who knew him before could hardly believe how altered he was.' Mrs Sutton shook her head sadly. 'I'm talking too much, I know I am. But you must know, if you are to call on them, how greatly that family has suffered. And that Jonathan Alleyn was one of the gentlest souls I have ever encountered. Before the war.'

'Gentle? Truly?' Rachel thought back to the violent fury in his eyes, and her hand went unbidden to her throat, where the marks of his fingers had only just faded. She swallowed, and could not make the two versions of the man meet up.

'Oh, yes. He was a sweet, kind boy. Young man, I should say. Thoughtful, and prone to introspection, perhaps, but bright and loving and full of joy. To remember him as I last saw him . . . oh, it breaks my heart!'

'When was that?'

'It must be four years past, now. We took my daughter along to see him. I thought . . . I thought a child might help to remind him that there is still good in the world. But he ordered us to leave, and bade us not return.' She sighed. 'To my shame, we have heeded his wish. Cassandra was so upset, so frightened by the way he spoke to us. I forgive him, of course, but I will not put her in that position again. I had hoped . . . I had hoped he would realise – there is still time for him to make a new life, to start again. To find a wife and have a family. It isn't too late. Though he seems older than his years, he is young enough to begin anew.'

'He doesn't seem to want to try,' Rachel murmured. Mrs Sutton might still see the sweet boy she knew in him, but Rachel had seen only a man, dark and mad and violent.

'No. I fear you're right. I hope it wasn't ill-mannered of me, to speak so much about them? But I sense that you are a gentle soul too, and will understand that I only hope to mitigate for him any . . . extreme impressions you might have formed.'

'It is a sad story indeed.' *And I look just like her. I look*

enough like this faithless Alice to make them both mistake me.
But I know of another. I know of another who also wore this face.
She swallowed against a sudden hollow feeling beneath her
ribs, a strange bubble of expectation. *Could it be?*

'Can you tell me, where did Miss Beckwith come from?
Who were her parents?' she asked.

'I cannot tell you.' Harriet shrugged. 'But you must come
to call, Mrs Weekes. Promise that you will,' she said impulsively.

'I do promise – it would be my pleasure, and I should very
much like to meet your daughter. Before my marriage, I was
governess to a family. I find that I miss the children a great
deal.'

'I should be delighted to introduce you to her. Oh, look
– it's nearly nine. Let's go in for tea before the mad dash
begins.'

There was already a crush of people around the tables of
food and drink that had been laid out beneath the arches at one
end of the tea room. People jostled and reached and chafed
with impatience, like a flock of pigeons around spilt grain.
Rachel and the captain's wife managed to snatch some jellies
and a glass of punch each before retiring from the throng to sit
in a quieter part of the room. They talked of simple things,
and Mrs Sutton shared harmless pieces of gossip about the
people they saw, introducing Rachel to some of them. They
were in conversation with a doctor and his wife when Richard
and Captain Sutton emerged from their card game, late on
in the evening. Richard was flushed, his eyes bloodshot in a
way that Rachel was fast coming to recognise, and she took a
steadying breath. He looked angry, and downcast, and was
barely able to be civil as he was introduced to the doctor and
his wife.

'Are we come too late for tea?' said Captain Sutton.

'No, I think not – but make haste, or it will all have been eaten,' said his wife.

'Mr Weekes – may I bring you something?' Rachel offered, since Richard didn't look like he had the energy left to fight his way to the food.

'No, indeed. My thanks. Unless it be a cup of punch,' he said, his voice low and sulky.

'Allow me,' said Captain Sutton, making his way towards the tables.

'Is everything all right, Mr Weekes?' Rachel asked, in a low voice at Richard's ear.

'Yes. I . . . I had little luck at the table, is all.' Richard found a weak smile for her. His lips were pale, and stood out against his reddened cheeks.

'Not too much was lost, I hope?' Rachel asked, carefully.

'Nothing that I can't recoup, at some later date.'

'Here now, have this to combat the heat in here!' Captain Sutton handed Richard a glass, and he gulped at it gratefully. 'And how have you enjoyed your evening, Mrs Weekes?'

'Oh, very much, thank you, Captain Sutton. Save for one thing, that is.'

'And what is that?'

'I have not danced once,' she said.

'Well now, that will not do at all, and if it does not offend you to stand up with so ancient a partner, I would be glad to escort you to the floor. By your leave, sir?' he asked Richard, as he held out his arm to Rachel. Richard waved them on with a sickly smile and sank into a nearby chair. They joined another couple in a well-known quadrille, which Rachel had learnt from Eliza's dancing master years before. Captain Sutton was a lively partner, more graceful than his appearance suggested, and Rachel was smiling and out of breath by the time the music stopped. 'There now – will that suffice?' he asked cheerfully.

On the way home, Rachel looked out of the chair's small window at dark streets and rain-streaked walls sliding past, and thought. Hearing the story of Jonathan's fall into madness made her much more sympathetic, both to his plight and the pain it must cause Mrs Alleyn; but if he had banished a good, close friend like the captain, why on earth would he wish to see her again? It could only be because she resembled his lost betrothed, Alice Beckwith, but apparently his urge was to hurt her for it, not to love her for it. But Rachel was curious, in a way she hadn't been before. Curious to know what he would say to her if they met again; curious to know more about the girl she so resembled. *My mirror image. My echo.* Harriet Sutton's words gave her courage, and the evening had been the most uplifting since her wedding day. She knew, by the time she'd helped Richard out of his sedan and up to bed, that she would go again to the Alleyns to find out.

* * *

On Friday the coalman came with his filthy wagon and sacks, his wheezy, broken-winded horse and his wizened face netted with sooty wrinkles. The coal cellar was underneath the pavement in front of the house, accessed by a door from the courtyard below street level. That door had a weak latch, and Starling took up her usual position, bracing it shut with her back as the coal was poured in through a small hatch in the pavement. With each sack that was upended came a thudding at her back, a pattering noise and a cloud of black dust that curled out around the door to gather in her hair and clothing. She felt sharp little grains in her eyelashes when she blinked. She braced her feet against the flagstones, feeling them slide where the stones were damp and slimy. *I am a doorstop*, she thought ruefully. *Alice brought me up a sister, Bridget trained me as a housekeeper, and now I am become a doorstop.* In the silence after the last load came down the horse coughed, and the coalman hallooed down to her. Starling stayed a while in the gloomy courtyard, quiet with her thoughts. She heard Lord Faukes's voice, unwelcome as it was: *But you were a starveling guttersnipe, so be content.* Ever with a smile in his voice to belie the barbs in his words.

Starling washed her face and hands under the pump, wincing at the water's bite, then stood with a stiff-bristled brush and swept the soot from her clothes and hair. Through the kitchen window she heard Sol Bradbury singing 'Proper Fanny' as she crimped the crust on an eel pie, and through the corridor window Mrs Hatton was berating Dorcas for something. Intrigued, Starling stepped closer to the window to listen.

'Oh, madam, please don't make me!' Dorcas quailed, in that shrill, wobbling voice of hers.

'Dorcas, this cannot go on! I understand that Mr Alleyn is not an easy man to serve, but serve him you *do*, and those rooms must be cleaned at some point. The stink in there is starting to crawl out underneath the door, for heaven's sake. There must be some forgotten dinner plate or something in there, going foul. At least go up and find what it is, and clear it out. Throw the windows open for as long as you can . . .'

'But he has devilish things in there, Mrs Hatton – *wrong* things!'

'There's nothing in there that can hurt you. You know as well as I do how rare it is for Mr Alleyn to come downstairs. We may not have this chance again for some time . . .'

Starling blinked, unsure whether she'd heard correctly, then she rushed inside to where the two women were standing.

'I'll do it, Mrs Hatton,' she said hurriedly.

'Thank you, Starling, but really, Dorcas is the housemaid, and she must—'

'Is he truly come downstairs?' she interrupted.

'That he is. He has a visitor.' There was interest in Mrs Hatton's voice, however much she tried to hide it. For a moment the three women stared at one another in wonder at this unlikely turn of events.

'I'll see to his rooms,' said Starling, and went up the stairs on nimble feet.

She crept over to the parlour door and listened for a moment, to check that it was true. Sure enough, Starling heard three voices within – Jonathan Alleyn, his mother, and another female voice that she didn't recognise. She wasted no time wondering but hurried on, climbing the stairs two steps at a time. The visit might be short, and even if it wasn't Jonathan might conclude his part of it at any moment. She burst into his rooms, holding her breath, and ran to open the shutters and the windows. The smell was quite awful. Grudgingly, Starling hooked the remains of the rat out from under his desk with the poker, and cast it into the fire. She could still be cleaning his rooms when he came back up, that would cause no outrage; she could not be caught searching them, however. Opportunities to do so were precious rare, since he spent so much of his time ensconced within. Even when he'd passed out with drink, she didn't dare. He woke with the ease of a soldier, as readily as a guard dog. Several times she'd been sifting silently through the papers on his desk, only to look up and find his eyes on her, watchful and unblinking. She shivered at the memory. His silent scrutiny was somehow worse than his rages. Starling had no idea where he kept the letters. He had all of Alice's letters, she was sure of it – the ones she had written to him, as well as the ones he had written to her; the ones she'd kept in her rosewood box, which had vanished from her room right after she had. *Right after he killed her.*

She opened the drawers of his desk in turn, running her fingers through the contents. Papers and journals; bills, receipts and military missives; small instruments like magnifying glasses and tweezers, and other things she could not guess the purpose of. One drawer was filled with tiny metal pieces – cogs, wheels, screws and spindles. It rattled as if full of money when Starling opened it, and she frowned, pausing to listen for any sound of his approach. Her heart thumped in her ears, sounding like footsteps. She continued to search until the desk was exhausted, but there was no sign of the rosewood box, or of a bundle of letters. Cursing, Starling went to the shelves next, which were laden with books and more strange instruments, and the glass specimen jars that so terrified Dorcas.

Jonathan had acquired them some years earlier. He'd gone to watch the dissections of several human cadavers at the hospital, though his mother declared such things an abomination; he'd been friends, for a while, with one of the doctors she sent to see him, who had dark theories about opening the skulls of living patients. Then the jars had started to appear – pale shapes preserved in alcohol solutions. A two-headed piglet, all wrinkled and white; a grey thing of wriggling, convoluted ridges, with two halves and a stem, which reminded Starling of the huge fungi that sometimes grew on the floodplain at Bathampton; a tiny creature that almost resembled a human baby, though its head was far too big and its body too small, and its eyes were nothing but large dark shadows either side of the translucent stub of a nose. The liquid in the jars sloshed as Starling reached her questing hands behind them, and her skin crawled away from them. She did not like to think about their origins, or how they would smell if the lids were opened up.

Then, from beneath her feet came the unmistakable sound of the parlour door opening, and footsteps in the hallway. Desperately, Starling returned to the desk and scrabbled through the jumbled papers and detritus on top of it. She nicked her finger on a scalpel, and left a drop of her blood on the blade. She heard the click of boot heels on the stone stairs. Then she saw a letter, just one; unsealed, the paper dog-eared and wrinkled. She stuffed it into her pocket and rushed into the bedchamber, where she was shaking up the eiderdown as Jonathan Alleyn came back into his rooms. Starling held her breath. He stopped as soon as he was through the door, as if trying to work out what was different, then turned his head towards the open shutters, the raised windows. She waited for the barked command for her to close them, but to her surprise Jonathan walked slowly over to the curving bay window, and stood in front of it, looking out at the damp, crisp autumn day.

Starling cleared all the dirty plates and glasses, all the empty bottles and filthy clothing from the room. She emptied the night soil from the pot, swept the floor and rubbed the furniture, relaid the fire and replaced all the candles. And all the while she could feel the letter in her pocket, swinging with her skirt, threatening to rustle and give her away. She itched to make her escape, to find a private place, and read it. When she was done she thought to just slip away, but at the doorway she paused. Curiosity gnawed at her, almost as strong as the urge to read the letter she'd stolen. Cautiously, Starling walked up behind Jonathan. He had not moved from his place by the open window, and stood with his arms hanging limply by his sides.

'Sir? Should I close them up now?' she asked. Jonathan did not reply. She stepped a little closer and peered around at his face. His eyes were shut and he was breathing as slowly and deeply as one asleep. Was it possible to sleep on your feet? Starling wasn't sure. A moist breeze scurried in from outside, and pushed at his hair and the untidy loops of his cravat. It smelled of wet grass, of damp stone and mushrooms – of the deep autumn that had settled over England. It was cold enough to pucker Starling's arms into gooseflesh, but Jonathan looked almost serene. At once, she thought of ten different ways she could rouse him, anger him, disturb him. But she did none of them; she had the letter to read, so she slipped quietly from the room and went down to the coal cellar for privacy.

* * *

Rachel halted as the Alleyns' front door closed behind her, and took a deep lungful of fresh, chilly air. She could hear the distant bleating of sheep on the high common, the tuneless clank of the bell-wether's clapper, leading the herd. If she shut her eyes it was almost like being out of the city entirely, like being at Hartford Hall, perhaps; at the far end of the long oak avenue that ran, straight as an arrow, across the parkland. For a moment she longed to be there, to walk with the illusion of never having to return to any of it – her old job at Hartford, or her new job as Mrs Weekes. The thought troubled her. She opened her eyes to reality with a sinking feeling inside. Her second meeting with Jonathan Alleyn had been almost as unsettling as the first, especially in its outcome; for although there'd been none of the violence and peril of before, that time she had left convinced that she would never return, whereas now she was leaving having pledged to. Her throat was as dry as paper, and she swallowed with an effort; she felt strangely light-headed, and her thoughts refused to coalesce. Stepping into the house behind her felt like stepping out of time and place; into a world where the rules she was so familiar with no longer applied, and anything might happen. It was exhausting. She put a steadying hand on the railings as she descended the steps at last.

Movement in the courtyard below caught her eye, and she looked down to see the red-haired servant crossing from the coal cellar to the kitchen door.

'You there!' Rachel shouted down to her. The girl froze and glanced over her shoulder, looking as guilty as sin. When she saw Rachel, her eyes widened in surprise.

'What are *you*—' she began to say, then closed her mouth and moved to go inside again.

'Wait!' Rachel called. She leaned over the railings to get a better look at the girl, and was surer than ever that she'd been the one at the Moor's Head on her wedding day. 'I must thank you,' she said. At this the girl turned again.

'Thank me, madam?' she said.

'Yes. It was you who . . . persuaded Mr Alleyn to unhand me, when I first met him last week. Wasn't it?' The servant looked uneasy, and hesitated before she replied.

'Aye, madam.'

'Were you watching us, then? And listening?' said Rachel, to which there was no reply. 'No matter. I am glad you were. I am glad you were there. And thank you for helping me.'

'Very good, madam,' the girl said curtly. She turned to go again.

'Wait – didn't I see you at the Moor's Head? A few weeks ago, on the day I was wed. Didn't you serve us wine that day?' The serving girl turned again, and looked so angry that Rachel knew she was right.

'You must be mistaken, Mrs Weekes,' she said grimly. Rachel didn't press her further; she was already sure she was right, though she couldn't say why it bothered her so much to know.

'Will you tell me your name?' Again, the servant seemed to seek a way not to answer before conceding to.

'Starling,' she said. 'I must get on, madam. There's much work to be done.'

'Well. You have my thanks, Starling,' Rachel called as the girl vanished through the door. *Mrs Weekes, she called me. So she knows exactly who I am, too.*

She found Richard in the cellars at Abbeygate Street. With the onset of autumn, he had taken to lighting a little brazier in the middle of the room to keep the casks and bottles at an even temperature. The room smelled faintly of cinders and smoke, amidst the wood must and wine smells of the stock. It was a strangely restful place, only ever softly lit. Richard was drawing off white wine from a barrel into a bucket. The smell of it was sharp and vinegary, and he wrinkled his nose. He'd rolled up his sleeves, and in the wan light his hair shone softly, and the skin on the backs of his broad hands was smooth and tanned. Rachel watched him for a while, soothed by his methodical movements as he worked, and the mild, diffuse expression on his face. In that moment, she could see what it was about him that she was trying to love. She took a long, slow breath, and sought to fan this tiny flame.

'How now, Mr Weekes?' she greeted him. Richard looked up with a smile.

'My dear. Is aught amiss?'

'No. I only wanted to tell you about my latest visit to Lansdown Crescent.'

'Oh yes?' To the denuded barrel of wine he added a bucketful of fresh milk, then a handful of salt and one of dried rice. Then he began to stir the mixture with a long pole. Rachel watched, fascinated.

'What are you doing to that wine?'

'It's foul.' Richard grimaced. 'This whole batch from Spain tastes like horse piss. This treatment will improve it no end, given a few days to work.'

'Won't the milk turn sour? And spoil it further?' she asked, Richard shook his head.

'It will settle out. You'll see. Now, tell me of your visit.'

The sounds of sloshing and the gentle clonk of the pole against the barrel filled the cellar. Rachel seated herself on the corner of one of the racks, and drew a pattern in the sawdust with the toe of her shoe.

'Mr Jonathan Alleyn came downstairs to talk to his mother and me, on this occasion,' she said.

'In truth? That is good, good. So he is not so very unwell?'

'Perhaps not. Or, perhaps not all of the time. He does limp badly, however.' She did not say that he had seemed like a dead man still standing, from the pallor of his skin and the unhealthy sheen upon it; and the way his eyes shone like glass, and the bones of his face and hands stood proud beneath the skin. She did not say that the sight of him had made her recoil.

'And what did he say this time?'

'He apologised for . . . his ill-behaviour last time. He said he had been suffering a great deal that day from the pains in his head, and that it hadn't been the best time for me to visit.' At that point he'd glanced quite coldly at his mother, and there'd been anger in his eyes that was older and deeper than this polite reprimand. When he'd looked again at Rachel his face had shown . . . something. Something she hadn't expected, and wasn't sure of. A slight awkwardness, almost sheepishness. He'd said he had little recollection of what they'd spoken of that day, but that he had a knock on his head he couldn't account for, and remembered her running from the room in haste. At this he'd grimaced, one corner of his mouth pulling to the side in displeasure.

'And what else? Did Mrs Alleyn say aught of note?' Richard asked, still stirring the barrel. The air had ripened with the odd, unhappy smell of wine and milk combined.

'How long must you stir that brew?' Rachel asked.

'Half an hour or more, to be sure all has been taken up. Go on, tell me of Mrs Alleyn.'

'She was obviously delighted that her son had come downstairs and was willing to meet and take tea with us.' A brittle kind of delighted, which was poised at all times to revert to nerves, to remonstration, to apology. 'We spoke of our interests, and I told them of my love of poetry and reading . . . Mr Alleyn agreed that reading could be a greatly soothing balm to a troubled mind. He also declared an interest in philosophy, and expressed regret that he is unable to read a great deal any more.'

'Oh? Why can't he?'

'It's too great a strain on his eyes, he says, and brings on the pains in his head. He finds that he can't concentrate to read more than a page of printed text.' She paused in her recounting of the conversation, just as the three of them had paused, and Rachel had seen an idea, a tremulous hope, come upon Mrs Alleyn. *Perhaps* . . . she had begun to say, and Rachel had known at once what she would suggest. *Perhaps you might come and read to my son, Mrs Weekes? From time to time? You have a pleasing voice, and a clear diction* . . . Rachel had swallowed, but with them both watching her, the mother alight with hope and the son bewildering, unreadable, her instinctive refusal had died on her lips. For a moment she'd wondered at this, at being welcomed so readily into the circle of so great a family. She, the wife of a wine trader. But then, with a blink, Mrs Alleyn had added: *You will be compensated for your time, of course, Mrs Weekes.* An employee then – governess to a grown man; companion to an invalid. Rachel had felt slighted, even somewhat hurt, to be reminded so bluntly that she was not their equal, and was not expected to give her time freely, out of friendship. 'I have been asked to return and read to him. As a . . . regular habit. Mrs Alleyn has offered to remunerate me for my time. I thought . . . I thought that perhaps it would be more seemly to refuse.'

'To refuse her request?'

'To refuse the payment, Mr Weekes. One does not rise in society by being in the employ of those higher than oneself, after all,' she said. 'Better to be unpaid, and therefore charitable. Better to be there as a . . . friend and acquaintance, rather than as an employee.'

For a while there was quiet but for the clonking and sloshing of the barrel.

'I can see the sense of what you say, Rachel,' Richard said at last. 'But . . . that you alone should be invited there, and not the both of us together, on more than one occasion, tells me that this is how we are viewed already. That this is what Mrs Alleyn had in mind for you all along – that you could be employed in service to her son. For if it was merely to be sociable, why was I not invited back with you?' Rachel made no reply. She hadn't guessed that Richard would see their position so clearly. He was ever ready to climb, it had seemed, rather than to admit that the Alleyns were too high to reach. 'And, in truth . . . an extra income would be most welcome,' he added.

'Indeed? But I thought your business was . . .'

'My business increases, but so do our . . . outgoing costs.'

'Which costs, Mr Weekes?' Rachel asked, carefully. Richard had the good grace to look away, and frown uncomfortably.

'The extra housekeeping we have taken on. The extra . . .

food, your new clothes, and . . . sundries,' he muttered, not meeting her eye. *The money you lose to drink and the gaming tables*, Rachel thought, and an angry blush coloured her face, that she alone should be blamed for their want of funds.

'Well then, I suppose I shall have to accept. I have no wish to become a financial burden to you, husband.' She stood, smoothing the back of her skirt and turning to go upstairs.

'Rachel,' Richard called. She turned, expecting an apology, or some words of thanks. 'Be sure to let me know, when you discover it, how much she intends to pay you.'

Rachel filled the kettle from the pump then went up to the kitchen and set it on the stove with quick, angry hands. It was perfectly reasonable that the wife of a working man should be paid to provide some service to a wealthy family, and yet, in truth, she had thought to leave employment behind her and devote herself to being a wife, nothing more and nothing less. It was not truly Richard she was angry with, more herself — that she had been foolish enough to think herself invited as an equal, albeit the lesser of equals. And she was afraid. The thought of being alone with Jonathan Alleyn, of perhaps being in his rooms again, made her pulse speed up and her thoughts scatter. The memory of his hands around her neck, and the unbreakable strength of them, was too fresh. She was not sure she could do it, in spite of his calmer demeanour this time. And when they looked at her, both of them, they saw her echo; they saw in her the memory of another. *Is it reading they want, or is it Alice's face?* Under Jonathan's gaze she'd felt unsure of what to do with her expression, or her voice. It felt as though anything she said would sound like a lie; like she had something she ought to hide, when she did not. Nothing felt natural any more, not even breathing. The air simply sat in a lump at the top of her chest, and made her feel dumb. *He loved Alice Beckwith, who had this face. He can tell me of her.* It was that, more than anything, which urged her to return to him.

Rachel brewed a pot of tea, then went to the window and looked out over the city. To the north, on the hill, she could see Lansdown Crescent. She could see the curved bay front of the Alleyns' house. She could see, just, the exact windows of Jonathan's room. In reverse, it would be impossible to pick out the Abbeygate Street house – the jumble of buildings was too confusing. How well this reflected their lives, also, she thought: the Alleyns grand but set apart, easily recognisable and yet isolated too; then she and Richard, part of the commingled soup of humanity pooling in the river valley, in the heart of the city. She wondered if a man could really mourn a betrayal for so long – for twelve long years. She wondered if losing Alice could truly be all that ailed Jonathan Alleyn.

Unbidden, the red-haired serving girl with the name of a bird came into her mind. *Mrs Weekes, she called me. She knows who I am, and it* was *her at the inn, at our wedding feast.* Rachel tried to work out what nagged her memory about that, and then realised it – the girl had been as struck by her appearance as Mrs Alleyn and her son had. *She saw Alice too, when she looked at me. She knew this Alice well.* Rachel wondered how she might talk to the servant, about this girl who'd worn the same face as her, and had disgraced herself for love; because the shadow in her mind had been ever more alive since she first heard of Alice. That distant voice, that echo, grew ever louder, and begged her attention, until Rachel sometimes caught its movement as a flicker in the corner of her eye. As with mirrors, she didn't dare turn to look because she knew it would vanish, and she so longed to have it near. To have her near. *Could it be?*

* * *

January 11th, 1809, Corunna, Spain

My Dearest Alice,

I scarcely know how to write to you, my love. In truth, I can scarcely write to you, the cold has injured my hands and made it near impossible. We have reached the coast at last, we are at Corunna, but there are no ships. The ships were supposed to await us here but there is nothing but the wide ocean horizon — how unimaginably vast it seems, after so long a time spent watching my own feet marching. The French are close behind us. We face the prospect of having to fight them here, when we have been starving for weeks, and frozen half to death. My heart is so heavy, my love, only thoughts of you keep it beating. Suleiman is dead. Bravest, most valiant and noble creature. Oh, how it grieves me! I cannot bear to relate to you the manner of his death — suffice to say it is a bitter injustice, a most terrible injustice, when he made it through the mountains with us, all the way, as so many others fell or gave up. He was steadfast, the most courageous creature I have ever known, and a truer friend I never had, other than you, dear Alice.

I know I am cowardly to despair. We have reached the coast, after all, when it seemed for some weeks that we would not. The men are in grievous poor shape. They are thin, and exhausted, and much beset by frostbite and illness. We have lost thousands on the march through the mountains. I have seen . . . oh, but I should not write of what I have seen, because I would not wish to pain you. But I have seen things, and done things, which will haunt me ever after. I have done things, my dearest. Things I can never tell you. There is such a stain of shame upon my heart, I fear you will perceive it and love me no longer. And then I would die, Alice. I would die. A shadow of dread looms over me, and it is the sure knowledge that I am worthy of you no longer. But I will not speak of it, and can only hope you will forgive me. Yours *is the sweetest and best soul I ever knew. Can you forgive me a weaker one? A corrupted one? The Spanish call us 'Caracho'. It means something foul. It is a curse word. It is a name we deserve. I await the means to send you this letter. I long to see you, or to have a few words from you.*

Yours most faithfully,
Jonathan Alleyn

Post script, January 13th. The ships are coming, Alice. This letter will travel the first leg of its journey to you with me. I will send it on when I land; we are bound for Brighton, I believe. We will be two weeks at sea, all being well, I will see you soon. To write those words makes my spirits soar.

The paper of the letter was as creased and stained as a blacksmith's hands; one small sheet, the writing cramped and filling the margins, Jonathan's lettering as hard as ever to read. There was a smudged thumbprint in the bottom right-hand corner, in some reddish brown substance Starling didn't like to touch. Soon it would have to go back. That very evening, in fact, when she took up his supper tray. If he happened to notice it gone, or guess that she had taken it, he could dismiss her, long association or no, and then she would have nothing, and be nowhere. But the date of the letter made her hands shake, and made the back of her throat ache.

We will be two weeks at sea, he had written, on the thirteenth day of January. Alice had vanished on the eighth of February, 1809. That was the last day Starling had been happy, out of all the long days that came after it. The last day everything had been as it was supposed to be; and everything after was humiliation and fear, and a chaos of grief and anger. February the eighth, 1809. And the day after that, Jonathan came to the farmhouse door, all desperate and grim, like some part of him had died. The deranged ghost of himself, eyes wild with something like fury, something like despair, something like guilt. *A fine alibi, to demand to see the person you have murdered*. On the eighth day of February, Alice had gone out alone first thing in the morning. She went to meet Jonathan, Starling knew. She knew it like she knew the sky was above her head and the earth was beneath her feet. Alice went to meet Jonathan, and could not forgive his blackened soul, or these things he wrote of, that shamed him so. And so he killed her. Starling shut her eyes, feeling such bitter rage and disappointment welling up inside her it was almost unbearable. By itself, this letter told her nothing new, and could not prove his guilt. She ground her teeth together as she jammed it back into her pocket.

Suleiman. The word whispered in her memory; she remembered learning it for the first time – rolling it around her mouth until she had committed it to memory. Few other words had such a clear provenance in her personal lexicon. Suleiman was Jonathan's horse, and she first saw him, and learned his name, on a late summer's day in 1807, the year before Jonathan set sail to Portugal to fight the French. She remembered sitting in the meadow grasses by the river with Alice, counting bumblebees and damsel flies with bodies like blue enamel darning needles. Then they heard the cattle stir, disturbed from their grazing as Jonathan cantered nearer. He grinned down at them as he reined to a halt, and the horse blew out hard through flared nostrils. Starling scrambled to her feet and backed away, and the horse reared up on its hind legs, startled. Alice's face lit up in admiration; she went fearlessly to lay a calming hand on the horse's shoulder. Its neck was an arch of muscle and blood vessels beneath a coat that shone like polished wood.

'Easy, boy. 'Tis only Starling and she'll not hurt you,'

Alice murmured. 'Oh, Jonathan! He's *magnificent*! What's his name?'

'His name is Suleiman,' Jonathan told her, and they both laughed.

'What's so funny?' Starling demanded, cross that she had been afraid of the horse.

'Suleiman the Magnificent,' said Alice, as if that explained everything. Starling scowled.

Jonathan dismounted and began to relate the horse's pedigree to Alice, and Starling stopped listening. She walked as close to the animal as she dared. It wasn't like the farm horse or the barge horses that went plodding by every day, or even like the grey mare Jonathan usually rode. Suleiman was bright bay, his coat a rich gingery brown but for his legs and nose, which were glossy black. His mane and tail were black too – what was left of his tail, anyway. Like the barge horses', it had been docked to six inches. Suleiman flicked this inadequate stump at the flies that settled on his flanks, and the fact that he could not reach them made him more restless still. Starling put out tentative fingers and touched his nose, which felt like the finest suede leather. The horse blew damp air onto her hand, and Starling looked right into his eyes, and was smitten.

'Can I ride him?' she asked, interrupting Jonathan.

'Well . . . I'm not sure that would be wise, Starling. He is very sensitive, and strong,' said Jonathan. He showed Starling his hands – there were blisters and shreds of pulled skin between his fingers from battling with the reins.

'Oh, please! Please let me! Just here in the meadow. I'll only walk him . . . I promise not to fall off.' Jonathan still argued that she might get hurt, but Alice persuaded him, blushing when Starling hitched up her skirt and petticoat, showing them both her long drawers as Jonathan boosted her into the saddle.

'You are too grown up for that, now, Starling,' Alice said. 'If you ride again it must be with the side saddle.'

Jonathan kept careful hold of one rein, and Suleiman rattled his teeth against the bit and pulled for his freedom. He seemed perplexed by such a small jockey, and danced from side to side, casting looks over his shoulder as if to ask after the meaning of it. With her pulse racing, Starling knotted her fingers through the coarse black hair of his mane, and hung on. The scent of crushed grass rose up around them, ground beneath Suleiman's hooves. His slightest movement made her wobble in the saddle, and fight for balance, but for a few heavenly moments she rode the magnificent horse, and she loved it, and she loved Jonathan for letting her. In the end, Suleiman lost patience with walking in small circles, and danced into a canter. Starling gave a small yelp and slithered off to one side, landing with a thud in the long grass. Alice rushed over to her, but Starling was laughing, delighted.

'Will you teach me to ride, Mr Alleyn?' she said breathlessly. 'Oh, will you? Please, please?' Jonathan glanced at Alice, who smiled.

'I see no reason why not,' he said, and Starling loved him even more. 'But not today. Today, we picnic.' He reached into the saddlebag, and drew out a large pork pie wrapped in a handkerchief, and a bottle of beer.

After they'd eaten, they lay side by side in the grass. The sunlight was strong, dazzling; it cast a brilliant halo around everything, so that their faces were too bright to make out, and expressions had to be guessed from laughter and words, from the silhouette of a smile. They were at a place where the river curled in a long, lazy arc through the meadow, and a shallow shelving beach of muddy pebbles had formed, the water eddying gently past. Starling lay on her back and blew dandelion clocks, watching the weightless seeds drift away into the blue. Alice and Jonathan were taking it in turns to read sonnets, back and forth. Their voices were hushed and private, carrying messages only they could unravel; the rhythm of the words lulled Starling quiet for a time. When silence fell she rolled her head to one side and watched Jonathan. He was staring away into the distance, lost in thought. A trickle of sweat wound through the hairline at her temple, and she rubbed at the tickle.

'Can I paddle, Alice? I'm boiling. Please?' she said, sitting up and squinting at her.

'If you're careful, and don't go out into the current.' Starling grinned as she wriggled out of her dress and boots. 'What were you thinking about, just then?' Alice asked Jonathan. He shrugged.

'Nothing. Everything,' he said, and then smiled. 'Sometimes my thoughts run away with me, and I get caught in the twists and turns of them.' He cocked his head at the river. 'How about it?'

'You can't mean . . .'

'I'm roasting as well, and you must be too.' He grinned.

'I haven't been into the river since I was thirteen! It's not . . . suitable,' Alice protested, smiling.

'There's nobody around to see. I know how modest you are, Alice Beckwith. A swim won't alter that.'

'Hurray!' Starling cheered, as they both got to their feet and began to shed their shoes and stockings. Alice lowered her face as she unlaced her dress, looking up at Jonathan through her eyelashes. The air between them seemed to thrum. As the girls waded into the water their white petticoats billowed up around them, swelling with air. 'We look like dandelion seeds,' said Starling.

The river's cold stole their breath. Alice took the longest time to submerge herself. She stayed in the shallows, smiling uncertainly and exclaiming at the feel of mud between her toes. Shadows marked the ribs at the top of her chest, and the thin ridges of her collarbones. Wisps of pale hair hung around her neck, and water droplets sat like jewels on her skin. Starling took all this in, admiringly, and when she looked at Jonathan he was staring too, with an expression of complete surrender.

'I bet I can swim to the other side and back,' he said, paddling his arms beneath the surface.

'No! You mustn't!' Alice's voice was wrought with alarm at once. 'You mustn't try! The current is very strong, even in the summer. Jonathan, don't!' she cried, when he cast a speculative look across the water. She sounded close to panic.

'All right, I won't,' he said, calmly enough. He waded closer to the bank, then pulled up a handful of green weeds and came after Starling with them, grinning like a fiend; she squealed and tried to flee through the dragging water. Alice laughed, and the moment of her fear was forgotten.

Before long a small wooden boat came along, carrying two men; a younger one pulling the oars and an older one tending to their nets and lines and eel traps.

'Do you know them?' Jonathan asked, as the boat approached. Alice looked anxious for a second, then relaxed and shook her head.

'No. I never saw them before. Did you, Starling?' Starling shook her head.

'Then we should play the simple country hobnails, and say that we know no better,' Jonathan declared. 'Well, Starling, can you manage it? Can you talk like a hobnail from the village?' He smiled at her.

'Aye, sir,' Starling replied, in her best Bathampton accent. Alice grimaced. Soon the dip of the oars brought the boat alongside them, and they halloed the fishermen quite cheerfully. The younger man grinned bashfully at Alice, and waved to them, but the older man tutted and darkened his face.

'Have you no shame, young 'uns?' he muttered. ''Taint decent, baring yourselves for all to see.'

'We b'ain't bare naked, sir,' Starling replied. 'Why, these 'un drawers o' mine reach fairly down past the knee bone, see.' She lay back in the water and waved her feet at the river men, and Jonathan dissolved into laughter. He had a low, pleasing laugh; it bounced along, like a ball dropped onto a hard surface.

'Hoggish wench,' the older fisherman muttered, and resolutely turned his face away as the boat passed them by.

Starling was giggling when she felt Alice's hands grasp her around her ribs.

'These 'un drawers o' mine?' Alice echoed. 'Where on earth did you learn to talk like that?' The question hung for a moment in the summer air, and both were reminded of the first lost seven years of Starling's life, before she'd found Alice.

'You were quite brilliant, Starling,' Jonathan declared, still laughing. 'The finest hoggish wench I ever heard.' They stood close together, the water up to their waists and the reflections of it dancing in their eyes and under their chins. Starling glowed with Jonathan's praise, and had a feeling inside as though her heart was swelling up to bursting. They stayed that way for a moment, and when Starling looked down she saw that Jonathan was holding Alice's hand with fierce resolve beneath the water's surface; their fingers woven together tighter than the reeds on the riverbank. They gave each other a long look, and Starling noticed how fast the rise and fall of Alice's chest had become. Embarrassed, pleasantly scandalised, she flung herself backwards into the water again, sending up a huge plume of water to soak them.

When Alice and Starling returned to the farmhouse later that afternoon, hand in hand, Bridget took one look at their bedraggled hair and the wet patches on their clothes, and widened her eyes in outrage.

'You've never been in the river, Alice!' she gasped. Alice chuckled.

'But it was the perfect day for it, Bridget. You should come with us, next time.'

'You'll not catch me submerging myself like that – it's not wise, miss, not wise at all. What if you've taken a chill? And look at the grubshite you've made of your clothes!'

'Bridget!'

'Pardon my language, miss, but, *really*!' Bridget's admonishments followed them into the house, and continued as she filled the washtub to rinse the river from them; but the invectives soon lost their heat, met with the girls' indefatigable good cheer. Starling was careful not to wash too well because she liked the mineral smell of the river on her skin, and in bed she cupped her hands to her face to breathe it in, feeling a wonderful echo of that swelling feeling she'd had, lulling her to sleep.

The short time Starling had spent astride Suleiman that day turned out to be her first and last riding lesson. After that, Jonathan was away with the army, training and preparing, assembling his kit, then away to Portugal, in the summer of 1808. The times that he did come to the farmhouse without his grandfather he wanted to spend with Alice, not teaching Starling to ride. She had never paused to think about what happened to Suleiman, not when Alice had vanished and everything got turned upside down and destroyed. *I cannot bear to relate to you the manner of his death*. Starling swallowed, and every time she read or thought of the words Jonathan had written she felt a tug of deep sorrow, of angry outrage, that the world had turned out to be so ugly, and so cruel, when Alice had taught her to think it was fair and lovely. It was a cold and heavy feeling.

Was this the letter that had convinced Alice to separate herself from Jonathan? Had it caused some crisis in her? She had been harder to read, full of fear and nerves and sudden storms of weeping after Jonathan set sail, and worst of all in the last three months before she vanished, following her fateful decision to visit Lord Faukes in Box. The last three months before Jonathan came home again, all black inside, half mad with grief and violence; a stranger wearing a familiar face. *No wonder she loved him no more, no wonder he killed her for it.* Starling played this scenario over and over, until it started to feel like fact. Perhaps letters like this one had been what killed Alice's love for him to begin with – *I have done things . . . things I can never tell you. There is such a stain of shame upon my heart . . . I am worthy of you no longer* – and then when she saw him again, it was confirmed. Something had happened to Alice, in those last three months. Some spark inside her had died, and though she was clearly full of secrets, they no longer lit her up and made her flit about like a firefly. They were heavy on her shoulders, and exhausted her; and when Starling asked her, late at night, what the matter was, Alice only shut her eyes and said *I can't bear to tell you.* Starling had been left to wonder what could possibly have been so bad. Being kept in ignorance had been torture then, and it was torture still.

That evening, Starling slid the letter back into the mess on Jonathan Alleyn's desk as he lay on his bed with the drapes closed, so she couldn't even see him. His rooms were darkened again, the shutters latched. There was no sound at all, and at the faintest rustle of paper as she returned the letter his disembodied voice came across to her, like a ghost:

'Touch nothing on my desk. Leave me be.' Bridling, Starling put down an uncorked bottle of wine for him with a loud report. It was ordinary wine – she'd run out of the strengthened stuff Dick had once mixed for her. She could only hope that Jonathan would drink enough of it to damage himself. There was a slice of chicken pie on the tray she'd carried up as well; she picked up the plate, tipped the pie into the fire. As she crossed towards the door she paused, and turned to face the closed drapes.

'Whatever happened to Suleiman? Your horse?' she asked. There was a long, loaded silence, and she began to think he would not answer.

'Suleiman . . . my good friend. I . . . We ate him.' Jonathan's voice was thick with revulsion, with sorrow. Starling swallowed convulsively; his words caused a lightning bolt of horror and rage to shoot down her spine.

'*Murderer!*' she hissed. 'You will burn for it!' She flew from the room, tears springing in her eyes.

* * *

Captain and Mrs Sutton's lodgings were in a tall, narrow townhouse on the north-east side of the city. As Rachel walked across town, the frigid air seemed to press needles into her skull, just between her eyes. The mist on the inside of the bedroom window had become a fine layer of ice crystals, tiny and perfect and dead. On days like this at Hartford Hall, in the heart of winter, the chambermaid would have been in to Rachel's room to stoke up the fire an hour before it was time to rise. The soft sounds of her doing so would reach Rachel, comforting and familiar, as she lay nestled beneath the thick eiderdowns and blankets on the bed.

Rachel was shown into the Suttons' parlour by an elderly female servant who had tired eyes and a faded dress. It was a small room, but well furnished. Harriet Sutton had been sewing, but she put down her work and rose with a smile.

'Mrs Weekes, how good to see you again. Tea, please,

Maggie. Unless you'd prefer coffee, or chocolate, Mrs Weekes?'

'In truth, some chocolate would be lovely,' said Rachel.

'I agree. Something to ward off this wretched chill wind. Chocolate for both of us then, Maggie.'

'Very good, madam.' The old woman curtsied slowly, as if not sure of her knees.

'Now, come and sit by the fire, Mrs Weekes – you look quite blue!' Mrs Sutton took Rachel's cold hands in her warm ones, and drew her forward to sit in the fireside chair.

'I've never known it be so cold this early in the season,' said Rachel.

'Aye. It bodes ill for a hard winter. I pity the poor what is to come,' Harriet said gravely. Then she smiled. 'And we will have to go to the assembly rooms more often, just for the warmth.'

'I'm not sure I will be there much. I don't think Mr Weekes enjoyed it a great deal last time,' said Rachel, carefully. After the losses he'd made at their last ball, they could scarcely afford to go again soon.

'But the Mr Weekes I know loves nothing better than a dance, and good revelry!'

'Well.' Rachel shrugged. 'Perhaps he grows more sober as time passes,' she said. She remembered the stiffness of Richard's arm beneath her own; the fixed, distracted look on his face. She had a sinking feeling inside. In all, he had grown less and less jovial, less and less cheerful, with each day that had passed since their wedding. 'How long have you known my husband?' she asked.

'Oh, a good many years, now. When Captain Sutton first went into the army, and became friends with Jonathan Alleyn, that was when he first met Mr Weekes.'

'Oh? While Mr Weekes was at their house, perhaps? On business?'

'Well,' said Harriet Sutton, looking slightly uncomfortable. 'Not exactly business, no. Mr Duncan Weekes, who I am sure you must know, was coachman to Lord Faukes, Mrs Josephine Alleyn's father. For years and years. After his wife died, Duncan Weekes and your husband had their lodgings above the coach house. This was not at Lansdown Crescent, you understand, but at Lord Faukes's great house, in Box. Your Mr Weekes grew from a boy to a man during that time. But I am sure he must have told you as much?'

At that point the servant came in with a tray and their cups of chocolate, and Rachel was grateful for the chance to compose herself. *Small wonder then, that Josephine Alleyn thinks of me as her servant, since I am indeed wedded to one of her servants. An ostler, he said his father was.* She thought back to Richard's stories, his confessions to her during their brief courtship, when he had seemed to lay himself bare. Yet how carefully and completely he had concealed this truth about himself. With a jolt, she realised how little she might really know her husband.

'In truth, no. He had not mentioned it. There is some . . . bad blood between my husband and his father. Mr Weekes does not speak to me of Duncan Weekes. I hope I might reconcile them. Perhaps I will manage it, in time,' she said, in a strained voice.

'Oh! Forgive me, my dear Mrs Weekes, if I have spoken out of turn! I didn't mean to talk about your own family as if I knew better.' Harriet took Rachel's hand and squeezed it, to make good her apology. Her expression was open and mobile, and once again it put Rachel at her ease. She felt that here was a person with whom she could speak freely, with no fear of misunderstanding. *Trust. She inspires trust, and how greatly I need such a person close to me.*

'But in this case you do know better, that much is clear. There's no need to apologise,' said Rachel. 'It is my impression that Mr Weekes would rather forget his . . . start in life, and focus on his future.'

'A wise man, then, and a philosophy we should all espouse. Our birth should not define us so much as what we do thereafter, surely?' said Harriet.

'But society runs contrary to that very idea, though it is a pleasant one.' *But I am not a gentlewoman any more, though I was born one.* 'In this country it seems that those who are born lowly must remain lowly, no matter how they strive or what they achieve; and some that are born gentlefolk remain so in spite of their base actions and debauchery,' she said. Harriet Sutton's expression grew troubled.

'We live in an unjust society indeed, to be so wilfully blind,' she murmured. 'I think you are speaking of Mr Jonathan Alleyn, when you speak of base actions.'

'The family are a great deal on my mind, in truth. I am to return there to act as reader and companion to Mr Alleyn,' said Rachel, and smiled slightly at the expression of disbelief that flooded her friend's face.

'But . . . I am all astonishment, my dear! I had never thought . . .'

'Nor I, after my first encounter with the man! Here's the secret, though – it seems that I bear a strong resemblance to Alice Beckwith.'

There was a pause, and Harriet sipped her drink delicately.

'I do not understand,' she confessed at last.

'Nor I, Mrs Sutton. But both Mr Alleyn and his mother reacted strongly in . . . recognition, when they first saw me. And their servant too, who must have known Miss Beckwith. And so, for some reason, he can tolerate my presence. His mother thinks it would do him good to be read to. She thinks it would soothe him, and . . . aid his recovery.'

'But . . . this is most strange, Mrs Weekes! I am delighted, of course . . . at this sign of improvement in Mr Alleyn. But I cannot think how a reminder of – forgive me – a person who betrayed and wronged him so terribly would be of help.'

'Nor I, Mrs Sutton, nor I. But there it is – I am to return there on the morrow and read for him,' said Rachel, feeling herself tense up at the idea. *And if he flies into a rage again, and kills me this time, at least I will be paid for my trouble*, she thought. *But he knows. He knows all about Alice*, the echo whispered, keenly.

'My dear, I hope . . . I do hope you can help him. Few men find themselves in such a dark place as he. How it would gladden all our hearts to hear that he can be woken from his nightmare.' Harriet Sutton's tiny face was serious and sombre, but her voice betrayed little hope, and Rachel felt the knot of tension in her gut tighten ever more.

'Come, now, on to the main reason for my visit – other than to see you again, of course, Mrs Sutton. But you did promise to introduce me to your daughter,' said Rachel. Harriet Sutton beamed, and went to the door to call. Cassandra Sutton was a thin, delicate little girl, tall for her age of eight years. She had a soft, olive-toned skin and greenish eyes, and hair as black as crow feathers.

'How do you do, Mrs Weekes?' she said shyly, and Rachel was enchanted.

'Well now, this must be the prettiest little girl I have ever seen,' she said warmly, and Cassandra fidgeted, pleased and embarrassed. 'How do you do, Miss Sutton?'

'Very well, thank you, madam,' the child replied with immaculate manners.

'Come, Cassandra. Come and sit with us a while.' Harriet Sutton held out her hand to her daughter and the girl hopped onto the couch beside her. Her small, even face was dominated by a pointed nose and thin, dark eyebrows; there was something elfin and endearing in her appearance, and not one jot of Eliza Trevelyan's pride or sullen temper.

'I should very much like to have a daughter like you. But my husband would rather have a big strapping son, to work alongside him,' said Rachel.

'Perhaps you could have both?' Cassandra suggested. 'I should very much like to have a brother.'

'Well,' said Harriet, her smile turning a little sad. 'You might have one, one day. We will have to wait and see what God has in store for us, won't we?' The look she gave Rachel was full of quiet resignation, and Rachel understood that there would be no more children for Captain and Mrs Sutton. From the age her new friend and the captain appeared to be, she guessed that their marriage had weathered a good few barren years before Cassandra was born.

'I had a brother,' said Rachel, and wished at once that she had not. She swallowed the sadness that choked her whenever she thought of Christopher. 'His name was Christopher,' she added, because there was a silence after she'd spoken, and both mother and child seemed to know instinctively not to ask where her brother was now.

'Christopher is a good name. We have a bear called Christopher, don't we?' Harriet put her arm around her daughter and squeezed. 'Now, why don't we go into the music room, and you can show Mrs Weekes how well you've been learning to play your guitar?'

After her visit, Rachel went to Duncan Weekes's lodgings, rapping her cold knuckles on the flaked and splitting door, and calling down at his small window. She had promised to visit again, even though she had little news to give, and she was deeply curious too – she wanted to ask her father-in-law about his time in service with the Alleyns, and about Richard's upbringing with them. After a while it seemed clear that the old man was not at home, and nobody else came to open the outer door to her. She walked on, towards Abbey-gate Street, thinking hard, trying to guess why her husband would have kept the nature of his long acquaintance with the Alleyns from her. Could it be as simple as not wanting to admit, out of pride, that he had been their servant? Or their servant's son? But then, he had told her about his father's lowly profession, and even boasted at how far above it he had risen. Perhaps he would rather have Rachel think he'd built his own success, and not been hoisted into it by a charitable former employer. He had told her that Mrs Alleyn had been a patron, and loyal customer . . . now it was a good deal clearer why such a grand lady should concern herself with the business of a young wine merchant.

Rachel walked quickly, agitated. Her breath streamed behind her, a wake in the cold air. She intended to confront Richard, and insist that he tell her everything about his relationship with the Alleyns. But he was not in the cellar, or upstairs either, so she had little choice but to wait. He got back after dark, and reeking of wine, though she could not tell for sure if that was due to the amount he had drunk, or the splashes his work left on his clothing. He smiled and kissed her cheek, but his face darkened when she asked him about the Alleyns, and about his father's job as coachman.

'I told you as much, already,' he muttered, sitting in a chair to pull off his boots and warm his damp feet by the fire. The rank smell of his stockings drifted over to Rachel.

'No you didn't, Mr Weekes. You told me only that your father had been an ostler, and Mrs Alleyn an important patron of your business.'

'Just so. If you had asked me more, I would have disclosed it. But you have had the whole story already, it would seem. Some might consider it disloyal, to ask others for gossip about your own husband.' He leaned his head back and gazed at her, eyes heavy with fatigue, but watchful.

'I did not ask about you, I asked about the Alleyns. Since I am soon to work for them, too. Mrs Sutton understandably assumed that I knew of your association with the family.'

'Well, what matter if you had not had the full story? It changes nothing.'

'Mr Weekes, I—'

'You what?' Richard cut across her, two short, hard words. Rachel flushed.

'I don't understand why you felt you had to keep this from me. That's all.' *And why you are so loyal to the Alleyns, and yet so touchy at any mention of them*. Richard shrugged, and shut his eyes.

'It has been a long and wearying day, my dear. Let us have no more of this. Is there no food in this house, for its master?' Rachel waited, in case he would say something more or she would find the nerve to speak on. When neither one happened she rose, frustrated, and went to prepare him a supper plate.

The following day was stormy. A strong wind blew out of a slate-grey sky, clearing away the smog of coal smoke and mist, and carrying flecks of biting sleet that felt like splinters on Rachel's face as she walked to Lansdown Crescent. She walked as slowly as she could, to postpone her arrival at the Alleyns' fine house, with its dead air and watchfulness, its strange, sad occupants. She took several deep breaths, and reminded herself of her duty to her husband; her sense of charity towards Josephine Alleyn; her desire to learn about Alice. She had no idea how long she was expected to read to Jonathan Alleyn, or to sit with him, but she hoped not more than an hour or two at most. There was no binding agreement; she could leave at any time. She was employed there, but she was not a servant. All these things she reminded herself, as she climbed to the front door.

Josephine Alleyn saw her first. She was by the canary's cage again, speaking words of soft entreaty to the bird. The canary cocked its head at her, eyes sharp and unblinking, but it said nothing.

'Ah, Mrs Weekes. It is good of you to come. My little bird here is silent and sad. Nothing I can feed him or say to him seems to cheer him,' she said wistfully. She passed the bird another sunflower seed, but it only looked at it, and did not take it.

'I understand that whistling to them sometimes encourages them to sing,' said Rachel. She hovered by the door, unsure whether to go further into the room or not.

'Oh? A pity. A lady should never whistle. Such a coarse habit, and it creases the mouth. Perhaps Falmouth might be persuaded to give it a try. But then, I never once heard a jolly sound come from that man, in more than twenty years of service. I fear his company might make my poor canary even sadder.' Josephine looked over at Rachel with a wan smile.

'Some other music, perhaps? Do you play, Mrs Alleyn?' *Anything but the shroud of silence in this house.*

'I used to. My father loved music, and I often played the piano for him before I married, and then after my husband had died, when I returned to live with him. My husband died when Jonathan was only five. Did you know that? Poor boy, he really never knew him. Lord Faukes was more like a father to Jonathan than a grandfather.'

'He was lucky, then, to have such a grandfather.'

'Lucky? Yes . . .' Josephine sighed, and fell into thought, and Rachel waited uncomfortably.

'Will I be sitting with your son in this room, Mrs Alleyn, or in some other?' she asked at last.

'What? Oh, no. He will not come down. I will take you up to him.' The older lady turned and walked slowly towards the door, her face immobile, betraying nothing of her thoughts. Rachel's heart sank. *Back to his rooms then, to the darkness and the vile smell and the feeling of being confined, just like that poor canary.*

She tried to remain calm, as they climbed the stone stairs in silence. Josephine Alleyn walked with her all the way to her son's door, and by the time they reached it she was wearing an equal measure of hope and doubt on her lovely face. Rachel tried desperately to think of Jonathan Alleyn as he had seemed the last time she called – apologetic, un-comfortable, and even nervous – rather than as she had first met him: violent and inebriated. They almost seemed like two distinct people. *Oh, let him be sober at least.* She would not stay if he was drunk, she decided there and then. There would be little point in reading to him if his mind was addled. Josephine Alleyn knocked on her son's door and then opened it, then stepped aside and ushered Rachel in, alone. 'Perhaps the Bible, if all else fails,' Mrs Alleyn whispered, before she closed the door. 'Perhaps the Bible would help him back into the light.'

The room was in near darkness again, and at once Rachel was on edge. The stink of death and decay had gone, how-ever, so she was able to breathe more easily. She turned, and saw Jonathan Alleyn sitting in an armchair in the bay window. His long legs were thrust out in front of him, his elbow rested on the arm of the chair, fingers pressing lightly into the side of his face.

'Mr Alleyn—' said Rachel, nerves making her voice blare out abruptly. Jonathan quickly raised his fingers in protest.

'Please, not so loud. Do come and sit, Mrs Weekes.' He gestured at a wooden chair that had been placed opposite him, near enough for her hem to brush the tips of his boots as she sat down in it. It was cool by the window; a draught crept around the shutters, and Rachel shivered.

'It will be very hard for me to read with so little light,' she said, more quietly.

'To read?' he said. A strip of light lit one of his watchful brown eyes, and sculpted itself into the contours of his face – the hollows in his cheeks and beneath his brows. His scrutiny again gave her that conspicuous feeling, that sense that all her words and expressions were false. *It is her he sees.* As if reading her thoughts, Jonathan Alleyn frowned. 'In truth, you are not so very like her. Like Alice. It is only a . . . an initial resemblance. You are taller, and narrower, your eyes are more grey than blue. Your hair is . . . your hair is just as pale as hers; your face . . . remarkably alike. But much of the similarity goes once speech and expression animate your features,' he said. Rachel felt absurdly disappointed, almost insulted. *But much time has passed; the years will work changes.* 'When I first saw you my vision was blurred . . . the headaches do that sometimes.'

'Well, I never claimed any connection to Alice Beckwith . . .'

'No more you did. You came in ignorance. I . . . I must apologise again for my reaction. For laying hands on you. It was inexcusable.' He spoke in a flat voice, with no marked emotion or expression, and only a slight frown to give his words credence. Rachel began to form an acceptance of his apology, but it wouldn't come. She laced her fingers in her lap and studied them.

'Laying hands on me? You half strangled me.' The words burst out, unbidden. Shocked at her own frankness, she saw a look of surprise and then despair fill Jonathan's face.

'I barely remember,' he muttered. 'It has vanished into the dark spaces.'

'Well,' said Rachel, not quite understanding him. She

rearranged her hands. 'How are you today? You're not suffering a headache now?'

'No, madam. Though the term "ache" scarcely gives a true idea of the sensation. It is more like a knife, twisting slowly in my skull. Like a thunderstorm, caught between my temples.'

'Have you consulted a doctor over it?'

'My mother has sent every doctor, quack and hedge witch in England to me at some time or another,' he snapped. 'All they do is bleed me, which makes me weak, then tell me to rest. None of it does any good. Only wine . . . only wine eases it. For a time.' He shut his eyes for a moment then leant forwards suddenly, moving so quickly that Rachel jumped. 'It's the things I have seen, you understand? It's the things I have seen and the things I have done, clawing away at my mind like rats!'

'Things . . . things you saw in the war with the French?' Rachel ventured, cautiously.

'Oh, how much you know, about the war and what happened there, and about Alice . . . How much everybody knows and how all the voices chatter on and how well informed everybody is about my infirmity! About my very *thoughts*!' he snapped, leaning back again, disgusted.

'In truth, sir, I know very little. I was only trying to—'

'You know nothing,' he stated flatly.

Stung, Rachel sat silent for a moment. There was a slight sound from the far end of the room, where a doorway led through to his bedchamber. She thought at once of the red-haired servant. *Starling*. Was she watching them again? Keeping guard?

'It was nothing. Only the house shifting in this wind,' said Jonathan.

'Last time . . . last time I was here there was a girl,' said Rachel. Jonathan grunted.

'Yes, that one. She gets everywhere. Sneaks around this house like a cat, far too bold for her own good.' He shut his eyes and pressed his fingertips into his temple again.

'A curious name. Has she no other?'

'No. She is a curious girl, given her curious name by another girl, the sweetest that ever lived.'

'You mean . . . Miss Beckwith? Did Starling belong to her, then?' said Rachel, puzzled.

'You are not here to question me about Alice Beckwith.' He spoke in that flat, adamant tone again, cold and hard as steel. Rachel swallowed to ease her dry throat.

'Why am I here, sir?' she asked eventually, steadily.

'You're here because my mother will not stop trying to fix what cannot be fixed. You're here because you bear a passing resemblance to a woman I loved, a woman I would have married, a woman who—' He cut himself off, took a deep breath. 'I don't know why you're here. There is no need for you to be. You may go.'

'I understood I was here to read to you. To assist you in that, when it is beyond you these days?'

'To assist me?'

'Yes. What would you like me to read?'

'You didn't bring something with you? Something wholesome and healing, something that will be good for my soul? Psalms? A book of sermons?' The question was sour. *He wishes me gone.* For a second Rachel almost stood up to leave, but something kept her in her chair. It would feel like failure, she realised, should she leave so soon, having achieved so little. *Give every endeavour your best effort*, her father had said, over and again, usually in reference to a page of unconjugated Latin. *But what is my endeavour here? To help this man, or to know what ails him? To know Alice, who changed everything.*

'I'll choose something from your shelf, shall I?' she said, in as light a tone as she could muster.

Jonathan said nothing as she went over to the wooden shelves that filled one wall of the room. She ran her eyes along the spines of his books, many of which were dusty and faded, and had names she could barely understand, or which were written in foreign languages. There were other things on the shelves as well – strange implements, mechanical toys and little jointed wooden figures, like the ones her mother had sometimes used for her drawing studies. There were the three glass jars with their pale, fleshy occupants that seemed to look back at Rachel. She recoiled from such dead, unnatural scrutiny. For a while, she was so intrigued with her exploration of the shelves that she forgot her purpose in looking. She ran her fingers along a smooth wooden tube, nine inches in length and screwed together from two sections, widening at one end like a funnel.

'It's for listening to a person's chest. To their heart, and their breathing, and all the strange mechanisms of the body.' Jonathan spoke quietly, close behind her. Rachel hadn't heard him approach, and tried not to show her unease.

'Oh,' she said.

'A Frenchman has invented it, lately; a man by the name of Laennec. Shall I show you? The sound is quite incredible. As though skin and bones and flesh have been peeled away, and the heart is left naked to be examined.'

'No, I don't want that,' said Rachel, alarmed. 'Your mother told me that you hated the French, and all things French. That you would not even have French wine to drink.'

Jonathan's expression darkened. 'She knows nothing of what I think, nor how I feel. It is quite astonishing, how much she misunderstands . . .'

'I believe it pains her a great deal that—'

'Stop. You know nothing, Mrs Weekes, and you make

yourself sound foolish.' Rachel bit her lip angrily, and said nothing. She took a step away from him, along the shelf, until her eyes fell on a tiny toy mouse.

It was life-sized – a little more than three inches long, with a delicate whip of a tail. Its body was made of thin, over-lapping scales of copper, the edges crenulated to mimic the look of fur. Its tail was a piece of leather, stiff enough to stand out behind it, everything else was made of the same bright copper but for its eyes, which were round jet beads, large and lustrous. It was attached to a piece of ebony wood, as though it had been walking across it when it had frozen, and turned to metal. Rachel picked it up gently, and examined it. The detail was exquisite. Individual horse hairs had been attached to give it whiskers; it had tiny copper claws, and its ears were tiny, perfect circles.

'You like it?' Jonathan asked, his tone softening.

'It's charming,' said Rachel.

'Look – see what it does.' He took the copper mouse from her, turned it around and wound a key that fitted into the wooden base, and then held it out on his palm. As the key wound down, the little mouse moved. Its feet pattered along as though it was running, then it paused, and lifted its nose as if to sniff at the air. Its tail curled higher and it sat back on its haunches, front paws dangling under its chin. Then it returned to all four feet and ran on. Again it performed this cycle, as Rachel watched, delighted; then after a minute or so the spring wound down and the mouse fell still.

Rachel looked up, smiling.

'I have seen something like this before,' she said. 'A schoolfriend of mine had a box, and when the key was wound, the scene on the lid came to life, and little skaters slid about on a frozen lake. But it was just a flat scene, not a real creature like this. It's wonderful . . . where did you come by it?'

'I made it,' said Jonathan.

'Truly, Mr Alleyn? How came you by such skill?'

'I was trying . . . I read a treatise on such mechanisms by a Swiss man, a maker of clocks. And I have taken apart several other such toys, to learn how they function. Most of my efforts were failures, but then this little mouse . . . continues to run.' His tone was strange, almost embarrassed.

'It is exquisite, Mr Alleyn. And a fine skill to have taught oneself as a hobby, to be sure,' she said encouragingly, but her words had the opposite effect. Jonathan frowned, and turned the copper mouse over in his hands.

'A hobby?' He shook his head and thought for a while. 'The philosophers have it that animals have no souls. That without a soul, the body is just a machine, like this. It performs mechanical functions with no thought, no governing mind. There was an automaton built by a Frenchman, the *Canard Digérateur* – do you know of it? The digesting duck? It can eat grain and digest it, just like a real duck. Does that not prove that animals are mere machines?' He paused, and Rachel shook her head, baffled. 'But if they have no souls, why is their blood hot, like ours? Why do they show fear? Why do they hunger? Why do they fight for life? Why will a cow stand and fight a wolf rather than let her calf be taken?'

'I do not . . . but animals cannot have souls. It is written . . .'

'In the Bible? Yes. A great many things are written in the Bible.'

'Surely, you do not doubt the word of God?'

'I doubt God a great deal, Mrs Weekes, as would you, had you seen and done what I have seen and done. And if animals have no souls, than perhaps neither has man. Perhaps we are all but machines.'

'You cannot truly think so.'

'Can I not? What can you understand of what I think? You have no knowledge of what man can do to his fellow man. I tell you, if there is a soul then there is also a beast in all men, which would take over all thought and deed if it could, and wreak havoc.'

'There is not a beast in *all* men, sir,' Rachel protested quietly. Jonathan's voice had risen as he spoke, and she feared to provoke him. His words frightened her; they sounded like a warning.

'You're wrong,' Jonathan said abruptly. He looked down at the copper mouse, and then thrust it into her hands. 'But keep this trifle, if it pleases you. Let it remind you of what I've said today.' He strode back to his chair in the window and threw himself into it. Carefully, Rachel put the clockwork toy back on the shelf where she'd found it.

Desperately, she scanned the books for something appropriate to read, and was relieved when she finally spotted a small volume of poetry by Dryden. She took it down and returned to sit opposite Jonathan Alleyn. His head was tilted back and his eyes were shut. As Rachel began to read she wondered if he'd fallen asleep, but he interrupted her at once.

'You choose poetry over philosophy, over science and reason? How like a woman.'

'I am more accomplished at reading poetry than the more . . . esoteric tracts you have available.'

' "Yet when the soul's disease we desperate find, Poets the old renown'd physicians are, Who for the sickly habits of the mind, Examples as the ancient cure prepare." Is that what you hope? That my soul's disease can be cured with poetry?'

'Not cured perhaps. Only cheered. Who wrote that verse you spoke?'

'Sir William Davenant.'

'Then you must know some poetry, and take pleasure in it? Or you did, at one time?' said Rachel.

'I knew another, who did,' said Jonathan. He closed his eyes wearily, so Rachel began to read again. She kept her voice low, and her tone soft, and read for half an hour without any reaction from Jonathan Alleyn, save for at one verse. When she read:

' "I feed a flame within, which so torments me, That it both pains my heart, and yet contents me: 'Tis such a pleasing smart, and I so love it, That I had rather die than once remove it" ', she saw a flicker of movement, and looked up to find him watching her through barely opened eyes. Her voice faltered and she lost her place in the text, and felt herself foolish and clumsy. Then she read on, and Jonathan closed his eyes once more, and when she got up to leave she was sure he was sleeping.

Rachel shut the door behind her, and with the quiet click of the latch felt herself sag. Her head felt light and was throbbing softly, and her stomach rumbled. She hadn't eaten anything at breakfast, such had been her nerves over this appointment, but it was more than that that ailed her. It was him, and his torment; the shifting dark things behind his eyes, and the way he wore his rage for all to see. *To keep the world from seeing something else about him?* He seemed to leach the strength from her, with his gaze that was so full of things she did not understand that it might as well be empty, and the hard, uncompromising way he spoke. He made her manners and her poise and her decorum seem like paper cut-out things, painted and unreal; and without them to cover her, she felt bare. Rachel went downstairs and knocked softly at the parlour door, but there was no reply. She tried the other receiving rooms, but they were similarly empty. She stood alone in the cavernous hallway for a moment, unsure of what to do. It seemed rude to let herself out, to leave without a word. In the end, she turned towards the back of the house, and found the servants' stair that led down into the basement.

At the foot of the stairs was a broad, bare corridor leading left and right, lit by candle lamps in wall sconces which guttered at her arrival. From the right came the herby, smoky smell of the kitchen, along with sounds of industry. Rachel's stomach growled again, and she turned towards it. It was a wide, vaulted chamber, dominated at one end by a massive inglenook containing the stove and bread oven, and a roasting fire in an open grate. She heard the pop and sizzle of hot fat, the creak of the jack wheel turning in the chimney. A squat woman with meaty arms was cracking eggs into a basin, humming to herself and quite unaware of Rachel. As Rachel drew breath to speak, the woman glanced up.

'And who might you be, dithering in my kitchen?' she asked. Rachel stepped forwards.

'I have been visiting with Mr Alleyn, and I . . . I could not find anyone upstairs . . .' The cook wiped her hands on her apron and curtsied inelegantly, looking flustered and annoyed.

'Beg pardon, madam, I had not known you . . . But you should not be downstairs, as a guest . . .'

'No – I know. My apologies. But, perhaps . . . I am not quite a guest, you see. I am in the employ of the household, for my visits.' Rachel took a step further into the kitchen and glanced at the fire where a joint of pork was turning.

'Well, you should no more be below stairs for all that, madam. Go on up, if it please you, and I'll call for Falmouth to see you out . . .'

'I was wondering if I might have a word with Starling? And perhaps . . .' Rachel could not quite find the courage to ask the cook for something to eat; the woman was clearly irritated by the intrusion into her domain. There was a basket of pears on the table. Rachel eyed it wistfully, and was sure that the cook noticed her gaze, but she did not offer her one. Rolling her lips together so that her chin puckered, the woman went to the doorway to call along the corridor.

'Starling! Someone wants a word with you!' There was

a pause, in which Starling did not appear, and the cook muttered a curse under her breath. 'She's in a world of her own of late, that one. Go back up, madam. Please. I'll send her up to you,' she said.

'No, it's quite all right. No need to fetch her, I shall go along and find her,' said Rachel, returning to the corridor. The cook paused, and then shrugged.

'Last door at the end, on the right.'

Rachel went along and knocked at the last door she came to; since it was open, she stepped through it. The room was split into two, and through the inner doorway she saw the red-haired girl, down on her knees, putting a bottle of ale into a jute sack. The girl jumped up when she heard Rachel come in, quickly kicked the sack underneath the bed and then turned with flaming cheeks and furious eyes. Rachel took a step back and forgot what she had been about to say.

'This is my room,' the girl blurted out.

'I know. I . . . beg your pardon.' Rachel joined her hands awkwardly, and then remembered that she was the girl's superior. She drew herself up, several inches taller than Starling. 'I want to ask you some questions. It won't take long. I am sure you have . . . duties to attend to.' Rachel glanced down to where the corner of the jute sack was still visible, poking out from beneath the bed. Starling glowered at her, but there was fear in her eyes as well. A loose tendril of ginger hair hung in front of her face, and moved in time with her breathing.

'Questions about what? Madam,' said the girl, curtly.

'About Mr Alleyn – I understand you have known him the longest of all the servants. And about Miss Alice Beckwith.'

'Alice?' Starling faltered. Her eyes widened, and some of the anger left her. 'You know about Alice?'

'Precious little. Only that she treated Mr Alleyn very ill,

and is partly to blame for his malaise. And that . . . I look like her. Or so I am led to believe.'

'She never treated him ill! She never treated anyone or anything ill, not in her whole life!'

'You knew her well?'

'I . . . she raised me. As a sister.'

'A *sister*?'

'Aye, a sister! Partly. As a servant too, perhaps . . . I knew her from when I was a child.'

'And . . . do I look very like her?' Rachel asked, almost shyly. *Like the girl a man loved so much that losing her has ruined him.* Starling stared at her with an expression Rachel could not read.

'That you do, Mrs Weekes. At first. You are older than she was when she disappeared, of course. And . . . your expressions are different. Your voice. It is a passing resemblance, nothing more.'

'That's just what Mr Alleyn said,' Rachel murmured. At this, Starling blinked, and incredulity flooded her face.

'He speaks to you about her? About Alice?'

'But a little. Perhaps he will speak more in time.'

'Then . . . you are to call again?'

'Yes.' Rachel drew her shoulders back, and tried to sound resolute.

'And . . . he does not alarm you?'

'Why should he?' said Rachel, and then felt foolish, since it was this girl who had prevented Jonathan strangling her a little over a week ago. 'He does not alarm *you*, that much I know.' She remembered the hearth brush striking Jonathan across his head. How could a servant act that way, and yet not be dismissed?

'I've known him a long time indeed,' said Starling, flatly.

'What was she like? Alice Beckwith?'

There was a long pause, and though Starling's eyes were

fixed on Rachel it seemed that they looked right through her, into the shadow behind her that flickered on the wall. For a while, Rachel thought she wasn't going to answer, but then she took a quick, deep breath.

'One day we went to have tea with the vicar and his wife in Bathampton . . . The place was newly built, and the vicar that proud that he showed her the whole house, even down to the servants' floor and the kitchens. Alice was pleased enough, and saw nothing inappropriate in being below stairs. She gave herself no false airs.' At this, Starling flicked her eyes over Rachel. 'She didn't see servants or lord and ladies, poor people or rich people. She only saw *people*. In the kitchens, Alice noticed the dog wheel, set up to turn the spit, with a little white dog that had to run and run to turn it, hour after hour. If it got tired the cook would put a hot coal in behind it, so it had to run or be burned. Alice wept when she saw it. She wouldn't let it continue a second longer.' Starling smiled, but looked sad. 'She made such a fuss with her crying and her accusations that the dog was released at once – the vicar had little choice. She brought it back to the farmhouse and nursed it, and the vicar's kitchen maid had to turn the meat until they had a clockwork jack installed instead. That was what Alice was like. She could not bear to see cruelty, and there was no cruelty in her. Not a jot. She was too good for this world, and people who speak ill things of her are far wrong.' Starling broke off her story and wiped her hands unnecessarily on her apron. She took another deep breath and looked down at the floor, eyebrows drawn together. *And this girl misses her still*, Rachel thought.

'I must get to work now, Mrs Weekes,' Starling said at last.

'Could we talk again, perhaps?' said Rachel, catching the girl's arm as she went to go past her.

'I daresay,' Starling muttered, and pulled her arm away;

she vanished into the stairwell on quick feet. Rachel waited a moment, and then went back to the kitchen and caught the eye of the cook.

'Get what you wanted, madam?' the woman asked, still clearly nonplussed by her presence.

'Yes, I suppose so. After a fashion.' She paused, and felt her conscience prick her. 'I thought I ought to tell you . . . when I went into the girl's room, I am sure I saw her concealing something beneath her bed. A bottle of ale from the pantry, it seemed,' she said.

'Starling? I'm sure you're mistaken, madam. Do go on up, and I shall call for Falmouth . . .'

'No, I am not mistaken. She was stealing, I am certain of it,' Rachel insisted. The cook gave her a steady, blank look.

'I am sure you are mistaken, madam,' she said tonelessly. Rachel's cheeks flamed.

'Well, then,' she said, flustered. The cook said nothing more, and only watched her, so Rachel turned and went back to the stairs, fleeing the woman's disrespect.

The rescued dog had been a small, wire-haired terrier with short legs and the tips of both its ears missing, most likely burned away. They named it Flint. It had lost patches of hair here and there, so that pink skin showed through. It stank, and shook constantly, and its breathing was laboured. When Starling held her nose and wouldn't stroke it, Alice gave her a disappointed look that stung her.

'Shame on you, Starling. It's not the dog's fault it has been brought so low. Where is your pity?' she said, so Starling stroked the dog's head, and it licked at her fingertips. 'See.' Alice smiled. 'See, he likes you.'

'You reeked like a ferret when we first took you in,' Bridget pointed out. She had a soft spot for dogs. They made Flint a bed in a warm place, and for three weeks he lay in it, wheezing, rising now and then to potter around the kitchen and cock his leg against the furniture. Alice nursed him as best she could, but still he died, and when he did she wept till she wore herself out, and had to go upstairs to lie down.

'Alice must have loved Flint very much,' Starling said to Bridget, as they scrubbed parsnips for lunch. Bridget grunted.

'She only needs an excuse, sometimes, to let out what's inside her. She only needs a reason to release it, and reset the balance. Best just leave her to it.'

'What do you mean? What's inside her?' said Starling. Bridget ignored her, and carried on scrubbing.

Later, Starling took up some tea and lay alongside Alice for a while, drawing patterns on the backs of her hands, which Alice found soothing. Starling thought about what Bridget had said, but couldn't fathom her meaning.

'Flint's gone to heaven now, hasn't he, Alice? Do animals go to heaven?' she said, carefully.

'No, dearest.' Alice's voice was sluggish and dull.

'Why not?'

'Because the Bible says so. Only humans have souls which can go to heaven.' Starling thought about this for a while.

'That's not fair,' she concluded, at last, and Alice dissolved into fresh tears.

'No, it's not fair. It's too unfair that he should die now, when he had found kindness and rest. It's *too* unfair! If I had only known sooner that such cruelty was going on when I had the power to stop it . . .' Starling tried desperately to think of a way to change the subject, to divert Alice from her misery. 'Alice, after I came here, did anybody come to find me? Did anybody come looking for me?' But this question, a matter of simple curiosity to her, made Alice weep anew.

'No, dearest,' she said, shaking with grief. 'Nobody came for you.'

'I'm glad they didn't,' Starling said quickly.

'Are you?'

'I don't care who they were, not really. Sometimes I like to imagine them, but . . . I only want to stay here with you, so I don't need to know about them.'

'You only want to stay here? For ever?' Alice turned her head to face Starling, and opened her bloodshot eyes. 'You only want to live in ignorance of your true heritage, your true family? You only want to go on at the whim of one man, who has the power to prescribe your life to you, though you know not why?'

'Who, Lord Faukes? He doesn't prescribe my life . . .' Starling trailed off. *Does he?* she wondered. 'You prescribe my life, Alice. You're my big sister, after all.'

'You are no more free than I am, Starling.' Alice sniffed, and stared at her intently. 'You and I are every bit as trapped and used as poor Flint, on his wheel. Don't you see?' Starling was mystified. Life at the farmhouse held everything she thought she needed. She could think of few ways in which it might improve. 'But I will find a way,' Alice whispered then, and a spark kindled in her eyes. 'I will find a way to change it, and Jonathan will help me.'

'What's Jonathan going to do?'

'He's going to marry me,' Alice whispered, and she shut her eyes again, and seemed more serene. Starling was still trying to puzzle out her meaning when she realised that Alice had fallen asleep. She watched her sister's pale and lovely face for a while, suddenly feeling as though there was much she did not know.

The following month was June, and Bridget packed up some clothing, and several pots of home preserves as presents, and prepared to make an overdue visit to her niece in Oxford.

'Now, you'll be all right? There is plenty of food in the larder – I've left you a mutton pie, and the peas are coming all the time – keep picking them. There's—'

'Dear Bridget, you're only going for a week! We shan't starve, nor the house cave in,' Alice interrupted her. 'Besides, you've been training Starling these past four years – what kind of teacher would you be if she couldn't cope with a few simple meals in your absence?'

'Hmm.' Bridget seamed her lips together for a moment, and then nodded. 'Well, then,' she said, tying the ribbon of her straw hat under her chin and hefting up her basket. 'Behave yourselves.' With that she went out and climbed up beside the yardman in their little wagon; he was to take her up to the Bath road, where she could catch the stagecoach. Alice and Starling stood side by side to wave her off, and once she was out of sight Alice turned to Starling, and smiled.

'Well,' she said. 'What shall we do today? Since it's holiday time you don't have to do your lessons. Not until Bridget gets back.'

'And can we have chocolate this evening?'

'We can. Every evening!'

'Huzzah!' Starling shouted, running out across the yard into the sunshine, and sending the chickens scattering.

Later that day Alice went for one of her solitary walks, just for half an hour or so while Starling put a slab of pork belly in the oven to roast, and shelled peas to go with it. When Alice got back she was secretive – Starling was wise to it in an instant; a misaimed pea bounced across the work top and rolled onto the floor.

'What is it, Alice? Is Mr Alleyn coming? Have you seen him?'

'I have not. But . . . a little bird told me that we should make ourselves look festive, and be waiting on the far side of the miller's bridge by middle morning tomorrow.' Her eyes were dancing with excitement, a happier countenance than any she'd worn since Flint died. Starling hopped from one foot to the other in agitation.

'Who says so? What little bird? Is it Jonathan? Where are we going?' she demanded.

'I don't know, dearest. But I think it will be fun.'

'Will we visit away from Bathampton, do you think?' This was something Starling longed to do. The world, only heard and read about, seemed impossibly huge and thrilling to one who had no memories before the farmhouse.

'We'll just have to wait and see, my chuck,' said Alice.

It took a long time for Starling to succumb to sleep that night; her anticipation of the day to come kept her mind alight and humming, and got her up at dawn. She was out and about before the yardman, even; while the air was still as cool and fresh as rainwater, and dew soaked the summer grasses. The sky was a pale, pristine blue, so high up and far away that looking up felt like falling. Swallows and house martins arrowed across it, adding their wheeling voices to the dawn chorus. Starling could smell the pea flowers and lavender in the kitchen garden; the damp stone of the farmhouse; the sweet greenery of the meadow; the familiar, reassuring stink of the muck heap. The chickens muttered at her as she reached beneath them for the eggs, but it was so early that not all had laid yet. She tipped the previous day's kitchen slops into the sow's trough and stayed awhile to stroke her piglets, which had skin as soft and pink as her own ears. But after all of that the shutters were still closed over their bedroom window, and Alice was therefore still abed, so Starling went to pester the horse in his stable. She could not be still.

After breakfast Starling chafed even more, as Alice washed her hair for her and combed it dry, tucking and fussing her red curls into their proper places. She put on her best white cotton dress, spat on a rag and rubbed her leather shoes into a semblance of cleanliness. Only then, when much primping and styling and beribboning was done, did they quit the house and set off towards the bridge. They paid the toll to cross and went up the lane towards Batheaston, and there waited in the shade of an ash tree because the climbing sun had grown hot. At the sound of a single set of hooves approaching, Alice's hand on Starling's shoulder squeezed; Starling looked up at her, grinning, as Jonathan Alleyn came into view, driving a small trap with a pretty spotted pony in the traces.

'Good day, fair cousins,' he called to them, with a wide smile. His dark hair had been pushed back by the breeze;

there was a light tan on his skin from the bright spell of weather.

'And to you, cousin,' Alice replied, pointedly.

'Why are you calling each other—' Starling began to say, but got an elbow in her ribs from Alice. 'Ouch! You didn't have to! Where are we going?' she asked, as Jonathan held out his hand to help them climb up in turn.

'We're going somewhere where nobody will recognise any one of us, or know that we are not three cousins, out together for the day. And . . . we're going to a fair,' said Jonathan. Starling gasped, and goggled incredulously at Alice, who was beaming. Bathampton had a May Day fair; it was a small event, where the village children danced ribbons around the pole, tea and ale were drunk and ferrets raced, and that was enough to make it a gala day for Starling. Jonathan clicked his tongue at the pony, and they moved off. 'Bridget left on her visit as planned, then?' he said.

'She did, and will not be back until Tuesday next. And . . . Lord Faukes?'

'He and my mother are in London this month and I find myself quite recovered from the slight head cold that prevented me accompanying them.'

Alice and Jonathan chattered and laughed as the spotted pony walked up and down the hills, and trotted along the flat, covering the eight miles north and east towards Corsham. Starling paid little mind to what they said, she was too busy staring around at the rolling hills, all bright and summer green; at the farmhouses and hamlets they passed; at the village of Box, with its stone cottages and pretty gardens. A good way back from the road in Box, she saw the dormer windows, gabled ends and tall chimney stacks of a very large, grand house, hidden by a screen of cypress trees.

'See, there,' said Jonathan, pointing to it. 'There is my grandfather's house, where I live.'

'But I can hardly see it . . . can't we drive up to it, just for a second?' said Alice, eagerly. Jonathan shook his head.

'I dare not . . . I'm sorry, Alice – I mean, cousin. The servants would surely see us, and wonder. And they cannot be relied upon to say nothing at a later date.'

'Oh.' Alice's disappointment lasted seconds; soon she was merry and laughing once more. Starling looked back at the massive roof, and had the peculiar feeling that the house was watching her in return.

Corsham was a bigger town than Starling had ever seen before. It had an ancient high street between undulating stone houses, paved with buff slabs and cobbles. There were flags and flowers hanging from every shop front and lamp-post, and the scent of food was everywhere – hot pies, strawberries, fresh fudge and cinnamon buns. Starling's mouth watered as she breathed it in; her stomach rumbled audibly, and Jonathan laughed.

'Famished already, little coz? Fear not. I have a fistful of pennies with me, for this very purpose. You can eat whatever you wish.'

'Anything I wish? Truly?' Starling breathed.

'Not more than one cone of fudge, and one of honeycomb, or you'll be sick,' Alice qualified. The high street and the square by the church were crowded with people and stalls; everything was for sale, from gloves to garden tools and corn dollies; jam to pig's ears and liver pills.

From the church square, a long carriage drive led up to the towering, intricate walls of Corsham Court, a house so huge and elaborate that Starling could only stare at it in amazement.

'Who lives there?' she asked.

'A man called Methuen. We dine there, sometimes,' said Jonathan. At this, both Starling and Alice turned to stare at him in near disbelief. It suddenly seemed inappropriate that they should be in his company.

'You have been invited to dine . . . in that house?' Alice murmured. She'd gone a little pale, and Jonathan looked confused for a moment.

'Oh – but have no fear, Miss Beckwith. Cousin Alice, I mean.' He smiled reassuringly. 'The family are not at home. There's no chance of my being recognised.' They walked on, and neither of the girls spoke. For a while, their Jonathan seemed a different creature entirely, and they were in awe of him, until he looked across and smiled his slightly bashful smile, and so went back to being the man they knew.

'What's it like inside?' Starling couldn't help but ask. Jonathan shrugged.

'Opulent. Ugly, for the most part. In the richest possible way. As you would expect, from what has been done to the outside of the house. He has some very fine paintings, however.' The silence resumed, Starling and Alice both hoping that Jonathan wouldn't realise that neither one of them had the first idea what to expect of the interior of such a place.

A pipe, fiddle and drum band were playing in the square, and people had begun to dance; simple country dances that involved a good deal of spinning, promenading and galloping. The dancers' faces grew red and sweaty in the heat of the day, but it didn't slow them any, and the spectators clapped and stamped out the time, on and on. The three of them meandered from one end of the fair to the other, seeing all there was to see, grazing from the food sellers, admiring the hawkers' wares. Starling ran this way and that, panting for breath, wanting to see and do it all at once. She was bewildered and enthralled by the myriad of strange faces, the crush of people, the noise and throng and chaos. It made her heart race and her head spin. She felt, for the first time in her life, like a citizen of the wider world, and she loved it. She only slowed for one thing — a song of perfect loveliness. In a quiet corner on the edge of everything, an Irish girl was singing with an old man to accompany her on the fiddle; they'd placed a grubby felt hat on the ground in front of them, and a few coins had gone in. They were battered and weather-worn, their clothes were worn out, but the fiddle had a hoarse, bittersweet timbre, and the girl's voice was as unadorned and beautiful as any of them had ever heard.

'*My young love said to me, my mother won't mind,*' she sang, and all who heard her stopped to listen. '*She placed her hand on me, and this she did say: it will not be long, love, till our wedding day . . .*' Alice glanced at Jonathan, and caught him studying her. A blush flared over his long cheekbones, and he looked away, abashed. As the Irish girl's song ended, and her spell was broken, Jonathan rummaged in his pocket and found a coin for the hat.

'Come,' he said. 'Let's go back for another of those delicious gooseberry pies.'

Soothed by the song, Starling quietened a little. She straightened her skirts and tried to walk with more decorum, like a proper young lady — moving through the fair, stepping neatly between and around the other revellers. When she glanced back, Alice had taken Jonathan's arm; they walked with their eyes on each other, not on where they were going — they followed Starling blindly. She was their pilot and captain, just then, so she changed course, humming the song she'd just learnt, and led them back to the lady with the marshmallow, and the liquorice-flavoured fudge. Later on they walked a distance across Corsham Court's parkland, opened to the public for the day, and rested in the shade of an ancient oak tree. They were full of food and laughter and sunshine, and drowsy from it all; shooing lazily at the buzzing flies, watching the brilliant light flicker down through the leaves. There came a roar from the edge of the park, as the winning tug o' war team pulled the losers into a mud patch; a sudden crescendo of noise and applause that pattered and echoed against the back walls of the townhouses.

'I wish every day was like today,' said Starling. Jonathan had lain back with his head on his arms, and shut his eyes; Alice sat as close to him as she could without touching. They'd stopped calling each other 'cousin' so ostentatiously, since nobody was listening. There was nobody there to tell them they shouldn't be; they were at their liberty, for once, and unconcerned.

'And I,' Alice agreed.

'Except we would all be as fat as your old sow if it were so,' said Jonathan.

'No, indeed.' Alice laughed. 'We would dance it all away.'

'*It will not be long, love, till our wedding day,*' Starling sang softly. 'I loved that song, didn't you?' She picked the feathery seeds from a stalk of grass and scattered them to the balmy air.

'I did. Very much,' said Alice.

The sun grew fat and was lowering in the west before they returned to the paddock by the inn where the spotted pony had been turned out for the day. He was dozing with one rear hoof tipped on its toe, occasionally whisking his tail at the midges; he seemed a trifle put out to be called upon to move. Starling fed him a piece of fudge to cheer him up. Behind them the band and the dancing went on, though many of the stalls had been packed away.

'Can't we stay a bit longer?' said Starling, as Jonathan lifted the collar over the pony's head; but she yawned as she spoke, and Alice smiled.

'I think you've had enough excitement for one day, dearest,' she said. Starling didn't argue. Though she wouldn't admit it, her head was pounding from all the sunshine and sugar; it felt too heavy for her neck, and she longed to put it down somewhere. The sounds of the fair receded behind them as they moved off into the failing light, with bats flying silently over their heads. Starling nestled into Alice's side, and felt her sister's arm settle over her shoulders; she shut her eyes, and knew herself safe. The rattle and sway of the trap, and the creak of its wheels; the soft, soft air, and Alice's arm around her, like armour. She glanced up only once and saw Alice resting her head on Jonathan's shoulder. Above them a few faint stars had come out, and Starling wished that the journey would never end. She wished to not arrive back at Bathampton, because just then everything was exactly as it should be; everything was perfect.

'You want to watch that one,' said Sol Bradbury, slapping egg wash onto a pie crust with broad, messy brushstrokes. 'Came in here bold as brass and told me she'd seen you stealing.'

'She never said so?' Starling replied, shocked.

'She bloody did. You need to be more careful. If Dorcas or Mrs Hatton ever sees then that's the end of you, and naught I can say will save you. I sent Mrs Weekes on her way, but you'd best hope she says nothing to the mistress.'

'She'd better not, or I'll see her off.'

'Oh? And how will you do that if Mr Alleyn half throttling her didn't scare her none?' said the cook. Starling frowned and said nothing for a while. She crushed peppercorns in a pestle and mortar, pushing so hard that the stone surfaces creaked together, and set her teeth on edge. *How dare she?* She could hardly believe the woman's temerity. She seemed such a thin, pale thing, so prim and bound up with manners above her station. Her voice was so quiet, so modulated, Starling couldn't imagine her ever shouting, or cursing, or arguing. And yet she was dogged, and determined, and she kept coming back. Starling hadn't considered that, when she'd contrived her meeting with Jonathan. She'd thought only of planning the moment, of gauging his reaction, of hoping to prise some revelation from him. Now it seemed she was stuck with Dick Weekes's wife turning up when she was no longer wanted. Starling was almost sure that Mrs Weekes had gone straight out after her visit to the kitchens. She was almost sure she hadn't stopped to speak to anyone else about what she'd seen below stairs. It seemed best to get rid of the evidence, however.

After the brief dinner service was done, and still simmering with an anxious kind of anger, Starling took the jute sack from under her bed, and made a quick inventory. There was the beer she'd purloined earlier that day, to go with the jars of pickled eggs, a thick slice of dry bacon, some figs, almonds and half a wheel of hard cheese, almost down to the rind but still with some edible parts. Starling went into the kitchen on soft feet and pinched the leftover bread, already sliced for upstairs and going stale, then she set off with her haul, ducking quickly out of the basement door even as she heard Dorcas's weary footsteps shuffling on the stairs. It wasn't the best time to go, it wasn't the right day. She wasn't expected. *How dare she.* Starling cursed Dick Weekes's wife with silent vitriol as she marched down the hill into the city.

* * *

Rachel was dawdling outside the Roman Baths. The early evening was already chill and dark, and a raw breeze angled through the damp streets, but Rachel had grown weary of sitting in the silent house, waiting for Richard's return. So she wandered the nearby streets instead, watching people and horses and carriages; gentlemen emerging from the baths with their damp hair steaming; children playing in the gutter, keeping an eye out for anything that was dropped or would be easy to steal. They played in the drifts of dead leaves beneath the plane tree in Abbey Green, throwing them up into the air and laughing as they fell like rain around them. Rachel smiled as she watched them, and wished for a child of her own. Something to devote herself to. She eavesdropped on snatches of conversation, and carried a basket over her arm in the pretence of being out on some errand, but even as this cheered her up she felt herself becoming a parasite, drawing on the lives of others. She'd been searching her purse for the pennies to buy a baked apple from a man with a handcart full of hot coals, when she saw Starling hurrying by, unmistakable with her red hair catching the torchlight; pretty in spite of her sour expression.

Weeks after her move to Bath, Rachel still saw precious few faces that she knew. The Alleyns' servant was walking down Stall Street, heading south at a smart lick that made the woollen skirts of her dress billow and flap. Tucked under her arm was a bulging jute sack, which Rachel recognised at once. Her heart picked up with some nameless excitement, and without thought she left the apple seller and made after Starling as quickly as she could. This girl had spoken the only kind words about Alice Beckwith that Rachel had yet heard, and she found herself wanting to hear more. Then she remembered the humiliating way the cook at Lansdown Crescent had treated her, and found herself equally keen to know the purpose of the bag of stolen food. The girl was easy to spot in the weaving mass of people, but she moved quickly, straight-backed and with her chin jutting out in front of her, like a challenge to the world; Rachel almost had to run to keep up with her. Her pattens made her clumsy on the cobbles, and she skidded as she hurried along.

At the bottom of Stall Street Starling didn't pause, carrying on into Horse Street and then over the river via the old bridge. There she slowed, and turned to the east, to where the river curled northwards and the canal branched off it. She seemed to search amongst the boats and barges there. Rachel waited in the shadow of the bridge, and then followed at a safe distance. The wharf side was all mud and filth; her feet sank so deeply that she felt it seeping through the seams of her shoes, in spite of her pattens. The smell of the river was foul, even with the weather as cold as it had been; a dank, fishy reek, with putrefaction at its heart. Rachel took shallow breaths, following as discreetly as she could as Starling went along the wharf, speaking to the boatmen in turn. *She means to sell her stolen goods, then?*

It was mostly men, down on the wharves; men working and talking and making deals; spitting, eating bread from dirty handkerchiefs and swigging from bottles. A few gaudy young women loitered here and there, with messy hair and smudged rouge on their faces. They smiled and called out to the workers, and with a jolt Rachel realised that they were whores. She suddenly noticed some of the men giving her curious, measuring looks, and one of them grinned a mouthful of ruined brown teeth at her. Rachel pulled her shawl tighter around her neck, and kept her eyes down. She almost turned to flee back over the bridge, back to safety, but her nameless, insistent curiosity was stronger. Starling had stopped to speak to one man aboard a barge. A thick-legged patchwork horse stood by patiently, harnessed to the craft, and Rachel crept closer, straining her ears to hear what they were saying. Their breath steamed around them, pale in the torchlight.

'That's too much – come now, it's a short enough distance,' Starling told the bargeman, who was wizened and dirty. In the darkness it was hard to make out what his boat carried, but from the looks of him, Rachel guessed it was coal.

'I needn't carry the likes of you at all, if I so choose,' the man pointed out, but his face wore half a smile.

'You're a rogue, Dan Smithers. A penny, then, and a song as we go.'

'A penny, and a taste of your lips.'

'A song is all you'll get from my lips, or I'll gut you with your own hook. Take it or leave it.' Starling put her hand on her hip, and the bargeman laughed.

'I bet you would, an' all. Hop aboard then, for I'm behind time leaving as 'tis.' Starling tucked the sack under her arm and jumped lightly onto the deck. Dan Smithers called out to his horseman, and the animal threw its weight into the harness. The barge eased away towards the mouth of the canal, from where it would pass beneath the pretty iron bridges of Sydney Gardens, and then out of the city. Starling settled herself down on top of the cargo, and as the boat vanished into darkness Rachel heard her voice, surprisingly sweet, drifting back over the water, singing a sad song about lost love.

Not selling the food then, but taking it somewhere – to someone? Resigning herself to not knowing, Rachel hurried back from the waterside, over the bridge and away from the bald, ugly stares of the river men. Against the pale yellow horizon, the black skeletons of trees stood stark on distant hills, and Rachel was suddenly saddened by her own curiosity about the red-haired girl, by the urge she'd felt to take part in her life, when she had no business to. She walked quickly back to Abbeygate Street, and only once she was standing in front of the shop, looking up at the lit parlour window that told her Richard had come home, did she realise that she didn't want to go inside. She stood on the pavement, staring up stupidly, as if she had any other option. Richard might not necessarily be drunk, she reminded herself. He might be sweet, and tired, and tender for once. But he would want to lie with her, as he always did, and the prospect left her cold. *How else do you hope to get with child, then?* the echo voice chided her gently.

For a minute or two she stood on the pavement, and absurdly wished herself aboard the barge with Starling, drifting steadily out of the city, rather than going into her home, and to her husband's bed. The servant girl always moved with a purpose; always had a steely gleam in her eye. She was not cowed, even when Rachel caught her thieving. *Whereas I am constantly cowed. By my husband, by Josephine Alleyn, and her son. And her cook.* Rachel's shoulders sagged wearily at the thought. And as she stood there, she remembered something

Starling had said to her earlier that day. *She was too good for this world.* She remembered the serving girl's obvious grief, and the significance of the words became plain to her. *Starling believes that Alice Beckwith is dead.* Rachel had a sudden strange feeling in the pit of her stomach, like a warning, and she waited a while longer in the street, trying to decipher it. But the night breeze bit at her fingers, and the streets were emptier now, and she could not linger for ever. So she squared her shoulders, and lifted her chin like Starling did, and went inside to Richard.

His mood was light and affectionate, and Rachel felt some of her anxiety dissipate. Richard took her hand and smiled as she came in, and led her to sit with him on the sofa. He had closed the shutters, and banked up the fire; the room was close and cosy with warmth and low light.

'How are you, my dear Mrs Weekes?' he said, leaning his head back to look at her. With the firelight glowing on his skin and hair, and curving into the contours of his face, he was angelic. It was hard to imagine the angry way he sometimes spoke to her. *There is a beast in all men;* that was what Jonathan Alleyn had said. But he had been speaking about himself, and Rachel refused to believe it.

'I am well, Mr Weekes. How was business today?'

'It was brisk, and that's good. More and more families arrive every day now, for the season, and thanks to word of mouth, and most especially word of Mrs Alleyn's mouth, my new Bordeaux is much in demand, as is a sweet rose port, lately in from Lisbon.'

'That is excellent news, indeed.'

'It is all happening, Rachel. Just as I'd hoped . . . I have you, the best wife I could wish for, and my business grows . . . The house is transformed by you, come alive. And soon we will have a finer place, not one over the shop . . . a house we can fill with children.' He smiled, and put one hand to the side of her face. His fingers smelled of wood dust and wine-steeped cork, and Rachel shut her eyes, leaning into him.

'Yes. I should like that very much.'

Richard's other hand came to rest on her belly, warm and heavy. His touch was somehow proprietary and reverent at the same time, and this time she welcomed it.

'And what of you? How went your visit to the Alleyns today? Less upsetting than the last time, I hope?' he said.

'Yes, much less so.' Rachel thought of the awful things Jonathan Alleyn had said to her, and the way he snapped; the way his eyes filled with rage and pain at a moment's notice. And then she thought of the copper mouse, and how he'd fallen asleep to the sound of her voice. She was unsure what she wanted to say to Richard about it – he was so strange and volatile when it came to Mrs Alleyn and her son. 'He seemed content to be read to. I stayed perhaps an hour with him . . . and there were no mishaps, not like before.'

'That is excellent. Excellent, Rachel. And . . . you were paid?'

'I was not. Mrs Alleyn made no mention of it before I went up to her son, and afterwards . . . afterwards I could not find her. I saw only the servants. Speaking of which, I saw one of them just now, doing something rather peculiar.'

'Oh? Saw one of which?'

'The Alleyns' kitchen maid – the red-haired one, who I also saw at the inn on our wedding day. She helped me the first time I met Jonathan Alleyn – she helped me when I was attacked. But I saw her just now, taking a barge boat out of the city with food she had taken from the house.'

'How can you possibly know this?' Richard took his hands away from her, sitting forward slightly.

'I saw her. I saw her at the house, taking something – a bottle of ale. She was putting it into a sack, and then just now

I saw her taking that sack and boarding a barge on the canal . . . I'm certain of what I saw, and yet . . .'

'What?'

'When I tried to tell the cook about it, the woman would hear nothing of it. Do you think I ought to tell Mrs Alleyn?'

'No.' Richard rose abruptly and walked to the window, even though the shutters were closed. His back was poker straight, his arms folded.

'What? How no? Surely—'

'It is not your business!' Richard kept his back to her, speaking to the chipped paint and woodworm holes of the shutters. 'And it is scarcely any way to repay the wench if she did indeed help you.'

'I know. But, surely, if the girl is thieving . . . If she is being stolen from, Mrs Alleyn—'

'You told the cook, and that was dutiful. You need do nothing more. It is not your place to involve yourself in such things.' His voice was hard, flat. 'And how did you happen to be down at the river, to see this girl board a boat?'

'I . . . well, I saw her in the street, so I . . . followed her,' Rachel said reluctantly.

There was a silence. Richard turned to face her, and with a jolt of fear she saw the anger again, suffusing his face like a rising tide.

'I am sure there are better things you could do with your time than run around after serving girls, on business of their own that is none of yours. Wouldn't you agree?' he said softly.

'Yes, Richard.' Rachel blinked, and looked away. But after another pause, she could not help but speak again, could not help but try to explain herself. 'I only wanted to . . . confirm to myself, whether or not the girl was up to no good . . .'

'I will hear no more about it! You are to have nothing to do with the likes of Starling! Do you hear me, Rachel? You are to have *nothing* to do with her!' He ground the words out, and she could no more fathom the cause of his anger than she could think of a way to assuage it. When she opened her mouth nothing came out, and she was forced to try a second time.

'Yes, Mr Weekes. I understand it.' It was little more than a whisper. Richard gave a single curt nod, and strode to the foot of the stairs.

'I am to bed. Are you coming?' He held out a hand to her, one that trembled ever so slightly. *Is that just anger, or something else?* Rachel rose without a word, feeling like a fool who erred and knew not why. As he lay her down with impatience in every caress, Rachel realised that he'd named the girl. *Starling.* He'd known exactly who she'd been talking about, though he'd always professed ignorance when Rachel had mentioned the girl before. *He knows her.* For some reason, this realisation made her eyes fill, and she couldn't tell if they were tears of confusion, or pain, or anger. *There is a beast in all men.* She shut her eyes tight, and thought of the copper mouse; its little feet running, its bright and beady eyes. She thought about it all the while, until Richard was asleep and she could breathe again.

* * *

Jonathan Alleyn was so quiet in the days after Mrs Weekes's visit that Starling began to worry. His black mood, his state of disarray, was like a downward spiral that once halted could be hard to jerk back into motion. She wanted him weak, and vulnerable, and restless. She *needed* him to be so, because that was all that mattered to her. It was all she could do. So she spent the day wondering how to torment him, and decided that she needed to start, as she ever did, by making him drink. Plain wine was not strong enough; she needed something else. Once he began drinking, he would fall back into despair. She thought of Dick Weekes, and the way he had brushed her aside. *For that pale cow, who has helped not a jot.* Starling ground her teeth, and refused to be thwarted. She'd been peeling potatoes; when they were done she swept the skins into her apron and carried them out to the midden, then went downstairs, right down into the bones of the house, where the leaching damp caused the stone walls to powder and weep green mould.

Before, Dick had doctored the wine for Jonathan with some clear, tasteless spirit he got in from Russia; she didn't know what it was called, or where she could come by more. The remnants of the house's wine stock was laid down in the low, cramped cellar beneath the kitchen. The front few racks had some newer bottles, supplied by Dick, but further away from the foot of the stairs were racks holding odd relics – bottles left by residents from a previous time. A time when the house was alive and occupied; when there might have been guests for dinner, and card parties, and small dances in the front parlour sometimes. The sawdust on the floor had rotted down to a hard mat that smelled of fungus and made Starling's eyes itch. She searched for something she could add to his wine without spoiling the taste of it, but there was only some ancient brandy, which stank to high heaven when she pulled the cork. She put it back in disgust, and went up to the still room. There was proof spirit there, used by her and Sol for making lemon water and spirit of peppermint. She uncorked the bottle, but hesitated. *If he should keel over dead . . .* That's what Dick had said. *He will not, surely?* Starling stayed frozen a moment more, caught in an agony of indecision. Then she took a tiny sip from the bottle. It scorched her tongue, made her cough and spit. She restoppered the bottle and hung her head in defeat.

She went down to the Moor's Head, but Sadie was cross and tired, and had no time to listen to her. Starling glanced around for familiar faces, but the only ones she saw belonged to people she had no wish to speak to. So she left again, and walked slowly along the street until she came to the foot of the abbey, a vast hulk of medieval architecture that dwarfed the new townhouses surrounding it, like a bear sleeping amidst cats. She gazed up at the carvings around the doorway; the massive Gothic window above. There was a stone ladder on the right-hand side of the façade, with tiny angels climbing its many, many rungs. *That is like life*, Starling thought. *An endless ladder, and sometimes it is too hard to keep climbing.* Suddenly, she felt very small. She felt small, and lost, and unbelievably tired, standing in the dark at the foot of the huge building. She swayed, and for a second she was seven years old again, starving and beaten, standing outside the farmhouse at Bathampton, too weak to take the final step towards it. The city rushed around her in a giddy blur, she tottered, and would have fallen if strong arms hadn't stopped her, appearing from nowhere to catch her under her arms.

Bewildered, Starling twisted around and found Richard Weekes looking down at her with a strange expression on his face. The starry sky wheeled behind him, the buildings and street were a blur, and for a moment his face was the only thing she could see, the only thing that made sense. With a cry, she threw her arms around his neck, and held on to him tightly. An inexplicable sob made her chest clench painfully. After a moment, Dick disengaged her arms, his fingers gripping tightly when she tried to hold on to him.

'Leave off, Starling!' he said, with a shove that made her stumble again.

'Dick, I—' Starling broke off, and shook her head to clear it. For an awful moment, she'd been about to declare her need for him.

'What are you doing, standing here mooning up at the abbey at this time in the evening?'

'I was just . . . I was walking back. It's none of your business what I do, is it?' She took a deep breath to steady herself, drew back her shoulders and ignored the treacherous little voice inside her head that said: *Let him want me again. Let him.* But though Dick did reach out to her then, it was to take her arm in a painful grip and give it an angry wrench.

'It is my business when what you do involves my *wife.*'

'What are you talking about? Let go!' Starling pulled against him, but it only made him hold her tighter.

'I'm talking about the way my wife keeps having cause to mention you. She's seen you here, she's seen you there; you've helped her with Mr Alleyn, she's seen you stealing, and taking a barge out of the city . . . what in hell are you playing at? I *told* you to stay away from her!'

'What? She's seen me do what?' Starling frowned in confusion. 'I'd have nothing to do with her if it were up to me! How is it my fault if she comes creeping around the Alleyns' house? If she spies, and follows? How can I help that? It was *you* that brought her to meet them, *you* that brought her into my way!'

Richard paused, and seemed to think, but he did not let her go. Starling's arm was going numb where he held it; a tear slid down her cheek and she hoped he would not see it in the darkness.

'Why were you watching her? Why were you in the room when she met Mr Alleyn?' he said at last.

'It was a good job I was, or he might have killed her! Haven't I always told you what he's like? He's a *murderer*, as she nearly found out first hand—'

'You're up to something, Starling, and I want to know what it is. Speak.'

'Are you drunk? Leave off!' Starling tried to twist away but Richard caught her other arm as well, and shook her.

'Speak! Are you trying to turn her against me? Have you

spoken to her about me, about us? If you have, I swear, I shall—'

'I've said nothing! As little as I can! It's *her* that seeks me out!'

'I don't believe you. You knew of her visit to Jonathan Alleyn – her first visit. You knew to spy on them . . . what was the meaning of it? I will hear it, Starling, or I will have your teeth out . . .' He spoke vehemently, with his face thrust into hers; flecks of spittle flew from his lips to land on her. *He spits on me now, like this, when just weeks ago it was kisses that left such traces on my skin.*

'There's something . . . there's something about her you don't know. That you can't know . . .' Starling said reluctantly. He shook her again.

'What?' The word fell hard, like a blow.

'She looks . . . she looks just like Alice. Alice Beckwith.'

'What are you talking about?'

'Your Rachel Weekes looks just like Alice Beckwith! My mistress, slain by Jonathan Alleyn!' Starling swallowed, breathing hard. 'That's why he near killed her.'

There was a moment of stillness then. Starling waited, trying to ignore the pain in her arms; Richard stared into her face and some unreadable expression smothered his anger for a second. But only for a second. He released Starling, pushing her away so hard that she staggered. Then he laughed a bitter, joyless laugh that echoed across the square.

'Alice Beckwith!' he cried, and then laughed again, throwing his head back and appealing to the heedless sky. 'I will hear no more about Alice bloody Beckwith! Dear God, Starling, you have plagued me with her so much her very name sets my teeth on edge!'

'You wanted to know the reason they invited her back, and the reason he flew at her, and the reason they have arranged to keep her visiting . . . well, there is the reason.

You wanted it and I've given it to you. Alice Beckwith. Mrs Weekes is the spit and image of his lost sweetheart. Now you have the truth of it don't harp on at me if you like it not,' said Starling. Dick ran his hands through his hair and down over his face, then folded his arms and glared at her.

'I know how Mrs Alleyn feels about that girl – the Beckwith girl . . . What reason could she possibly have to encourage her son in his obsession?'

'She thinks it will help him, in the long run. For he has a visitor now at least, some link to the outside world. If she must put up with Mrs Weekes's face to get him that, then it seems she is willing to.' Again, Richard paused to think.

'And you knew of this – you knew of this likeness from your first sight of my wife.'

'Of course. It was like seeing the dead walk. She chilled my blood, truth be told; though your wife is older, of course, and not as fair.'

'You saw her first of all, at our wedding feast. Did you . . . did you have anything to do with our invitation to Lansdown Crescent? With me being asked to present my wife to Mrs Alleyn?'

'Well, you didn't think it was through any merit of *yours*, did you?' said Starling, recklessly. Richard clamped his jaw shut and looked away. In the dark, she couldn't see the blush she was sure would be mottling his skin. She swallowed, and felt her tenderness towards him coming on in the guise of regret, and shame for mocking him. She raised a hand to touch his arm but thought better of it. 'Dick, I'm sorry. I didn't mean . . .'

'Didn't mean what?' His voice was cold.

'I didn't mean to . . . keep this from you. But you broke with me, and told me to speak no more about Alice . . . I only wanted to see if . . . to see if seeing her brought out some confession in him. In Mr Alleyn. I thought that if he saw her, he would—'

'You're behind it all, then? This is all *your* plan? And what is that plan? Do you intend him to fall in love with my wife? For her to betray me for that mad cripple? Is that how you plan to be reunited with me?'

'What? Are you simple? No, as I said, I only—'

The blow caught her off guard; it came backhanded, across her right cheek, and it knocked her to the ground. The world spun around her again; she tasted blood in her mouth. She grazed the heels of her hands against the filthy flagstones of the abbey square, and could feel grit in the cuts, stinging. Fury made her forget her fear and she glared up at Richard, baring her teeth as she struggled to rise.

'Stay, or I will knock you down again.' Richard held his knuckles in front of her face in warning, so Starling sank back to her knees, chest heaving, eyes snapping with rage. 'Now hear this – you will not approach my wife. You will not speak to my wife. You will mind your business and your tongue, and you will say *nothing* of Alice Beckwith to her. If she learns about it, then I will know where she got it from. I will not have you infect her with your madness, Starling.' He stepped back and looked down at her coldly. For a second, Starling thought he would kick her. She braced herself to dodge it but he only turned and walked away, boot heels pounding the stones.

Just then a party of young people walked into the square, chattering and laughing, and Starling silently thanked them for driving him off. She began to rise but her legs were watery and weak. So she stayed there, and wrapped her arms around her knees, feeling the freezing ground numb her skin through her skirts. Her head was throbbing from the knock he'd given her, and she found one of her back teeth loose, wobbling in the bloody gum. She laid her left cheek against her hands, and stared into the shadows at the foot of the abbey. *But Rachel Weekes already knows about Alice.* She resolved to avoid Richard Weekes from then on. It would mean no more visits to the Moor's Head, or to Sadie. *Where then shall I go?* Silent stone faces stared down at her from the abbey walls, and gave her no answers. Her breath steamed in the moonlight. *This ladder is too tall for me.* She stayed a long time, and lost herself in reverie. She thought of sunshine and soft hands; she thought of the lovers' tree.

1808

It was during the last summer of Alice's life that Starling discovered the lovers' tree. She was out with Bridget, running errands in Bathampton on a warm, lazy sort of day in July; soft white clouds sat sedately in a powder-blue sky. The housekeeper was getting leaner and wirier with each season that passed; she carried her basket over an arm that was nothing but bone and sinew beneath freckled, weathered skin. There was more grey than brown in her hair, and her face had started to sink inwards, hollowing out between the bones of cheek and jaw. But this paring down only seemed to make Bridget tougher, and quicker. She walked with smart steps, and was terse with all the shopkeepers and craftsmen they dealt with, not stopping to gossip when Starling wanted to dawdle and look around her.

She especially wanted to dawdle around the butcher's shop, in spite of the iron stink of blood and offal, because Pip Blayton, the butcher's son, was just a year older than her at thirteen, and she found herself curious about him. Pip was tall for his age, and his shoulders were starting to widen. He looked like he'd been stretched; his body was long and clumsy, but his face was nice, in spite of the pimples that scattered his forehead. He had sandy hair that he hid behind whenever Starling looked at him, dipping his chin so that it fell over his forehead as heat torched his cheeks. Even though Starling was still small she had tiny, budding breasts and a slight curve in her hips that hadn't been there before. Her face was still her face, but it was subtly different, changing in tiny ways that made it more of a woman's face, less of a child's. Starling liked to see Pip blush; she liked to watch him trying to ignore her. And when she smiled at him, Bridget gave her such a censorious look that it made her smile wider.

'Who are you, Grinagog, the cat's uncle? You mind where you flash that rantipole smile of yours, Starling. You'll get yourself in trouble, soon enough,' Bridget said, as they carried on away from the shop.

'What kind of trouble?' Starling was deeply curious about this.

'Never you mind.'

'If I knew what kind, maybe I would know how to stay out of it?' she pointed out.

'If you knew what kind, you'd rush into it ever the quicker. I know you too well, my girl,' said Bridget, which only made Starling even more curious.

After five years with Alice and Bridget, there was a good deal Starling was curious about. The farmhouse and the village of Bathampton were her whole world, and however much she loved that world, it had begun to seem a little small. She often thought wistfully of Corsham, and the fair Jonathan had taken them to the year before. She wanted to feel that excitement again, that sense of belonging to a loud and colourful throng of people. Sometimes, Starling walked the other way along the canal – west, towards Bath. It was only two miles to the edge of the city. She walked until she could see its rooftops and crescents, and there she would stop and stare, watching ribbons of smoke rise from a thousand chimneys; seagulls wheeling around the markets and middens; church spires thrusting up towards heaven here and there; and the huge towers of the abbey. On days when a soft west wind was blowing, it carried the faint rattle of hooves and cartwheels on cobbled streets, and the yell of men's voices along the wharf. The city seemed like a huge and wonderful mêlée after the sedate, ordered pace of things in Bathampton. It was almost frightening, but at the same time deeply compelling.

But when Starling asked Alice if they could go into Bath on a visit, Alice's face always fell. She tried again, one spring day when they had both walked far to the west, along the river, and were gazing at the clustered buildings of the city together.

'I should like to, Starling. But Lord Faukes says we should not,' Alice said.

'But . . . why not?'

'I cannot say, dearest. He says he thinks it would be too great a strain on me. On my heart.' Alice looked down at her hands, at her fingers, which were slowly shredding a posy of bluebells. 'And that the city is no place for innocent young girls. So perhaps because it's more that we would have no escort, no acquaintances . . .'

'But . . . couldn't he take us with him one day? Or Mr Alleyn?'

'I have asked.' For a moment impatience made her words clipped, but then Alice hung her head and her voice lowered to almost nothing. She looked ashamed. 'But I'm afraid the answer is no.' She took Starling's hand and squeezed it apologetically, and Starling didn't understand what Alice could possibly have to be ashamed of. They stood in silence for a while, and Starling thought hard about what she would say next.

'Well, we need not tell them. It's an easy enough distance to walk – it wouldn't take long. We could go, you and I, and explore, and say nothing to Lord Faukes, or to Jonathan, though I'm sure Jonathan would not betray us.' Alice smiled slightly, but then her face fell serious.

'Of course Jonathan would not betray us. But you would have us deliberately disobey the man who keeps us? The man who let me take you in, when he had no cause to other than kind indulgence?'

'But . . . we went to Corsham fair last year, and that we kept a secret from him. Wasn't that disobedient too?'

'Yes, perhaps it was, but he had never specifically said to me that I should not go to Corsham, as he has with Bath.'

'But he would never hear of it, Alice—'

'But we would have done it, nevertheless. We would be the betrayers, don't you see? And we would always know it. And besides . . . the chickens always come home to roost, as our good Bridget would say. A lie will always come back to haunt you. If somebody should see us, and word of our disobedience reach Lord Faukes , , , well then, how kindly do you think he would feel towards us? We who owe him our home and our food and our well-being?' She smiled faintly at the look of sullen disappointment on Starling's face; leant over to kiss her forehead. 'Don't pull such a cross-patch face, Starling! What is there in Bath that we do not have here, in Bathampton?'

'I don't know! That's why I want to go! Why must you always be so obedient to him? How can you not want to explore—'

'I am obedient because I would have a roof over our heads – yours and mine!' Alice said angrily. Starling blinked, stunned. It was the first time Alice had ever raised her voice to her. 'Of course I want to explore – of course I want to go abroad, and go to dances, and make new friends! But I am told I may not, and I have no choice but to obey. Don't you understand that?'

'He would not be so very angry, would he?' Starling mumbled.

'Would you care to chance it?' said Alice, fixing her with a warning gaze.

'Maybe.' Starling shrugged, half rebellious, half cowed.

'Well, when you are older, and independent of us, you may go where you please,' Alice said flatly, and Starling halted her argument at once, because this spoke of a time when she would not always be at Alice's side, and she did not want to hear of such a time.

Starling kicked the heads off a few blameless dandelions by her feet, and could not look at her sister. She felt a horrible kind of embarrassment to be scolded in such a way, and searched for some way to make things normal again.

'Alice . . . why is Lord Faukes your benefactor?' she asked, as lightly as she could. 'I mean, what happened to your real parents? Who were they?' Alice turned her head to look north, across the river towards Box and Batheaston. A soft breeze blew wisps of her hair around her chin, and fluttered the blue ribbon of her hat.

'I don't know, Starling,' she said, her voice soft and sad.

'Haven't you asked him?'

'Of *course* I've asked him,' she said, exasperated, and Starling sensed some hard kernel beneath Alice's decorum for the first time; some hungry thing too long ignored. 'He says my father was an old friend of his, a man he loved. My mother died and . . . in his grief my father would have given me away to strangers, and so Lord Faukes took me and kept me safe, and found Bridget to look after me. And then my father also died . . .' She turned to look at Starling, wistfully. 'Whoever they were, they are dead. Of that much I am sure. And I must have been a source of shame to my family, must I not, to be kept in ignorance even of my parents' names, so that I may never try to find their kin? My kin.'

'Are you a secret, then?' said Starling, scowling in thought.

'Of course I am. Have you only just realised?' Alice smiled bitterly. 'Jonathan is not even allowed to speak about me to his mother. Lord Faukes has forbidden it.'

'But why would he, Alice?'

'Don't you see, Starling? The only person who could tell me is Lord Faukes, and he will not. And if I demand to know, I risk his displeasure. So I am trapped. I will never know, and I must endeavour to be content at that.'

'Perhaps . . . perhaps when you come of age some bequest of your father's will come into effect, and you will find it all out, and have a fortune and a great house.'

'It is a pleasant enough story, dearest. But let us not pin our hopes too highly upon it.'

'But when you are one and twenty, you will be free to leave his care anyway, won't you?'

'If I choose it, yes. But where would I go, Starling? What would I do? I have nothing. I know nobody outside of Bathampton.'

'You have Jonathan,' Starling pointed out, doggedly.

'Yes. I have Jonathan. I have only Jonathan,' Alice said quietly, and then they walked back to the farmhouse in silence.

In the darkness late that evening came footsteps and the glow of a candle flame around the bedroom door, and Starling was awoken, and padded silently towards it to listen. The floorboards were cold beneath her bed-warmed feet; she pulled her nightdress tight around her. On the landing were Bridget in her night cap and Alice with her hair tied up in rags. The candle was in Alice's hand, held between them, lighting their faces from below so that their eyes looked hollow and unearthly.

'Why does he keep me here, Bridget? Who am I to him?' said Alice. Bridget's mouth was a tight, flat line; at her sides her arms hung tense and uneasy.

'You're his ward, miss. You're kept here in comfort, and in safety, and lucky for it.'

'Safety from what? And why am I his ward, and kept secret? Who were my parents?'

'That I cannot tell you.'

'Cannot? Or will not?' Alice pressed. Bridget said nothing, and Alice gazed at her with little hope or expectation. 'Where does the name Beckwith come from? My father, or my mother? Or is it a fiction, like everything else? I have asked in the village, I have asked people passing through, for years and years. Nobody has heard of that name, here or anywhere else.'

'It is your name. Be content with it.'

'Be content?' There was an incredulous pause. 'Are you his, Bridget, or are you mine?' Alice whispered.

'I am both,' said Bridget, and in her voice was some pent-up emotion, something that twisted in pain like a fish on a hook.

'I think I'm like a bird kept in a silver cage. Something charming for him to look upon, and even to love. But something owned, that will never have its own destiny, or the freedom it was born with.'

'Not all are born into freedom, Alice. Perhaps it is better to appreciate the silver cage, when others have a cage of mud and sticks.'

'A cage is still a cage, Bridget,' Alice said coldly. Starling held her breath, but they said nothing more. Alice went back downstairs, though it was bedtime, and Bridget stood for a long while, not knowing she was watched. Her mouth stayed in its tight, flat line, and her eyes gazed out through the wall of the house, into the far distance. Her face was as empty as a broken heart, and though Starling wanted to hold her, at the same time she knew she must never let on that she'd seen the older woman in a moment of such profound and terrible nakedness.

In the end, Alice's twenty-first birthday came and went

with no visits from lawyers or uncles or executors of hidden wills. Only Lord Faukes came, with gifts of white kid gloves and a beautiful evening gown of turquoise silk overlaid with the finest silver lace any of the three women had ever seen. A ball dress that Alice would have no occasion to wear. Lord Faukes bade her try it on, and she dutifully twirled and posed for him, and even danced with him a little on the parlour floor, though there was no music and he looked grotesque as her partner – too old, too fat. In his meaty hands Alice was doll-like, so fragile he might destroy her on a whim. Lord Faukes's face shone with pleasure at seeing her in the dress. Alice smiled and said again and again how much she loved it, but Starling still noticed the look of bitter disappointment behind her eyes, and the way her smile fell at once from her face when her benefactor's back was turned.

'Perhaps they don't know how to find you, and will come a little late with news?' Starling whispered into the darkness of their bedroom that night, when she could tell Alice was not sleeping.

'Nobody is trying to find me, Starling,' Alice replied, and Starling didn't argue because she thought it was probably true.

'Then we are sisters more than ever, Alice, because we are both cut off from the people who had us as babes, and our pasts are secrets that we shan't ever know about. But we are our own family, are we not?'

'We are our own family,' Alice agreed, but Starling could not tell from her voice what Alice was feeling.

On the sunny July day, a year after that, once Bridget had hustled Starling away from Pip Blayton at the butcher's shop, the pair of them walked past the George Inn and along the lane that eventually crossed the river and went on to Batheaston.

'We've to pay the miller for that flour he delivered on Monday. I didn't have the coins about me when he called,' said Bridget, when Starling asked.

'I can do it, if you want. You don't need to walk all the way with me,' said Starling, who loved the freedom to dawdle. Bridget was flushed and breathing deeply, so she paused and gave Starling a shrewd look through screwed-up eyes.

'You'll give Miller Harris the money, and nobody else, and no going back to make calf eyes at Pip Blayton?'

'Of course!' said Starling, with an almost straight face. Bridget rolled her eyes and hefted her basket higher up her arm. She fished some coins from her pocket, handing them to Starling.

'There, then. Go on and take it to him, and mind you hurry back. Good girl.' She gave Starling a nod and a purse of her lips, which was as close as Bridget generally came to smiling. On light feet, Starling carried on alone.

The bridge marched across the wide span of the River Avon on hefty stone arches. The water was deep and clear; its bed was cloaked with vibrant green weeds which wafted in the current, sheltering trout and perch and other fish. On the far side, coming from Batheaston, there was a toll house where a man with a face full of grog-blossoms sat and sipped brandy all day long, collecting coins from those who wished to cross. Starling hung over the parapet and watched the mill's huge wheel turning, throwing up jewels of sunlit water and a sodden, river-bottom smell of wood and minerals and muddy life. The slap and splash of it was hypnotic. Starling stared, the sun hot on the back of her head, until Miller Harris popped his head out and shouted at her. She paid him Bridget's coins and sauntered back over the bridge, stopping on the home side, facing west, to look for fish and throw in a few pebbles from the dusty lane. She almost didn't see Alice against the blinding brilliance of the sunlit water. Starling shaded her eyes with one hand, and looked again.

The figure was perhaps three hundred feet from the bridge, by the water's edge where the bank dropped steeply from the meadow. In the dappled shade along the bank it was hard to see her, but Starling was sure it was Alice. Nobody else was so lathy slim, had hair so arrestingly pale, or wore a dress the colour of lavender. Alice was picking her way gingerly along the water line, using the gnarled tree roots as stepping stones and the low branches as handholds. She stopped when she reached one tree, a weeping willow which snagged the shining water with its silvery tendrils. As she stepped beneath its branches, Starling lost sight of her. She moved a little further along the bridge to find a better vantage point, but from no angle could she see through the willow's draping leaves. Then, a moment later, she saw Alice emerge again, going back along the bank to the spot where she could climb up to the meadow. As she reached open ground, Alice looked around, as if to check for observers. Starling thought about waving to her but something stopped her, and instead she sank a little lower behind the stone parapet.

Starling knew she ought to go back to the farmhouse. Bridget would know she was dawdling, and would want help with the cleaning and their lunch. Alice had been heading that way; Starling could ask her what she'd been doing on the river-bank. A farm wagon pulled by heavy horses came rumbling over the bridge just then, so Starling had to move. But she didn't go straight home; she climbed over the fence and picked her way down through the trees to the meadow-marsh. The bank dropped four feet straight down to the water's edge but Starling was bolder and more nimble than Alice. She clambered down through the roots of the weeping willow, grasping at handfuls of snaking, whip-like branches, until her feet landed with a squelch in the mud where the water was lapping.

The tree's trunk had split into two early in its life; the partition began just a foot or so above the ground. The two parts of it had wrapped around one another, twisting tight together. Its bark was rough but looked as supple as skin; the trunks locked like mighty arms in a perpetual, sinuous embrace. The drooping branches shielded Starling all around, and turned the light a fresh green; it felt private, magical, like a fairy dell. Just above her head, Starling saw a dark crack between the two trunks. Some animal or disease had caused a narrow opening to form, a slight gape between the loving arms. Then Starling saw the carving, just beneath the opening. It was not new; the bark had healed and swollen around the cuts, so that they sat deep in the wood. Six or seven years' growth at least, Starling estimated, since the cuts were made. *Before I was even here. When I was still . . . wherever I was before.* It was a simple carving: two initials, *J & A*. The middle symbol had been carved with curving flourishes, so that it touched on both of the letters, joining them up. Starling's heart quickened with some strange emotion. She reached up, and slid her hand into the hollow.

She groped around inside, flinching as she felt an insect hurry away from her intruding fingers. There was a square of folded paper inside, and with her heart bumping even harder, Starling drew it out and opened it. There, in Alice's neat script, were the words: *Sunday, after church, before noon. My love.* Starling felt a jolt in her stomach, and there seemed to be a little hitch in the world, a little moment in which it stopped turning. She tried to swallow but her throat was dry. She folded the note back up, with fingers that shook, and then hesitated. She'd been about to put it back, but the same impulse that had stopped her waving to Alice now stopped her again. There were times, not many, when Jonathan came to visit the farmhouse with his grandfather; other times when he came to meet Alice and Starling somewhere, and Starling had always known that those meetings were to be kept secret from Bridget and Lord Faukes. Now it seemed that there were other visits, other meetings, of an even more secret kind. So secret that not even Starling could know of them. She sat down on a huge root protruding from the bank, noticing as she did so that the root had been worn smooth and clean by being sat upon many times before. Starling bit her lip in dismay, and with an angry little sound she started to cry.

She hated to cry; she almost never did. There was some latent memory in her, some buried knowledge of pain and fear so great that there had seemed nothing in the world worth crying over since then. But this betrayal cut with a poisoned blade. She wiped at her face and gulped and forced herself to stop. She had been included in their affair in so many ways – in their friendship, even in their letters, though Alice knew nothing of that; to find herself excluded from so much more was intolerable. Little cracks appeared in the very foundations of Starling's world, and she was suddenly afraid, horribly afraid; as though the cracks might gape open, swallow her down and cast her back to that time before the farmhouse, before Alice. Fear, anger, hurt; they swelled to a crescendo in the few short minutes Starling sat on the root beneath the willow tree. When they receded she felt calmer, and had a strange new hardness in her heart. She stood, and cast the note into the river. The water carried it swiftly away, twirling it, spinning it about. Starling watched until it slid out of sight, then she climbed back out into the sunshine and walked home with no one thought coming clearly to her mind.

Back at the farmhouse, Bridget was putting stuffed apples

into the oven, and hardly bothered to scold Starling for taking so long. A look was enough, weary and long-suffering.

'I'll fetch some angelica for the custard,' said Starling.

Alice was in the kitchen garden, sitting on a metal bench surrounded by rosemary and lavender, thyme and bay. She had her legs tucked underneath her and was reading a cloth-bound book of poems. She looked up and smiled as Starling came out to sit with her.

'And how are you, little sister?' she said with a smile. The sun made her eyes shine like the river. Starling nodded, and stayed mute. She couldn't seem to find any words to say. She sat on her hands on the edge of the bench, and kicked her legs back and forth, and could not look at Alice. 'Starling, what is it? What's wrong?' Alice laid down her book and reached out one hand to touch Starling's arm. For a second, Starling wavered, and felt treacherous tears prickling the top of her nose again. She wanted to demand to know why she had been excluded, not trusted, lied to. But then that new hardness seemed to get in the way. It sat at the top of her chest, like a plug, and stopped the words, the tears, from bubbling out. She glanced over and saw that Alice had kept one finger on the page she'd been reading. Marking it, ready to flip the book open and pick up again, as soon as Starling had stopped bothering her.

'Nothing,' she snapped, getting up from the bench. She bent, swiped up a handful of angelica flowers, and turned back to the kitchen door. 'Bridget needs me.'

Come Sunday the weather turned, bringing a warm, grey drizzle, solid from heaven to horizon as though the clouds had simply lowered themselves to ground level. The three residents of the farmhouse joined the villagers of Bathampton for the Sunday service in the ancient church of St Nicolas, and as they walked back along the canal, Starling watched

Alice carefully. There were pink spots in her cheeks, and her eyes were restless; she looked more animated than a person coming from an hour and a half in church should, but there was nothing else to give her away. Had Starling not known otherwise, she would never have guessed her sister had a secret, and this was another betrayal. This Alice seemed an entirely different person to the one in whom secrets fizzed uncontrollably, like the bubbles in beer.

'Did you hear Mrs Littlewood, calling us *the three birds from the hen house?*' she asked.

'Pay her no mind, Starling. She's a common scold, that one,' said Bridget.

'What does it mean, though?' Starling pressed.

'It means we haven't a man about the place, and it means she envies us, for she has Mr Littlewood to deal with and we all know what type of man *he* is,' Bridget muttered. Alice made no comment. The wet day made their hair and clothes hang limply. Alice had chosen a time when Starling and Bridget would be busy, preparing the Sunday meal. A time when she could slip away unnoticed, to walk or read, as she almost always did. How many of those times in the past, Starling thought now, had Alice in fact been keeping trysts with Jonathan?

As they returned to the house, unbuttoning coats and untying their hats, Alice paused.

'I might keep mine on, and walk on for a little while,' she said casually.

'Oh, can I come? I need to stretch my legs after sitting through that boring service,' said Starling.

'For shame, show more respect,' Bridget admonished her. 'I think the vicar gave an admirable sermon today . . . mind how you speak on the Lord's day.'

'Yes, Bridget. So, can I go with you, Alice? Please?'

Starling looked her straight in the eye, until Alice had to look away.

'Oh, but you hate the rain, dearest,' she said vaguely. 'And Bridget should not be all alone with so much work to be done.'

'It's not really raining . . . and you're only going a little way, you said.'

'I think . . .' Alice paused, fiddled with the front of her coat. 'I think you should be kind, and stay to help Bridget. I shan't be long.' She smiled sweetly enough at them, and then turned and wandered away without another word, pausing to wave from the gate.

'Mind you don't get soaked through, if the rain gets worse,' Bridget called after her.

'Or if it does, be sure to shelter under a tree!' Starling added, and had the unhappy satisfaction of seeing Alice's smile flicker.

Alice came back an hour later, damp, bedraggled and forlorn. Her hem was muddied and her face wore open disappointment, and at once Starling felt guilty to have made her sad. She thought of the little note, sailing heedlessly downstream towards Bath. 'Didn't you enjoy your walk?' she asked, and though she tried to sound easy, her voice was tight and wobbled slightly. Alice looked at her strangely.

'I enjoyed it well enough. The weather is perhaps . . . not the best,' Alice replied. Bridget grunted.

'Well, it weren't the best when you set out, so there's no shock in that,' she said, with a slight roll of her eyes.

'Indeed,' said Alice, with a small, strained laugh.

'Did you have to shelter under a tree?' Starling asked, and again that tightness was in her voice. Alice walked to the far side of the room and beckoned Starling over while Bridget's eyes were on the stove.

'You left your footprints in the mud, dearest,' she whispered, and Starling's guilty heart jumped into her throat.

'What do you mean? What mud? I never—' She broke off under Alice's steady, sad scrutiny.

'He did not come. I shan't see him now for weeks; he will be going to war soon and must stay with his company,' she said. Starling squirmed away from her blue eyes, from the hurt look in them. 'Starling, did you take my note?' she whispered. Starling said nothing; she only hung her head, shamefaced. Alice took a deep, unsteady breath. 'I know . . . I know why you might be angry with me,' she went on. 'I can explain why we had to keep everything secret, but not here, and not right now . . .'

'I . . . I don't know anything about a note.'

'Starling, please. Don't lie.' Alice spoke so softly, so sweetly, that Starling could hardly bear it. She thought of the lies Alice had told to her – lies of omission, lies of secrecy; all the years that had passed since she and Jonathan had carved their initials into the tree; all the times they had met, and kept it from her. Had kept their love – a special, better love – only for each other. She was so angry, so ashamed, it caused a pressure to build in the hard place inside her, as if the plug would not hold, and something would force its way out.

'It's not me who's the liar!' she cried, and Alice blinked in shock. Bridget looked up from the far end of the room.

'What's that? What are you two conspiring over, eh?' she called. Starling wheeled to face her, feeling off balance, almost frantic. She felt Alice's hand on her arm.

'Please, don't say anything!' Alice hissed. Her eyes were full of fear, and though Starling quailed, she could not stop herself.

'Alice has been meeting with Jonathan in secret! They're lovers! But he is engaged to Beatrice Fallonbrooke!' she blurted out. In the corner of her eye she saw Alice's hands fly to her mouth, her eyes going wide in horror. Bridget dropped her wooden spoon with a clatter, and stared at Alice with a terrible expression. Silence fell in the kitchen, and in it Starling was sure she could hear the cracks at her feet, the cracks in the world, opening even wider.

Rachel was ushered in to her next appointment with Jonathan Alleyn so quickly that she was still out of breath from the long climb up to Lansdown Crescent. The grassy slope in front of the buildings was still crisp and grey with frost where it sank into a shaded hollow; the sky was flat white with cloud, giving no clue as to where the sun might be. There was no breath of a breeze. Mrs Alleyn greeted Rachel at the foot of the stairs, as the butler took her hat, gloves and pelisse from her, and she smoothed the front of her dress. There was that same awkwardness between them, which Rachel was sure they both felt – of her being not quite a guest, not quite a servant. Neither one knew quite how to behave, nor was Rachel ever sure of the reception she would be given. The older woman was by turns warm then cold, stiff then easy, sharp then distant. Impossible to know.

'Perhaps you'll join me to talk for a moment, when you've finished your reading?' said Mrs Alleyn, as they turned to climb the stairs.

'It would be my pleasure,' Rachel replied. *And during that time I must somehow work out how to ask for my payment, or Mr Weekes will want to know why I have not.*

'I had hoped Jonathan would come down today, but . . .' Mrs Alleyn trailed off, apologetically.

'Men were ever stubborn, and wont to have things their own way.' Rachel smiled, to imply no criticism, but Mrs Alleyn's face went stiff.

'How right you are, Mrs Weekes,' she murmured.

Jonathan Alleyn didn't rise as she entered the room – he

hadn't before, and this simple omission put her on edge. She had never known a gentleman not rise for a lady's entrance; she didn't know if his failure to do so made him less the gentleman, or her less the lady. Jonathan had opened one fold of the shutters, and the window just a fraction, so that the frigid morning air drifted in. He wore only dark blue breeches and a white linen shirt, the sleeves of it rolled up. The fire had died in the hearth and the room was heavy with cold, scented with wood and the damp grass of the crescent. Rachel squared her shoulders and went over to him. She could see gooseflesh on his bare arms, but his face had a faint sheen of sweat, where it was not covered by several days' growth of whiskers. An empty wine bottle and a stained glass were on the floor beside him; the stale smell of his unwashed body hung about him.

'Mr Alleyn . . .' Rachel trailed off as he turned abruptly to look at her. He seemed to have trouble focusing his eyes. 'Are you well? You look feverish . . . It's so cold in here. Let me call for a servant to make up the fire—'

'No, leave it. I am too hot . . . only this cold is keeping me alive, I think,' he said, in a rough voice.

'But, if you have a fever, we must call a doctor to—'

'To bleed me? I have bled enough, Mrs Weekes. Please sit, and say no more on it. I am quite well.' Shivering slightly, Rachel complied. Jonathan's eyes followed her every move; they were the only lively thing in his gaunt face.

'I brought a book from home this time. It's the new poems by Keats . . . a wedding gift to me from my husband,' she said. 'And a selfless one, since I think he cares not one jot for poetry,' she added, more softly. *Perhaps my husband would prefer Byron.*

'Why would he, Mrs Weekes?'

'I beg your pardon, sir?'

'Why would Richard Weekes care for poetry? He is an

unlettered oaf, and a covetous fool, for all his pretty face. Or, at least, he was when I last knew him.' Jonathan took a deep breath and sat up straighter in his chair. He propped his elbows on the arms of it, steepled his long fingers in front of his mouth. His nails were bitten and ragged.

'Well, I . . . I suppose a person might change, and improve,' Rachel murmured. Only a few weeks ago she would have leapt to Richard's defence. Now it seemed loyalty enough to say as little as possible about him.

'They might. But such improvements tend to be skin deep only, in my experience. Tell me, how came you to be married to him?'

'How do you imagine, sir?' said Rachel, with some asperity. 'We met at the house of my former employers. I was governess in Sir Arthur Trevelyan's household, at Hartford Hall. Mr Weekes and I met when he came to discuss wine with Sir Arthur . . .' She thought back to that moment, the moment she'd seen love storm through Richard like an invading army. It gave her a strange pang almost like nostalgia, or perhaps regret.

'And it seemed a good match to you? You who are clearly educated, and have been raised a gentlewoman . . .'

'Aye, sir, it seemed a good match. I would scarcely have consented to wed if it had not.'

'I'm curious, that's all. I would understand more of the ways women think, if I could. More of the reasons why they act the way they do.' He gave her a tiny, wintery smile.

'Not all women act in the same way,' Rachel pointed out, carefully.

'No indeed, though everything they do has the one thing in common – that it is unfathomable to me.'

'What about the situation is hard for you to understand, Mr Alleyn?' Rachel felt tension clipping her words.

'Well, you cannot love him. I wonder what, then, made

him seem a good match, when he is . . . what he is, and you have all the semblance of a lady. Was it simply his handsome face?'

'I'm not a child, Mr Alleyn, to be so confused by good looks. A good many years have passed since you were . . . out in society. Perhaps a good many things have changed since then. And he loves me . . .'

'Does he? Truly?' Jonathan leant forwards in his chair with sudden intensity.

'Yes!' She thought of Richard's anger, of the way he sometimes spoke to her; his unwanted touch, and the way her body had begun to recoil from it. She hoped none of it showed in her face.

'And do you love him?'

The question hung in the air between them, and Rachel felt a flush begin to spread up from her neck. The choice was between truth and loyalty, between integrity and propriety, and it was not one she knew how to make.

'You cannot ask me such things,' she said at last, quietly. Again came his fleeting smile, as cold as the crystals of frost on the window glass.

'Your reticence is answer enough. And here I am torn – for I could not have admired you for loving such a man, yet nor can I admire you for marrying beneath you, when you did not love him . . .' Humiliation made Rachel angry.

'Why should it matter whether you admire me or not, Mr Alleyn?' she said stiffly. 'When we first met you told me that all women are whores, be it for coin, status or safety that we sell ourselves.'

'Did I say as much?' Jonathan leant back, his eyes sliding away uncomfortably. 'I can't remember it.'

'But you stand by it, perhaps? Well, ask yourself this, sir, if it is true: what *choice* does a woman have but to settle herself somehow, for one of those three things?'

'And which one made you settle, Mrs Weekes?'

'It is none of your concern. Your mother pays me to come here and read to you, and that is what I shall do.'

'Whether I will it or not?'

'Do you wish me to leave?'

'Far be it from me to thwart another of my mother's *great* plans.' He leant back with a scathing wave of his hand.

'You are too kind, sir,' said Rachel, stung, in spite of herself. Jonathan watched her steadily for a moment, through narrowed eyes. Then he blinked, and his eyes softened.

'Forgive me,' he said curtly.

In the uncomfortable silence that followed, the sound of children's laughter drifted up through the window from the street below. Clearing her throat, Rachel began to read. As often happened, she soon got lost in the words, in the beauty and intensity of the images they conjured, and time passed rapidly, without her noticing. She felt a deep sense of calm, of being outside of herself, and of the world. Her heartbeat was slow and steady until Jonathan interrupted her, as she was halfway through 'La Belle Dame Sans Merci'.

'Enough. Please. Read something else,' he said hoarsely. Rachel returned to the cold gloomy room with a start, and to the thin, haunted figure sitting opposite her.

'You do not like the poem?'

'It speaks of things I have no wish to hear about. Enchantment, and betrayal . . .'

'But I have not yet read to the end, you will see that—'

'He is alone, is he not, and driven half mad by his love?'

'Well . . . yes. In truth,' Rachel admitted.

'No more of it, then. 'Tis a lie, that misery longs for company. The suffering of others does nothing to ease my own.'

'And what do you long for, sir?' she asked. Jonathan stared at her for a moment, as if bewildered by the question.

'I want what I cannot have. I want to unsee things I have seen, and undo things I have done . . .'

'And surely you know that can never be done? So another way must be found.'

'Another way?'

'A way to be at peace with what is past, and to . . . turn your back on it.'

'Really? Another way?' Jonathan laughed then, but it was a bitter sound. 'And if those things took the very heart and soul of you, and left only the brutish parts? What other way is there then?'

'No one but God can take your soul,' said Rachel.

'Aye, madam – God, or the devil.'

'You should not say such things. I'm certain—'

'No, you are not certain. You are naive, and inexperienced. Go now, and leave me in peace. I made no promise to hear a sermon.' He shut his eyes and pinched the bridge of his nose with his fingers. With anger making her hot in spite of the chill, Rachel stood and walked smartly over to the door, where she paused.

'I'm no child or servant, sir, to be commanded *stay* and *go*,' she said, her voice tight with emotion. 'Perhaps I know nothing of you, and what you have seen, but do not forget that the reverse is also true.' She shut the door behind her with greater force than was needed.

Josephine Alleyn was in the garden. The sun had burned through the low cloud and mist and was slanting down, touching the dying plants with a lemon-coloured light, the ghost of summer's warmth. The garden was as wide as the house, and twice as long; surrounded by high walls and laid out in the Italianate style, with pathways curving this way and that between dwarf box hedges and naked rose bowers. An ornamental pond was at the centre of it all, its fountain still and silent, a thin sheet of ice over the black water. Mrs Alleyn was sitting in the far corner, where the sunshine was strongest, and she cut such a lonely figure that Rachel felt a stab of pity for her. She was well wrapped in furs and woollen shawls, but she was not reading, or writing, or drawing; she was simply sitting, with her face turned to the sun and her eyes closed. Rachel cleared her throat quietly, so as not to alarm her.

'Forgive me, Mrs Alleyn,' she said. 'I have finished with Mr Alleyn for today.' Josephine Alleyn opened her eyes and blinked at the light. The sunshine was so bright that it smoothed the years from her face, and Rachel was struck again by her beauty, which in her youth must have been truly exceptional. For a long moment Mrs Alleyn did not speak, and Rachel waited uncomfortably, her toes going numb in her shoes.

'Mrs Weekes. Thank you,' she said at last, and her voice was thin and frail.

'Are you quite well, Mrs Alleyn? Shall I call for somebody?' said Rachel. The older lady waved her hand, and seemed to come back to herself.

'No, no. I was only . . . lost in thought, for a moment. The older one gets, the more power memory has to enthral, I find. To enthral, and sometimes to overpower. Do sit with me a while, Mrs Weekes.' She twitched her cloak to make room for Rachel to sit down beside her. The stone bench was bone-achingly cold. 'How did you find him today?'

'He was . . . calm. He seems to have a touch of fever, however. It would be prudent, perhaps, to watch him these next few days, in case it turns any worse.'

'Yes.' Mrs Alleyn blinked. 'Yes, I will do so. I will be sure he is checked,' she said.

'Forgive me, Mrs Alleyn . . .' Rachel began. 'I can't help but notice that your son seems to be . . . resentful of you, for some reason? When it seems to me that you have only ever supported him in his infirmity . . .'

'Resentful?' The older woman smiled sadly. 'That's a gentle euphemism, my dear.' She turned her face to the sun again, and took a steady breath. 'In truth, he barely tolerates me.'

'But why should it be so? He can't blame you for the war, or for his abandonment by Alice Beckwith.' Mrs Alleyn winced at the mention of Alice's name.

'Of course he blames me, Mrs Weekes. Children always blame their mothers, sooner or later. Even if he can't put into words what it is that angers him so . . . We raise them in love, you see. We raise them in love, and teach them to find the world a wonderful place. And when it is not, they feel betrayed. They feel as though we have betrayed them. So no matter how much we love them, how much we try to make all well for them, sooner or later they blame us, and are wroth with us.'

'That is a sorrowful thought, Mrs Alleyn,' Rachel murmured.

'Indeed. We are a sorrowful little family these days, Jonathan and I.' Mrs Alleyn turned to Rachel with a touch of urgency, as if needing to mitigate. 'I tried to warn him, you see. When I found out about his . . . liaison with that girl, I tried to warn him that she was beneath him. That she was unworthy of his heart and not to be trusted with it. He wouldn't listen of course. Young men never do.'

'You had objections to the match?'

'Objections? Alice was little better than a farmer's child! She was my father's ward – an act of kindness on his part, performed for an old acquaintance when the girl was born in . . . unfortunate circumstances. She was merry-begotten, you see – nobody's daughter. She was of no name, of no connection, of no fortune. Jonathan was betrothed to another, from birth . . . Foolish boy; he threw the match over for a wench only kept from ruin by my father's good heart.' Mrs Alleyn shook her head angrily. 'Oh, he wept over it, he was sorry to grieve us, but he would not give her up. Thank heavens the war took him off before he could do anything as foolish as marry her.'

Rachel absorbed these words, and was puzzled. *Thank heavens the war took him off? The war that near destroyed him?* There was a touch of steel about Josephine Alleyn, she saw then; a touch of the indomitable.

'So, when Miss Beckwith abandoned him in his absence . . .' she ventured.

'He blamed me, of course; though I had no contact with the wretched girl. Still he blamed me, as the one who always told him that she was not worthy of him.' *But he loved her. He loved her enough not to care.* Rachel said nothing for a while, feeling a strange sense of outrage on Alice Beckwith's behalf. *She was nobody's daughter.* Those words gave Rachel a faint prickle of joy. They spoke of mysterious origins, of a foundling child. *Yes*, whispered the echo in her mind. *A child that was lost.*

'May I speak frankly, Mrs Alleyn?' she said.

'You may, Mrs Weekes. Manners and propriety have little place in this house any more, as you have must already have gathered.'

'Whether it is the war that has done it, or his treatment by Alice Beckwith . . . or whether it be those two things combined, it seems to me that your son has lost faith in the world, and in mankind. As you yourself have said, he seems to feel betrayed, and wishes to have no part in his own life any more.'

'You think . . . you think he wishes to die?' Mrs Alleyn breathed, stricken.

'No, madam! No indeed. I think he wishes . . . to have

nothing more to fear. To never expose himself to the risk of further pain. But in hiding away as he does, he traps himself with his memories and his nightmares. In truth, I believe the biggest, perhaps even the only, barrier to his return to health, and to a normal life, is that . . . he does not wish for any such return.'

Silence fell in the garden, and Rachel waited fearfully, worried that she had said too much. A robin flew to the top of a nearby pergola, feathers puffed for warmth, and treated them to a cascade of liquid song. The air was so still that Rachel saw the tiny wisp of its breath as it sang.

'You see things very clearly, Mrs Weekes,' said Mrs Alleyn at last. There was a note of despair, a note of defeat in her voice. 'I suppose my next question must be, can you think of any way to change his mind?'

'In truth, I cannot.' Never had Rachel felt less qualified for any task. 'But you told me that it was unusual, and progressive, for him to even consent to see me, and be read to. So I will continue to, if you wish it. I will challenge his despair however I can, though I can make no promise of success.'

'I wish it, thank you, Mrs Weekes.' To Rachel's surprise, Josephine took her hand. The woman's fingers were profoundly chilled, and her grip first tightened and then loosened, as if unsure of itself. *How long has it been since she took anybody's hand?* Rachel swallowed, loath to say what she was about to.

'I beg your pardon, Mrs Alleyn; I wish that I did not have to mention it, but . . . my husband is bound to query me later on, over . . . your offer to reimburse me for my time with your son . . .' Rachel hung her head, embarrassed.

'Poor girl. You are too good for the likes of Richard Weekes,' Mrs Alleyn muttered. She pulled her hand from Rachel's and turned away from her slightly, as if to distance herself again. Rachel's head came up in an instant, and it was Mrs Alleyn's turn to look uncomfortable.

'I understood that you thought highly of my husband, as your former servant. That you had done a great deal to aid his elevation to a man of business . . .' Rachel said, too quickly, feeling something like panic. Mrs Alleyn pursed her lips, and when she spoke, it was coolly.

'I spoke out of turn. I meant no slight to Richard, only a compliment to you, my dear. For what he is, Richard has done very well. He has worked hard and deserves the rewards. But you are a finer wife than he could ever have hoped for, and I know he would agree with me. Forgive me. I have known him a good deal longer than you, but I forgot myself to speak so freely about him in your presence. I spoke too truly when I said that manners and propriety had abandoned us here.'

'Why have you helped him so much? Why do you still keep ties with him, when he left your service so long ago?' said Rachel. Mrs Alleyn's mouth twitched to one side, but it was not a smile. It was a curious expression, a mixture of warmth – even affection, or the remnants of it – coupled with distaste.

'Richard Weekes . . . was always deeply loyal to me. He served me faithfully throughout some turbulent times in my father's household. I value loyalty, and always reward it. That said, much of his success is due to his own diligence, and is none of my doing.' Her tone brooked no argument.

'Of course.' Rachel thought of Richard's nerves when they had first come to call at Lansdown Crescent; she remembered the way he had bowed so low, and trembled. Her mind was alight with enquiry.

'And you shall have money to show your husband. Come now, let us go in, and I will deliver it.'

'You are too kind, Mrs Alleyn,' said Rachel.

Josephine had grown stiff from the cold, so Rachel helped her to rise and they walked back into the house arm in arm. A flash of flame red caught Rachel's eye as they reached the steps, and she looked up thinking that the robin had returned. But it was Starling she caught a glimpse of, turning hurriedly away from a small window halfway up the house. Rachel's skin prickled. *She was watching me again. This girl who so offends my husband that he will not confess to knowing her.* She remembered Richard's command that she have nothing to do with Starling. She remembered his anger flaring, his voice rising, and afterwards the rough way he had handled her in bed, not looking her in the eye. She tensed as she contemplated what he might do or say if he found her out in what she was about to do, but in the end it didn't make her hesitate.

As the front door of the grand house closed behind her, Rachel darted quickly through the little gate in the railings and down the servants' stair. She knelt by the courtyard door and took out the note she'd carried with her from home that morning, written after Richard had left the house. Fingers shaking with nerves, she pushed the paper under the door and was up the stairs again with such haste that her feet slipped on the smooth stone – for a heart-stopping moment she thought she would fall. She paused to catch her breath, then crossed the street and set off down the hill into Bath with more decorum, wondering whether Jonathan Alleyn would be watching her from his window as she went. She resisted a powerful urge to turn and look.

*   *   *

Starling went to the abbey in the grip of mixed emotions. She was excited, and curious, and also afraid; pleased, and for some reason angry as well. Like as not the anger had to do with the tone of the missive. *I would speak to you again. Meet me* . . . Starling was ever wont to resent being ordered. She wrapped her shawl around her tightly, wedging the corners beneath her arms. The inside of the huge building was always cool, even in summer. The heat of a sunny day couldn't penetrate the thick walls; walls so ancient that the stones seemed fused with dust and age and the slow grinding of gravity, so that the abbey was no longer like a manmade thing, but a structure pushed up from the bones of the earth. In winter, the cold seemed to radiate up from the floor, down from the ceiling, and in from all four corners of the echoing space within. A verger was drifting from place to place, lighting candles; a few pews were occupied by the pious and the homeless, and a thin man who stank of the midden was sweeping the floor. The scratch of his besom only seemed to deepen the hush around it. In the shadows beneath the organ loft, Starling saw the person she had come to meet.

Rachel Weekes was standing beside a massive pillar, shifting from foot to foot with her face pinched up in worry. Starling felt her disgust increase. The woman could not have looked more conspicuous, more as though she had a secret. Her arms were folded tightly against her tall, narrow body; her face was white under a faded green hat that matched her faded pelisse. Starling strode up to her with such purpose that she had the satisfaction of seeing Mrs Weekes flinch, and draw back. *For this chicken-breasted creature Richard takes to beating instead of loving me.*

'Thank you for coming,' said Mrs Weekes, quietly. 'After I left the note, I wasn't sure if . . .' She trailed off, uncomfortably.

'You weren't sure if I could read?' Starling guessed. She felt her mouth pull to one side in disgust. 'Well, I can. Better than most. And I've a fair hand, as well,' she added.

'I'm sure you have,' said Rachel Weekes, and Starling felt her irritation rise again, to be caught bragging.

'Well, I'm here. What do you want?' she said. Rachel Weekes was looking at her strangely, and Starling remembered the bruise on her face. A pinkish bloom where Dick had hit her, that had swollen the cheekbone and made the eye on that side bloodshot.

'Did somebody beat you?' the woman blurted out, all sudden consternation. Starling took a moment, deciding what and what not to say.

'Aye, somebody did; a blow, not a beating. For having spoken to you, madam. So let us have the reason for this meeting made plain, so I can be away and nobody the wiser.'

'Somebody hit you for talking to me?' Rachel Weekes sounded incredulous. 'Who?'

'Can't you guess?' said Starling. She glared at Mrs Weekes, and had the satisfaction of seeing, in her eyes, that she could indeed guess.

'I don't believe you,' she whispered.

'Oh, I think you do.' Starling watched the woman shift uneasily. She took a deep breath. 'What do you want with me? He told me never to speak to you again, nor approach you. I don't think it occurred to him that you would approach me.'

'You and my husband are . . . you are . . .' She could not bring herself to say the word.

'We were lovers. Yes. Not since you wed though.' Starling cast a brief look at the crucifix over the altar, in case Jesus could hear her.

'How long before we wed did you . . . did it . . . cease . . . ?' The woman's voice was a strangled whisper, shaking with emotion. Starling did not flinch.

'Two days before. He wed you still wearing the scent of me, I do think.'

Starling's heart clenched at the cruelty of her own words, with the thrill of being able to wound her rival so. *I was wounded, too.* But in the next instant, she felt deflated. Mrs Weekes put out a hand to steady herself against the wall; her face had turned ashen, and was so full of horror that Starling at once felt the need to make amends. She tried to resist it. *Alice would embrace her, and call her sister, and comfort her. But I am not Alice.* Still, she felt her resolve waver and her anger seep away. The woman looked abject in her misery. Starling almost put out her hand, but could not quite do it. 'Mrs Weekes . . .' she said, but was unsure what else to add. The woman raised her eyes, expectantly. 'Aren't you angry?' said Starling, eventually. 'Aren't you angry with me? With him?'

'I am angry only with myself,' said Rachel Weekes, her voice tight and trembling. 'I've been a fool. An utter fool. And it cannot be undone, can it? It *cannot!*' She dissolved into a storm of tears. The verger looked over at them curiously, and Starling shushed her, herding her further back into the shadows.

'Shh! Quiet, people are looking. What can't be undone?'

'The marriage!' Rachel Weekes gasped, between sobs that shook her chest.

'Well, no. That much is true. I was fool enough to love him but not fool enough to marry him, at least,' said Starling, almost to herself. *Though I would have, if he'd asked. I'd have been fool enough then.* At this, Rachel Weekes grew calmer, and stopped crying.

'You loved him?' she said. Starling glared at her in silence. 'Then he has treated you very ill . . .' She looked at the bruise on Starling's face, and seemed poised to begin weeping again. Starling tried to distract her from it, and was surprised to hear Bridget's words coming out of her mouth. *Two mothers I had, one soft, one hard.*

'Well, there's no point crying over spilt milk,' she said wryly.

To her surprise, Rachel Weekes laughed; a startled snatch of laughter.

'My mother used to say that,' she said.

'Everyone's mother says that sooner or later, I reckon,' said Starling. 'What's done is done; there's nothing between him and me now. As far as I know he has been true to you, since you wed.'

'No.' Rachel shook her head. 'I have been much deceived. But then, perhaps I deceived myself most of all,' she murmured. She sounded calmer, dejected. Starling felt a stab of worry.

'Don't challenge him about this, will you? Don't tell him we've met, for pity's sake! It would go ill for both of us. You must swear not to tell!'

'I won't tell. I won't . . . challenge him,' said Rachel Weekes.

'I can't stay here all day – I must get back to the house. Was this what you wanted from me, then? To know that you married a knave?' said Starling.

'No, that was not it . . .' Mrs Weekes wiped her face with gloved fingers, and took a deep breath. 'I wanted to talk to you about Jonathan Alleyn. And about Alice Beckwith.' Starling froze at the mention of both their names together. She couldn't remember when she'd last heard them spoken in the same breath. *Jonathan and Alice. J & A; carved into the flesh of the lovers' tree for ever.* She swallowed.

'Well? What of them?'

'When we spoke before, at the house, you said to me that Miss Beckwith had been too good for this world.'

'I spoke the truth. What of it?'

'Do you think her . . . dead, then?' Rachel Weekes had stopped crying, and now a strange light was in her eyes, a strange eagerness that Starling mistrusted.

'I know she is dead.'

'How do you know? Were you still in touch with her, after she absconded?'

'After she . . . ? No, you don't understand a thing! She never absconded. She never had another lover, and she never left her home with another . . . She was killed! That's the truth of it!' Whenever she spoke of it, Starling's pulse quickened with desperation; the terrible frustration of knowing the truth but being believed by no one. But Rachel Weekes's eyes had gone wide with shock.

'She was killed? You mean . . . murdered?'

'Aye, murdered! By Jonathan Alleyn!'

'By . . . God above, you cannot mean it?' Rachel Weekes said breathlessly.

'I would not say such a thing lightly.'

'But . . . what happened? Will you tell me?' she said. Starling stared at her for a moment, and realised that nobody had ever asked her to describe that day before.

The last time Starling ever saw her, Alice had been winding the front of her hair into rags before bed; patiently wrapping each lock around a strip of cloth, and then twisting it up and tying it near her scalp. The back of it she left to hang loose, down between her shoulder blades. When she unwound the rags in the morning, the curls were never quite as neat as she wanted them – her hair was too fine, too wilfully straight. Most nights Starling didn't wake when Alice came up, but that night, that last night, she woke from a dream of running and never tiring to see her sister at the dressing table, fixing her hair in this way. At once, Starling felt safe. Her dream, though it had almost been wonderful, had left her with the uneasy feeling that she was not quite normal, not quite real. But there was the smooth pallor of Alice's skin in the mirror, and the way she curled up her toes and crossed her feet to one side of the stool, and everything was real and right again.

The morning sun woke Starling, casting a spear of light across her face through the gap between the shutters. Low, chill, winter sun that told her she had overslept. It was early February, the year 1809. Alice's bed was already empty, so Starling hurried out of the blankets, wincing at the cold in the room, pulled on her everyday wool dress and stockings, and went downstairs to help. Bridget was at the stove, cooking drop scones for breakfast in a black iron skillet.

'Hey ho, Bridget,' said Starling, yawning. 'Where's Alice?'

'Up and out already, far early this morning,' said Bridget, always curt and grumpy at that time of day – her back ached, the first hour or two she was up. 'I heard her go. She's not let the hens out or fed them,' she grumbled.

'I'll do it.' Starling swung her shawl around her shoulders, tied her hair in a knot at the nape of her neck and stuffed her feet into her pattens. There was frost on the ground and in the trees, frost sparkling on every tendril of wild clematis that grew along the front wall of the yard. Her breath made miniature clouds against the brilliant blue sky. Alice loved such mornings – crisp and still and beautiful; she didn't feel the cold as much as it seemed she ought. Starling searched, but Alice wasn't in any of the barns, at the sty or in the stable with the horse. She shielded her eyes and stared out along the river, looking for the tell-tale flash of colour that would mark Alice's approach – her bright hair, her blue dress, her pale pink shawl of warm lambs' wool, which she sometimes wrapped around her head when it was this cold, laughing and saying she would make a fine shepherdess. There was no sign. Shivering, Starling fed the hens and let them out of the coop, quickly gathered the eggs and hurried back inside.

Alice did not return in time for breakfast. Bridget and Starling ate it without her, neither one acknowledging any concern. Starling didn't want to betray herself, didn't want to be the first to say it; as though whoever first expressed fear would be responsible for giving it cause. But at lunchtime the two women, Bridget past fifty, and Starling just thirteen years old, gave up pretending that all was well. Gradually, they stopped going about their chores and drifted to the kitchen window to look out in hope. The sun had melted the frost by then; the world was green and brown and grey again, dowdy and unremarkable. Unable to hold her tongue any longer, Starling took a deep breath and turned to face the older woman.

'Bridget, where is she?' she said in a small voice. For a moment Bridget didn't reply. They exchanged a look of shared unease. Then Bridget cleared her throat.

'Go on into the village and ask a few faces.'

'It was so icy this morning . . . and it must have been dark when she went out. What if she fell? What if some harm has come to her?'

'Then we will find her and scold her for her lack of good sense,' said Bridget, curtly. 'Go on into the village.'

So Starling ran from the butcher's shop to the baker's, stopping everyone she saw along the way. She went along the river and along the canal, a good distance in either direction, asking fishermen and bargemen and rovers. She went across the bridge and asked the miller and the toll man; she knocked on the door of the parsonage, and checked in church. She steeled herself and went into the inn, which she had never done by herself before. She asked the serving girls, the inn keep, the travellers eating their stew and potatoes. By sunset she could think of nowhere else to go, no one else to ask. *She will be home in the kitchen when I get back. Some small mishap detained her, that was all.* She pictured Alice seated by the fire, with a hot cup of tea in her hands and a sprained ankle propped up in front of her. She pictured it so clearly that she ran back to the farmhouse in her haste, burst into the kitchen all breathless, and could not understand why the room was dark, the fire gone out, and Bridget still stood at the window with her face pinched up in fear. In that exact moment the ground seemed to shudder beneath Starling's feet, and everything suddenly seemed breakable. She felt queasy and helpless, and sharp-fingered panic scrabbled in her gut.

'We must send word to Lord Faukes on the morrow, if there is still no sign of her. He will know what to do,' said Bridget, in hollow tones.

Neither one of them could go to bed, so they sat in the kitchen through the night, cold and sleepless, until the sun rose once again. There was still no sign of Alice. Bridget paid the yardman's boy three farthings to run a message directly to Lord Faukes in Box, and half an hour later the rattle of the front gate roused the two of them from their chairs, hope flooding through them. The door was thrown open before they reached it, and the person that came through it stopped them in their tracks.

'What's the meaning of—' Bridget began to say, only to cut herself off in astonishment.

'*Mr Alleyn?*' Starling breathed, not quite believing it was him.

'Where is she? Where is she?' Jonathan Alleyn gasped, fighting for breath. He staggered into the kitchen, looking around wildly as though Alice might be hiding behind the table. There were cuts and gashes on the backs of his hands, crusted with filth. '*Alice!*' he shouted. And then the smell of him hit them, and shocked them even more. Starling clapped her hands over her nose and mouth.

'Saints preserve us! He reeks of the slaughterhouse,' cried Bridget. In truth, the stink he gave off was worse than blood. It was blood and rot and burning; excrement, putrefaction and filth. His clothes – his red army jacket and breeches –

were so stained and tattered it was hard to recognise them. His hair was long and matted, his face unshaven. He had always been lean but now he was painfully thin. Beneath the clothes his body was like sticks and shards; no softness, no flesh. What skin they could see behind the dirt and bruises was a ghastly greyish white. There was a long tear in the shoulder of his jacket, a messy darkness beneath that gave off the worst smell.

Gagging, Starling followed him as he crashed through into the parlour.

'Alice!' he shouted to the empty room. Starling stood in his way, forcing him to stop.

'Mr Alleyn! How are you here – here and not at the war? Where is Alice? Have you been with her?' she asked desperately. Jonathan looked down at her and didn't seem to recognise her at all. His eyes were feverish and wild; the hands that grasped her shoulders shook violently, but had an inhuman strength.

'Where is she? The letter she wrote . . . it cannot be. I won't believe it! Where is she?' His voice rose from a whisper to a shout, spittle flying from his lips. His fingernails bit into her.

'We don't know where she is! Do you know? Have you seen her? What's happened?' said Starling, her words garbled by tears that came on suddenly, half closing her throat. 'You're not well, Mr Alleyn . . . *please* . . .' But Jonathan shoved her to one side, and continued his search, trailing his stink behind him until it was in every corner of the house. When at last he came back to the kitchen, Starling stood shoulder to shoulder with Bridget, frightened and bewildered.

'I must find her. I must tell her . . .' Jonathan said indistinctly. He seemed to be losing control of his tongue; the sounds he made were strange and disjointed.

'He is afire with fever,' Bridget said quietly. 'We mustn't let him leave as he is.' At this, Jonathan's head whipped around and he glared savagely at them.

'Who are you? What have you done with Alice? *What have you done?*' he bellowed. It seemed to take the last of his strength. His hand was on his sabre, trying to free it from its scabbard, as he sank to his knees. 'You cannot keep me here,' he whispered. And then he collapsed.

Some weeks later, when the fear of harm coming to Alice had evolved into the agony of grief, the bitter torment of not knowing, Starling managed to see Jonathan again. She and Bridget had been made to quit the farmhouse in Bathampton, and Starling was in service to Lord Faukes, at the house in Box. She needed to be near Jonathan, since he was her best link to Alice. She needed to be near him, because he could set about finding her. He could stand up and deny the stories being told about her, and be believed. He could do *something*. And when Alice came back, and found the farmhouse at Bathampton let to strangers, she would come to Box second of all, Starling was sure. She would come to find Jonathan and Lord Faukes. She would come for her sister. For days Jonathan lay unconscious, and doctors came and went from his room. For days after that he would see no one. Starling was forced to wait, driven to distraction with impatience. When she did at last sneak into his room he was much changed. The stink was gone; he was clean, his wounds bandaged. He could stand, and walk – she had seen him. Yet he did not walk; he did not ride. He did nothing.

When Starling appeared in his room he did not seem to think it amiss. If he was surprised that she'd walked out of his secret life in Bathampton and into his everyday one in Box, he showed no sign of it.

'Mr Alleyn, why do you not search for her?' she whispered.

Since losing Alice, Starling was less sure of herself, less brave. She was less sure of everything around her, other than that Alice would not have abandoned her willingly. And she was horribly, horribly lonely.

'There's no point,' he said roughly, not looking at her. For a moment his mouth kept working, as if he would say more. He frowned; his eyes were swollen, and had lost their sparkle. 'She's gone,' he said, eventually.

'You cannot believe what they are saying about her. You cannot believe she had a lover, and has run off with him. You cannot!'

'Can I not?' he said, grinding out the words. He shook his head. 'The letter she wrote to me,' he said. 'I *wish* I could remember! And my lord grandfather, and my mother. All tell the same story. And even Bridget has confirmed it . . .'

'What? Remember what? What has Bridget confirmed?' Starling's heart felt weak and damaged. When it pounded like it did then, she worried that it might come apart. Her head ached unbearably, with disbelief, with shock, and desperation.

'She has left with another. She is gone.'

'She would *never*! You know that. Mr Alleyn, she loves you! She wants to marry you – it's all she's ever wanted! And she made me her sister . . . she would never just abandon us! Why aren't you out looking for her? How can you believe them? You know it's not true! You know it!' She grasped his arm to make him see. 'Someone has taken her! Or hurt her! Do something!'

'What would you have me do, Starling?' Jonathan wrenched his arm away from her. Two of her nails bent backwards and tore, but she felt nothing. 'Do you call my grandfather a liar? And my mother? Do you doubt what Bridget saw? Do you doubt the letter Alice wrote to me? Do you doubt every piece of evidence that she has run away?' His face was a snarl, and tears ran down it.

'Yes, I doubt them. How can you not?'

'You are a fool, girl. She no more loved me than she was sister to you. Both were lies! It was all *fiction*,' he said, and Starling recoiled, stung.

'What letter did she write to you? Where is it? Let me read it,' she demanded.

'I . . .' He hesitated, frowning. 'I have lost it.'

'Lost it? What did it say?'

'I . . . I cannot remember. I was not . . . I was not myself . . .'

'But you are well now, sir. *Please*. You must do something. You must try to find her. Anything could have happened to her – gypsies might have taken her . . . or robbers left her injured somewhere . . . You must search, Mr Alleyn! You can't believe what they are saying!'

'Enough! I will hear no more. She's gone! Do you hear? She's *gone*.'

'No! No, she's not. She wouldn't,' Starling moaned, tears blinding her.

'Yes. She is gone.' Just then, Jonathan stared into her eyes with such conviction and despair that Starling felt the seeds of a terrible suspicion germinate.

And as the months passed, and Jonathan returned to the war in Spain, and no word ever came, her suspicion grew and grew, flourishing like weeds in the waste ground of her grief. For even if Starling allowed herself to think that Alice would abandon her, she did not believe that she would go so completely, and never send word. Never send a note to say goodbye, or to explain why she had acted in secret. But no word ever came, and nobody in the house at Box would even speak of Alice Beckwith, and Starling could not understand why Jonathan, who had loved Alice, would believe what was said about her. She did not *believe* that he believed it. So, when she thought back to his ravaged eyes and the cold, bitter way he had said *she is gone*, it seemed that he must know more. That he must know things he would not say.

There'd been blood on him when he came to the farm-house that day, blood aplenty. Spatters and smears of it, all over his clothing. And he had been raving, unhinged; he had spoken of a letter that none but he had seen or read, the contents of which had upset him terribly, yet which he now claimed he could not remember. Still some part of her kept its trust in him, though; kept it for three more years until he came back again, his leg wound finishing the war for him. Some part of Starling would not believe Jonathan could harm Alice. Until that man she no longer knew hit her for mentioning Alice's name. Until she heard him say it out loud, clear as day. *She is dead*. Then all trust vanished, and all hope with it.

There was a pause after Starling finished her story, and she glanced over her shoulder to make sure the verger and the caretaker weren't listening. Rachel Weekes seemed dumb-struck. She shook her head minutely.

'How can that be? Mrs Alleyn says her son got word of Alice's disgrace while he was fighting overseas . . . He wasn't even in the country. Or do you say he killed her after she ran away?'

'No, no.' Starling shook her head in frustration. 'Mrs Alleyn lies, to cover for her son . . . she doesn't want it to be true, of course she doesn't. She's a noble lady, but as a mother her first loyalty is to her son . . . He *was* returned! Alice got word that the men were returning, and stopping in Brighton to recover from the fray. She wrote to him there . . . I know not what she said. But he came to Bathampton the day after she vanished. The very next day!'

'Wait,' said Rachel Weekes, shaking her head. 'I can't follow you . . . he killed her because she loved another?'

'No!' said Starling, louder than she'd meant to. Several heads turned towards them. 'No, she had no other lover. She never did – I would have known about it if she had.' Starling felt the tiniest pull of doubt as she said this. She remembered what Bridget had said – what she'd claimed she'd seen. She thought of the way she'd betrayed Alice to Bridget after she discovered the lovers' tree, and shame smouldered in her gut. Could Alice have hidden things from her, after she proved herself so untrustworthy?

'Why then would he kill her?'

'I . . . I think she might have tried to break it off with him. Their engagement, which had been a secret one. I know his family did not approve of the match.'

'Indeed not.'

'After Mr Alleyn had gone off to the war, Alice went to Lord Faukes's house in Box, one day. Where Mrs Alleyn lived, with Jonathan as well. She was never the same after she came back from there that day. I think Lord Faukes told her plainly that she could not marry Jonathan.' *And what Lord Faukes wanted, Lord Faukes got.* Starling pushed the memory away, her gorge rising. 'There must have been some grave reason, some terrible threat . . . or perhaps it was something Jonathan had said or done – perhaps *he* was the betrayer! But whatever the reason, I think she wrote to Jonathan to break it off.'

'This is what Captain Sutton has told me. That Mr Alleyn had a letter from her in Brighton, and he left at once for Bathampton.'

'Who is Captain Sutton?'

'A friend of Mr Alleyn's, or was. They were in the army together, and my husband is acquainted with them. I have . . . become friends with his wife.'

At the mention of Richard Weekes, both of them fell silent for a moment. Starling felt her cheeks grow hot. She felt absurdly embarrassed, and jealous, that Rachel Weekes should share an acquaintance with Jonathan that she knew nothing about. *Folly. He is not your pet, nor your prisoner.* But in truth, that was how she had come to think of him – as her possession. He was at the centre of all her thoughts; him, and what he had done.

'There is the proof of it,' she said, half strangled. *Why, Alice? Why?*

'She said Jonathan took the news very badly indeed.'

'Yes. Badly enough to kill her.'

'But surely . . . he would have been discovered in his crime, if he had done something so terrible? Her body would have been discovered somewhere . . .'

'Not necessarily.' Starling swallowed against a sudden hard lump in her throat. 'If he cast her into the river, and she was swept a goodly way before she was found . . . if she was found at all . . . nobody would know who she was. And nobody was looking for a body . . . they all thought she'd run away with another, because that's the story that was put about.'

'Put about by whom?'

'By Jonathan Alleyn, and his mother. By Lord Faukes. By the gossips in Bathampton, who had always wondered about poor Alice, and jumped at the chance to malign her.' *By Bridget. Oh, how could you, Bridget?*

'I still don't understand why you think otherwise,' said Rachel Weekes. That strange urgency was still in her eyes, fiercer than ever.

'I *know* otherwise, because I knew Alice. She would *never* have betrayed Jonathan. She would never have betrayed anybody. She loved him, and she was true to him all her life. She loved her home, and she loved . . . she loved me, and Bridget. She would never have gone off and left us all. *Never.*'

'You are quite certain.' It was not a question, and a sudden calm came upon Starling. *She does not scoff; she listens.*

'I know it like I know the sun will rise in the east,' she said.

Rachel Weekes was watching Starling with a kind of steady amazement. Her tears had left her face mottled, but her eyes had dried; she seemed to consider several different things to say before choosing.

'Jonathan Alleyn is a tortured soul . . . he said to me he wished to undo things he had done. And there is much violence in him, I have seen it. But to do so evil a thing . . . You truly believe it? You would have it that Mrs Alleyn lies to cover his crime? That she has done so all these years?'

'Yes, she lies. Of course – what else would a mother do? Jonathan is all she has in this world, after all, especially now her father is gone.' *In that, we are alike; though our hearts be worlds apart.*

'When did Lord Faukes die?'

'He's seven years in his grave.' *Seven years I pray God he's spent roasting.* Starling fought the urge to spit at the mention of him. 'Jonathan Alleyn loved Alice, once. But he was different after the war – he was not the same man, nor has been since. You saw how he behaved, when he first saw you! He might have killed you too.'

'Aye, he might have,' Rachel murmured. Her eyes were distant, thoughts racing behind them. 'But why have you not denounced him, if you are sure of his crime?'

'A public accusation?' said Starling, in disgust. 'Who would believe the word of a servant over people like them? Nobody. And I would lose my position, and all access to the man. Why do you ask me all of this? To know the man you are sent to comfort?' Starling demanded, suddenly suspicious. Rachel Weekes shifted her feet, looking almost sheepish.

'Yes, to know him . . . to know what I am to deal with. But also to know . . . to know Alice. The one whose face I share. The one he loved so dearly. Tell me, who were her parents? Mrs Alleyn says she was nobody's daughter.'

'She said that?' Starling chewed her lip for a moment. 'Alice herself often wondered, but none of us knew who her parents were. Lord Faukes would never disclose it.'

'And he was the only one who would have known, I suppose.'

'He and the parents themselves, whoever they were. But to know Alice you need know only this: that she was all kindness, all decency; all generous and gentle soul.' Starling took a deep breath, teetering on the slippery edge of the chasm of grief inside her. She feared that if she fell in, she would never climb out again. She collected herself. 'Alice would have forgiven Jonathan for killing her. That's what she was like. She forgave people . . . there was no malice in her. No rancour or spite. To know Jonathan Alleyn you need know only this, that it is truly a fine line between love and hate.'

'Then I am wed to a liar, this we know, and am possibly in the employ of a murderer,' said Rachel Weekes, as she absorbed these words. Her voice was heavy and wretched, but she did not sound afraid. Starling looked at her curiously.

'Then you believe what I have told you? That he killed her?'

'We . . . we have not yet had the full story of what passed between them, I am sure, and I pray it is not so. But I believe he could have.'

For a long moment the two of them simply stood in the abbey's pooling shadows and watched each other. Starling was not sure what else she should say, and it seemed that Rachel Weekes was also confounded.

'It would not be wise for us to meet again,' Starling said quietly.

'But I will be at the house many times. I will be there this Wednesday . . . if you want to talk to me again.'

'It was you who wanted to talk to me, remember?' Starling pointed out, and saw Rachel Weekes flinch, stung.

'But I am well placed, am I not, to try to discover the truth of the matter?' she ventured.

'Why would you want to do that?' Suspicion flared in Starling again.

'Because——' Mrs Weekes broke off. Her eyes searched Starling's face, as though the answer might be there, and Starling felt something tremulous in the pit of her stomach, like sparkles of joy that faded as soon as they lit. *Ye Gods, but she is the very image of my sister.* 'I have thought, since I first entered that house, that it seemed frozen; sleeping, or perhaps only waiting,' said Rachel Weekes. 'Now I understand what it was that made time stop. It was Alice, and the way she vanished. She haunts that house . . . she haunts Jonathan Alleyn and his mother. Such secrets . . .' She paused, shook her head slightly. 'I . . . I am told I must keep going there, but I . . . I *cannot* do so, and not know the truth,' she said vehemently. 'The truth will set us free,' she murmured. 'Perhaps it could set me free.'

'I don't think the Bible was referring to such dark truths as these,' said Starling. Rachel Weekes frowned, in obvious thought.

'But twelve years have passed since Alice was seen . . . In twelve years you have found out nothing new?' she said.

'Twelve difficult years, I assure you.' Starling scowled defensively. 'I stayed on in their service only to this end . . . only to keep my enemy close. It is nine years since Mr Alleyn got back from the war for good, and he was more than half mad when he did. I had conversations with him then that he claims not to remember now — not remember at all. Then for years he was near insensible with opium . . . He dreamed four years away, and drank the rest . . .'

'He does not remember that time? Then . . . is it not possible . . .'

'That he does not remember killing her?' Starling shook her head. 'I do not believe it. Perhaps he wishes to forget, but I do not believe that he has. That he *could*.'

'Then it is this knowledge, you believe, that torments him so?'

'Should it not torment him to know that he slew the one person who loved him best in all the world?'

'But he knows what you suspect of him? Then . . . how can you be safe there? How can you not fear what he might do to you?'

'You need not fear for me. I can manage Jonathan Alleyn.'

'It has been so long since Alice was lost,' said Rachel Weekes. She studied Starling with wide, pitying eyes, and Starling recoiled. No one had looked at her that way in years; Alice had been the last person to. It made her feel vulnerable, somehow weaker, as though she might crack. 'How have you borne it?' the woman asked.

'What choice have I had?' Starling replied, curtly. *What have I become in those years, that I cannot stand to be comforted?* 'If Mrs Alleyn knew what I was about . . . But she lies for him, I know. She knows more of the truth than she lets on.'

'Perhaps she also lies to herself,' said Rachel, softly. 'A mother's love is a powerful thing. I have . . . I have begun to know the lady, a little. Perhaps, in time, she might speak.'

'You must not say anything of what I have told you! Not to them . . . they must not know that I know, or in an instant they would be rid of me!' Panic made Starling's voice rise.

If they send me away, if they do that, what have I then? She had the sudden, fearful sensation of losing control.

'I shan't speak of this to them. I . . . I don't know what I will do.'

Starling thought quickly. It had been a relief to speak the truth and pass on her suspicions; she had not bargained on recruiting an ally – a person with her own ideas and plans. A person easily shocked, and likely to betray herself. *She could ruin everything.*

'Do nothing,' said Starling. 'It would be better if you didn't see him any more. If you went no more to Lansdown Crescent. It would be safer for you, and easier for me.'

'I *must* go. My husband commands it, and I would feel . . . duty bound to Mrs Alleyn to do so, even if he did not. What should I do?' said Mrs Weekes. Starling took a moment to decide, chewing the inside of her mouth. Her unease remained; the sudden fear of unanticipated change.

'If you would be a friend to me, then I . . . Mr Alleyn has Alice's letters. All of her letters, his letters to her as well. She kept hers in a rosewood box about as long as my forearm, and in all the chaos of the days after she vanished . . . only once I had recovered my wits enough to look for it did I find it gone. No one else would have taken it, and I have seen him reading them, upon occasion. He clings to them as though they might assuage his guilt. There could be some clue in them, as to what manner of thing made her break with him. For if it was grave enough that she would do that, then it is grave enough that he might kill her for the same. For insulting him.'

'Do men kill over insults?' asked Mrs Weekes, softly.

'Only every day. See if you can find where he hides the box, and in it the other letters. For all the times I've searched his rooms, I've found it not – it must be in some secret place.

If you can find it out, tell me. I need to know what she wrote to him in Brighton.'

'All right. I will try.' Rachel Weekes's expression betrayed scant hope of success.

'Say nothing of this! To anyone,' Starling whispered fiercely. Rachel Weekes gave a quick, anxious nod, but made no move. *She hardly knows where to go next, or what to do.* Starling left her there.

She was loaded with a new and different mix of emotions as she ducked out into the crowded square. The fear was still there, but the anger gone; a nagging foreboding now, and the excitement even stronger, and beneath it all the unease that came from having so long trusted nobody, and suddenly finding trust assumed by another. *Why should she trust me any more than I her? And yet she does. She does not scorn the things I told her. She does not side blindly with the Alleyns, as she might.* As if the world had lurched slightly and come out of its old rut, it suddenly seemed as though the future would be different; life would change. But for better or worse, Starling couldn't tell. *Isn't that what I intended when I brought her into that house? For twelve years they have woven such lies that I have not managed to penetrate them. Could she be the one to do it?* Starling did not trust the woman, nor understand her one bit, but she felt less alone than she had before; less alone than she had since she was parted from Alice.

* * *

Rachel walked with little idea of her destination. She was distracted; she left her feet to find their own path and they stopped on a quiet corner of an unswept street, where rubbish and muck were piled high in the gutters and only the ice on the puddles kept her feet dry. A starving cat came to sniff her shins, hoping for food, but when Rachel lowered her hand to stroke it, it ran away. She leaned against the wall and shut her eyes for a moment, trying to marshal her thoughts. She'd known even before the girl had spoken. She'd known as soon as she'd seen the bruise on her face, and had thought of the way Richard had named her, in his anger. *Starling*. Named her even though he'd made every effort until then to deflect Rachel's interest in the girl, and feign blindness to her existence. And she was pretty enough, though her face was pert and her red hair dishevelled. There was a sharpness about her; the liveliness of her expression spoke of intelligence, and wit. But Starling was afraid of Richard too; it was clear from the way she'd made Rachel swear to not reveal their meeting. *It would go ill, for both of us.* Rachel took several deep breaths to calm down. *And he was with her right up until we wed. As we courted, and he said he could not live without me. And she loved him. Did he love her? Could he have, if he beats her now?*

Long minutes later the cold begin to work on her, stiffening her fingers, making the joints ache. To keep herself from thinking about Richard, she thought about Jonathan Alleyn instead. Somehow, during her visits to him after the first one, she had written off his violence towards her as an aberration; he'd been so much calmer since, more sober. Black tempered, and alarming, but never violent again; yet she couldn't deny that she'd witnessed that tendency in him, even if Starling's story hadn't had the ring of utter conviction. And all her conversations with him told her one thing above all – that he was tortured by regret and self-loathing. *Could he have killed Alice? Is that what torments him so?* The thought made her mouth go dry, and anxiety flutter in her stomach. *Let it not be so*. Yet she was confounded to find that she feared him no more now than she already had; though the thought of how she would even begin to discover where he kept Alice Beckwith's letters was already troubling her. The one and only time she'd mentioned Alice's name, he had cut her off abruptly. *At least he is no worse than he appeared to be when I first met him, unlike someone else.* She stood up from the wall and set off with greater purpose, towards Duncan Weekes's house.

The old man had been sleeping, though it was early in the evening; he opened the door with a befuddled expression and his cap still on, blinking owlishly. His cheeks were rough with coarse white stubble; he smelled of stale skin, tallow and brandy.

'Mrs Weekes . . . dear girl . . . I had not expected you,' he mumbled. He stood up straighter, but it caused him to wince.

'Forgive me, I . . . I wanted to talk to somebody. I shouldn't have called at this hour . . .' Rachel stammered. Duncan seemed to focus on her face; on her puffy, red eyes.

'Come, come.' He ushered her into the chilly room. 'Are you all right? Has something happened?'

'No, that is . . . yes . . .' Rachel put her hands to her face and tried to keep hold.

'Please, sit, Mrs Weekes,' Duncan said kindly. 'Be easy, you are safe here.' Rachel glanced up at this; it seemed an odd thing for him to say. As though he expected her to be unsafe elsewhere. 'You look chilled to the bone. Can I pour you a tot of brandy, to warm you?'

'Yes, please.' Rachel noticed that he poured himself one as well, and swigged it down before he handed hers to her. She sipped it, felt the fire in her throat, and coughed. Duncan smiled briefly and set about reviving the fire, which had all but burnt out while he slept. The few sticks and coals he tipped onto it were the last in the bucket.

'Ah,' Duncan murmured, indistinctly.

'I will fetch more, if you tell me where the bunker is?'

'No, no. Do not trouble yourself,' he said, and looked so uncomfortable that Rachel suddenly guessed the truth.

'There is more coal, isn't there? You do have more?'

'Not today, not today,' he said, with fragile good cheer. 'I've been in a bit of bad bread, lately. But tomorrow I have some work, down on the wharf. I shall buy coal when the day is done, and be warm as toast by nightfall.'

'But what of tonight?'

'Well. I have your company to warm my heart, do I not?' He smiled wearily as he sank into the chair opposite her, and Rachel felt tears well up in her eyes again.

'Mr Weekes . . .'

'Here now, none of that. Tell me what troubles you, my dear, and do not fret over me. I'm a tough old bird, you'll see.'

'I . . . it's Richard. My husband.' *And your son.* Rachel was suddenly unsure whether to continue, but Duncan gazed at her with such sympathy that the words were out before she could stop them. 'I found out that he . . . he has been wenching. Right up until the very moment we wed!' She hung her head, ashamed, and wept again as much from embarrassment as sorrow.

Clumsily, Duncan Weekes put out a gnarled hand and patted hers.

'Oh, my poor girl. And my foolish boy!' He shook his head.

'What should I do?' said Rachel, desperately.

'Do?' Duncan Weekes smiled sadly. 'Well, you can do nothing, my dear.'

'Do nothing? But . . . but he has . . . he has . . .'

'He has kept his wedding vows, you say?'

'As far as I can discover, yes.'

'That then is something to be thankful for, is it not?' said the old man, softly.

'*Thankful?*'

'My dear girl, young men with pretty faces – and even those without them – will always know more of . . . the world, than young ladies. It was ever so. The world is full of rantipole girls who'll accept a promise, or even a compliment, as betrothal enough to consummate. Of course you're shocked — you have been brought up good, and virtuous. But a good many young women have not that advantage, and are led more by their senses than their good sense, if you follow me. Richard has always drawn the morts to him; and like any young man, full of vigour and good health, to expect him not to indulge himself would be like setting sweet flowers before a bee and then bidding it not to sup.'

'Then such behaviour is to be condoned? Accepted?'

'Condoned, no, not at all. I say only that it would be a rare and virtuous young man who approached the altar on his wedding day as pure as the day he was born. Perhaps it is behaviour that is to be . . . expected. The sadness here is that you have found it out, and been wounded by it. Far better that a young lady continues in marriage happily unaware of such past transgressions.'

'You mean to say that ignorance is bliss?' said Rachel, bitterly.

'Sometimes, aye, it is.'

'Then restraint and virtue in men is naught but an illusion.'

'Not an illusion, a reality, my dear. It perhaps only wants, now that you know of his folly, an adjustment to what you can understand as virtue. I say again, he has kept to his vows to you — that is something to take comfort in, surely?'

'Perhaps,' said Rachel, listlessly. She glanced up, and Duncan Weekes smiled apologetically. 'I should not have brought this complaint to you. You are his father. It was wrong of me, and I'm sorry.'

'No, it was not wrong. You are to come to me whenever you need to.'

'Nothing is turning out the way I had envisaged it,' she murmured.

'Ah, my dear girl – nothing ever does! Only try to forgive my boy. What's done is done, and can't be altered. He loves you, I am sure of that.' Rachel considered this, but said nothing.

They sat in companionable silence for a while, as the coals began to seethe and smoke in the hearth – the brandy warmed Rachel far more than the meagre fire. Through the ceiling and walls came a faint, sweet song, repeated over and over, and the thin wail of an unhappy baby. Rachel fumbled in her pocket and drew out her purse. There was money in it to buy supper, and she passed it all to Duncan.

'What's this?' he said startled.

'Please, take it. Take it and buy some fuel for your fire.'

'You need not provide for me, my dear. Thank you, but I—'

'Please take it, or I will be forced to go myself to buy the coal, and then I'll have smuts all over my dress. Take it. It's not right that Richard and I dine in warmth by a merry hearth, while you shiver here alone; and I have had my fill of wrong things for today.'

'You have a kind heart, Mrs Weekes.'

'Please, call me Rachel. We are family, are we not?' Duncan Weekes's face showed his pleasure, even as he fingered the coins uneasily.

'I do not think Richard would thank you for giving me this, Rachel.'

'He will not hear of it.' *With luck, he will not notice.* 'I'll say I bought ribbons with it. Ribbons always befuddle a man, my mother used to say. They know that women must have them, but cannot fathom out the why.' She smiled, and Duncan chuckled. Rachel finished her brandy and rose to leave, then a further thought occurred to her.

'May I ask you one more thing, sir?' Mrs Alleyn said something to me that lingers in my mind. She said that Richard had been exceptionally loyal to her, during a time of strife. I understood that she meant in years past, while you both were still in her service. Perhaps it is not my business, but I am curious . . . I wondered if you knew when she might mean?'

She arranged her skirts and shawl, and only then realised that the old man hadn't answered. She looked up, and was struck by the expression on his face. Duncan's jaw hung slack, a little open; his eyes were huge and uneasy.

'What is it?' said Rachel, startled. Duncan shook his head slightly, and closed his mouth.

'I cannot say,' he said, his voice rough. He cleared his throat nervously and rubbed the palms of his hands against his shirt. Rachel stared at him.

'Mr Weekes?' she said. 'Do you know what time she spoke of?'

'No, child. I do not know. Whatever it was, it's long past now. I would not trouble yourself with wondering.' He could not look her in the eye. He patted his pockets as if searching for something, and ran his tongue over his cracked lips.

'Perhaps you're right,' she said softly. *What frightens him in my enquiry?* 'It was only a passing curiosity.' Duncan Weekes sagged visibly in relief, and nodded. She took her leave of him and went back onto the deadened street, where the darkness was complete, the sky a fathomless black. She walked back to Abbeygate Street with a sense of foreboding that bordered on fear. She thought of the welt on the side of Starling's face; she thought of the two of them lying together, all the time Richard had been courting her. She had no idea how she would react when she next set eyes on her husband.

The house was in darkness, and Rachel waited a while in the kitchen, with dinner set out all around her. She found she had no appetite for it, as the evening grew old and Richard did not appear. Her own relief at his absence troubled her too much. *I am bound to him, for all time. What will life be, if I am already pleased when he keeps away?* She went upstairs to bed, and sat awhile with her trinket box on her lap, carefully unpinning the lock of her mother's hair from the lining and holding it to her lips. The hair was smooth and cool; scentless, unfeeling. She shut her eyes and tried to conjure Anne Crofton into the room; tried to hear what advice she would give her daughter. *I must learn to love him, there is no other choice.* She knew that her mother would have said something similar, if she could. She sent out a different prayer instead. *I might have found her, Mother. Tell Papa – I know you are with him. I might have found her. And she will anchor me, when now I am cut adrift.*

For a second, Rachel could almost hear her mother – the gentle creak of the boards beneath her tiny, slippered feet; the swish of her skirts and the soft sound of her breathing. But when she opened her eyes the room was empty, of course, and she felt the ache of despair, like a bruise that didn't heal, but grew deeper all the while. A memory came to her then, unexpectedly – of her mother's voice rising in fear. Rachel concentrated, frowning, trying to make it clearer. A sunny day, and water sparkling; excitement, laughter. Her father's hands around her ribs, lifting her; and then that shout from her mother, high and panicky, and in its wake was emptiness. Nothing more would come but the shine of summer colours on water: blue and green and white.

Rachel wanted to sleep with the lock of hair in her hand, but didn't dare in case she ruined it somehow. In case the ribbon came undone, and scattered the precious stuff. She pinned it back to the velvet, stowed her box away in the drawer, and went to bed. When Richard came in it was night, Rachel didn't know the hour. The room was frigid, and pitch-black. He came in with no candle, stumbling and loud, and landed heavily on the bed. Rachel lay perfectly still with her knees drawn up in front of her and her elbows tight to her ribs. She fought the urge to scramble away from him, and tried to breathe evenly, so that he would think her sleeping.

'Rachel,' he said, his whisper loud enough to rattle the darkness. He reeked of spirits. The mattress sagged as he leaned over her; still she did not move, nor speak. 'Rachel.' He pulled her shoulder, trying to roll her towards him. For a second she resisted, but then realised she could not do so and yet feign sleep. So she let him turn her onto her back, and could not keep her breathing steady. It juddered in her chest. She felt his lips on hers, his skin ice-cold from the frosty night; felt his hand brush clumsily across her breasts, cupping each one and squeezing, too roughly; he moved it lower, to her crotch, and pushed his fingers inside her, and the casual, thoughtless way he did so appalled her. Yet still she did not move; she barely breathed, paralysed now by the dread of what he would do next, whether she was sleeping or awake. She felt entirely powerless to stop him, to dissuade him. She *was* entirely powerless in that, and always would be. But then he sagged bonelessly against her, his head heavy on her chest. 'Oh, *why?*' he murmured, indistinctly. 'Why can't you love me?'

Rachel held her breath and made no reply. She had no reply to give him, after all; only that she had wed in hope of coming to know and love him, but that the more she knew him, the less she loved. Soon he was asleep, still lying heavily across her, making it impossible for her to either escape or rest.

After meeting Starling in the abbey, and hearing what she'd had to say, Rachel felt Alice's absence even more. As though the gap she'd left was a tangible thing, a space with edges and depth and echoes; as unfathomable as the way she'd vanished, so completely – like a murmured word in a crowded room. Rachel felt it everywhere she went, but nowhere stronger than in the house on Lansdown Crescent, where the residents wove their lives, one way or another, around this gaping hole. Treading carefully on such dangerous ground. But Rachel felt it in her own home, too, where Alice had never been. Strangely, she felt the girl missing from her own side; she felt Alice missing from her memories, and from her dreams of the future.

Rachel visited Jonathan Alleyn twice each week, reporting to his mother afterwards, when she could be found. The lady of the house was often secreted away in some part of the house that Rachel didn't know. She sensed that Mrs Alleyn was lonely and might perhaps welcome somebody to talk to; but at the same time, she had not been made welcome enough to feel comfortable knocking on doors in search of the lady. The weather grew ever colder, and stormier. Rachel came to dread the wind, rolling down the hill as she climbed to Lansdown Crescent, making the strenuous walk even harder; blinding her eyes and tugging at her clothes. She wore the weather like a garment by the time she arrived – stained and dripping for rain; pink-cheeked and sniffling for frost; dishevelled and breathless for wind.

Rachel saw Starling more often than she saw Mrs Alleyn. The red-haired servant seemed to have free run of the house, though she was a kitchen maid. She was a near constant presence; appearing in the corner of Rachel's eye, flitting up a stair, or beckoning her from the servants' door to come and exchange a word. And since there was far more to be said and done at the Alleyns' house than there was in her own, Rachel came to anticipate her visits with a kind of eager anxiety. She thought about them whenever she wasn't there; about what had recently passed, and what she would do on her next visit.

Richard was away from Abbeygate Street more and more, and when he was home didn't seem to notice her increasing preoccupation. He rarely asked what she did at Lansdown Crescent; only took the money and pocketed it with a distracted smile, and bade her always to send his warm greetings to Mrs Alleyn.

Rachel's visits were sometimes very short; far shorter than the time it took her to walk there. On one occasion, Jonathan was asleep when she knocked softly and entered; slumped over his desk with a quill in his hand, ink stains all over his fingers. His crossed arms hid what he'd been writing; an empty wine bottle sat next to him, and a stained cup. Rachel had the idea of looking for Alice's box of letters then, but the thought of being caught doing so made her skin crawl. *Besides, Starling said she'd already searched. I must find some way to ask him.* Often he sat dumbly while she read, gazing out of the window or directly at her with a startling intensity, saying nothing. When he did that, Rachel found her heart racing in such frenzy that it made her voice shake, and spoiled her reading. Sometimes, she found herself stealing glances at him when his attention was elsewhere; at his face, his hands, his body inside his clothes. That he was a murderer, and that she could sit so close to him, seemed unreal. Each time she thought it a jolt of fear and amazement went through her.

One mild Wednesday afternoon, Rachel walked in on Jonathan in the grip of one of his headaches. He was sitting in the dark with the shutters latched, and when she opened the door the light from the hallway made him recoil. He was at his desk with his head gripped in his hands, trembling; his skin pale and shining with sweat. When Rachel asked, shocked, if she should leave him, he could only give a curt nod, keeping his mouth and eyes tightly shut. Another time she walked into one of his nightmares. He was in his sleeping quarters, and Rachel hesitated to go near him, for decency's sake; but the noise he was making was terrible to hear, and she worried that he might be feverish again. She lit a lamp and, steeling herself, went to his bedside. He was lying on it fully clothed, and there was no evidence of him having been drinking. He was panting and his body made panicky movements – arms and legs jerking as though he was trying to run from something. His head twisted to and fro on his neck, and he was muttering, spitting out odd words that made no sense.

'Mr Alleyn,' said Rachel; quiet and fearful. She cleared her throat and said his name again, more strongly. 'Mr Alleyn, wake up. You're having a bad dream . . .' At the sound of her voice his body went still, but he continued to breathe rapidly and gave a low moan, as if he was in pain. Tentatively, Rachel put her hand on his forearm and squeezed gently. 'You must wake, sir,' she said. And in a heartbeat, he did just that.

His eyes flew open, and he lunged towards her, catching her hand as she tried to retract it.

'Is she dead? Is she dead?' he said, in a voice that rasped. Fear washed coldly over Rachel. She remembered his hands around her throat on their first meeting, and the way she'd felt her own death come crowding in like a swarm of flies.

'Mr Alleyn, please let go. It's only me. Mrs Weekes . . . you were having a nightmare.'

'I tried to make it right,' he whispered, still clasping her arm. His eyes looked through her, tortured and afraid. His body was wracked by a sudden sob, and Rachel knelt down, trying to prise his fingers from her arm.

'Tried to make what right, Mr Alleyn?' He caught her other hand too, squeezing her fingers. Tears streaked down his face.

In spite of her fear, Rachel's heart softened at the sight of such anguish, and she stopped struggling against him.

'It was only a nightmare, Mr Alleyn. Rest now. You're safe here.' *But am I? This man is a killer.* But in that moment he didn't look like a killer; he looked like a frightened boy. Gradually, Jonathan let himself be soothed, and was asleep again within moments. The next time Rachel called, he seemed to have no memory of the incident.

Starling seemed impatient, as if she had expected some instant revelation. Often, the girl appeared by Rachel's side as she left the Alleyns' house, and walked partway down the hill with her, always taking her on some hidden route through a tiny alley rather than being seen out on the main street. She walked briskly to keep up with Rachel's longer strides, and tucked her hands into her armpits for warmth. Rachel always asked to hear something else about Alice; always wanted to know her better. Starling seemed happy to talk about her, as though she'd long wanted the opportunity to do so. Her face lit up when she did; a warmth and animation that sloughed off her habitual expression of suspicion and displeasure. So Rachel learnt of Alice's penchant for marzipan, and hatred of oysters; her skill at the piano and her flat, tuneless singing voice; her grace, and intelligence. How she had educated Starling, as her own governess had educated her.

'Mrs Bouchante, she was called. A widow, from France. She taught Alice until she turned sixteen and then left, so I never met her. Alice said she smelled of bitter almonds, and that her skin was as dry as a lizard's,' said Starling, with a smile. Rachel heard about Alice's colour blindness, and her heart that fluttered and kept its own time; about her love of animals, and the little drawings she did of the insects and flowers they saw along the riverbank. 'I wish I had one to keep. To remember her by. She sent most of them to Lord Faukes.'

'What was Lord Faukes like?' asked Rachel one day. 'Mrs

Alleyn says he was a good and great man.' Starling stopped in her tracks at this, closing off in an instant.

'He was all guts and garbage; a man who took without asking. He's good now he's dead, and I'll say nothing else about him,' she snapped. 'See you again, Mrs Weekes,' was all the farewell she gave as she turned and walked back up the hill, leaving Rachel startled.

When Rachel next saw Jonathan, he was restless and unable to keep still. He had deep shadows under his eyes, as he paced from chair to desk to window and back again, limping on his lame leg. Rachel watched him uneasily. His movements were jerky, and unpredictable. He spent a good deal of time rummaging in the drawers of his desk, searching for something with a frown of distraction.

'What are you looking for?' she asked at last, exasperated. Jonathan looked up with a start, and then froze as if confounded by the question. He stood up slowly, his hands hanging limply at his sides.

'I . . . do not remember,' he said, troubled.

'Please, come and sit down. Have you not slept?'

'No, no. I cannot sleep. I do not sleep,' he muttered, and began leafing randomly through the papers on his desk. 'The note. The note from the lovers' tree,' he said quietly. 'I was looking for it. I thought . . . I thought perhaps I had read it wrong. Perhaps there was something in it, some clue I had missed.'

'The lovers' tree? What is that? What note?'

'The note! Not written by my hand, and not by hers . . . whose then? *That* is the question!' His hair was falling into his face and he scraped it back impatiently with fingers that shook. *He is exhausted.* Without thinking, Rachel moved towards him. She put one hand on his arm to still him, then took his hand and drew him towards his chair, surprised by the warmth of his skin.

'Mr Alleyn, please come and sit down. Come and sit with me. You are overwrought,' she said softly. *And now I hold that hand that would have choked the life from me*, she thought, wonderingly. *He would have killed me, and I am told he has killed another. Why then can't I feel that, in my heart? Why don't I believe he is a murderer?* As if caught off guard by her touch, Jonathan let himself be led. He sat down on the edge of the chair, still frowning absently, and when she took her hand away she felt his fingers cling to hers, just for a second, as though he would have liked the touch to remain. That harrowing look of pain and regret was in his eyes, and Rachel felt pity gnawing at the unease he caused her.

'You were looking for a note from Alice? A note she left you?' Rachel asked. With a swell of nerves, she saw her moment to ask. 'Perhaps it is with all the other letters? I will search for it amongst them, if you tell me where?' The words sounded so duplicitous to her own ears that her mouth went dry, but Jonathan didn't seem to notice.

'Other letters? What other letters?' He shook his head, and when he spoke his voice was heavy with despair. 'No, it was a note *for* Alice. Not written by me, but left in our secret place. A place only she could have told him about. The other . . . person.'

'The lovers' tree? It was a place you used to meet at?' she asked, and Jonathan nodded. 'And this . . . other person, who left her a note. You think that it was a sweetheart?' *Starling swore it could not be so. But if he saw a note?*

'I was told . . . I was told she'd been seen with another. I did not believe it, not for a heartbeat. Still, I do not . . . And yet . . . and yet . . .' He shook his head, perplexed. 'I found a note left for her, with a time and day to meet. It was not signed . . . but it was not in her hand. Who, then, was she to meet?' he said, in quiet desperation. Rachel thought for a moment, her strange but ever strengthening loyalty to Alice Beckwith shaping her answer.

'It could have been entirely innocent, could it not, Mr Alleyn? People are ever quick to impugn a lady for the most harmless of gestures . . .'

'That's why I wished to read it again! But I can't find it . . . I've looked everywhere . . . I searched all night. What if I . . . what if I never saw it? What if my mind is playing tricks on me again?' He chewed savagely at his lower lip, and Rachel saw a thin line of blood spring up where he tore the skin.

'Stop. Stop doing that.' She took his hand again, pulled it away from his mouth. 'You're exhausted, and you need to eat something . . .'

'I will not eat until—'

'You will eat, sir. I will see you do so, or I will come no more; for I won't sit by and watch you sicken.'

'Watch me sicken?' He almost laughed. 'Madam, I sickened years and years ago.'

'That much I can see, and perhaps it is time for you to stop revelling in it so,' said Rachel, crisply. Jonathan frowned as she went to the door and called to Dorcas to bring coffee, bread and cheese.

'Let me have some wine if I must take something.'

'It's not yet noon, sir. And there are more than enough wine-soaked men in my life as it is.' Jonathan watched her steadily as she came to sit back down. 'Do not eye me so, sir. I know your opinion of my husband well enough; I'm sure I don't need to explain any further.'

'You are different today, Mrs Weekes. You are bolder.'

'I am tired too, Mr Alleyn.'

'The kind of tired that sleep does not cure?'

'Yes. That kind.' For a moment they looked at one another, and neither one blinked.

'Then perhaps we begin to understand each other,' Jonathan murmured at last. Rachel looked away, suddenly self-conscious.

When the tray was brought up Rachel had some coffee as well. She cut a thick slice of bread and topped it with cheese for Jonathan, and watched him steadily while he ate. He seemed to recover his appetite as he did so, reaching for more without her prompting. The hot drink steamed the window glass, obscuring the view of brown autumn trees and city roofs. It gave the impression of the room closing in around them, isolating them from the rest of the house, the rest of the world. Rachel was surprised to find this comforting.

'You said to me before that you wished to unsee things you had seen, and undo things you had done,' she said at last. 'Will you tell me which things?' Jonathan stopped eating at once, letting the last piece of bread fall from his fingers.

'Why would you wish to hear such things?'

'Because . . . because I do not understand you, Mr Alleyn. But I wish to. And because I think, perhaps, long years of holding these things to yourself, and staying silent, have not helped you to forget them. Perhaps if you spoke of them, if you shared them . . .'

'You would take up half my burden for me?' he said bitterly. Rachel watched him, silently. He chewed his final mouthful and swallowed it laboriously. 'Such things are not fit for a woman's ears.'

'Oh, what is a woman, but a human being?' Rachel replied, irritated. 'You haven't borne the knowledge with any great stoicism, or grace. Why should I fare any worse than you?' Jonathan stared at her and, slowly, his face filled with something like dread, and she understood that some part of him wanted to speak, and yet feared to.

'It is not the knowledge I must bear, but the deeds,' he said. 'I have never spoken of them.'

'Try it, sir. Only try it, and then let us see,' she said.

'I don't know where to start.' Rachel thought quickly; to ask him outright about Alice would get her nowhere.

'Tell me how your leg was injured. Tell me of that battle,' she suggested.

'Battle? No, indeed. It was at B . . . *Badajoz*.'

His voice failed him, as if the word were too much; it was spoken in a hoarse whisper, raw and fearful. 'It was no battle. It was a hell on earth, a heinous orgy of destruction and grief . . . No.' He shook his head vehemently. 'I cannot start there, for that is the end, not the beginning.'

'Tell me of the beginning of the war, then. I was still young, at that time. My father didn't encourage me to hear much about it, but I saw news of our victories on the side of the mail coach. They would decorate it with ribbons, too.'

'You were still young? As was I, Mrs Weekes, as was I. I was that concerned with assembling my baggage, and with turning out my horse just so, that I'd given almost no thought to fighting. To why we were going; to what a war would be. I had not known what it would be. Jars of coral tooth powder and pomade, with silver lids – that's what I spent my last few days trying to find. Isn't that a perfect folly? That's what I thought I needed. A jar of hair pomade with a silver lid.' He shook his head incredulously.

'You were a cavalry officer, then?'

'Yes. Moths – that was the first thing. Do you believe in signs, Mrs Weekes? Portents, I mean?' he said intently, leaning towards her with a gleam of desperation in his eyes, as if he could somehow change any of what had passed.

'I . . .' She had been about to deny it. 'I should not; yet I see them, sometimes.' *The morning of my wedding, when that thrush sang its heart out, keeping its eye on me. Trying to warn me.*

'Enlightened thought calls them the product of a weak and

superstitious mind. But perhaps we do not yet understand all there is to know about this world, and this life. I think such signs should be heeded.' Jonathan nodded gravely. 'The first sign I saw was the moths. I took a wound – you will laugh to hear how. Some fierce battles were fought, that first summer of 1808. We fought the French in Portugal, before we even crossed into Spain. We landed like conquering heroes and told the Portuguese people their time of oppression was over, even though we'd already lost men and horses in the surf, trying to land the boats . . . Before we even set foot on the peninsula, we lost men. But still we thought we were invincible. On the very first march, men fell out of line in the heat. I remember looking at the dust cloud above us and thinking we would all be smothered beneath it. The troops were green novices, weakened by the sea crossing. They'd joined up for a wage, or a meal, or for the glory the recruiters told them would be theirs; and I was as green a novice as any of them, for all I was an officer, and mounted upon a fine horse. My first wound . . . my first wound was a scorpion sting.'

Afterwards, he knew to shake out his boots before putting them on in the morning. The sting felt like a jab from a red-hot needle, in the arch of his left foot; he kicked the boot off and watched, revolted, as the half-crushed creature limped away. It was yellowish-brown, about the length of his thumb. He examined the wound but there wasn't much to see at first – a small hole leaking clear fluid, around which the immediate area had gone white, the outer area a mottled red. The pain of the initial sting soon faded, to leave a low throbbing only. Jonathan rinsed his foot with cold water, then pulled on his boots and thought no more of it.

A battle was brewing; they were at the village of Vimiero, and the French were coming. His blood rose at the thought – he had yet to be tested in any real way against the enemy; he was excited and afraid; he was keen to know how he would prove himself as an officer. Within two days, however, Jonathan could think of little else but the pain in his foot. Had he been an infantry man, and not mounted on Suleiman, he would not have been able to march. He would have been left behind, his company command replaced. At the end of the second day he slept with his boots on. He was sure that if he ever got his left boot off, he would certainly never get it back on again. His head was pounding, he felt weak and dizzy. The foot with the sting was so hot he worried that it might set fire to his stocking. It felt huge, heavy, and very wrong. He kept the boot on for a second reason too – he didn't want to look at his foot.

Then came the heat and fury of the battle at Vimiero, and Jonathan learned how he would prove himself in the fray – capable, outwardly calm, while inside his heart shuddered in outrage. When it ended the British were victorious, the French routed and in retreat, though there were heavy losses on both sides. Wellesley and several other senior officers wanted to pursue them, all the way to Lisbon. They were denied this by high command; the French were to be allowed to take their wounded and retreat unmolested. They were even, eventually, to have the use of English ships to leave Portugal, a decision for which the British commanders would be recalled to London to give account. On the strewn and smoking battlefield, French and British soldiers greeted one another as they searched the fallen for men they could save. They shared a few words, a laugh, a pinch of tobacco. Dazed and exhausted, Jonathan watched them with a growing sense of unreality; for if the men did not hate one another, how could they kill one another? Why would they? He was baffled by it; felt apart from the rest of them for being unable to understand. That was his first real taste of battle, and it left him numb, bewildered, and frightened.

When he dismounted from Suleiman at day's end, Jonathan couldn't even set his left foot down. Captain Sutton, his company second in command, noticed the way he grimaced and hovered the leg. He forced Major Alleyn to sit down on the crumbled remains of a village house, and when pulling at the boot caused him to scream in agony, Sutton cut it from his leg instead, using a short, sharp utility knife. The stink that emerged with the bloated foot caused them both to blench. Captain Sutton helped him to the field hospital, gave him brandy and then left to return to the men.

The surgeons worked in open-sided tents under big, yellow lamps. They worked right through the hot night, engaged in what was often a futile battle to save the gravely wounded men. Since his foot was not life-threatening, Jonathan sat to one side and waited his turn, watching in mounting horror. The surgeons sawed and they stitched; they dipped their hands inside men to pick out shrapnel, they fished for musket balls with long forceps; they plastered over belly wounds, no matter what damage had been done inside the man. When they ran out of plaster, they packed wounds with cotton rags and the shirts of dead men, and when they ran out of those they did not pack them at all, but left them open to the night sky and waited for the men to die. Which they did, crying piteously for God or their mothers until their voices left them. The night clamoured with the sounds of their agony. Jonathan sat, and he watched, and he waited. It took around twenty minutes to amputate a leg through the hip joint, he learned. Only a stick of wood kept that man from biting through his own tongue. There was nothing to relieve pain but watered-down rum, which the men vomited back up in their shock. The smell of blood and rum and bile was everywhere, impossible to escape – to breathe was to breathe it in. Sweat ran from the surgeons' heads into the wounds they were trying to close.

It was near sunrise before Jonathan was seen to. He climbed onto a table upon which, moments before, he'd seen a man pass his last moments with blood and piss leaking from his shattered body. He felt the man's fluids seeping through his own shirt and breeches. The surgeon took one look at his bloated foot and then glared at Jonathan with disgust dawning through the wooden exhaustion on his face. He looked *disgusted* that Jonathan should trouble him with so trivial a wound, and Jonathan was disgusted with himself as well. He was disgusted with the war, and the ways of men, and the whole world. He stared up as the surgeon cut away his stained stocking. Underneath, his foot was darkly purple, huge and stinking; a crusted layer of pus had dribbled from the scorpion sting and dried on his feverish skin. It smelled like foul meat and corruption. Calmly, the surgeon took up his bloody scalpel and sliced open the skin around the sting, so that all the poison and filth inside could run out. A splatter of rank and rotting blood, to join the unspeakable mess on the floor. Jonathan was too exhausted, too shocked at the pain to make a sound. He gazed up at the lamps, and that's when he noticed the moths. Huge black moths, the biggest he'd ever seen – the size of the palm of his hand. They circled the lamps, drawn to the light, on wings as black as pitch and so velvet soft that they made no sound at all. In his near delirium, Jonathan saw them as the souls of the men who had died that night, trying to find a way back into the light, into life. He took them as a sign, a stark warning, that they were all dead men.

'I should have heeded that warning,' Jonathan said to Rachel. 'I should have fled. Better to have been called a coward outright, perhaps, than to have carried on, and been a part of what came later. To this day I cannot abide the smell of rum . . . The smell of it returns me there, to that night, and it's like a nightmare I can't wake up from.' Jonathan's face was colourless in the wan light of the day; beads of sweat had broken out on his forehead. For a while Rachel feared he might faint, but he did not; he stayed hunched in his chair. Rachel swallowed, struggling for something to say.

'I have heard it said that war changes a man; that he is forced to address his own true nature, his own essence, by the extremity of his situation . . .'

'War changes a man, it is true. For the most part, it changes him from being a person to being meat. Meat and offal, to be left lying for flies and stray dogs to consume.' He glanced up at her. 'You flinch at this, Mrs Weekes? It is the truth, and you wanted to hear it.'

'I know I did. And I do. The truth is important, for nothing festers like a falsehood, this much I know.' She watched him as she said this, in case it would have some effect on him, but there was nothing. Only his dark, pained eyes in his pale face, and the sense of a vast tide of feeling pent up behind both, causing chaos there.

'Some things are worse than falsehood, I think. Some falsehoods can be kind,' he murmured.

'You carry a great weight of experience inside you. A great weight of bad memory.'

'So great I can never be rid of it, and it taints everything I have done or will ever do since. I can do no right, now; not after the wrongs I have done. After Badajoz . . . after Badajoz I did a kind thing. A good thing, I think, though many lies were woven around it. It was the last thing I did in that war, my last action in it, and with it I hoped somehow to begin to make amends. But I can't think of it without thinking of everything else, of what compelled me to do it. Every single thing I have done since the war is tainted by the things I did during the war. Do you see?' Suddenly, he clasped his head in his hands as if it hurt him. 'I could give everything I owned to a poor man in the street, and it would not be generosity. It would be a symptom of my guilt, my disease.'

'In war a man is compelled to fight, and to kill. It is duty, sir, not sin,' Rachel ventured.

'Compelled to kill, yes. To kill in battle, when under attack, or in the defence of others. Would that that was all I did, during those years.'

'You mean to say you killed when you should not have? You killed . . . innocents?' she whispered.

Jonathan's eyes bored into hers, and when he spoke his voice was as cold and sharp as a blade.

'I have seen and done things that would send you screaming from this room, Mrs Weekes.' Rachel's heart beat faster; nervous tension made it hard to breathe.

'In war—'

'On the march towards the Spanish border in the autumn of 1808, after we had allowed the French to leave the field, defeated and weakened, or so we thought, they fled before us, destroying everything in their path. All food, all water supplies, all shelter. We came to a village where every last soul had been put to the sword, for the crime of having us come to their aid. A young girl . . . a young girl, not more than fourteen or fifteen lay in the middle of the street. Her face was comely, even in death. She had been crushed beneath a vast stone that they'd placed on her chest so that she could neither breathe nor move as they ravaged her. Who knows how many times – the lower parts of her body were a ruin. Nearby lay the corpses of a man and woman, and of smaller children, three or four of them. Her parents and siblings, it seemed, who had been made to watch this most brutal spectacle before being slain themselves.' He paused and swallowed convulsively, and Rachel fought to keep her horror from showing.

'A while later, two or three miles from the village, we came upon a French infantryman who'd been left behind by his comrades. He was wounded in both legs – not severely, but he'd grown too weak to carry on. But he had a good deal of life left in him. He lived a good long while.' Jonathan gazed at Rachel, and now his eyes were quite empty. 'There was a man amongst our foot, an Irishman called McInerney. The raped maiden had borne a likeness to his daughter, he said. The wounded Frenchman lived long enough to plead for mercy as McInerney took off his skin, a strip at a time. A good many of us watched him, including myself; we did nothing to hinder him. But this bloody revenge did nothing to slake the men's anger. If anything we grew angrier still. That beast part had awoken in each one of us, and every vile thing we did and saw from then on only made it stronger. That is what war does to men, Mrs Weekes. That is what it did to me.'

'Enough!' Rachel gasped. Her hands flew to cover her mouth. She'd been trying to show no reaction but this was too much, and the room was spinning. Jonathan gave her a pitying look.

'Now you wish you hadn't urged me to speak. I should apologise, because you had no idea what you were asking, but I cannot. I live with these things. This is what I know the world to be, and if you understand that, then you will understand why I want no part of it.'

There was a pause in which neither one of them spoke. Rachel struggled to compose herself.

'Don't cry, Mrs Weekes,' Jonathan said quietly. He reached out as if to cover her hand with his, but she snatched it away and saw him retreat, turning in on himself again.

'Forgive me . . . it is only that . . .' She shook her head, helplessly.

'It is only that I repel you now, more than when we first

met, though my room stank of death that time – one of Starling's little pranks – and I near killed you.'

'No! It is only that . . . when the fight is to stay in command of oneself, the slightest kindness from another can . . . can be the ruin of composure. Is it not so?' She blotted her eyes and looked up to find the ghost of a smile on Jonathan's face.

'And you wonder why I baulk from telling it all to you. You wonder why I baulk from that kindness,' he said bitterly.

'I'm quite all right, Mr Alleyn. Only unaccustomed to hearing . . . such things.' She took a deep breath. Jonathan had sunk back in his chair and was gnawing at his lip again. 'You need to rest. You need to sleep, sir,' she said.

'You have some measure, now, of what I see when I close my eyes,' he replied.

'Perhaps a tonic of some kind . . . a sleeping draught?' Jonathan shook his head.

'Such oblivion is dangerously compelling, Mrs Weekes. For . . . for years I relied on tincture of opium to liberate me from this. It brings on a wonderful kind of living death . . . a release from all thought and care. At one time I lay near to death because if it. Only my mother saved me then, removing the stuff from me, and leaving me to suffer in its absence. She saved my life, I think, though I did not thank her for it at the time. I'm not sure I thank her for it now. It would be simpler to die, I sometimes think.'

'Our lives are God-given,' Rachel said softly. She shrugged. 'It is not for us to decide when we relinquish them, and what would be simpler is not pertinent.'

'Is that so?' he said, his mouth twisting in disgust.

He stared blackly at her for a moment, and then erupted out of his chair. 'You say it is for God to decide, then? Does God put guns in men's hands? Does God make men rape young girls to death? Does he take aim with flying shrapnel and artillery fire? Does he place one fateful finger on each man on a battlefield and say "fever, gangrene, dysentery"? No!' His voice had risen to a shout, and Rachel didn't dare reply. He seemed to tower over her so she stood up, knotting her fingers in front of her to keep them still, and watched as Jonathan strode to the bookcase and fetched down one of the large glass jars he kept there. It took some effort to lift it; the liquid inside sloshed. Rachel could sense the weightiness of it, and inside was a wrinkled, knobbed thing, trailing tentacles from its underside. 'Do you know what this is?' he said.

'No,' Rachel whispered.

'This is a man's brain. He was a criminal – a murderer, in fact.' Rachel stared at it in horror.

'How . . . how came you to have such a thing?'

'I befriended one of the doctors my mother sent to me. An anatomist. He thought he could cure the pains in my head by cutting a hole in my skull the size of a sovereign, to relieve the pressure. By exposing my brain to the sun and sky I would be cured, so he proclaimed. What do you think? Should I have let him?'

'Sweet Lord, no, he would have killed you, surely?' said Rachel. Inside the jar the brain was moving, the cords beneath it wafting like the sentient tendrils of some creature. She began to feel queasy.

'He said not. He said he had experimented up in London, upon a woman who'd been driven quite insane by the deaths of her six children. He thought the procedure would let the ill humours out of her mind, and restore her reason.'

'And did it?' Rachel's voice was near strangled.

'Well, she raves no more. She speaks no more either, nor walks, nor eats. They feed her through a tube, and when they stop, she will die.'

'Why do you tell me this?'

'I would make you *see*, Mrs Weekes. I befriended this doctor, though I did not let him carve my skull. I went with him to watch the opening of cadavers brought down from the gallows; I . . . I wanted to learn how the body worked. I wanted to find the place inside a man where the soul resides; I wanted to be sure, again, of its existence. Because otherwise we are just machines, aren't we? Like the digesting duck – like that copper mouse? So I watched, and I studied, and this is what I found out: we *are* just machines, Mrs Weekes! We eat and we sleep and we shit and then we do it all again, just like the other beasts that walk this earth. And when we die it is because another man has broken some part of us – removed some cog from the machine so that it may not run. And this, *this*—' He shook the brain in its jar so that the fluid sloshed and the lid rattled; he took one slow step towards her, then another. 'This is what decides it. Not God. Not fate. So I ask you, Mrs Weekes, if another man may decide when I should die, why then should I not decide it for myself?'

Jonathan Alleyn stood in front of her, eyes snapping; holding the jar out in front of him like some gruesome gift. His hands were white with the effort of gripping its smooth sides; shudders ran up his arms.

'We are not mere machines, sir. I am sure of it. Man was made for a higher purpose . . . in God's image . . .' said Rachel, shakily, fighting the urge to run from him. She could not take her eyes from the greyish thing, the dead thing, in the jar. *Is that truly what I keep inside my skull?* It seemed desperately wrong that it should have been torn away from its owner and kept in such a hideous manner, for living eyes to look upon. *Such things are meant to stay hidden.*

'In God's image?' Jonathan laughed then – a mirthless sound. 'Then God is a murderous bastard, Mrs Weekes, and you are a wilfully *stupid* woman.' Rachel flinched, cut by the insult.

'What then of love?' she said desperately. 'Where in that machine of blood and bone does love reside, Mr Alleyn?'

'*Love?*' he spat. He stared at her blankly as if he didn't know the word, and then his eyes blazed anew. Anger disfigured his face, turned his lips bloodless and thin, put deep furrows between his brows. It made him look bestial indeed. 'Love is an illusion. Love is a myth. Love is a story we tell ourselves to make living more bearable! And it is a *lie*!' he roared, lifting the jar high above their heads.

Rachel froze. Jonathan's sudden rage assaulted her like a flare of agony, so intense it slowed time, and made everything else hollow and unreal in comparison. In that moment, she glimpsed its black, ravaged heart; the look in Jonathan's eyes chilled her. *He can't even see me any more.* Then his arms came down abruptly, swinging with tremendous force. At the last second Rachel managed to take a step backwards, and so the jar exploded into shards at her feet, not over her head.

Silence rang in her ears. The reek of spirits rushed to fill the room, stinging her eyes and nose, bringing tears to blur her vision. There was a stinging from her leg, too – blood was welling from a cut above her ankle, a neat slice through stockings and skin. The murderer's brain had come to rest on the toe of her right shoe. When Rachel moved her foot she felt its soggy weight. It rolled away sluggishly, shining wet and looking more alive than it should. Her gorge rose; she shuddered and clamped her hands over her mouth. Jonathan was breathing hard, staring straight ahead without blinking; his empty hands hung at his sides. A sliver of glass had flown up and nicked his cheekbone, and a thin line of blood ran straight down from it, looking like a scarlet tear. Gradually, Rachel saw some awareness return to his expression; he blinked, and then his eyes widened, and he swallowed. As if released by this, she stepped past him hurriedly, her heel grinding a fragment of broken glass into dust. Her walk became a run, and she left him there, standing in silence, as she pulled open the door and fled.

At the bottom of the stairs two figures were waiting for her – Starling rushing from the door in the panelling, and Josephine Alleyn coming from the front parlour. Rachel stopped and leant on the newel post to catch her breath.

'Mrs Weekes! I heard a terrible noise, I feared . . .' Mrs Alleyn chose not to say what she had feared. Her face had worn panic, but soon resettled itself.

'He . . . the jar . . . I think . . .' Rachel fought for words. 'I am not injured,' she said.

'But, you are. Your ankle . . . come – come at once and sit down. Starling, why do you loiter? Send up some tea, and some warm water and cloths.'

'Madam,' Starling muttered, scowling as she vanished. Josephine led Rachel through to the parlour, and seated her on the couch.

'I do hope my son has not . . . What is that dreadful stench?' Mrs Alleyn recoiled, putting her fingers under her nose.

'Oh, I can hardly tell you!' Rachel cried. She felt the liquid sloshing around in her shoes, between her toes, and nausea washed through her again. 'It was one of his . . . specimen jars. The h-human brain. He . . . dropped it.' Mrs Alleyn leant away from Rachel, revolted.

'Please,' she muttered. 'Take off your shoes and stockings immediately. Falmouth! Take these things away. Clean and dry the shoes, if you can, but do not bother with the stockings – burn them. And send Dorcas to my room to find a clean pair for Mrs Weekes.'

'My thanks, Mrs Alleyn,' said Rachel, wearily.

The stockings that Dorcas brought were knitted silk, far finer and softer than Rachel's woollen ones. Josephine Alleyn watched her wash her feet and put them on with an expression that hovered between compassion and froideur.

'Tell me, Mrs Weekes, was this a deliberate attack by my son?' she asked, at last.

'I do not think so. That is . . . he meant to smash the thing, in his anger . . . but I do not think he meant to injure me.' *But he would have, perhaps, had I not stepped back. Without even knowing he did so.* The thought sent her a shiver.

'What had angered him so?'

'I . . . it was my fault. I spoke of love. I thought to . . . soothe him, to reassure him, when he had grown agitated. But the effect was quite the opposite.'

'Yes. It would have been,' said Mrs Alleyn. When Rachel looked up she found the older woman studying her. 'But you must know, Mrs Weekes – you who have also lost people – that love can be as cruel a thing as any under the sun.'

'Yes, I suppose it can be.'

'When I first invited you here to introduce you to Jonathan, I told you, did I not, that I sensed some strength in you?'

'You did, Mrs Alleyn.'

'That was the strength I sensed, for it is in me too. It is the strength that comes from suffering, and surviving it. My son does not have it, and so his wounds do not heal.'

'You speak of your own grief at losing your husband, and your father?' At this, Mrs Alleyn's face fell out of its steady composure for once. Her eyelids flickered down, her lower lip shook, just for a moment.

'I had but two years of marriage to Mr Robert Alleyn, before his untimely death forced me to return to my father. They were the happiest two years of my life,' she said, words weighty and cold with sorrow. In that moment, Rachel saw Mrs Alleyn differently. She saw a woman, alone and afraid, rather than a grand and powerful lady. Impulsively, she took the other woman's hand in both of hers and held it tightly, as much for her own comfort as for Mrs Alleyn's.

'I do fear that I shall never be that happy,' Rachel said, with quiet yearning. 'For such love – passionate love – I have never known.'

As though a door had closed, Josephine Alleyn retreated from her.

'Do not wish for it,' she said. 'Such love will use you ill, like as not. It used me ill. It used my son ill.' She stared down at their clasped hands so pointedly that Rachel released her hold, confused.

'But you would not wish to have never felt it at all, surely?' she said. Mrs Alleyn did not answer at once, and thoughts paraded behind her eyes.

'Perhaps, perhaps not. Perhaps I value the lessons it taught me, more than anything. The strength that losing it gave me. A woman needs that strength, to survive the ordeals this world will devise for us. The ordeals men will devise for us.' She said this so grimly that Rachel did not know how to answer.

When Falmouth returned her shoes Rachel immediately smelt the preserving spirits still on them. She didn't ever want to put them back on her feet, but saw little option. Mrs Alleyn wrinkled her nose and scowled.

'Well. You will have to wear them to go home, Mrs Weekes, I cannot lend you any of mine. I have always had very dainty feet, but yours . . . But then do burn them, and find yourself another pair. This should cover your expenses, and you may keep the stockings.' She fetched coins from a nearby drawer and handed them over.

'You are very kind, Mrs Alleyn.'

'But are you, Mrs Weekes? And are you kind enough?'

'I don't understand.'

'Will you come again to my son, in spite of this . . . latest mishap?' She asked it abruptly, almost impatiently. *If I say no, she will waste no more time with me.*

'I . . . I must have a chance to rest, and to think, Mrs Alleyn.'

'To think?' she echoed, and then waved her hand. 'Very well. Take your time, Mrs Weekes.'

When Rachel got home she gave her shoes to a pauper, and found that the foul smell had got into the stockings Mrs Alleyn had given her. She dropped them, pinched between thumb and finger, into a pail of soapy water; then sat near the front window and waited for Richard, lost in thought. Jonathan Alleyn filled her mind: the things he had told her about the war; the way he had lost control in his anger. *Is Starling right about him? Could he have done Alice harm, even if he didn't intend it, and doesn't remember it?* The thought was somehow more troubling to her now than it had been in the beginning. *But not killed her,* said the echo, in hope. *Not that.* If there truly had been a letter for Alice from some unknown other person . . . could that person not also have made her disappear? Or helped her to? *She could be alive.*

A knock at the door startled her up. It was a smut-faced boy with a note for her; she gave him a farthing and he scampered away. The note was written on a small scrap of paper, the torn corner of a bigger sheet. The ink was as black as soot, the writing well slanted and done with extravagant loops, untidily, as if hurried. The note contained few words, but those were enough to still her. *Forgive me. Jon.ᵃ Alleyn.* Rachel folded this tiny note into her palm and held it until the paper turned as warm and soft as skin. *The other note is the key to this – the note to Alice from the lovers' tree. Did she betray him for another? Is it the war that plagues him, or his secret guilt? I must know.*

For several days, she did not return to Lansdown Cres-cent. She needed to let herself settle, to take a breath, to understand what she thought and felt a little better. To understand why she kept Jonathan Alleyn's note tucked into her trinket box, and reread it as if it contained some important and complicated instruction that she needed to learn by heart. It had been too long since she'd visited Duncan Weekes, so she took him a beef pie, still warm from the oven. They sat to either side of his mean hearth and ate it from plates on their laps, with a mug of hot watered brandy each, talking about small things and pleasant memories. The old man seemed in good spirits, and Rachel was keen to clear her thoughts for a while, so she mentioned nothing of the Alleyns, or her difficult involvement with them.

She went with Harriet Sutton and Cassandra to buy new shoes with the money Mrs Alleyn had given her, on a day of such pervading chill that the chief topic of conversation was the distant dream of the coming spring and summer; the picnics and boat trips they would take together; the short-sleeved dresses they would wear, the flowers in their hat bands.

'With the coins she gave you, you could buy a far finer pair,' said Harriet, as the cobbler measured Rachel's feet, and she chose a style from his design book.

'I know. But this way we can all go and have tea afterwards, and I can treat us to cakes to go with it. If you would like to?'

'Oh, can we?' said Cassandra, her face lighting up.

'Those old shoes of mine were far too lightweight for walking right across the city two times in the week, as I now must. A simple, sturdy pair like this will serve far better.'

'And Mr Weekes will not mind? Your spending money on us?' Harriet asked this quietly, for Rachel's ears only.

'He will not know of it,' she replied. 'And if he did, why should he begrudge me the rare pleasure of entertaining friends? I know, in truth, that he wishes me to be out in society more.'

'Oh, I am sure he would not begrudge it.' Harriet smiled again, but her eyes showed some misgiving. 'But perhaps we are not quite the society he would encourage you into.' *She thinks of the money he lost at cards, and she knows it was not the first time. She knows how he hoped I would make him richer.* Rachel found that she was not embarrassed by this, but grateful for her friend's understanding. 'It is an adjustment, is it not?' Harriet went on, kindly. 'The pocket money my father used to give me was far more than I had to spend during my first years as Captain Sutton's wife.'

'Well, perhaps that is also true for me. But it has been many years since I had any money to spend whatsoever. Do not discourage me from enjoying a small bonus such as this,' said Rachel, with a smile.

'Oh don't, Mama! Don't discourage her,' said Cassandra imploringly. She turned from examining the many-coloured swatches of fabric and leather on the counter, her black hair swinging like a sombre pennant.

'Listen to how she pleads! I never knew a girl more enamoured of cake as this one,' said Harriet. 'Or one so spoilt by her parents to have become so.' Cassandra widened her eyes, quite artfully, her demeanour gravely slighted. 'See how she tricks me!' Harriet laughed.

'Cassandra, my dear girl, I can think of no better reason to trick your mother than for cake,' said Rachel mischievously. 'But in this instance you are quite safe — no such tactics are needed. Cake will be had.' The little girl went back to the swatches, and Rachel smiled at her mother. 'Let me, dear Mrs Sutton, to thank you for all of your many small kindnesses since we met,' she said.

But Rachel could not stay away from Lansdown Crescent

for good. Jonathan Alleyn took a deep breath when he saw her.

'I didn't think you would come again,' he said stiffly.

'Well,' said Rachel, as she stepped into his study. She wrinkled her nose. 'The stink of that . . . liquid still lingers.'

'The ethanol . . . I know. Starling has scrubbed and scrubbed, much to her distaste. But to no avail.'

'I daresay it will fade, in time.'

'As will the memory of what caused it, I hope. Mrs Weekes,' he said, looking down at the offending patch of floor. 'Mrs Weekes, forgive me. To behave in such a manner was . . .'

'Unforgivable?' she supplied. Jonathan glanced up in dismay, and relaxed a little when he caught the humour in Rachel's eyes.

'Yes. Unforgivable. But here you are. I am . . . glad.'

'Your temper is your enemy, sir. You must not let it command you.'

'Yes. It was not always so, but . . .' He rubbed at his face, then yawned uncontrollably.

'Have you still not slept since I saw you last?' said Rachel, incredulously.

'Perhaps I have . . . a little. I don't remember.' He looked up again with a bitter smile. 'Sleep is the soul's ease, remember, and I have none.'

'Let's not have this again. I do not believe we can lose our souls, or even that they can change. Like life, they are God-given, and immutable, and if I risk another of your rages to say so, then so be it. But perhaps the soul may be wounded; perhaps it may sicken, and retreat deep inside us,' said Rachel. Jonathan slumped, as if her words exhausted him.

'Some things are easy to say, more difficult to prove.' He turned away and sat in the chair behind his desk, staring listlessly at the clutter that covered it.

Rachel thought for a moment, and then went to the shelves. 'Do you mean to cast another of my specimens at me, in revenge?' said Jonathan.

'No. I mean to show you some proof.' She held out her hand to him, and in her palm sat the clockwork copper mouse. 'You were meditating on what made people, and animals, different from automata, you told me. Was it really necessary to craft such an exquisite toy in the process? Or did you do it for the pleasure of it?'

'I . . . I don't know.' He frowned.

'This is a beautiful thing, Mr Alleyn. Truly, a beautiful thing, and it came from within you. From your heart and soul to your hand.' Rachel wound the key and watched the little mouse run. Jonathan watched it too.

'I was thinking of Alice, when I made it,' he said. 'She loved . . . all creatures. Small, furry things; helpless things. She had a pet harvest mouse for a while, when she was a child. It had lost a leg to the farmer's scythe, and she nursed it. She kept it in a tinder box, and named it Harold.' He paused, watching the mouse run as if he'd never seen it before. 'Did you ever hear such a ridiculous name for a mouse?' He smiled at the memory. Rachel swallowed, ever uneasy in the face of his shifting emotions. They seemed to race through him like clouds in a blustery sky.

'There, then,' she said softly. 'It is as I said. Your soul is intact, sir. It's only your heart that's broken.' Jonathan Alleyn gave her a long look, and when the copper mouse stopped running he took it from her, and held it in his cupped hands. 'You . . . you slept once before, as I read to you, Mr Alleyn. I wonder if you might again?' she said.

'I'm in no mood for poetry, Mrs Weekes,' said Jonathan. 'And sleeping in this chair makes my body ache.'

'I brought something other than poetry to read today. Something to take your thoughts away from your own troubles, and fix them on far-off times and places. Why not recline, while I read it?'

'You mean to tuck me into bed like a child?'

'I mean to do no such thing. But if it's sleep we're aiming for, then you may take yourself to bed without fear of embarrassing me.'

Jonathan watched her steadily for a while, and then rubbed at his eyes so fiercely that he turned them red. He rose unsteadily and crossed to the far end of the room, to the doorway that led through to his shadowy sleeping quarters. There he paused.

'When I thought you would not come again, I . . . I liked it not. Will you . . . will you come again soon, Mrs Weekes?' he said. Rachel faltered to hear him sound so vulnerable. *Does he need me, now?*

'As soon as you wish it, Mr Alleyn,' she said. Jonathan nodded, and turned away from her. Rachel heard the bed creak as he lay down upon it.

'Whatever it is you plan to read, I'll hear precious little of it if you remain right over there,' he called out to her. Rachel approached the darkened threshold, and knew that she must not cross it. She fetched the chair from his desk and positioned it near the doorway, then took out the book she'd brought with her, brand new, the spine pristine.

'I haven't read this yet myself, so we will begin it together. It's a novel by Sir Walter Scott, and the title is *Ivanhoe*.'

'A novel? I don't care for novels.'

'How many have you read?' she countered, and was met with silence. 'As I thought. A good many gentlemen claim to have no interest and find no merit in a fictional story, when they haven't given themselves the proper chance to sample one,' she said.

'Men's minds have greater cares and responsibilities than women's. What is there to be gained from wasting time reading the fancies of others? Such things are for the entertainment of young boys.'

'Listen, and perhaps you will find out what's to be gained,' Rachel replied, tartly. There was a loaded silence from the unlit room, and so she began to read.

She read for an hour or more, until her mouth was dry and she had reached that state of deep tranquillity that came when she was carried away by a piece of writing. Finding herself at a natural pause in the text, she listened. From the darkness the only sound was of heavy, regular breathing. *He sleeps.* Rachel closed her eyes for a moment, filled with a powerful sense of satisfaction. Before leaving she sat a while in silence, and found herself wishing she might look in on him in his sleep, and see his face in repose for once, free from anger and fear and misery.

* * *

Starling had been waiting for Mrs Weekes to quit the house for a good long while. Her visits to Jonathan seemed to grow longer every time, and Starling struggled to find good reasons to remain within earshot of the front door closing. When at last she heard it, she darted quickly up the servants' stair and caught the woman's attention with a stifled hiss. Mrs Weekes turned quickly, with a startled expression that was almost like guilt. Starling was suspicious at once, and realised how flimsy a thing her trust yet was. It bothered her that she knew not what passed between Jonathan and Mrs Weekes in his rooms. *Does she keep things from me?* Mrs Weekes was so pale; walked with her back so straight and her shoulders so still. *She walks like a statue might. Like an effigy of Alice.* Next to her, Starling felt short and scruffy. She felt again like the guttersnipe she'd once been, and it made her prickly, defensive.

Together, they walked a short distance away from the

house, keeping close to the high wall of the garden so that they would not be seen from inside, then turned to face one another.

'Well, then,' said Starling, for want of a better commencement.

'Well. Your face has finally healed; I'm glad to see it,' said Mrs Weekes.

'I've healed far worse wounds in my time. You've said nothing to Dick Weekes? Good,' she said, when Rachel Weekes shook her head. 'And what did you discover from Mr Alleyn today? Have you found Alice's letters?'

'No. I mentioned them to him some days ago but he . . . he didn't know what I was talking about. Starling, I don't think he has them. He was looking for something in particular, though – a note he said he found in the lovers' tree. Do you know of such a place? He said there was a note to arrange an assignation, left in that place, but not written by him or by Alice – though it was addressed *to* Alice.'

'He's lying,' Starling said at once, though the news made her stomach turn over. *There can't have been.*

'He was confused . . . he seemed to think it might be a letter sent to Alice from the man she eloped with. He'd been searching for it in his room; he wanted to read it again in case it would tell him something new. But how could it, after so many years?'

'It's *you*, Mrs Weekes. The way you look so much like her . . . You're bringing it all back to him.' *As you are bringing it all back to me.*

'But why has he not mentioned this note before? To anyone?'

'It is an invention. There's no such note, and Alice had no other lover. He seeks to deceive you, Mrs Weekes!'

'It did not seem that way. He was not calculating. He was frantic . . . confused . . .'

'In what way confused?' Starling demanded. Mrs Weekes seemed taken aback by her tone – she was always so sensitive, yet so measured. It ruffled Starling all the more, and impatience gnawed at her every thought.

'He . . . he did say he wasn't sure he had seen this letter, truly. But it seemed to me that he had.' Rachel Weekes sounded uncertain.

'Well, how can you be sure if he had, if he is not sure and the note cannot be found?' said Starling, tersely. When Mrs Weekes made no reply she took a deep breath to calm down, clenching her teeth. *I should not have encouraged this woman to interfere*. Dick's wife was disturbing things – upsetting the fine balance she'd wrought between Jonathan's sanity and his madness; tipping it the wrong way. Rachel Weekes wore a reproachful look on her pale, serious face.

'He spoke of your pranks. "One of Starling's little pranks", he said, when he mentioned the stink in his rooms the first time I called. What do you suppose he meant by that?'

'How should I know what he meant? He is only half sane at the best of times, and hardly knows what he's saying.' Guilt nudged at her. Somehow, knowing that Jonathan was aware of her persecution made her feel almost embarrassed; like a child caught out.

'He doesn't seem mad to me. Only . . . disturbed,' Rachel Weekes said stubbornly. 'Sick in spirit.'

'Aren't they one and the same thing? You have a very forgiving soul, Mrs Weekes, or perhaps it is only a short memory.'

'I have not forgotten how he attacked me; believe me, I have not. But he was not himself that day. As I come to know him a little better, I can see that he was not himself.'

'And what of more recently, and the smashed jar? He was not drunk then – why did he attack you?'

'I . . . we were speaking of love and fate, and of . . . self-murder.'

'You condemned it?' said Starling.

'Of course I did,' said Rachel Weekes. Starling grunted.

'Well, that would do it.' She glanced up at the woman's incomprehension, and took a deep breath. 'He tried to end his own life. A few years ago.'

It was after his mother ordered all caches of opium removed from his rooms, and he was locked inside to rail and curse against her and God and the world. For days the door stayed locked, and nobody went in to him. Wild sounds of destruction were heard; vile curses bellowed out in pain and rage. Starling saw Josephine Alleyn standing with her back against his door, listening in silence, all ashen and clammy with anguish. When peace returned they opened the door just long enough to push through a tray of food and water. And so it continued.

It was weeks before Jonathan was well enough for life, such as it was in that house, to go on. He was skin and bones when Starling next saw him, appallingly thin. Death's head upon a mop stick. His sunken face was that of a stranger, and when he saw her shock he smiled bitterly.

'What's the matter, Starling? Don't you like to see me suffer?' The smile crumbled away; he hung his head. 'If Alice could see me now,' he whispered. 'If she could . . .'

'If she could see you now she would despise you,' said Starling, knowing it was not true. She fled into his bed-chamber, stood in darkness to catch her breath. The loud sound of breaking glass called her back out. Jonathan was a soldier; he knew which wounds bled the worst. He'd stabbed the bottle into the top of his thigh, near his groin, and his leg was already glossy with blood. For a second, Starling did nothing. For a second, she held the power of his life and death in her hands, and it filled her mind with fire, and rang in her ears. *No. You shan't rest.* She ran forwards, splayed her hands across the wound, shouted so loudly for help that it made her throat ache.

Rachel Weekes gasped; a sharp intake of breath as though she'd been slapped.

'He said I was wilfully stupid,' she said quietly. 'Perhaps he was right.' She shook her head. 'How great must his torment have been, to do such a thing? How deep his wounds must go.' Her words brought Starling back to the present, with the memory of that moment hurting her throat anew.

'What wounds he has he gave to himself. It is his guilt that torments him; and that violence is his *true* self – any gentility is but a mask.'

'Perhaps so.' Mrs Weekes looked sad, and seemed to think for a moment. 'He himself would argue that conclusion, I think.'

'Well, then – oughtn't he to know?' said Starling. There was a pause.

'Mr Alleyn has begun to talk to me, at least. To confide in me. He has begun to tell me about the war,' said Rachel Weekes, hurriedly, as if she couldn't bear the empty air.

'About the war? What use is that? You must make him confide in you about *Alice*. The war did not sit well with him, that much we all know. He came back mad and violent, that much we all know. Countless other men came back and managed to continue with their lives without resorting to the murder of innocents.'

'Did they?'

'Aye! Better, stronger men than he, I think.'

'Or less moral ones, some of them; less impressionable ones.'

'What is this? Why do you try to make him a poor lost lamb? I've known him near all my life, Mrs Weekes, so do not seek to tell me what he is!' said Starling, feeling horribly unnerved each time the woman spoke. It was like looking down from a high place, a feeling of losing balance, teetering. She couldn't trace the cause of it, so she summoned anger to burn it away, and had the satisfaction of seeing Rachel Weekes flinch. *She would turn my head, if she could. She would make me doubt the things I know.*

'I don't forget that. I only . . . I only tell you how I find him,' she said quietly.

'Then perhaps you are a poor judge of character, and situation, and should not pretend you can be of help to me; or to Alice.' Starling glared at her, and Mrs Weekes drew her shoulders back, taking a breath.

'I can be of help. I want to know what happened to Alice.' Starling thought for a moment before she next spoke, gazing at the garden wall.

'I read a letter of his – one he wrote to Alice from Spain, before he came back from the war the first time. Before he came back and . . . killed her.'

'And did you not find the others, with that letter?'

'No, it was on his desk, by itself. It must have been the last letter he wrote to her. In it he spoke of the shame he felt – that he had done bad things, and that if she knew them she would love him no more.'

'Yes. I believe he has seen and done much that haunts him.'

'I hope it haunts him! I hope he sees her ghost in every dark corner of the room!' *And I wish I did. I wish I saw her too.* 'If he speaks to you of the war, then try to find this out. Try to find out what he did that shamed him so, that first year of the war. I think he told Alice, and she could not accept it.'

'I'll try. He . . .' Rachel Weekes broke off, swallowing hard. 'He has told me things lately that made my blood run cold. Things he saw, the way the war was waged on the common people of the peninsula, as well as between the opposing armies.'

'It's never a pretty thing, I've heard tell.' Starling nodded. 'I have met soldiers old and new, and when they drink, they drink to forget.'

'Who did you take food to, the week before last?' Rachel Weekes suddenly burst out.

'What?' said Starling, startled. A rosy blush swept up from Mrs Weekes's neck.

'I . . . I saw you, in the city. That is to say . . .'

'Oh yes.' Starling fixed her with a flat glare. 'I've not forgotten that you told on me, to Sol Bradbury. Tattled on me for thieving.'

'Weren't you thieving?' Rachel Weekes retorted, flustered. 'I . . . I thought to do the right thing, in reporting it,' she said.

'Shows what you know about rights and wrongs, doesn't it? And Dick said you'd seen me take a boat. Why did you follow me?'

'I just . . . I happened to see you in the street, and I was curious. I saw you board a barge and go out of the city, and I—'

'And you what?'

'I envied you.' The words were little more than a whisper, and somehow they made all the ire in Starling melt away. She smiled, though she didn't quite know what pleased her.

'You *envied* me?' she echoed, and shook her head. 'You wouldn't say so if you'd smelled Dan Smithers's breath close to.'

'Perhaps not,' said Rachel Weekes, with a cautious smile of her own. *Do I frighten her?*

'I took it to an old acquaintance, fallen on hard times.' Starling paused, considering, before adding: 'One who knew Alice of old. Perhaps the only other person but me that recalls her fondly. That recalls her at all, outside of this household.'

'Will you go again to this acquaintance?'

'I daresay I will, in due course.'

'Could I go with you?' Again there was that urgency to the woman, that keenness that Starling did not quite understand, or trust.

'Why would you want to? It would bring down your husband's wrath, if he found you out.'

'He will not . . .' This was spoken with less certainty. 'I will be careful.'

'But why would you want to? It's a cold journey at this time of year.'

'I want to . . . be free of the city for a while. And I want to talk to another person who knew Alice. It might help me to understand her better,' she said. Starling considered her for a moment. She suddenly saw that Mrs Weekes needed something, very badly, but Starling had yet to divine what that thing might be. She shook her head.

'You want to understand her? She's dead, Mrs Weekes. You can't know her now, I fear. You're too late.' Her own words made Starling pause; they grazed the raw edges of her own grief. 'You speak as though you're infatuated with her, and yet you never saw her, nor spoke to her.'

'I see her in the mirror, you forget. And I see her in your words, and in . . . the words of others.'

'Differing accounts indeed, I am sure.'

'Truly. And I must know the truth, if I can find it out.'

'To what end though?' Starling pressed, doggedly. But it seemed that Rachel Weekes had no answer to this question. After a pause, and with a pleading look in her eyes, she said:

'I could bring food. I could bring meat and bread, to pay for my presence on the visit.'

'Very well.' Starling relented. *It could do no harm to me, surely? She risks more by it.* 'I will go again next Monday night, at around five in the evening.'

'On All-Hallows' Eve?'

'Are you afraid of ghosts, Mrs Weekes?'

'I think it might be wise to be.'

'That is the arranged time, though. Meet me over the bridge, on the south wharf. And don't be late, because I won't wait if Smithers is ready to depart. It's a wearying walk in the dark, if the boat has gone.' Mrs Weekes looked pleased enough at this, and though Starling kept a stern face as she turned away, she found that she didn't mind the idea of having the tall woman's company on the dark and joyless trip along the canal.

1808

In the kitchen at the farmhouse, there was a suspended, ringing moment after Starling blurted out Alice's and Jonathan's secret. When it ended she was sent upstairs, but she did not quite go all the way. She sank into the same spot by the banisters from which she'd first seen Jonathan and Lord Faukes, though it was harder for her to fit there than it had been, and there was such a restlessness in all her limbs it was near impossible to remain quiet or still. For a long time, Alice only wept, and that was the hardest thing of all to bear. She wept with a kind of frantic need that prevented Bridget from saying anything at all. Starling heard the scrape of chair legs on the kitchen floor, and the kettle coming to the boil on the range.

'Alice, child, stop now,' said Bridget, after several long minutes. 'Take a deep breath, slowly now. Be calm, be calm. Take a sip of tea.' She heard the trembling rattle of a china cup in its saucer.

'Bridget, you must not tell him! Promise me! Please, I beg you, for he will prevent us from ever seeing one another if you do, and he will like as not cast us out and we will have nothing and be ruined! And I will never see him again!' Alice gabbled.

'All this you knew, and yet you continued your liaison – you indulged your feelings, and encouraged them to grow. All this you knew, and also that I am employed by Lord Faukes, and must obey his commands.' Bridget spoke heavily, wearily.

'I indulged my feelings, and encouraged them to grow?

No, I am *compelled* by my feelings, Bridget! You must know, you must understand . . . haven't you ever been in love?' Alice's voice was shaking. Starling knew she would be pale, wild-eyed. *Do not let her take one of her turns because of what I said.*

'I fancied I was once, and it was no more prudent than this love you have for young Mr Alleyn. My father stepped in and prevented our becoming too attached to each other, and before I had shamed myself publicly. It was a painful separation, I shan't deny it. But now I see the sense of it, and you must see the sense of removing your affections from Mr Alleyn.'

'The sense? No, I see no sense in that! I see no sense in separating, or being kept apart, when our souls are wound tight together and have been these many years! You must have seen it? You must have known the way we feel for each other?'

'I've known it, yes. Anyone with eyes in their head would know it, seeing you together in the same room. Even Lord Faukes knows it, though he does not know you would disobey him like this, and meet with his grandson in secret – as I did not know it. Alice, what were you thinking? He is engaged to another! And even if he were not, he is destined to make a fine marriage, into a noble family.'

'Would I not make a fine wife for him?' said Alice, in a tone of such misery that Starling couldn't stand it.

'You are as fine to me and those that know you as any high-born lady, Alice, but that is not the way the world works, and no amount of love or wishing will ever change it. You have no name. You have no family, and no fortune. Jonathan is the son of a noble lady.'

'He does not love Beatrice Fallonbrooke! And he will *not* marry her; he has sworn it to me. These past three years, he has tried to remove himself from the engagement. Only his honour and duty to the lady prevent him from renouncing her publicly.'

'His honour? How honourable is it to lead you a dance like this, and break your heart, when he knows he cannot wed you? He will be cut off if he does. You would have nothing, and nowhere to go. All doors would close to you.'

'If we were wed, I would happily live under a hedge with him!'

'Foolish girl! Think! *Think* about what would happen!'

There was a long silence. Starling didn't dare breathe, and her chest burned. Her pulse was thumping painfully in her head; she tried shutting her eyes but it only got worse.

'Please don't tell him,' Alice whispered then.

'I am duty bound to. He will separate you, I fear. We will be moved away, too far for any secret meetings to take place.' Bridget's voice was flat, unhappy.

'Moved away? No! *Please*, Bridget . . . I won't survive it.'

'You'll survive it because you'll have to. What choice is there? Be grateful it was me Starling told on you to, and not Lord Faukes . . . I don't know what would happen if he found out the full story.' Bridget's voice was laced with warning. In the silence that fell again, Starling heard Alice draw in a deep, gulping breath. She thought then about running down to the kitchen, throwing herself down in front of them and saying something, *anything*, to undo what she had done, and mean their lives would not be turned upside down, and Alice's heart broken. She found that not a single muscle in her body would respond to the command. The numbness of sheer panic held her, and her shame was like a heavy weight pushing down on her.

'Believe me, I would rather not have to leave this house. We have been comfortable here, these twenty years . . .' Bridget muttered then. Alice gave a gasp.

'Then do not tell, dear Bridget! Pretend as though nothing

has changed! As though Starling had not spoken, or I had denied it all and you believed me!'

'I can't do that . . . if it were found out . . .'

'It will not be! How could it be?' Alice's voice was bright with desperate hope. 'Don't shake your head, Bridget – tell me you will stay silent, and we can remain here in Bathampton, and all will be as it was before!'

'Alice! This is not a game!' Bridget cried. 'Lord Faukes loves you, and has always been gentle with you. But make no mistake, he is a powerful man, and he will have things his way. I have seen how he deals with those who defy him . . . And in the not trifling matter of his grandson's marriage? You wouldn't be able to throw yourself into his lap and weep your way out of that one, mark my words.'

'He will not hear of it, Bridget.' Alice sounded calmer, and resolute.

'And you must swear to see Jonathan in secret no more. You must separate yourself from him. Swear it, Alice; because sooner or later these things are found out. They always are.'

'I . . . I—'

'Swear it to me, Alice, or I will have to report it now. You would leave me no choice. Jonathan Alleyn is not for you, however much you care for him.'

'Very well, then. I swear it.' This was spoken in a small, strangled voice.

'You must talk to Starling. I thought her loyal to you, to both of us.' Bridget gave a sigh. 'She has proved otherwise.' At this, Starling's limbs awoke. She scrambled up and flew down the stairs, running out of the house as fast as her feet would carry her, because she could not stand to hear what either one of them would say to her.

She roamed along the canal for a long time, then high onto the ridge above the western edge of Bathampton, from where

Ralph Allen's folly looked down – the turreted and crenel-lated wall of a sham castle, newly built to embellish the view from the gentleman's town house. Starling stared up at it and wondered at the power some men had, to change the world to suit them better. *When we others must just do as we are bid, and be meek and malleable.* She thought about what Bridget had said of Lord Faukes – *he will have things his way.* She remembered the sudden warning she'd felt, nameless and wordless, deep in her bones, during one of his visits a year or so before.

She'd fetched him a glass of port while he was alone by the fire in the parlour, and he'd taken hold of her wrist to prevent her turning away. Normally she stayed out of his sight as much as she could; she tried to draw as little attention to herself as possible.

'Wait a while, girl. Starling,' he said, smiling so that his cheeks turned his eyes into crescents. Starling did as she was bid. She pulled experimentally at her arm but his grip, though gentle, was quite unbreakable. She let her hand hang limply at the end of her wrist. In some hindquarter of her brain, she divorced herself from it completely; if she had to leave the limb behind to free herself, she would do it. She watched him in silence as his thumb moved around to press into the vulnerable underside of her wrist, where the blood was warm and close to the skin. He massaged her in small circles, considering, and the prickling feeling this gave her went straight to that hidden part of her mind that knew to bite, and kick, and run. She balanced her weight evenly on both feet, poised slightly on her toes, ready. She started to shake. 'Do not fear me, girl. Why should you fear me?' he said, with a chuckle. *I do not fear you*, Starling realised. *I hate you.* 'How old are you now?'

'Rising twelve, we think, sir,' she said reluctantly.

'Quite the little maid,' he said cheerfully, and laughed

again though his eyes never left her, and it was not mirth that filled them but a kind of hunger. Starling glared at him then, and let everything she was feeling fill her face. Lord Faukes recoiled, though he did not let go her hand. 'Mind your manners, little vixen. I had a horse once look at me the way you just did. I was forced to beat that mare bloody, so I was.'

'Yes, sir.' Starling looked down instead, because she could not keep the hate from showing.

'That's better.' Lord Faukes dropped her wrist and laced his hands across his gut, shifting his weight. The chair creaked. 'Remember who owns you, girl. Remember to whom you are beholden.' In that instant Alice came in from the stables with her cheeks glowing and her hair unravelled, and went to embrace the old man with a smile. For a second, Starling wanted to step between them – Alice had no idea how to bite or kick or run. But she could not, since there was no excuse to other than every instinct she possessed, commanding it.

Alice found her eventually, as the sky was turning milky pale and a sliver of moon had risen. Starling had found her way to the lovers' tree, and was sitting in the shadows on the protruding root, quiet and numb and miserable. She started to cry when she saw Alice approaching, because the shame was intolerable. Alice sat down beside her, all serious and calm. Her pale hair caught the last of the light, but her eyes were in darkness.

'Don't cry, Starling. I know why you told Bridget,' she said. 'I know why you were angry. You wanted to hurt me some, because I have hurt you, haven't I, dearest?' Starling only wept more, messily; snot and tears slid down her chin. Alice's arm went around her shoulders and squeezed. 'You are so quick and bright; it's easy to forget how young you are.' She sighed softly and fetched out a handkerchief to wipe Starling's face. 'You and I have been so close, since you first came to us. It must be impossible for you to understand why I met Jonathan in secret, as well as the times I met him with you, and at the house. It has to do with the kind of love we feel, and my . . . particular situation. Perhaps you understand a little more of that now, after hearing what Bridget had to say earlier on.' Starling glanced up and saw that her eavesdropping was no secret. She dissolved into fresh tears of misery; for a while Alice let her cry. A weak breeze shifted the willow whips.

'Now I need to know how close we are, Starling,' said Alice, after a while. She whispered the words, so that they seemed spoken in part to the darkness and the silent sliding river. Starling gulped and sniffed and tried to read her expression.

'What do you mean, Alice?' she said.

'I have sworn to Bridget that I will detach myself from Jonathan. I had no choice but to swear it. But I shall not do it. I *will* not do it!' Alice took Starling by the tops of her arms and stared into her eyes. 'You betrayed me before because you were hurt and angry. But you betrayed me to the one person who had best reason to keep my secret with me. Perhaps it was deliberate, perhaps not, but betraying Jonathan and me to Bridget was really hardly a betrayal at all.' Starling waited, hardly breathing. She'd never heard Alice sound so serious. 'I will *not* detach myself from Jonathan, and he will not detach himself from me. It would be utterly impossible. So I will break the vow I just made to Bridget, and break it willingly, and if the time comes that Jonathan and I must flee from our families to be wed, then I will go eagerly, though I should be disgraced for ever. I tell you this now because you will have guessed it, I know. If not at once then sooner or later. So I ask you now, Starling – will you betray us again?'

'Never!' Starling gasped.

'Think before you answer, dearest. It will be harder to keep this secret now. Bridget will be watching . . . she will doubtless make you promise to tell her if I do not keep to my word.' Alice's fingers clutched Starling's shoulders, gently but insistently.

'I will lie to her too, I don't care! But you must promise me one thing,' said Starling, desperately.

'What is it?' Alice sounded wary, worried.

'When you go . . . when you go away with Jonathan, you must take me along with you. You mustn't leave me!'

'Starling, dearest . . .'

'You *must* not leave me! Promise it!' Alice pulled her closer, and pressed a kiss to the top of her head.

'I promise it; and that is a promise I *will* keep.'

They waited until they were both calm, and composed, and resolute, before returning to the farmhouse, and to Bridget's stern unease. As they went in Alice turned to smile at Starling, and it was that smile that reassured her, and told her she was forgiven and loved. It was that smile that made the ground under her feet turn back to solid rock from shifting sand, and convinced her to ignore that sparkle of instinct that came again, with the shadow of Lord Faukes looming large in her mind; the urge she felt to take hold of Alice's hand and run, right then, immediately and far away.

1821

Overnight, frost had settled on every stone of the city, every leaf and blade of grass of Barton Fields, where Rachel and Richard met Captain and Mrs Sutton to walk. Mist lay thick over Bath, snaking along the river as though the water had breathed it out. It crept up the lower slopes of the city, so that only the upper crescents rose clear of it; an elegant harbour along a shifting white shore. Cassandra Sutton was swaddled in coat and woollen shawls, with gloves on her hands and leather boots laced high up her legs. She walked ahead and then skipped back to them, to show them whatever she'd found – acorns, or fir cones; once a massive horse chestnut leaf, golden brown and crusted with ice. The exercise made her cheeks pink and her eyes shine, and the child looked as vibrant as the spray of crimson hawthorn berries she next brought to show them.

'Cassandra, do not run about so, I beg you. You're a young lady now,' said Harriet Sutton.

'But if I run I'll keep warm,' the little girl pointed out, and smiled winningly at them as she turned and trotted away once more. Her teeth were a flash of white against the darker colouring of her face.

'Cassandra!' Harriet called after her, but her tone was amused, not reproachful.

'It does children good to run, and fill their chests with fresh air,' said Rachel.

'True enough. But Cassandra is coming to that age when I think I ought to instil a touch more decorum in her, perhaps.'

'Oh, she is but nine years old, is she not? I think she could safely be allowed to run wild for a couple more years.' Rachel smiled. 'When I was her age, my father still took me fishing for tadpoles. We would stand for hours in the muddy edges of a stream, dipping for the poor creatures. I think he longed for a boy, to take on such outings! Once Christopher was born, I was allowed to become his daughter, rather than his son. I was about Cassandra's age when that happened, and I turned out well enough, I suppose.'

'Indeed you did. You turned out very well indeed.'

Harriet looped her arm through Rachel's as they walked; Richard was walking further behind, with Captain Sutton.

'Harriet, may I ask you something?' said Rachel.

'Of course.'

'Does your husband ever talk about his time in the war? The war against the French, I mean?'

'In truth, very little.' Harriet Sutton sighed. 'I do not press him on it, since it seems to me that it pains him to speak of it.'

'Do you think it . . . troubles him? The things he has seen and done?'

'My husband is a good and kind man; I'm certain such violence troubles him. But he does his duty to king and country. His duty as a solider.' Harriet turned her head to look at her husband. 'The army needs men like my husband, to bring a measure of decency to the grotesquery of the battlefield.'

'Indeed.'

'What makes you ask?'

'Mr Alleyn has lately begun to speak to me of his time in the war. Of the things he saw and did,' said Rachel. *And they are things that turn my stomach.* 'I can't imagine how any man could come through the same and remain innocent of heart.'

'Yes. I have heard of other soldiers who find it impossible to return to their old lives when they come home. They find society meaningless; their days pointless; their wives and families . . . frivolous.'

'And what becomes of these men?'

'Gradually, they resettle, and find peace.' Harriet shrugged. 'Or they do not, and turn to drink and dissolution, or retreat from the world.'

'Or retreat into drink and dissolution, all three,' Rachel murmured. Harriet smiled sadly.

'What does he tell you?'

'Such things . . .' Rachel shook her head. 'Such things that I begin to understand why his memories torment him so. Why he has lost his faith in humanity.' *And then I read him a tale of adventure and chivalry, and he sleeps, like a child.*

For a while they walked in steady silence, watching Cassandra as she darted here and there beneath the naked limbs of a horse chestnut tree, filling her coat pockets with glossy nuts.

'I am glad,' Harriet said then. Rachel turned to look down at her diminutive friend, confused. 'Jonathan Alleyn's heart is good. I *know* this to be true. And war may change a man's mind – change his outlook and his behaviour, change the very way he thinks, perhaps. But it cannot change a man's heart.'

'But perhaps, if they behave badly enough, it matters not that their heart remains what it always was. Not everything – not every deed – can be forgiven, after all.'

'Can it not? Is that not what Christianity teaches?'

'I don't know.' Rachel thought of Alice, and the way she had vanished from the world. She thought of the Portuguese girl Jonathan had spoken of, crushed beneath a rock and ravaged. 'I don't know,' she said again. Harriet squeezed her hand.

'Don't give up on him, Mrs Weekes,' she said softly. 'Nobody has grown as close to him since he returned from the war as you are now. You are doing him good, I know it. And you are *doing* good, by your time and your . . . willingness to see past the wall he has built around himself.' Rachel nodded vaguely.

'I hear such things about him, from . . . others, that I hardly know what to think,' she said.

'You can trust my own account, I hope. I *know* him to be good.'

'But, *how* do you know, Mrs Sutton? How are you so sure?'

'I . . . I cannot say. Forgive me. Tell me, what does your husband make of your progress?'

'He makes nothing of it. He knows nothing of it,' said Rachel. 'He cares only for the wage I am paid by Mrs Alleyn. He never asks me what I do there, or how I fare.' Try as she might, Rachel couldn't keep the unhappiness from her voice, and alongside it was something new; something like contempt. She hoped that Harriet Sutton wouldn't hear it, but the look her friend gave her was troubled, and she didn't speak for a good few moments.

'The first year of marriage is a voyage of discovery,' Harriet said eventually. 'And perhaps it is inevitable that not all things we discover will be to our liking.' She smiled sympathetically, and Rachel looked away. Suddenly, her own distaste for her husband shamed her.

They had reached the end of the track across Barton Fields, and waited for the men by the path that would lead back into the city, and to a coffee house where they could warm themselves. Rachel smiled warmly at Richard to disguise her true feelings. His return smile was thin and uneven, as though he tasted something sour in his mouth, and Rachel's heart sank even further.

'Well, I think we've earned something hot to drink, and perhaps something sweet to eat, to warm us, hmm?' said

Captain Sutton, sweeping his daughter into his arms and touching the tip of his long nose to hers. 'Cassie! Your nose is like an icicle!'

'There's nothing so warming as having one's family around one, I think,' Harriet remarked to Rachel and Richard, who had linked arms without speaking to one another.

'Quite so,' said Rachel, but Richard spoke at the same time, and more loudly.

'I have found little warmth in my own, lately,' he said, then closed his mouth tightly, letting his eyes slide angrily over Rachel's face before looking away into the mist. Rachel was mortified and didn't know where to look. There she stood, arm in arm with her husband, their faces turned away and a wall of unspoken hard feeling between them.

Late in the evening, Rachel found herself wondering about Richard, and his habitual long absences at night. At first she had assumed he was with clients at inns or private houses, or with traders; that his frequent drunkenness was the result of toasting and sampling and the sealing of deals, or somehow otherwise linked to his business. But after his comment to the Suttons, she was no longer sure. Duncan Weekes had counselled her to be glad his son had not broken his wedding vows to her, and to forget about any prior indiscretion. *But what if he does break them?* She didn't dwell on the question, since the answer was *what if* indeed – she could do nothing to stop him, except to expose him and try to shame him into behaving better. But even that, she found, did not interest her. She was not interested in improving him. The realisation came as a shock, and if it was true then she should also be uninterested what he got up to when he was not at home. He would say it was not her business, and he would possibly be right. *But I would still know*, she decided. *I would know the full story of what I have wed.*

Rachel wrapped up against a light rain, only heavy enough

to glaze the cobbled pavement. She went from place to place with her brows furrowed and her hood drawn forward to hide her face from passers-by. She could not bring herself to enter an inn alone, but she peered in through windows, and through doors when they were thrown open by people coming and going. A cloud of talk and laughter and warmth and stink wafted out from within each time, and caused her a curious mix of revulsion and loneliness. She saw ruddy faces, and smiling eyes; she saw arguments and tears, and lovers dipping their heads together in secretive corners that the candlelight barely reached; she saw men drinking alone, staring at nothing, swallowing down mouthfuls of spirits like food. But she did not see Richard Weekes in any place she visited, and after two hours of searching she gave up, cold and oddly disappointed. *Do I want him to be a reprobate, then? To excuse myself for not loving him?* On the pavement she almost stepped on a man, sitting with his feet in the gutter.

'Beg pardon, sir,' she muttered, as the toe of her shoe got caught in his coat tails. The man swayed but made no reply, and Rachel paused. 'Mr Weekes? Is that you?' She bent down to see his face. There was a cut above Duncan Weekes's right eye, which had dribbled a crusted line of blood down to his jaw; he sat with his eyes shut and his mouth slack, stinking of brandy and piss. 'Mr Weekes – are you well? Can you hear me?' said Rachel, more urgently. She shook his arm and his head came up, slowly, eyes opening a fraction to see what trouble he was in.

'Rachel! How charming to see you, my dear girl. Do come in, come in. Sit by the fire and warm yourself.' His voice was a slur, hard to understand. Rachel bit her lip anxiously.

'We are not at home, sir. We are on the street by the Unicorn. What happened to your eye? Were you attacked?'

'My eye?' the old man mumbled. 'My eye?'

'Come, sir – you must rise. It's far too cold a night to be

sitting out like this, and we wouldn't want you apprehended for doing so. Come, I cannot lift you, you will have to help me.' Rachel grasped him under his arm and urged him to rise; his coat sleeve was wet through, and filthy. For a while Duncan didn't move, and Rachel was left to tug at him futilely, but then a pair of passing young men saw her plight; they hefted Duncan to his feet with ease, grinned and tipped their hats to Rachel when she thanked them. Slowly, she coaxed Duncan Weekes to walk. 'Let's away to somewhere warmer, somewhere kinder,' she murmured, as they stumbled along.

'Forgive me, child. Forgive a foolish old drunk,' Duncan said thickly, and then coughed; his chest sounded clotted and unwholesome. Rachel found her throat too tight to reply.

They were not too far from his lodgings, and when they reached the door Rachel patted his pockets until she found the key. His room was wholly black, and little warmer than outside. She manoeuvred Duncan onto his bed and then tried to light the fire, but found no coal or wood to do so.

'Didn't you buy coal, Mr Weekes? Didn't you buy some fuel with the money I gave you?' He only stared at her in abject apology, and Rachel understood what her money had been spent on. 'Well, then,' she said, helplessly. 'Well. Blankets, then.' She lit some candles, which gave the illusion of warmth with their yellow light; piled as many blankets as she could find on top of the old man, and fetched water and a cloth from the washstand to clean the cut on his face.

'I lost a hand of pontoon, when I'd bet a shilling. I did not have the shilling,' he confessed, trying to smile. 'Lucky he only gave me this small cut and not a sounder hooping, eh?' A bruise was spreading out from the wound, and he winced when she dabbed at it. 'It will make my head thump all the worse, come morning.'

'Oh, why do it? Why ruin yourself with drink, sir?'

Rachel exclaimed suddenly. Duncan Weekes's face sank down.

'It's like a command you have to answer, though you know the master for a base villain,' he said softly.

'You, and my husband, and Jonathan Alleyn . . . the stuff makes fools and firebrands of all of you!' She squeezed out the cloth in the bowl. The water was icy.

'Miserable fools, yes. It makes us lose the things we love most.' Duncan Weekes's rheumy eyes shone. The candle flames were caught in them like little sparks of life. Rachel stared into them.

'What happened to your wife, Mr Weekes?'

The old man sighed; shut his eyes for a moment before answering her.

'She'd been away one Christmas, to visit her nephew. I was meant to go to Marlborough, where her nephew would leave her, and accompany her on the last leg of the journey by stage. But I . . . I drank away my fare, and fell into a stupor. So she came back alone, and being last to board, since she had waited as long as possible for my arrival, she had no choice but to ride on the roof. We suffered a spell of bitter winter weather, at the time. Bitter. By the time the stage reached Chippenham, they found her . . . they found her succumbed to the cold.'

'Oh, Mr Weekes,' Rachel breathed.

'Grog is the devil itself. It was grog and my own weakness for it that killed her, sure enough. So you see, I can't blame my boy for hating me,' said Duncan, bitterly. 'But then, perhaps the devil is in us to begin with, and the grog only gives him free rein. Aye, perhaps 'tis so! It is in the Alleyn family. I have seen it. I have seen their devil for myself!' The old man's eyes widened, and he grasped her hand where she tended him. 'Oh, be careful, my dear! It worries me deeply that you have taken that man into your circle, into your life.'

'I have come to know Jonathan Alleyn better. I do not fear him as once I did.'

'Jonathan Alleyn . . . perhaps not, perhaps not. But the others . . .'

'But, there is only he and his mother remaining,' she said, confused. Duncan shook his head.

'They all have his blood. And she is her father's daughter, right enough,' he said, in a voice gone small and frightened. 'Richard will tell you . . . he will tell you I was dismissed from them for my drunkenness. That's what he will tell you. But it wasn't so. It wasn't so!'

'Why then, Mr Weekes?' Rachel whispered, squeezing his hand tightly.

'Because I *saw*! I saw them! And what I saw could not be mistaken. And they both knew it . . . they both knew what I'd seen . . . And I told her. I told her.'

'Told who what? What did you see?'

'I understood then . . . I understood them, then, and I was happy to go, after that. I knew how much my boy wanted to stay on, but I was happy to go after what I saw . . .' Oblivion was tugging at him, closing his eyes, making his words lose shape and sense.

'But what was it, Mr Weekes?' Rachel shook him slightly, desperate to know. His eyes opened again, struggling to focus on her face.

'Oh! Poor girl, I fear you have fallen into dark hands . . . dark hands. That family has evil secrets, and their hearts are black . . . I *saw*!' He sank back again, and his breath came rattling through his teeth, wheezing and rank. The smell of it made Rachel recoil; it carried the stink of infection. She felt her heart thudding. She held Duncan's hand and tried to warm it, but in the end hers only grew colder, and the old man slumbered on, restless but dogged, so she left him.

All-Hallows' Eve was a bright, crystalline day; the low sun thawed an early frost to leave everything glittering with water. From a thousand chimneys, a thousand ribbons of smoke rose straight up into the still blue sky. Rachel spent the short daylight hours writing a letter to the Trevelyans, stitching an old tippet into a better semblance of fashion, and trying to make pastry that was neither tough and leathery, nor too fragile to lift. All the while, she could hear Richard down in the cellar. A steady stream of callers came and went; she heard laughter and hushed discussions; the rumble of rolled casks, the creak of the barrow wheel as stock and supplies were brought to the store or taken away. *Today of all days,* Rachel fretted. She thought up half a dozen excuses she could give Richard for going out of the house so close to nightfall, and even wondered about sneaking out without seeing him at all, and she was so nervous about it as five o'clock approached that she ended up pacing the kitchen-cum-parlour from one window to the other, gazing out in search of answers.

She sighed quietly in relief when, at half past four, Richard came up to announce he was going out.

'Where will you go?' Rachel asked, in spite of herself. Richard looked impatient for a moment, and then unhappy. He crossed to her and kissed her cheek, raising a hand to stroke her hair.

'I have some business to attend to,' he said, and Rachel stifled the retort that she did not believe it. It would be to an inn, or a gaming table somewhere. She remembered what Richard had once said about his father – that he wouldn't be half so poor if he didn't drink his wages away. *Hypocrite. And you seem to increase such expenditure all the time.* With a pang she wondered if she was to blame for Richard seeking his entertainment elsewhere, but she wanted him to go out, after all, so she said nothing more.

'Will you be late?'

'I'll be as late as I need to be, Rachel,' he said, irritated. 'Don't wait for me, but eat, if you're hungry.'

'Very well.' *I just hope your business keeps you out later than mine will keep me.* Richard pulled on his gloves and left without another word. Rachel counted to a hundred once the door had slammed shut, then hurried into her own coat and gloves and headed for the river.

On the far side of the bridge she looked left and right, trying to pick out Starling's small figure from the crowd of river men and traders, urchins and apprentices. In the failing light the torches dazzled her eyes and made it hard to see. Behind her, the city bells began to strike five and she felt a flutter of panic, until a hand grasped her arm and she looked down into Starling's heart-shaped face.

'I thought you'd changed your mind,' she said, steering Rachel through the crowd by her elbow.

'No, I—'

'Hurry – he won't wait. Did you bring food?'

'What?'

'You said you'd bring some food.' Starling paused, and glanced at Rachel accusingly.

'I . . . I'm sorry. Richard was in the house until the very last moment . . . I couldn't. I was worried about getting away without him knowing.'

'Never mind.' Starling resumed her march through the muck and garbage of the riverside. They reached the same barge Rachel had seen Starling take before, and the girl went on board in one smooth jump. Rachel peered at the gap of inky water between the boat and the wooden jetty. 'Come on, then,' said Starling, seating herself on the sacks of coal. Rachel glanced at Dan Smithers, who gave her a lopsided grin that showed teeth gone brown; the upper and lower canines had worn away on one side into a perfect round slot for his pipe shaft.

'Make the jump, ma'am, if you would have a ride,' he said, still grinning. Squaring her shoulders, Rachel gathered her skirts and crossed the gap with a single long stride. She lost her balance, unprepared for the way the barge would move, and staggered forwards onto the coal sacks. Dan Smithers chuckled.

'A gentleman would have offered me his hand to board,' Rachel pointed out, coolly, but the bargeman only laughed.

'Aye, ma'am. No doubt a gentleman would 'ave.'

Starling smiled at her indignity, though not unkindly. When she was like this – unguarded, in her element, she had a kind of buoyant confidence that Rachel admired, and envied. There was something resilient and indefatigable about her. Soon they were sliding beneath the ornate iron bridges of Sydney Gardens, between steep stone walls. The voices of walkers and hawkers and sweethearts echoed down to them; disembodied words drifting like ghosts along the water. Rachel shivered and pulled her coat tighter around her. Then they were out of the city and in darkness, save for the lamps on the prow and stern of the barge – two single flickering flames to hold back the night. There was no sound but the soft slapping of water on the hull, and the muffled clop of the horse's feet. Rachel saw the first stars of the evening coming out, and excitement filled her; she felt as though she were escaping, somehow. *But you will only have to go back again.*

'It'll be a hard frost tonight,' said Starling, her words causing pale shreds of mist to obscure her face. She was sitting cross-legged, her face half lit by the lamp on the prow, fiddling with a loose thread that trailed from her mittens. *She is half a young lady, half a tavern wench.*

'How old are you, Starling?'

'Possibly four and twenty.' Starling shrugged.

'Possibly?'

'I've never known for sure. We always used my height to guess, but I was tall as a child and am not so tall now. So perhaps all our guesses were wrong.'

'Doesn't your mother know?' said Rachel, confused.

'I daresay she does, but since I've never known her, that doesn't help much.'

'You're an orphan?'

'I don't know.' Starling tipped her head to one side to look at Rachel, and continued. 'I walked into the farmyard one winter's day, wearing only rags. I was small – six or seven years old. Alice took me in, and cared for me.'

'But if you were six or seven, you must remember your life before that, surely?'

'I do not.' Starling shrugged again. 'I think I chose to forget; and forget I have. I sometimes have odd feelings, like warnings. Intuitions, you could call them. About people, or happenings. I think they might be lessons I took from that life before, but that's all I've kept. The intuitions, and the scars.'

'The scars?'

'It seems I was beaten a good deal.'

'Oh. That's terrible.'

'I have no memory of it, so it's no trouble to me.'

'And Alice decided to keep you? Did she try to find out where you came from?'

'Not very hard, if she did.' Starling smiled briefly. 'Not when she saw how I'd been treated. If they'd wanted me back, they'd have come looking, wouldn't they? I was only small. I couldn't have walked so very far in the winter, with no shoes on my feet. They must have been nearby, and as happy to be rid of me as I was to stumble into Alice's care.'

'So that's why you have such a singular name?'

'Alice used to say that the starlings had brought me to her. They were making a row, coming in to roost, and then there I was, barefoot on the muddy yard with feathers in my hair.' Starling smiled as she spoke, and Rachel saw how much she enjoyed this legend about her beginnings.

'So she raised you as her own?'

'As a sister, more or less. Alice was only seventeen or so herself when I appeared. It was a funny kind of upbringing – Alice treated me as her kin, and Bridget taught me how to be a good servant.'

'Who is Bridget?'

'She was Alice's housekeeper, but also her guardian, and her gaoler. She was employed by Lord Faukes . . .' Starling paused, swallowing. 'She was employed by Alice's benefactor to serve her, but also to keep her confined to the house and village of Bathampton. Alice never went further than the edge of it her whole life.' Starling turned her face away sadly, as a vixen's harsh shriek echoed across the water. 'Apart from one time,' she added, so softly that Rachel almost didn't hear her. 'It's Bridget we go to see tonight; she's old now, and infirm, and much reduced from when I first knew her.'

The cold was making Rachel wheeze; biting her hands and feet. Her teeth rattled together. Sudden movement in the lamplight startled her but it was only a barn owl. It ghosted along in front of them for a while, as noiselessly white as snowflakes, then vanished into the darkness like a secret. Rachel looked over and found Starling watching her with eyes gone huge in the lack-light.

'It's not much further,' she said, as the yellow shapes of lit windows came into view up ahead. 'Can you see the house?' She pointed, and Rachel made out some tall chimneys and the straight line of a roof, perhaps three hundred feet back from the canal. 'That's the house I grew up in. That was the house where we lived, the three of us. Child, maid and crone.'

'Is Bridget a housekeeper, still?'

'No, she's too ill to work; she lives on charity. She has no family of her own left. Only me.'

'She is lucky, then, that you take the time to visit her.'

'What else should I do? At times there's been little love lost between us but . . . she is there in my earliest memories, and she was kind, in her own way. She is my family, too. All the family I have now.'

'You could wed, and make your own family,' said Rachel.

'Perhaps I will, one day.' Starling looked down and picked at her glove again. 'The beard-splitters I meet aren't the kind of men I'd care to wed.' She glanced up apologetically, and Rachel was glad of the darkness to hide in.

When they arrived, Rachel disembarked more deftly than she'd boarded, and followed Starling onto a bridge across the canal. As the barge slipped away eastwards its lamps looked like tiny will-o'-the-wisps, dancing over the dark water.

'How will we get back again?' Rachel asked, suddenly afraid.

'If we're lucky, there'll be a boat heading west that'll let us ride. If not, it's a brisk walk back, not much more than an hour. We might even feel warmer if we walk. What time must you be back?'

'I don't know. Sometimes my husband . . .' Rachel paused. It was too easy to forget that Starling knew her husband well; perhaps better than she did herself. 'Mr Weekes usually stays out late,' she finished, in a stunted voice.

'Yes. That sounds like Dick Weekes. Always off cater-wauling,' said Starling, tonelessly. They made their way along the deserted village street. There were lights on in windows but no sounds of music or voices from within; Rachel found the stillness eerie.

'Where is everybody?' she whispered.

'Those that aren't in the pub will be tucked up indoors. It

is All-Hallows' Eve, after all. They've no wish to see their dead walking.' In the borrowed light of a doorway Rachel saw the flash of Starling's feral grin.

'I should quite like to see some of mine again. Even if they were in spirit form,' Rachel said softly. Starling's grin evaporated.

'Yes. So would I.'

At the top of the street they turned off onto a muddy track, pitted with frozen puddles and tunnelling between overgrown yew hedges. At the end of it huddled a row of three tiny cottages, single-storeyed, each with two small, square windows to either side of a narrow doorway, and a squat chimney poking up through the centre of the roof. They caught a whiff of the cesspit, and the reek of old ashes. Starling strode purposefully to the middle cottage and rapped her knuckles against the wood. She lifted the latch without waiting for an answer.

'Bridget, it's me! And I bring a friend with me.' She glanced briefly at Rachel as she stepped inside, as if embarrassed to have used the word *friend*. Rachel followed close behind her, hoping for warmth, but, like at Duncan Weekes's lodgings, the temperature barely rose inside the cottage. The air was stagnant; the only light came from a single candle on the mantelpiece, above a stove in which the last embers of a fire were dying.

'Bridget?' Starling called again, passing through a doorway on the right. Rachel waited in the first small room. The floor was bare, and the only furniture a crooked table with a stool tucked under it, a wooden cupboard, and a rocking chair which sat facing the stove. Everything felt stiff with cold, from the bones of the house to the very air itself. From the other room she heard the rustle of a straw mattress, and murmured words. 'You can come in now – and bring the candle,' Starling called.

Holding the candle before her made everything else recede into shadow, but Rachel saw Starling perched on a three-legged stool by a narrow cot bed, and in that bed lay a shrunken figure with cheekbones like knife edges and deep rings under its eyes; wrapped in so many layers of blankets and shawls it was hard to tell where the bed ended and the person began. 'Bridget, this is Rachel Weekes, lately married to Dick Weekes, the wine man. Mrs Weekes, this is Bridget Barnes. Come closer so she can see you.' Rachel did as she was told, noting how keenly Starling watched Bridget's face. *Of course. She waits to see her reaction to me. To this face which is only half mine.* But if Starling had been hoping for anything as dramatic as Mr Alleyn's response, she was disappointed. Bridget simply stared, without blinking, for such a length of time that Rachel found herself staring back, deep into the old woman's sunken eyes. They registered recognition, but no surprise; only a deep, slow-turning sadness.

'Well. I suppose there were only so many faces God could create. Sooner or later he had to make the same one twice,' said Bridget. She sounded breathless; her voice was thin and the air seemed to only penetrate the topmost portion of her lungs, so that she had to take constant small snatches of it. 'You're welcome here, Mrs Weekes. Though your presence might cause a stir, on this of all nights.'

'Thank you, Mrs Barnes,' said Rachel.

'We saw nobody, as we came to you. Nobody who might think her a ghost,' said Starling.

'It's Miss Barnes,' Bridget pointed out. 'I never did marry. Perhaps if I had I would be tucked up warm in the house of my son or daughter now, instead of in this sty; though I shouldn't complain of having the almshouse when there are plenty that haven't.' She stopped and took several breaths to catch up, coughing wheezily. 'The damp in the walls plays havoc with my chest,' she said, to nobody in particular.

'Well, I may not have a warm and comfortable house I can take you to, but I do have some things for you. Look here — some candle stubs, more beer, a ham bone, some dried fish and peas and . . .' Starling pulled an earthenware jar from her sack with a slight flourish. 'Honey! I didn't even steal it. I bought it for you, Bridget,' she told the old woman proudly.

'Well, now, I'm sure you didn't need to go and spend your money on me, girl,' Bridget muttered, but Rachel could see how pleased she was.

'No, I didn't,' Starling said haughtily. 'So be happy that I did, eh?' For want of somewhere to put it down, Starling sat cradling the honey in her lap. She reached out with one hand to twitch the bedclothes straighter, and as she turned her face away, Rachel saw it was etched with worry. *This woman is her only family, and she is a frail and expectant thing.*

Under Starling's direction, Rachel helped to carry in more wood from a pile behind the cottages. The eerie stillness in the shadows beneath the frozen trees made them hurry back inside.

'Is there no coal?' said Rachel, and Starling shook her head.

'There never is. I thought about bilking some from Dan Smithers, but though he's my friend he'll not carry me if he thinks I'm stealing from him.'

'I have some money. We should have bought some from him,' Rachel pointed out, opening the stove and feeding in some smaller twigs to get it started again.

'Open both vents on that stove, or it'll take an hour or more to light!' Bridget called from the bedroom. There was no water in the kettle, and with a sigh Starling went back out into the darkness, to the pump on the street, and Rachel was left alone with Bridget, feeling suddenly awkward.

She hovered in the front room for a while, until Bridget called her back to the bedside.

'Lord, I hate this darkness,' she grumbled. 'It's early evening, but could be the dead of night. My eyes can see to do nothing past four in the afternoon! And shan't now until April next.' Rachel took Starling's place on the three-legged stool.

'Spring does seem a long way ahead,' she said. Bridget grunted.

'You must forgive me for not rising. I'm not so much the invalid I seem, but today my chest is heavy and I have no strength. It comes and goes, some days better than others. Perhaps this will be my last winter; perhaps not.' She spoke matter-of-factly; without fear or self-pity. 'Your face wakes old pain. Old grief. Why have you come?'

'I am . . . employed at the Alleyns' household, on Lansdown Crescent. As reader and . . . companion to Mr Jonathan Alleyn . . .'

'To Jonathan Alleyn? So, Starling hasn't poisoned him yet, then, or slipped an adder into his bedclothes.' Bridget spoke scathingly.

'No. Not yet.'

'Well. I'm not surprised. For all her bluster and spite, she's a sensible girl. She has a good job there, and she knows it. Where else would she go, for heaven's sake, if she left the Alleyns?'

'I . . . do not know. She seems to hate him, though. Her master. And to hate the mistress a little as well.'

'She has to hate him; what else can she do? She blames him for Alice leaving us. Easier to think him a murderer than to accept the other idea.'

'You do not think he did it?'

'No. But who can know, especially after all this time? There were so many secrets, so many meetings that I knew nothing about. I turned a blind eye as much as I could. Who was I to thwart their plans? Lord Faukes would have cast us all out if he'd found it out, but Alice loved Jonathan so keen – loved him like breath. And I loved Alice.' She shrugged; coughed a little.

'It seems most who knew Alice loved her. All but Josephine Alleyn.'

'All who knew Alice loved her. Josephine Alleyn met her only once; her hatred was for what Alice *was*, for what she represented, not for Alice herself.'

'And what was Alice to her?'

'A scandal, of course. A rich man's by-blow with no name of her own, born in shame.' Rachel's heart squeezed in her chest.

'You know of Alice's birth?' she said, her throat going tight with nameless fear.

'It doesn't take a genius to fathom it. She was placed into my arms one day, a little girl with a sunny smile and hair like silk. Lord Faukes brought her, and put her into my arms, and I saw the way he favoured her. What man has tenderness for a child, unless it is his own blood?'

'You say Alice was Lord Faukes's child?'

'I cannot prove it, and it was never spoken of. But why else do rich and powerful men sponsor nameless young children? And keep them tucked away, out of sight and mind?'

'How old was she when he brought her to you? How old was Alice when you saw her first?' Rachel pressed, leaning forward and pinning Bridget with her gaze. The old woman frowned in thought.

'Small, still. Not more than three years of age. I never knew where she'd been before that – I knew better than to ask.' Suddenly, Bridget's eyes swam and her mouth twisted up, and when she spoke tears misshaped the words. 'I was as much of a mother to that girl as whoever it was that birthed her. Mother and nurse and servant. Does Starling ever think of that? She goes on like she's the only one that misses her.'

Rachel shut her eyes. *Three years old. Abi . . . was it you?* She struggled to keep her composure.

'Do you . . . do you think Alice is dead?' Bridget looked up sharply at her strangled tone, then shook her head.

'She ran away. She had enough cause to, if she'd come to accept that she could not marry Mr Alleyn. I never heard from her again after that morning she went out. She loved to walk . . . it wasn't strange that she went. I heard the door swing just after dawn, before the sky was proper lit. I thought to myself, "I do not need to rise just yet. Alice has gone out, she will bring the eggs on her way back in. Starling will light the fires." That's what I thought, as I lay there all lazy and warm. And that was the last sound I ever heard from my Alice. She should . . . she should have sent us word! She must have known how we'd worry, and that we would have kept any secrets she wanted us to. She should have sent us a word.' Bridget settled her chin as she spoke, but there was more pain than rebuke in her voice.

'It surprises you that she did not?'

'Yes. But then,' Bridget shrugged. 'Letters get lost.'

'The Alleyns are sure she eloped with another, but Starling insists that Alice had no sweetheart other than Jonathan. That she would never have been untrue to him . . .'

'She deceives herself,' said Bridget, abruptly.

'What do you mean?'

'I don't like it any more than she does, but I know what I saw with my own eyes. I saw Alice, with another man.'

'What other man?' Rachel asked, her heart beating harder. *Let her be alive.*

'Don't you think I'd have sought him out if I knew? I was . . . pleased. I saw him only once, from the back. They'd been talking on the bridge by the inn, and then he went off towards the toll bridge. Their talk was lengthy and . . . impassioned. A quarrel, almost. I saw him from far away as he went, and only from behind, but I was glad. Surprised, to be sure, but glad. She couldn't have Jonathan, you see. They must have told you? Josephine Alleyn must have told you? Jonathan was forbidden to marry her; she was nobody. She might even have been his own kin . . . but even if that weren't so, she was too far below him. I daresay they made plans to run away, or to wed in secret, but they'd been in love since they were bairns. He'd have done it already, if he was going to. Wouldn't he? That's what I tried to tell her, though she wouldn't hear me. If he truly meant to wed her, he'd have done it long before. Loving him was only ever going to break her heart. So when I saw her talking to this other one, I was glad.'

'Who was he? What did he look like?'

'He was *nobody*! He was a stranger who asked her for the time of day, nothing more!' Starling's voice was tight. She stood in the doorway with the full kettle in one hand and a sloshing pail in the other, knuckles crimson from the cold and eyes glittering with anger.

'I know what I saw, Starling! There was more to it than that!'

'You know no such thing! What would you know?'

'What would I know, who raised her up and knew everything she did – even the things you thought you kept secret?'

'They were planning to run away! She and Jonathan! And they were going to take me with them . . . If you saw her speak to some man, then perhaps he was helping them, somehow. Perhaps he was a friend of Jonathan's come to bring her news of a plan he didn't dare write down.'

'If you believe that you're naught but an idiot, girl!' Bridget snapped, and then coughed, and spoke more softly.

'Why go searching for a complicated answer, when there is a simple one right in front of you?'

'Because,' said Starling, and then stopped, swallowing. 'Because Alice *loved* me. She called me her sister. She wouldn't have just left me here – left me to Lord Faukes. She *promised*.'

'She loved you, for sure. And she loved me, in her own way. But we all thought she loved Jonathan Alleyn more, Starling, and yet she betrayed him. I *saw* her, and I know what I saw.'

The two of them stared at one another. Their argument had the weary, scarred sound of one that had been had many times before, and hurt them both every time. Starling turned away to put down the pail and set the kettle on the stove. Rachel sat in silence, huddling into the shadows by the bed, still electrified by the news that Alice had come into their lives aged three, not newborn. Her heart thumped so hard that it seemed to shake her all over; Bridget turned a beady eye on her, and seemed to see it.

'But you have not answered my question, Mrs Weekes,' she said. Rachel looked up at her, feeling absurdly guilty. 'Why have you come here?' In the silence that followed the question, Rachel sensed Starling's listening ears. Suddenly, she wanted to tell them. She wanted to tell somebody what she dared to hope, but that hope was such a fragile little thing – a house of cards that could tumble down if someone trod too heavily close to it. But if she spoke it out loud, it might also coalesce. It might also make it true. Rachel swallowed, licked her lips, and spoke.

'I had a sister. Her name was Abigail. A twin sister, identical to me,' she said. In the other room, the silence grew even more acute.

'Her favourite colour was blue; I remember that quite clearly. Lavender blue; and mine was yellow. On our last day together, Mama tied back our hair with ribbons to match our favourite dresses — lavender for Abi, primrose for me . . .' That warm and sunny day; a day of light and air as soft as a gentle caress on your skin; a day of whispers and secretive giggles, caught behind small hands. Their brother Christopher was not yet born; the two girls were their own whole world, and their parents were the stars around which they spun. They had two languages — one for each other, and one for other people. A language of intuition and odd, fluting syllables; in truth they barely needed to speak at all, since the one knew instantly what the other wished to say. They were old enough to walk and run, to climb onto chairs and down steps. They were old enough to loves stories and songs, and to play games with their dolls and toy horses. They were old enough to have a favourite colour, and a favourite food, but they were no older than that. That day they were going to visit their grandparents, a destination not quite as exciting as the carriage ride that would take them there.

The girls loved to ride in the carriage. They could never sit still and straight on the leather seats, as they were instructed to. They fidgeted and bounced here and there, and craned to watch from the window; they knelt on the seats, and played on the floor as it rocked and rattled. Their mother, Anne, just smiled and took pleasure in their delight; she told their nurse not to reprimand their antics too firmly. The girls loved the horses, too. Before setting off, they each took a turn in their father's arms; he held them near the animals' blinkered heads and let them stroke the coarse whorls of hair between their eyes.

'Take care to keep your fingers far from his mouth, Abi,' warned their father, John Crofton. They loved the pungent smell of the horses, particularly when they'd been running awhile and had sweat foaming on their powerful shoulders. The horses had bright chestnut coats with white legs and cream-coloured manes and tails. Their father had got them for a good price because red horses with four white legs were said to be unlucky. *Tosh and palaver*, said John Crofton. The little girls dreamed of being allowed to ride outside, on the box, sitting next to the whip. Then they could watch the manes fly and hear the hooves strike and the wheels clatter; they would feel the wind streaming in their hair and see the world rushing by, like flying.

But even their libertarian mother was adamant – they could not ride on the box, and they weren't allowed to lean out of the window unless the carriage had halted or was moving very slowly, with no trees or hedges nearby to snag them or lash at their eyes. At the ford was one good place, since the crossing was always made cautiously. The road slipped into the By Brook and vanished along the rocky bottom to emerge the other side, muddy and rutted, some thirty feet away. It was early in the summer and spring had been full of downpours; there were still days of torrential rain, after which the landscape gently seethed when the sun returned, steaming as it warmed and dried. So the By Brook was running high; it was deeper than usual at the ford, and faster. The water shone; a green, unbroken skin undulating over the rocky bed, reflecting the vibrant colour of young beech boughs overhead. They heard the coachman, Lenton, holler to the horses, an elongated *ea-sy* that slowed the carriage. They heard the first great splashes as the horses started into the water.

'Me!' the girls shouted at once, each desperate to be the first to look out. Their father smiled indulgently.

'Rachel first, since you were first to pet the horses before we left, Abi.'

John Crofton dropped the window as low as it would go, and held Rachel's small body on his knee so that she could curl her fingers over the sill and stick her head out. Droplets of water landed on her face like rain, kicked up by the horses. She gazed down at the white plumes where their legs churned the river, and smelled their sweat and the clean river scent; the sticky leather of the harness. The water came well above the horses' knees, covering their white socks. Their tails trailed in it, tugged downstream. The carriage slowed right down, and wobbled side to side over unseen rocks. Rachel looked up at the back of Lenton's grey head. He was sitting straight, knees wide; tweaking at the reins, keeping them slow. Then the carriage tipped slowly, the left wheel riding up high onto some obstacle on the riverbed. It inched up to a high point and then stopped altogether. Rachel gripped the sill tighter as she was pulled towards the other side of the carriage. She felt her father's hands tighten around her middle. She felt thrilled, and yet safe.

'Hup now. Easy on, easy on.' The coachman's voice stayed low and calm; the horses leaned into their collars, but the carriage stayed stuck.

'The wheel must be wedged in some crevice,' said Anne Crofton. 'Can you see anything?'

'Hop down, little girl, and let me look,' said their father. But Rachel didn't want to relinquish her vantage point, and hung on.

'I want to see! My turn!' Abi cried suddenly. She reached up and grabbed the window's edge. She jumped, pulling on her arms to lift herself up. All of her weight was against the door. At that moment the carriage jerked forwards, and righted itself abruptly, and in the next instant the latch popped open, the door flew wide, and Abi was gone.

'*Abigail!*' Their mother's voice was a piercing, incredulous shriek. For a sickening moment Rachel was also airborne; her father's hands tightened convulsively, gripping her ribs so hard that it hurt. There was water and the wet, black side of the carriage beneath and behind her, then she was inside again, thrust far back into a seat and left.

'Abigail – catch her! Lenton, catch her, man, *catch her*!' John Crofton was in the river, over his knees and struggling against the current. He lurched, could not find safe footing; had to keep one hand back to grip the wheel for support. The horses tossed their heads and plunged at the sudden noise and movement; Lenton was caught up with them, wrestling with the reins.

'Abigail! Oh, my baby! My baby!' Anne Crofton was hysterical; Rachel hardly recognised the sounds coming out of her mouth. Her mother was leaning out of the carriage with her arm flung out and her fingers splayed as though she might somehow reach Abi and pull her back to safety. But the river was fast, and deep enough, and the girls were only just old enough to climb onto chairs and down steps, not out of heedless rivers. Rachel stood behind her mother in the unsteady carriage, and looked out. Far down the river, where it curved out of sight beneath dappled green trees, a fragment of lavender blue was racing out of sight.

'She drowned?' Starling's voice made Rachel jump; all the grim inevitability of the story was in it.

'We had to think so. We grieved as if she had . . . but we never found her, you see. We never found her . . . body. My father and our man went the whole length of the By Brook, to where it joined the Avon – here, at Bathampton – asking in every village and cot along the way. But nobody had found a little girl, alive or dead, in the water. We were so young; I remember that day only as snatches of colour and sound and scent. I don't remember her falling, not exactly, but I remember the colour of her dress, and how pretty it looked in the water. And I have always had the feeling . . .' Rachel paused, and took an uneven breath. 'I have always had the feeling that she wasn't gone.'

'So when you were told about Alice Beckwith, who you looked so similar to, you thought it could be her? Your sister?' said Bridget.

'The accident happened not ten miles from here in the By Brook valley, and that river runs here, to join the Avon! And now you tell me that Alice was brought to you aged three years or so . . . don't you see? It has to be her!'

'Poor girl.' Bridget was shaking her head. 'I can see why you would want to believe it. But you have a similar look to her, not an identical one, and Alice was some issue of Lord Faukes's, I'm convinced of it.'

'But you don't *know* it!'

'No, I do not know for sure. But don't agitate yourself over it so, Mrs Weekes!'

'Don't agitate myself, when I may have found my sister, lost to me these twenty-six years?' Rachel felt panicked, desperate; she felt Abi fading, slipping away from her. *Stay, dearest.*

'But you have not found her,' said Starling, a grim silhouette in the doorway. Her voice was hard, and even. 'Alice is long dead. You have not found her.'

Rachel sat in silence for the rest of the visit. She rose from the bedside and went to sit by the stove, which was finally giving out a little heat, as Starling made a soup of the dried fish and some barley she found in the cupboard, and took a bowl of it to Bridget. She watched as Starling put a smooth lump of stone on to heat as she swept the floors, then wrapped the stone in rags and slid it under the blankets near the old woman's feet; then she brewed a pot of tea and sweetened a cup with honey for each of them. All the while, she and Bridget exchanged comments about her work and the Alleyn household, and what provisions and charity might come in before Starling next visited, and who had been caught with whom, canoodling behind the church. There was no more talk of Alice or Jonathan, or the other man in Alice's life; as if a truce had been called until the next time. There was no more talk of Abigail, and Rachel sensed them parting around the subject like a stream around a fallen branch; as though she had brought something shameful, embarrassing, to the cottage. She said nothing, feeling cowed and angry, and foolish too. *What if it is not folly to believe it? Jonathan found a note . . . and Bridget saw another man. What if she ran away, and is alive somewhere?* The thought was so sweet it was almost unbearable, and Rachel swallowed hard. *Even if she didn't remember me, she would know me as soon as she saw me.*

There were no boats heading west, so Starling and Rachel walked back to Bath along the towpath, side by side. The moon in the icy sky made everything strange and grey; the canal, the landscape, their skin and eyes – even Starling's bright hair. For a long time neither one of them spoke. They walked quickly, the cold clenching in their chests.

'Will we pass the lovers' tree?' Rachel asked, at last. Starling shook her head.

'No. It stands back the other way, towards the river. And it would be folly to go so close to the river's edge in darkness. If you stumbled in at this time of year . . . We can go another day, in the light, if you want.'

'I would like to.' There was a silence before she spoke again. 'It must have been terrible, not knowing what happened to Alice. Terrible then, and terrible now.'

'Yes,' said Starling, with a note of suspicion in her tone. 'But I do know what happened to her.'

'But you are not sure. It . . . it can be a way to grieve, I think. Or rather, a way to postpone the grief, and to divert it. After my little brother died my father chased after every doctor in England for an explanation. For a definitive answer

– what was the illness that took him, how did it work, where did he acquire it, how might it have been prevented. It . . . it drove him to distraction for a while, but it did not bring Christopher back.'

'I know she's not coming back,' Starling whispered tersely. 'I only want justice for her.'

'If she is dead then justice does not interest her. It is only for you that you seek it.'

'Should her killer go unpunished, then? Should his crime stay hidden?'

'No. I only mean that . . . that perhaps you ought not let your grief blind you. You ought not let it insist upon an answer when perhaps there is none. Or perhaps you truly have it already.'

For a moment Starling made no reply, and when she did speak her voice was low and angry.

'What answer?'

'Why didn't you tell me that Bridget saw Alice talking with another man?'

'Because it means nothing! It was innocent! Alice was pretty . . . men often tried to catch her eye.'

'But Bridget knew her as well as you did – wouldn't she know what she saw? And what of the note Mr Alleyn spoke of, from the lovers' tree? Don't the two things together perhaps suggest that—'

'No! No, they do not! It's all a veil, can't you see? You want her to have run away because you want her to be your sister, and living. But she did not; and she is not!' Starling's voice rang out loudly. She quickened her pace as if wanting to leave Rachel behind.

'You . . . you cannot have it both ways, you know,' said Rachel, striding to catch up with her. It was a thought she hadn't entirely meant to voice, but there was no way to take it back. She braced herself for Starling's response.

'What do you mean?'

'You cannot have Alice flawless, and yet murdered by Jonathan Alleyn. He cannot have all the blame for her vanishing.'

'Speak plainly.'

'They loved each other, that much is known. They were in love for years. Do you mean to tell me Alice would reject Jonathan when he came back from the war, because he was disturbed? Haven't you told me she was a most forgiving woman, and kind-hearted to all?'

'Yes. She was.'

'Then would she have rejected him if he came back in a poor state? Even if he had done bad things in the war?' There was silence. 'Would she?' Rachel pressed.

'No.' The word was small, and unwilling.

'Then what cause would he have to murder her?' Again, silence. 'The only possible cause would be that she did indeed try to leave him for another.'

'No! Faukes must have frightened her into it, somehow.'

'But she was quite prepared to defy Faukes and elope with Jonathan, you told me. You don't want it to be so, and I understand. But Bridget saw her speaking with another man, and Jonathan found a note – an invitation to meet, written to Alice in writing he didn't know.'

'That is no proof! Where is this note, then?'

'If he did not find it, Starling,' Rachel said gently, 'what other reason could he have to harm her?'

They walked on for a while, their steps steady and measured in the dark. Rachel felt oddly calm, oddly removed from the scene she inhabited. She felt as though she was gliding past the world, drifting along to one side, powerless. A pair of watching eyes. *Just like on my wedding day. I exist only on the edges of this.* 'There is another explanation.'

'What?' Starling leapt at this small offering.

'*He* did not kill her.'

'Then who did? This other man she met?'

'So you can conceive that she *was* meeting another? That she loved another? Then can't you conceive that she ran away with him, in truth? That she was too ashamed to face you and Bridget because of it; too ashamed to face Jonathan? She wrote to him to break it off. Captain Sutton was there with him in Brighton when he got that letter.'

'She would not leave us. She would not leave *me*. Jonathan killed her!'

'Only if she was untrue to him. That could be the *only* reason. Don't you see, Starling? You can't have it both ways!'

'And this is how you honour the one you hope is your lost sister?'

'I would rather have her faithless, and cowardly, than dead,' Rachel said softly.

'Alice was neither of those things!'

'Then you prefer her to be dead?' The words were pitiless to Rachel's own ears, and she awaited an angry rejoinder that didn't come. After a minute or so Starling blew her nose, and Rachel saw her cheeks all silvery wet.

'I wish you hadn't come,' said Starling, quietly. Rachel couldn't tell if she meant on the visit to Bridget that night, or to Bath, and into Starling's life. She heard an echo of her own loneliness in the words; wanted to put her arm around the girl, but didn't dare.

'What did you mean when you said Alice left you to Lord Faukes?' she asked instead. Starling didn't answer, but Rachel noticed the way she tensed, her shoulders curling inwards just fractionally, as if to absorb a blow.

They paused at the foot of the bridge that would lead them to Bath's inner streets, as though unwilling to return to their lives in spite of the late hour, the cold, and the unease between them. Rachel thought of Richard, and what she would say if she found him home, waiting for her. *That is my life, in spite of my reluctance. I chose it and I can't change it. He is my only chance for a family.* It was an unavoidable truth. *Unless. Unless I can find Abi.* She followed Starling's gaze to Lansdown Crescent, in the high distance, and knew then where she would rather go. The realisation hit her like a slap, a jolt that went right through her. *Should we switch places?* But if Starling had once wanted Richard Weekes, Rachel knew she wanted him no longer. She was clever enough for that. *Her will is bent on proving Jonathan Alice's murderer. Now I must bend to proving he is not.* Their parting glance was full of unspoken things, and Rachel didn't ask, though she wanted to, when or if they would meet again in private. She tried not to dwell on how much she would rather have carried on at Starling's side, to Lansdown Crescent, to the dark and disordered rooms on the second floor, and their dark and disordered inhabitant. *Be alive, Abi! Be alive, and run off, as Bridget believes. As all others believe. Let Jonathan not be your murderer, and me not destined to lose you twice.*

The house above the wine shop was empty and unlit. Relieved, Rachel let exhaustion swim into her body; from the cold, and the wearying intensity of all she had heard and said that night. She went slowly up to the bedroom with a taper to light the lamp, undressed and brushed out her hair. Her stomach felt hollow, but she didn't want to eat. She closed the shutters and went to the dresser where her trinket box was kept. She craved her mother's advice like never before. Seconds later her heart fled her chest, sinking like a stone. The box wasn't in its normal place. She scrabbled through gloves and stockings, combs and neckties; through each of the drawers and then throughout the rest of the room, though she knew she hadn't put the box anywhere else. But there weren't that many places to search, and soon she was forced to stop, sit down on the bed, and accept that the box, with her mother's lock of hair pinned inside, had gone. At once she guessed its certain fate, and then she wished even more to be Starling, and free; rather than Rachel, and trapped.

By the time Richard returned the abbey bells had rung eleven and the streets outside were quiet; Rachel's anger was cold and hard, unlike anything she had felt before, and underneath it was a bud of fear that threatened to bloom – the fear that wherever her treasure had gone, it might not be retrievable. It made her incautious; she didn't notice that Richard was frowning even as he came into the room, face flushed, skin clammy in spite of the cold outside. She didn't notice that his shirt had been pulled loose from his belt, that his knuckles were grazed and crimson. She rose to her feet and met him with a tumble of tight words.

'Where is it? My trinket box?'

'Your what?' said Richard, but the guilty cast his frown took told her the truth.

'It was my mother's. If you've sold it you must get it back.'

'Leave me be, can't you? I have had a trying time of it this evening.'

'I daresay you have. It must be a trying business, staying out so late all the time, and drinking so much. Where is it? You had no right to—'

'I had no right? You are my *wife*, Rachel. Or had you forgotten? Everything you once owned belongs to me.'

'That box was precious to me! It was my mother's before it was mine! You knew how much it meant to me.'

'It was just a thing, Rachel! An object that served little purpose in itself, but which has paid a number of bills.'

'Your bills, not mine! Your debts from the gaming tables, I don't doubt.'

'Mind your tongue, Rachel. I won't be wedded to a shrew,

and I won't be spoken to like that in my own house. Or out of it. Not by you, or anyone.' Richard's face darkened still. A vein ran up the middle of his forehead, cast into relief by the lamplight; it spoke of something building up inside.

'What did you do with what was inside?' Rachel was shaking with fury; her mouth was dry.

'There was nothing inside – naught but a scrap of paper, and those earrings, which fetched a little extra.'

'A little extra? They were worth a great deal, you *stupid* man! And the lock of hair? Please tell me you kept that. Please.'

Rachel shut her eyes to await his answer – she couldn't bear to see it writ large across his face. So she didn't see his fist before it hit her, slamming into her mouth and jaw. She sat down abruptly, put her hands to her face in shock. There was a moment of ringing numbness and then pain bloomed through her head, squeezing like a giant fist until she thought it might crack the bone. There was blood on her fingers when she brought them away, blood in her teeth and on her tongue; a metal taste of iron and salt.

She looked up at the sound of footsteps. Richard loomed over her. She thought he would put out his hand to help her up, but he did not.

'Never speak to me that way,' he said, in a voice she barely recognised. He was shaking now – a tremor of barely held violence. His fingers twitched, and Rachel waited for a second blow. It did not come. Richard turned away from her, fetched a handkerchief from the drawer and tossed it at her. The blood from her lip left scarlet kisses on the linen. She had never felt more alone.

Unsteadily, Rachel got to her feet.

'If you insult me again, I will . . .' Richard trailed off, glancing at her, and she saw his tension begin to ebb away, and shame come to fill its shoes.

'You'll what?' she said. *Beat me harder, like you beat Starling?* A wave of misery crashed over her, because she realised she wasn't surprised that it had come to this, nor so soon. She was not surprised that Richard had hit her. *And he will hit me again, that is a certainty.* She felt utterly defeated.

'You are my *wife*. You must show me the proper respect, Rachel! It's not my wish that things be this way between us.'

'Respect cannot be beaten into a person.'

'I disagree, and I pray you do not make me prove it,' he said coldly. Rachel shivered, a sudden clench of fear twisting her inside.

'There was a lock of hair in the box. Pinned to the lining. A lock of my mother's hair, and the last piece of my family in my possession. Is it gone then, with the rest?'

'I saw nothing inside but the earrings.' At this, Rachel did begin to cry. The tears were hot and blinding. 'Such keep-sakes are worthless, in truth,' Richard said gruffly.

'It was not worthless to me!'

'If you were a better wife, a warmer one, and more loving, I would not be gone as much. If you had widened our circle, as you were supposed to, I would not need to pay as much for my entertainment. Instead the only friends you make are madmen, or existing acquaintances of mine who can afford but a single bottle of sherry come Christmas!'

'So this is my fault? My fault you are dissolute and drunk, and fritter away your money at the tables?'

'*Yes!*' Richard's sudden bellow was shocking. Rachel felt a dribble of blood ooze onto her chin. 'Come now and make amends. Come and be my *wife*.' He held out his hand to her, turning to the bed.

I will die before I let him take me tonight. Rachel stepped towards him, closer to the light. She left the blood on her chin, and let her mouth open to show her bloodied teeth. She could feel her bottom lip swelling, the cut stinging like a burn. She stared at him, steady and cold as the grave, and did not take his hand. After a moment, Richard dropped his hand and turned away, as if he couldn't stand the sight of her.

* * *

Alice would never have left me to Lord Faukes. But of course, Alice hadn't known what that man was like – her ostensibly kindly benefactor. *He will have things his own way.* Starling wondered, as she rose from her cold and sleepless bed the next morning, if Bridget had known when she gave Alice that warning just how right she was; how vile and corrupt a man Lord Faukes had been, whom Alice treated like a grandfather, and kissed and embraced whenever he came to call. Aged twelve, Starling had come to think of him as like a fruit gone bad, still keeping a glossy thick rind to give the appearance of wholesomeness, when inside the flesh was a rotten pulp, riddled with worms, eaten away by decay. The thought of it made vomit burn in the back of her throat. *Never was a man less deserving of Alice's kisses. And Rachel Weekes asks me what did I mean by it. She hears things all too clearly.* Starling remembered all the times Bridget had bade her keep out of Lord Faukes's way, all the times she'd sent her hurrying from the room on some errand when the old man had tried to talk to her, or take her hand, or give her some titbit. She remembered the way Bridget had hovered and stared when Alice embraced the old man; poised, watching, fighting the urge to pull Alice away. *She knew. But if she thinks Alice was Lord Faukes's child, what danger could she have imagined her to be in from him?* Starling decided not to think about it; not to think about Lord Faukes. She even shut her eyes to banish the images, but her memories spun on nonetheless. She stumbled on the stairs; grabbed at the wall for support.

Nine days after Alice had last been seen, Lord Faukes

came to the house in Bathampton and Starling found out just how completely her world had ended. The atmosphere inside the house was unbearable, like a breath held so long that it threatened to burst. Bridget was silent and as grim as the grave; already in mourning, already shut off from the world – from Starling, who was still waiting in mounting terror and confusion for Alice to walk back through the door. For she had to, surely; she had to. When they heard the sound of a horse approaching, both knew it would be news. Starling ran into the yard, so overwrought with relief she thought she might scream. She thought it was Alice returned, and when she saw that it was Lord Faukes she thought he must have brought word of her; news of when she would be coming back. Bridget stayed seated at the kitchen table, only lifting up her face to show the new, deep lines criss-crossing her skin, as though grief was a whip that lashed at her.

Before their master was even off his horse Starling was at his side, closer than she would normally stand, made careless by need. But she didn't take his hand to implore, or even touch his sleeve. The rot beneath the rind; she could still smell it, however distracted she might be.

'You have word of Alice?' she said, and did not curtsy or bid him good day, or wait for him to speak first. Lord Faukes glared at her, long and steady, as he handed the reins of his horse to the yardman. He walked on towards the door, and she trotted alongside.

'She did not manage to make you any less brazen-faced, then, eh?' he muttered, distractedly. Once indoors, he handed Starling his hat and gloves and went through to the parlour to sit down. 'Bring me brandy, girl. Bridget, I would speak to you.' His voice was grave, but even. The women, old and young, glanced at one another. They could read nothing from his words, so they did as they were bid. When Starling took in the brandy, Bridget was already standing in front of him with her hands laced together, quite still and re-signed. Starling wanted to stay but Lord Faukes said brusquely: 'Be gone with you, little wench.'

For ten minutes Starling waited alone in the kitchen, and just like the first time she'd waited for news from the parlour, time grew sticky and slow, stretching itself out near to breaking point, like a string of tar. They seemed unbearably long, those last few moments in her life in which Starling had hope; the possibility of joy. When Bridget came out her face was grim and still, giving nothing away. Starling rushed to meet her.

'Bridget, tell me. What news is there? Where's Alice?'

'I don't know where she is, child.' Bridget pressed her lips together briefly, clamping off the words. 'But she's gone, and I think . . . we must be ready not to see her again.'

'What? What do you mean? There is news, then? Tell me it!' Starling gripped the older woman's hands, felt how cold and dry they were. Like there was no blood beneath the skin at all.

'Come in here, Starling, and stop clamouring so. I will tell you what you need to know,' Lord Faukes called from his chair, the same parlour chair he always chose, though his hips wedged into it tightly, his flesh moulding into the wood and fabric. Half reluctant now, Starling went to stand in front of him. 'Bridget. I have a yen to eat veal for supper. Go into the village and see if there is any to be had.'

'Sir, I doubt that at this late hour there will be any—'

'Go on and look for some, I say!' His sudden bark burst the bubble of decorum that had perched, fragile, over the household. Starling felt a warning again, scratching away at the back of her mind as though it wanted out. But she *had* to know what he would tell her about Alice. She was caught, like a fish on a hook. Bridget glanced from her master to Starling and back again, her clenched knuckles even whiter, spots of crimson in her cheeks and her eyes full of some desperate want that she could do nothing to fulfil. With wooden steps she made her way to the door and went out of the house, not even pausing for her coat or hat, or for coins to pay the butcher.

Only once they were alone did Lord Faukes look up at Starling, and clear his throat.

'Alice has disgraced herself beyond redemption. She will never be welcome here again; I shall have no more to do with her.' He spoke without anger, but also without doubt.

'What disgrace? What do you mean? Where is Alice?' Starling pleaded.

'You will not see her again.' His words landed like blows, each one shaking her more than the last.

'What?'

'She has run away with a man; a lover. Feckless, ungrateful girl. She has eloped to be wed, since she knew I would not allow it. There. It is as painful to me as it is to you, I hope you realise. She has deceived us all as to her true nature. Or perhaps she was corrupted by the wild influence of another. Or others.' At this he gave her a steady look, hard and considering. 'Tell me truthfully. Did you know of this liaison? Of her plans to behave to so ruinously?'

'I don't understand.' Starling shook her head. 'She has run away with Jonathan? But . . . he was here after she went missing; he came looking for her . . .'

'What nonsense is this, with Jonathan? Of course not with my grandson! He would not act so wrongly! I don't know the name of the man she has gone with. If I knew it, believe me I would find them all the faster. Jonathan is at Box even at this moment, deeply upset by it all. I do not deny that I knew of some . . . attachment between them. A cousinly affection. But the idea that the two of them would collude in such a way is . . . preposterous.'

'But they planned to marry! They have written to each other and spoken and thought of little else since I have known them!'

'Written, you say?' said Faukes, eyeing her severely.

'And . . . and she has taken nothing with her – no clothes, none of her possessions . . . all are still here!'

'Of course she's taken nothing – you shared a room, did you not? She could hardly pack a trunk without you knowing it, could she? Whoever she has left with, she must think he has the means to clothe her anew.'

'But Jonathan . . . Alice . . .' Starling struggled to set her thoughts in order. She put her hands to head to keep them all in. 'Alice loved Jonathan! She would never run away with anybody else!'

'Do not contradict me, wench!' Faukes shouted, his face mottling with blood. 'It's more than you deserve that I take the time to explain the situation to you!' He thumped the arms of the chair with his hands, making the frame of it shake. He was as solid and strong as the wood itself, Starling thought. She rolled onto the balls of her feet, ready. *None of this is true.* She was as certain of it as she was of her own heartbeat.

'Forgive me, sir. But I . . . I . . .'

'You do not want to believe it, any more than Bridget did, or Jonathan or I. But it does no good to deny facts when they are put plainly in front of you. The girl has made a mockery of all she has been given, and she will have nothing more from me or my family. This house will be let. I will see you and Bridget put into positions elsewhere, if you will accept my help with due gratitude, and be good and obedient, the pair of you. And you will speak no more of Alice Beckwith. The girl is dead to me; I will not hear her name.'

'How do you know, sir?' Starling whispered, her throat too tight for speech. 'How do you know of this elopement?'

'She wrote a letter, delivered to my house in Box.'

'May I see the letter?'

'So, she taught you to read? No, you may not. I flung it into the fire, it angered me so. There. Take this bitter news and be reconciled to it, for it cannot be changed. Perhaps I might find room for you in my own household. Eh? What do you say to that?' Lord Faukes levered himself out of his chair as he spoke and stood over her, head and shoulders taller. Starling took a step backwards. 'I shouldn't mind seeing such pretty, flaming curls every day.' He reached out a hand as if to catch a lock of her hair, and Starling stepped back again.

'No!' she managed to cry.

Her backward step made her catch her heel on the corner of the couch. As she fought for balance he dealt her a back-handed blow to the side of her head that made her ears ring, and she twisted as she fell, landing hard on her stomach across the arm of the couch, which drove all the air out of her in one rushing exhalation. Before she could think or try to rise she felt the weight of him bearing down on her. His hand was on the back of her neck, gripping hard, pushing her face into the seat so that she could hardly breathe, let alone fight him. She reached over her shoulder, nails scrabbling at his sleeve, seeking skin. She couldn't reach any, could not make her arms bend behind her to find his cheek or eyes or mouth; any soft part she might have been able to injure. She had nothing to bite but the dusty fabric in front of her face. Her own breath was hot and suffocating, clamped over her nose and mouth like a swaddling cloth.

'I've tamed wilder things than you, girl,' said Lord Faukes, his voice tight with lust and amusement. 'But fight on, if it please you. The harder won victory is always the sweeter.' Starling felt air touch the backs of her legs as her skirt was lifted; felt her skin bruised as her drawers were torn away; felt that bone-deep warning, that knowledge she should not have had of what was coming. Knowing it made it hurt no less, and made it no less shaming. Her vulnerability, her failure to prevent what was happening filled her with a terrible rage, as incandescent as it was futile. She shrieked it out into the muffling cushions – every curse and threat and insult she knew, and then wordless cries when his thrusting began, tearing into her. It was not over quickly. Lord Faukes was not a young man; he took his time to take his pleasure.

Sometime afterwards, Bridget rushed in, eyes and mouth wide open, to find Starling still leaning over the arm of the sofa, staring at nothing, her jaw knotted tight at the hinges as she ground her teeth together.

'I knew it . . . I knew it as soon as I saw him ride past me, all red in the face and loose in his limbs! The foul old *bastard*! May he rot!' Bridget cried; the first and only time Starling heard her curse somebody. 'May he *rot*! Are you injured? Can you rise?'

'Don't touch me,' Starling ground out, and she felt Bridget hesitate, startled at her tone. There was a pause, a measured beat in which Bridget changed tack, subtly and effectively.

'Well, you can't stay there all day, bung upwards and bleeding on the carpet. Come up and let's get you clean.'

'I won't ever be clean. And let the carpet go to bloody hell. Let the next lot worry about the stains on it, for we won't be here much longer, he says.'

'No more we will. But clean you shall be, Starling. The traces they leave can always be rinsed away.'

'Not always. That was not the first time.'

'I guessed as much.' Slowly, Starling peeled herself up from the sofa, standing gingerly. Blood and seed ran down her leg and she shivered in revulsion. She met Bridget's gaze, saw that the older woman was near as aggrieved as her by what had happened.

'Only Alice stopped him until now,' she said, and Bridget nodded.

'Forgive me. You couldn't know the danger. I'm sorry I went out.'

'I knew it. And you had no choice but to go.'

'I had a choice, but I was too much the coward to take it.' Bridget's breath suddenly hitched in her chest; she thumped a fist into her ribs and groaned. 'But no more! *No more!* I will call him master no more!' she cried out, then made a sound like a sob but dry, hollow.

'Don't cry, Bridget. Help me to wash instead. You're right – I can't stand the stink of him on me.'

'How much older than your years you sound, Starling.' Bridget scrubbed her face with her hands, then let them fall to her sides. 'You always did. Come then. I'll put water on to heat, and fetch the tub.'

Starling sat in the tub with her body stinging, the hot water too harsh on the lesions and bruises; she felt calm, almost dead.

'How will it be without her, Bridget?' she murmured.

'We have no choice but to find out, my dear,' said Bridget; a term that had always been reserved for Alice, until then. 'You're not bleeding each month yet, are you? At least there should be no child, then. And you are not a child any longer, Starling. You must choose where you would go, what you would do. This will not be the only time – that much I can assure you. If you continue to accept the wages of that man, this will not be the only time.'

'You will go your own way, then, Bridget?'

'I will. And take you with me, if you'll go.'

'What about Alice? How will she know where to find us?'

'Alice is gone, girl. One way or another. Though it breaks my heart to say it.'

'She will come back, I know she will. She wouldn't just go

and leave us. And what about Jonathan? She'd *never* leave him for another! You know it as well as I do!' At this she saw Bridget pause, and choose not to tell her something. She had no will to demand to hear it. But she decided there and then that she would stay in Lord Faukes's service. That she would stay near Jonathan, in a place that Alice would return to. Bridget seemed to know it too.

'I would have kept you with me. Kept you safe and found you work. Remember that, in the times that are coming,' said the older woman, gravely.

'You can't keep me safe. Only Alice could do that.' She didn't mean to be cruel but she saw the remark hit home. Bridget's face pinched, and she said nothing more, fetching more hot water and clean towels in silence. Starling sat and she thought and she waited. She waited to find out how life would be from then on.

I must find her last letter. Starling carried on up the stairs without thinking, to the second floor of the house on Lansdown Crescent. She didn't pause to check where Mrs Alleyn was, or Mrs Hatton, or Dorcas. A smell of cinders and baked fish lingered in the stairwell. Never once had she believed that Alice had written a letter to Lord Faukes, to tell him of her elopement; she knew a bare-faced lie when she heard one. Her thoughts were troubled, turning this way and that, trying to fix on something clear. *Damn Mrs Weekes and her theories.* Could she be Alice's sister? When Mrs Weekes had described the way her infant sister died, Starling had remembered Alice's sudden fear on the day they'd swum in the river at Bathampton. Remembered how close she'd come to panic when Jonathan suggested swimming out into the current. Could that have been a distant memory, resurfacing? A nameless warning, like those that Starling's early years had left her with? Starling shook her head, muttering refutations beneath her breath. *Alice was* my *sister. Rachel Weekes muddies the water, nothing more. She is a fantasist!* The reason why Jonathan killed Alice was in Alice's last letter to him, sent to Brighton, and it was not that she had fallen in love with another. It had to be something else, something which had brought him hurrying back to Bathampton; something which had turned him wild and mad.

She was at his door and breathing hard, and then inside without knocking. At the sound, Jonathan came from his bedchamber with his shirt untucked and rumpled, his hair a mess in front of his eyes.

'Starling? What's happened?' he said, tilting his head at her; his tone so normal, so understated that Starling took a step backwards. Time and reality skidded around her. *Here is the man I hate. Does he not know that I hate him?* 'Are you well? You're so pale.'

'Am I well?' She reeled slightly, putting out her hands for balance. 'This is all wrong,' she murmured, dizzily. Past his bedraggled figure, on the cluttered desk, was a knife. A pewter blade, dull in the low light; a blunt instrument for the breaking of seals and the splitting of figs. Blunt, then, but still lethal, if used with enough force. Starling stared at it as Jonathan watched her, bewildered. Three steps were all that were needed, she calculated. Three quick steps, a turn and a strike, and whatever truths he knew would bleed out of him and drip through the fancy plasterwork of the ceiling below. She rolled onto the balls of her feet, balancing herself.

'Starling,' said Jonathan, pinching the bridge of his nose with his thumb and forefinger. He sighed. 'You remind me of her sometimes. Did you know that? Just in your . . . gestures. Your facial expressions. Just sometimes.' Starling blinked, and lost sight of the knife behind a haze of tears. She shook her head vehemently.

'I wish you had died instead of her!' she said. Jonathan didn't flinch.

'So do I,' he said.

* * *

The proper thing to do would be to stay indoors until the cut and swelling on her lip had fully healed, but Rachel found she cared less and less for what was proper. One side of her chin was greenish grey with bruising, and the cut had knit into a stiff black line. As he dressed, Richard kept his eyes turned away from her, and wore his guilty scowl.

'You will not go to the Alleyns looking like that,' he said, pulling on his boots.

'I have an appointment. I will keep it.'

'But, your face . . .'

'What of it?'

'You should send a message and say you're unwell,' he suggested, as sulky as a child. Rachel felt a whole new emotion just then, one she had never known before – an exhausting blend of fear and contempt.

'But I am quite well, Mr Weekes. And I'm sure my appearance will cause no particular outrage in that house,' she said stiffly. Richard didn't see fit to argue further; he went down to the shop without another word and Rachel was left to wonder if that was how things would be between them, for the rest of their lives. *Anger, violence, disappointment. For both of us, it seems.*

By the time Rachel had climbed to Lansdown Crescent the sun had turned the milky sky a blinding white, and behind that a touch of blue was beginning to glow. Frost furred all of Bath's window glass; the air was entirely still. November was promising to be cold and sharp. Jonathan rose from behind his desk when Dorcas showed Rachel into his rooms; he smiled, but it melted from his face when he saw her.

'What happened here?' he said seriously.

'A small mishap, nothing more.'

'He beats you?'

'This was the first time, and my fault, in part. I quarrelled with him.'

'The first time is rarely the last. What was the quarrel about?'

'I—' Rachel broke off, unsure if it would sound petty and sentimental to him. 'It was a trifling thing, to be sure. I had a silver box that belonged to my mother. And inside it I kept a lock of her hair, pinned to the lining. The box is . . . sold.' It still made her sad, and somehow more alone.

'Sold by your husband, without your knowledge?'

'Yes. A childish thing to mourn, I know. But mourn it I do.'

'Perhaps, but to have a piece of the child you were can be a precious thing,' said Jonathan, softly. 'I can scarce remember what it was to be a child. Who I was then, before all of this . . .'

'Perhaps it does no good to. The temptation is always there to imagine what that child would make of me now. Of the life I have chosen for myself.'

'Nobody can know the outcome of things, before they are begun. You should not blame yourself,' Jonathan said quietly. Rachel turned to gaze out of the window, where the sky was now brilliantly blue. The rooms around her seemed stifling in comparison.

'Come. Let's go out for a walk. I can't bear to stay cooped up inside today.'

'I don't go out.' Jonathan shook his head with a frown.

'I know, and it's high time you did. Come. The fresh air and exertion will do us both good.'

'I don't care to be seen. My leg, and all the tattlers . . .

And I can't abide crowds,' he said. Rachel thought for a moment.

'How about sheep? Can you abide sheep? I daresay they will have nothing much to say about you, or your leg. Come. I insist.'

Dorcas and the butler, Falmouth, watched in undisguised amazement as Jonathan came downstairs and asked for his coat and hat. They watched in more amazement as he left the house, squinting in the sunshine, with Rachel on his arm.

'They will run and tell my mother I am cured,' he said drily. He kept his arm, and Rachel's hand on it, clamped tightly to his ribs, and Rachel felt the tension running through him.

'It is only a walk,' she said carefully. 'Quite a common-place thing.' Jonathan kept his eyes fixed on the ground in front of him, ignoring the glances they got from passers-by — gentlefolk and dallying servants both.

'People are staring,' he muttered. 'Damn their eyes!' His weak leg twisted and buckled slightly as he walked, giving him a jolting, uneven stride.

'Let them stare. They're most likely looking at my lip and wondering if I kicked you in the leg to retaliate,' said Rachel. Jonathan laughed. It was the first time she had ever heard it, and straight away she loved the sound, and the way it bounced along. In the sunlight his skin was terribly pale, but the shadows under his eyes and cheeks looked less severe. She could see the grey running through his dark hair more clearly, yet at the same time he seemed younger, as uncertain as a youth.

They reached the far end of the crescent and passed through a gate onto the high common. The grass was ankle-length and tussocky, drenched in dew and frost-melt, glitter-ing in the sunshine. They walked for twenty minutes or more, climbing steadily, until the city was behind and below them, and the only sounds were the occasional bleats of sheep and piping of birds. The uneven ground was hard work for Jonathan, and he had been so long without exercise that he was panting by the time they stopped and turned to look back. The dew had soaked their feet and the hems of their clothes. Rachel's toes were damp and numb, but she didn't mind it at all. The blood was thumping through her veins; she felt warm, and well. They stood side by side to catch their breath, and squinted down at the tangled streets of the city, where the last shreds of mist lingered like ghosts.

'This is as far as I have been from my rooms in nine years or more, I think,' said Jonathan.

'No wonder you've been so unhappy,' said Rachel. Jonathan looked down at her, but said nothing. 'I prefer to look the other way – away from the city. To look at the far horizon. Somehow it always makes problems seem smaller,' said Rachel. Jonathan turned obediently to the west, where the River Avon shone like a discarded silver ribbon, winding through fields and trees still clad in the remnants of their autumn colours.

'I came to Bath with my mother because I didn't know where else to go, or what else to do. I didn't care, because I wanted to die,' Jonathan murmured. 'Now it seems I will never leave.'

'Of course you could leave, if you wanted to.'

'And go where, and do what?'

'Wherever you choose; whatever you choose. Take a wife, begin a family. You have that freedom; you have that choice. Don't you see? You can do that. You need not stay trapped here, as I must.' *If I persuade him well enough he will do it, and I will see him no more.* The thought jolted her heart. *Better that, though, than him continuing in torment.*

'The rules are harsher for women than men.' Jonathan narrowed his eyes against the light, and they were unreadable.

'But you could still leave him, if you were strong enough to do so.'

'And go where? And do what?' She smiled, sadly. 'I would be a pauper, reduced to beggary, or whoredom. I would have no employment, no society. No. I have no choice but to remain by my husband's side.' Whatever lightness of mood she had felt suddenly vanished, and she took a deep breath.

'Then I will remain as well,' he said. 'Who else would sit and read tales of adventure and derring-do to me, a mad cripple?' He smiled, and Rachel smiled back at him.

'You are not mad, or crippled,' she said.

'Then what am I?' he asked.

Wounded. Haunted. A killer. The person I most yearn to see.

'You are a good man, war wounded and much troubled by the past.'

'And you are the soul of tact and diplomacy,' said Jonathan. 'Do you think I can't see the other thoughts that whisper to you behind your eyes?'

'What do they whisper?' she asked. *He sees me?* In response Jonathan only smiled again, took her hand and raised it to his lips, pressing a kiss into her chilly skin. Rachel felt the touch of his mouth right down to her bones, like a burn or a bruise, but sweeter. For a moment she couldn't remember how to breathe. *Because a week or so past he might have killed me, and now he kisses me?* she wondered. *No*, said the echo, *only because he kisses you.* She suddenly thought how Starling would react to his gesture, and felt a little sick. As if he sensed this, Jonathan dropped her hand at once. He looked at her for one second more, his expression shifting, ambiguous, then he turned to the horizon again.

'May I ask you something delicate, Mr Alleyn?' Rachel said weakly.

'I think you have earned the right to.'

'What makes you so angry with your mother? I mean,

long years living together under . . . difficult circumstances may well breed discord, I know, but it seems to me that there is more to it than that. That you blame her for something,' said Rachel. Jonathan folded his arms, shielding himself. He did not break off his stare into the west.

'Yes, I do blame her. She is the reason . . . I think. I mean, I can't know because I know she lies, and does not tell the whole truth even when she deigns to tell me some of it. But she is the reason Alice wrote to me.'

'I don't understand.'

'Alice's last letter to me. She wrote to me, a letter that reached me in Brighton.'

I know. Rachel managed only in the last instant not to say this out loud.

'She said . . . she said we had to part. That we could never be together, or marry. That it would be an *abomination*. That was the word she used. Abomination. To describe our love, that had been as strong and blameless as the sun since we were just children. She said . . . things between us could never be as they had been before. We should not meet again.'

Bridget was right, Rachel knew in that moment. *Why else do rich and powerful men sponsor nameless young children?* And if Alice had been Lord Faukes's child, she would have been Jonathan's aunt. *Oh, poor girl, if she found that out.* Rachel swallowed, she shut her eyes for a second, and Abigail flickered in the far corner of her mind, ever fainter. Rachel reached for her. *Josephine could have been wrong. Perhaps Lord Faukes only adopted her. Found her, and adopted her*, she thought desperately.

'And there was more . . . I know there was! If only I could *remember* . . .'

'You do not have the letter still?'

'I can hardly remember that day. I had just got back to Brighton . . . I was injured, exhausted, half mad, half starved.

I can barely remember my journey back to Bathampton at all. It's like some strange, dark dream. And when I came to myself I didn't have the letter in my possession. I must have dropped it, or cast it away. But – *abomination*. I remember that word; I did not dream it.' He shook his head. 'It was the retreat back to Corunna, you see . . . from the moment we marched into Spain, it was near impossible to write, and when I did write there was nobody to take the letters. She had no word from me for weeks and weeks, so she went to Box to see if they had news,' said Jonathan, shaking his head slowly. 'Oh, *Alice!* Why did you do that? If only she hadn't. She must have thought that they would welcome her – she must have thought that they'd find common ground, in their love and fear for me. She wasn't to know that my mother – and my grandfather – had rules she couldn't hope to know about.'

'So your mother told her something to make her flee?' *How much has he guessed?*

'Yes. When I arrived back to find her gone, they spun me the yarn that she had run away with another, and forsaken me. Mother told me she'd left a note, to my grandfather, to explain and apologise. They said she was a disgrace, a pariah, and I was to forget her.'

'But you didn't believe them.'

'When my mother lies, I can tell. She has lied all her life, and though I can't discover the truth, still I *know* she lies.' His voice had turned hard and angry.

Rachel thought hard, searching for sense in the conflicting tangle of all that she had heard said.

'But you said to me, some time ago, that you'd found a note from Alice's . . . new companion. A note for her, to arrange an assignation.'

'Yes, I . . .' He broke off, and frowned. 'I'm *sure* I did. But it was . . . I was not myself in those days. I have forgotten much . . . there are stretches of time I can't account for. Dark spaces. They are one of the things I brought back from Spain with me. Dark spaces.' He shook his head again, and Rachel felt a chill go through her. *The first time I came to read to him, he said those words to me — dark spaces. When he could not remember throttling me.* She thought of the brain in its heavy jar, teetering above her head, and the blank, blind look in his eyes. 'But the note has gone, if I did find it. It has gone. Perhaps I destroyed it. Perhaps I . . . never saw it. A nightmare, it might have been. Brought on by the lies my mother and my grandfather told.'

'Starling suggested as much.'

'What?'

'I . . .' Rachel hesitated, unwilling to reveal the extent of her contact with Starling. 'We have spoken, Starling and I. She was curious about my face . . . my resemblance to Alice.' She held her breath but Jonathan sounded sad rather than angry.

'Yes. She loved Alice as much as I did.'

'She does not believe that Alice was keeping other company. That she ran away with anybody else.'

'I know. She thinks I killed her.' He looked at Rachel and smiled at the shock on her face. 'We have had many years in which to fling hurtful and violent things at one another, Starling and I.'

'But, she also told me . . .' Rachel paused again, unsure if it was right or wrong to speak. 'They had a housekeeper. Bridget Barnes.'

'Bridget saw Alice speaking with another man, shortly before she vanished,' said Jonathan.

'You know already?' said Rachel. Jonathan was still breathing deeply, his chest rising and falling emphatically.

'Yes. My grandfather got it from her, and told me. But still, I . . . won't condemn her. I *know* when my mother is lying. Whoever this man was, and why ever Alice went away with him, she can only have thought it was for the best. They must have deceived her in some way. Or perhaps taken her against her will.'

'But you always seemed so angry with her – you seemed to blame Alice for abandoning you!'

'And I did, for a time. Perhaps I still do, in darker hours; for I cannot think why she would go, and why she would stay away all this time. What could have been so terrible that we could not have surmounted it, together? So then, I think again – they must have forced her away somehow.'

'Why would they, when she had been prepared to break it off with you? Your family didn't want the two of you to wed. Alice went to them and revealed your intentions, and something was said to frighten her. She wrote to you to break it off. Why then would they go further?'

'I don't know! Don't you think I've asked myself these things, time and time again? The only people who know are Alice and my mother. One cannot tell me, the other refuses to.'

'So you think . . .' Rachel was finding it hard to speak. Her voice was trapped in her throat, choked by her heart. 'You think that Alice is still alive?'

'Yes, of course. I pray that she is. I would rather . . . I would rather have her alive somewhere, in love with another, sparing me not a thought . . . I would rather that than she be dead. Only Starling ever thought that would be better.'

'So would I,' said Rachel, but quietly, and Jonathan didn't seem to hear. They stood a while, each lost in thought, with the sun shining in their eyes and a buzzard circling high overhead, riding the warm air as it rose from the hill. Rachel let her arms hang down by her sides and tried not to wish that he would unfold his arms and take her hand again. She felt childish, foolish, to think it. *What would I gain from such a gesture?* Again, the echo answered her, as softly as a pent breath gently released. *Everything*.

1808

By early November it had been more than six weeks since any news of Jonathan had reached the farmhouse in Bathampton. When he'd come to tell them, that summer, that he was going to Portugal to fight the French, Starling hadn't had the first clue where Portugal was, or why the French should be there instead of in France, and they'd spent a while hunting out the atlas and poring over maps of Europe. Her betrayal of Alice after her discovery of the lovers' tree seemed forgotten, as did their plans to run away. The war with France had postponed everything, and as if she guessed as much, Bridget had met the news of Jonathan's departure to the Peninsula with a kind of sombre relief. Jonathan was pulled in half; spoke in one breath of glory and duty, and in the next of how much he would miss them all, and long to return. Whenever he mentioned it, Alice's eyes swam with tears which she refused to shed in his presence. But once he'd taken his final leave of them, they fell like rain.

Jonathan's letters came each week, sometimes in twos and threes. He wrote nearly every day, but the letters were sent in groups, as and when they could be. He filled every available inch of the paper, the writing so cramped it was harder than ever to decipher. They came smeared and splodged sometimes; they came smelling of smoke, or gunpowder, or the prickling scent of dust. One came burnt, with an uneven black ring through the middle and a reek of cinders, the words inside the circle lost for ever. Alice snatched them all up and devoured them, and once she'd read each one to herself several times, she would read them out loud to Bridget and

Starling; but always with pauses, gaps where she censored the words, and glanced up at Bridget with a look at once apologetic and defiant. And then the letters stopped, and they could only wait. After two weeks without word, Starling got bored and turned her attention to other things. But for Alice, the burden of waiting got heavier and heavier every day.

She woke Starling up one night, while the room was black and cold. She hadn't lit a candle, and her grasping hands seemed to come from nowhere, like the darkness itself come alive. Starling scrambled back, trying to break away.

'Hush, hush! It's me!' Alice whispered, tense and urgent. Her throat sounded tight.

'What's wrong? What's happened? I can't see anything!'

'I had a terrible thought, dearest.' Her voice was a homeless, breathy thing. 'What if Jonathan has been killed? If Lord Faukes has had word of him . . . perhaps he would not think to inform us. He doesn't know of our . . . bond, after all, does he? What if that's it, Starling? What if he's dead and they haven't told me?' Starling could think of nothing to say, and the invisible hands gripped her wrists ever tighter, until the nails cut in. 'I shall have to go there. I shall have to go to Box and ask.'

'Alice, no! You're not allowed!' said Starling.

'But I must know,' said Alice, and then she said nothing more.

Come morning, Starling and Bridget woke to find Alice gone. With nerves making her stomach feel watery and ill, Starling told Bridget where she had most likely gone. Bridget's lips turned bloodless and pale. It was less than five miles to walk to Box, but steep, and might take Alice an hour and a half if no traffic agreed to carry her. After three hours, Starling began to watch for her, keeping an eye out of the nearest window, whatever room she was in. Bridget was grim and silent, and worked with a single-minded intensity that betrayed how anxious she was.

'Lord Faukes loves Alice,' Starling said to her at one point. 'He will be kind to her, I think.' But Bridget merely grunted.

'You know little enough of men, or of the world, Starling no-name.' Which put Starling's nose out of joint so that she resolved not to speak to Bridget again until Alice got back. Just half an hour later, Starling was watching from the kitchen window when she saw Alice's familiar willowy figure approaching.

'She's back!' she shouted excitedly, forgetting her vow at once. Alice marched across the yard and through the door, shoulders stooped and chin dipped into her chest. She turned and slammed the door shut behind her, then stood swaying, leaning forwards until her forehead touched the wood.

'What is it? Is he dead then?' Bridget demanded.

'Bridget! Don't say that!' Starling cried.

'Better to know. Well, Alice? What news?' But Alice only stood with her face to the door, and did not answer. When Bridget and Starling turned her, they were shocked. Her face was ashen, almost grey; her lips had a bluish tinge, eyes wide and staring. She shook so badly that the tremors were more like convulsions, jarring through her body.

'*Alice!*' Starling threw her arms around her.

'Leave off, girl! If she's faint that won't help!' said Bridget. With her ear pressed to Alice's chest, Starling heard her heartbeat, racing and stuttering, just as it had the first night Starling had met her. It skipped beats, then fired in short, staccato bursts; a pause and then a flurry, with no rhythm, no pattern; it felt as though a small and desperate animal was trapped behind her ribs. Then there was a long pause between beats, longer than the others, and Starling looked up as Alice's eyes rolled back in her head, and she crumpled to the floor.

The doctor came and bled Alice into a white porcelain bowl; he told them she must rest and drink dark ale to fortify her. Alice slept deeply for twenty-four hours, her face so white and her body so still that she might have died. Starling crept into the room now and then, to reassure herself with the gentle waft of Alice's breath on her cheek. When she woke up they fed her, and made her drink beef broth. They washed her, and brushed her hair, but for two days Alice said nothing, and only stared straight ahead. There were shadows under her eyes like bruises, smudged purple; faint blue veins crawled under her skin. Starling built up the fire in the grate but it did nothing to banish the chill and the gloom from the room. At the end of the third day she crawled onto the bed to lie beside Alice.

'He's dead, isn't he?' she whispered. She could think of nothing else that might have rendered Alice so low. 'Bridget believes it. Is it true?' She couldn't imagine it; couldn't imagine Jonathan not existing any more. Real people didn't die; not real people that she had seen and touched and spoken to. She could not grasp the weight of it, but it gave her that same watery, sick feeling, churning inside her. 'Is he dead, Alice? Is that what Lord Faukes told you?' She didn't really expect an answer but she got one, though Alice's voice was a puny murmur of sound.

'No, Starling. Jonathan is not dead. Not that they had heard.'

'Oh, *Alice*!' Starling cried, joyfully, turning to embrace her. 'Then why are you so sad? Did he chastise you? Lord Faukes? Was he cruel? Even if he was, even if we have to leave Bathampton . . . well, it doesn't matter because Jonathan will come back and marry you and look after us. All will be well, Alice!' She beamed at her big sister. 'All will be well.' But Alice shook her head minutely, and two fat, swollen tears dropped onto her cheeks, one from each eye, in perfect unison.

'No. Nothing will be well. I am . . .' She blinked, searching for the words. 'I cannot marry him. I can never marry Jonathan.'

Starling waited while Rachel Weekes went in to Mrs Alleyn, to give her usual report on her visit with Jonathan. The reports had been getting shorter and shorter, though the visits grew longer and longer. Starling had a strange feeling about that. A kernel of mistrust in her gut; hard and bitter as an apple pip. *And now they walk out together, arm in arm. I wanted her to torment him with that face, but she heals him.* She was restless with frustration. All her years of hard work, all the little punishments she had meted out; all of it was being undone by something she herself had set in motion. When she heard the front door close she darted out and up the servants' stair, glaring at Rachel Weekes as they moved away together along the garden wall.

'What are you doing? Are you on his side now?' Starling snapped, the words surprising her. She hadn't been aware of thinking them.

'What?'

'Walking the high common like . . . like . . .'

'Like what?' said Rachel Weekes. She seemed distracted, and Starling noticed her split lip, the bruise on her jaw.

'What did he beat you for?' she asked, in all curiosity. It seemed that Rachel Weekes's marriage had followed the same course as her own liaison with Dick, only more rapidly. She still felt angry with the woman for marrying him, but now it was because she'd been stupid enough to saddle herself with him. Rachel's attention settled onto her more steadily.

'What's wrong, Starling?' she said levelly.

'What do you mean?' Starling was taken aback by her tone; affronted. 'You know what's wrong. I thought you wanted the same as me – to find out why he hurt Alice, and to prove it. But now I think what you want might have changed, mightn't it? What now, are you in *love* with Jonathan Alleyn?'

'No,' said Rachel, with a kind of startled outrage that spoke volumes.

'Hard luck if you are. You're married to Dick Weekes, until God parts you. And Jonathan loves *Alice*, not you.'

There was a pause, and Rachel stared hard at Starling until she could hardly bear it. The weight of the taller woman's gaze seemed to crush her.

'What have I done to you, to make you try to wound me so?' she said.

'You were supposed to be on *my* side!' Starling sounded childish to her own ears. She folded her arms in disgust, to hide the tremulous, unhappy feeling that was growing inside her. 'Tell me what you found out today.'

'I asked him about Alice's last letter to him. He said she called their love an *abomination*. She said they should never see each other again.'

'Abomination . . . I hardly know what that means.'

'It means that Bridget was right, perhaps, about Alice being Lord Faukes's child. If the love she and Jonathan had was incestuous . . .'

'No.' Starling shook her head. The idea made her sick to her stomach. 'Alice couldn't have been Faukes's child. No man so vile could sire such a sweet girl.'

'What did he do to you? Lord Faukes, I mean?'

'What do you think he did? What do all men of power do? They take without asking.' Starling heard the bitterness in her own voice; the ugliness. Rachel Weekes's face reflected her pity, and disgust. Starling spoke on, to deflect it. 'What of your lost sister – what of that? Now you say it was not her?'

'I . . . I want it to be. I want Alice to be Abi . . .'

'But she could be . . . she could be, couldn't she? If she *was* Lord Faukes's, wouldn't he have had her from birth? Wouldn't he have brought her to Bridget sooner?' *What are you saying, mindless fool? Alice was your own sister, not hers.*

Starling sighed sharply through her nose. 'Anyway, it matters not, and can never be known for sure. But do you believe now that Mr Alleyn killed her? That he had reason to?'

'I don't . . . I don't know.' Rachel frowned, and looked down at her hands. She cradled one in the other, and rubbed her thumb over its surface as if to check for a wound or a mark. 'He spoke of . . . dark spaces. Dark spaces in his memory.' The words, spoken reluctantly, sent a thrill through Starling.

'It is as I said — see how he begins to build the story that he was out of his mind, and can't remember doing it? That's what he's hiding behind, and how he'll end up forgiving himself.'

'No. I don't think he'll ever forgive himself. He's no longer sure he saw a note to Alice. The one he said he found in the lovers' tree. He says it might . . . have been a nightmare.'

'I knew it! I *knew* it.' Starling's throat was aching tight; she thought she might scream, or laugh.

'What of the man Bridget saw her talking to?'

'What of him? We will never know who he was. And anyway, it was innocent. It was nothing.'

'Why should Alice argue with a man in the street?'

'It matters not! He is almost ready to confess to you! I am certain of it. You must press him more. When will you come again?' She grasped Rachel's hand to force her concentration, her words tumbling eagerly, shaking with excitement.

'And what then?'

'When he confesses? Then I will . . .' Starling trailed off. There was such a sudden, ringing emptiness in her head that she noticed the damp, gritty smell of stone all around; she noticed the chill in the air making her nose run, and the stinging under her thumbnails from peeling oranges that morning. She had no idea how to answer Rachel Weekes's question.

'Have you tried asking him?'

'What?' Starling whispered, distracted.

'The things you want to know . . . have you tried asking him at any time, in all the twelve years since you both lost her?'

'Yes, of course I have! I asked, over and over, in the beginning. But he was only ever silent about it – about her. About everything!'

'Fresh back from the war, he would have been? Full of misery and guilt and the horror of it . . . And I wonder how kindly you asked him, Starling. And were they questions, or accusations?' Rachel Weekes made the reprimand so gentle that Starling barely noticed the sting. 'Have you asked him since, or have you only sought to keep him as mired in despair as you could?'

'He deserves no kindnesses from me. Or anyone.'

'Are you sure?' Starling thought on it a while. She knew the answer; she had always known the answer. He deserved no kindnesses – and hadn't this pale facsimile of Alice near enough confirmed his guilt, just now? And yet Starling stayed silent, and was silent for so long that the time to reply came and went. Mrs Weekes took her hand and squeezed it in parting, and as she walked away Starling was left with the ghost of her warmth on her fingers.

Since you both lost her. Rachel Weekes's words flew around in her head like snowflakes, settling on her with a freezing touch, time and again. *No.* I *lost her.* He *took her.* Starling went up to Jonathan's rooms with cheese and grapes for his lunch, without even being asked, and found herself standing in front of him. He was in his chair by the window, where she most often found him of late; his back turned to the dark, cluttered contents of his rooms so that he could watch the world instead, with light on his face and his eyes far away. A trail of footprints led the way to him, flecks of grass and damp autumn leaves that had come in on his boots from the common. When he looked up at her his face was calm, and he almost smiled to see her. Starling clenched her fists and this fledgling smile vanished. He seemed to tense himself, ready for whatever she would throw at him. *Have you tried asking him?* So many questions sprang into her mind, and each one gave her a feeling of pressure behind her eyes. She blinked furiously at it. *Why did you kill her? How did you kill her? Where did you hide her afterwards? How can you bear to draw breath? Why should I not kill you too?*

'Why . . .' she began, her voice so constricted she had to try again. She was confounded by everything she might ask. Jonathan gripped the arms of his chair as if he might leap up and flee, but his eyes were clear. *He is sober. When did I last look into his eyes, and see them sober?* 'What . . . What did you do, on the way to Corunna, that shamed you so? What did you do, that made you hate yourself so?'

Jonathan stared at her in silence. If he deduced that she had read his letter, he gave no sign of it.

'You have told me often that I will burn in hell,' he said, eventually. Starling held her breath. 'But I have seen it already. I have seen hell, and it is not hot. It is cold. As cold as dead flesh.'

'What do you mean?' Starling whispered.

'You have never asked me about the war before.'

'I . . . you did not want to talk to me.'

'I did not want to talk to anybody. Not until Mrs Weekes made me.'

'She . . .' Starling swallowed; could not tell what she felt. 'She said I should ask you the things I want to know.'

'And this is what you want to know? Then you shall hear it,' said Jonathan. Suddenly, the look on his face made Starling want to stop him, made her want to not hear it, but it was too late. He took a deep breath; began implacably.

'Before the retreat came the advance, of course; in the autumn of 1808. We advanced into Spain divided, with no maps, poor supply lines and only some ill-informed Portuguese scouts to guide us. It was folly, before it even began.' He paused, shook his head. 'But orders had come from London, and had to be obeyed. The army was to be divided into three parts to travel more covertly; those three parts were to take three different routes, and reunite at Salamanca.' The man in high command, Sir John Moore, was overheard to mutter of the recklessness of it. The sky and ground were still dry, and a dense pall of dust hung above the army, but Jonathan felt a deep foreboding. He realised that it would be a miracle if all eventually reached Salamanca before the winter, and without starving to death. Huge, black moths beat their silent wings in his mind.

He rode Suleiman to a high ridge and sat for a while with Captain Sutton at his side, watching the long columns of men and wagons and horses as they moved out. Most of the men were cheerful, pleased to be on the move. He heard snatches of song and laughter; the roll and beat of the marching drums; the high-pitched whistling of piccolo flutes – sweet sounds above a background din of squawking chickens, lowing oxen and rumbling, creaking wooden wheels. The women – wives who'd drawn lots in London to be allowed to follow their men; prostitutes, washerwomen, gin sellers and mysterious hangers-on – had been told to stay in Portugal.

They'd been warned of the hardships ahead — the columns were travelling light; there would be no wagons to carry them, they would have to follow on foot, and there wouldn't be enough food. Still many of them followed, as stubborn and single-minded as the pack mules many of them were leading. Jonathan watched them pass by behind the men, skirts already filthy to the knee, and he feared for them.

'Why do they come? Why didn't they listen?' he said to Captain Sutton, and the captain gave a shrug.

'They travelled all these many miles to be with their men. What have they in Portugal to stay for? It is an alien land, and if they stay not with the army, then there is no point at all in their being here.'

'We will never manage to keep all fed.'

'We must hope to find food as we go. Fear not, Major; I am sure we will bring them through it.'

But the captain didn't sound sure; he sounded full of the same doubt that Jonathan felt. When the weather broke and the rain started, the air itself turned grey and the ground was soon a quagmire. The mud was a hindrance to those at the very front of the lines. To those behind, when many hooves and feet had churned it already, it was a sucking, debilitating nightmare. Jonathan checked Suleiman's feet every evening, cleaned and dried them out as best he could; but he could still smell the rankness of thrush taking hold, and feel the heat and swelling of mud fever in the animal's heels. It was the same for the men — they were not dry from one day or week to the next. It was impossible to keep tents or kit, skin or boots clean; the mud got everywhere. They stopped singing; the pipers stopped piping. Their feet bloated, blistered, cracked. In startlingly quick time, the chickens were all slain and eaten. There was no food to be found in the barren landscape, and what farms and villages they passed had most often been gutted and laid waste by the retreating French. All their enemies had left them were horrors and corpses. At the end of each day's march, as Jonathan tried to care for Suleiman's feet, he whispered to his horse of the warm stables awaiting them in Salamanca; the sweet meadow hay that would be piled high in his manger; the oats he would have in his nosebag, fresh and tasty instead of mouldy from the constant damp. Suleiman shivered and heaved a sigh as he listened to this, as if he didn't believe it, and Jonathan's own stomach rumbled as he spoke.

Moore's section of the army, with Jonathan, Captain Sutton and their company within it, was the first to reach Salamanca, in late November 1808. They were weak, exhausted, underfed. They were rife with dysentery, sickness and lice, and they were told to be ready to move again at once, because a French force ten times their number was at Valladolid, a mere four or five marches away. French numbers in Spain swelled all the time; Napoleon himself had arrived to lead in the centre and south – the emperor was quite determined that Spain would remain a part of his empire. When Jonathan heard this news he felt a cold fist of fear in the pit of his stomach. He was ashamed of his reaction and tried to hide it as he passed on the alert to his company, though he saw it mirrored in some of their faces. Others showed excitement at the prospect of a fight; some were clearly furious, though Jonathan could not guess at what; some showed nothing but weary acceptance. A drawn-out, hollow expression, which made their eyes look dead.

'It will be a relief, will it not – to fight at last instead of marching?' said Captain Sutton carefully, as he and Jonathan shared a flask of wine in the captain's billet later on. Naked candle flames juddered and flapped in the draughty room, sending shadows careening up the walls. Jonathan looked Sutton in the eye and knew that the captain saw his fear. He knew, but did not despise him for it. Still Jonathan flushed with shame as he raised his cup.

'A relief, indeed,' he said, then drained the drink down. Wherever a wine cellar had been discovered in the city, it had been raided. Huge barrels had been rolled out into the streets and drained, and sat empty with a few collapsed, insensible men around each one. More than one man had drunk himself to death already. And still the cold rain fell.

'Without fear there can be no valour,' said Captain Sutton, softly. He was older than Jonathan by fifteen years, and had seen battles and wars before this one. He was a good man, and kind; he helped his inexperienced senior officer wherever he could, and Jonathan was grateful, even though this care made him feel like a child swimming out of its depth.

In the middle of December they quit Salamanca again. Sir John Moore had resisted for as long as possible, hoping for the other army contingents to reach the city; hoping for the arrival of Spanish allies to reinforce them. None came. But then word came that the French had moved south; that they thought Salamanca deserted, and had no idea of the British force in occupation there. There was a chance to strike an unanticipated blow; a chance to divert the French from harrying the beleaguered Spanish in the south, and Moore took it. He marched them north-west, towards Saldana, where a famous commander called Soult, dubbed the Duke of Damnation by the men, was in command of a large French force. After a stationary month, one of few comforts and scant food, the men were almost happy to march again, especially if there would be a battle at the end of it – the waiting wore them down; they wanted to fight. Jonathan thought of the violence and death they had seen so far, and couldn't understand their eagerness. But he kept this to himself, close-guarded; just like he kept his doubts and all his misgivings about his chosen career to himself.

'It will soon be time to give the enemy a taste of our mettle, men – and our steel!' he bellowed to his company, and they gave him a resounding cheer as they marched. The words were bitter in his mouth, and sounded hollow in his ears. Behind the saddle, Suleiman's ribs arched out, plainly visible beneath his too-thin coat. When the wind blew the horse shivered, but did not baulk. Jonathan felt the shudder pass up through his own body, as though he and his horse were one being. *Lend me your courage, brave friend.*

Jonathan wrote to Alice constantly, and managed to resist telling her of the fear he felt, and his disgust at the bloodlust of his compatriots. He managed not to describe the way they all seemed to be growing less and less human as the weeks wore on. They grew more bestial, more brutish and cruel – even in their most basic characteristics: they were hairier, ragged, and they stank. The war was shaping them to its own ends. He wrote none of that, and instead wrote of the longing to return to her which occupied his every waking moment, and haunted his dreams as well. Then their surreptitious march was cut short – they encountered a company of around seven hundred French cavalry, and engaged them in a short and brutal fight which finished when the French were all slain. Thus Soult was alerted to their march on Saldana, and their whereabouts.

Word was sent south; the main French force halted, turned, came back for them. When Jonathan was passed the dispatch with this news, he felt his guts turn watery and his legs soften with panic. He bit it down and awaited orders, but they had no other choice than to flee. Within days they might be surrounded by so many thousands of French that any battle would be a massacre. There was no choice but to retreat, back to the coast in the west. On Christmas Eve 1808, the British turned towards the mountains. The officers had to herd their reluctant men – the troops wanted to stay and fight the Duke of Damnation, or Napoleon himself – to fight *anybody*, rather than climb a mountain range in wintertime, with no supplies. They knew that the mountains would be every bit as deadly as any such battle might be.

Jonathan was sure he could feel the French behind them. He sensed them like a huge black cloud, or like a wave about to break over their heads. He had the constant unnerving feeling of being watched, crept up on. He gave short shrift to his disobedient men, although he stopped short of having them flogged. Men under other officers were not as fortunate. Some took a hundred lashes for a muttered complaint; two hundred for straying away from the columns; three hundred for cozening mutiny. They were left with their backs in tatters, unlikely to live, and loving their commanders no more than before. *Run!* Jonathan wanted to scream at them. *What is the matter with you? Run, while you can!* The words stayed trapped in his mouth, straining to get out, as the rain turned to snow and the wind grew teeth and claws. His men took the obvious conflict within him as a sign that he hated the order to retreat as much as they did. It made them love him more, and if he'd had any laughter left he would have laughed at this irony.

It was cold enough to freeze the blood in their veins. Each night the snow set with frost, turning hard and razor sharp. Men who had lost their boots in the sucking mud of the plains now walked barefoot, on feet gone black with frostbite, shapeless with swollen bruises. One man had worn his right through to the bone. He was kneeling in snow, looking down a rocky slope at the milling French not far below them, when Jonathan came up behind him. The smooth, grey knobs of his heel bones protruded through the lacerated soles of his feet. The sight gave Jonathan a dizzy feeling, as if he teetered on the lip of a precipice, and was about to fall. When the man saw him looking, he grinned at Jonathan.

'A fair sight to frighten the Frenchies, eh, sir?' he croaked, in a voice as broken as his body. 'Don't fret for me, sir; they pain me not at all.' There was a dull, feverish light in his eyes, and Jonathan moved away without talking to the man, afraid of him because he was clearly dead but still marching; dead but not yet aware of it.

To begin with, the rearguard of the British force was harried constantly. Again and again they had to turn, draw up lines, and repel the French pursuit. *Make ready! Present! Fire!* Shouted out, over and over again. Jonathan heard the four words in his sleep, and woke with his hand curled around the hilt of a sabre he wasn't holding, his arm aloft, ready to fall to the accompanying roar of musket fire. He led one short, vicious fight to hold a river crossing, after which the little stream was left crammed with corpses, both French and British. Jonathan surveyed the scene with his ears ringing from the guns; the burbling water sounded like music, like silver bells. There was smoke in his eyes and mouth; his throat was so dry he couldn't swallow, and there was nothing in his canteen. He went to the water's edge and knelt in the freezing mud, and scooped up water that was colder than ice, and red with blood. He drank it down nonetheless. It soothed his throat, and tasted of iron. On the far bank lay a young French soldier, still just a boy. He fed the red waters from a wound to his face – half of which was missing. But the boy lived for a little while longer; Jonathan met his eyes and found he couldn't look away. He sat down in the filth and stayed with this dying lad, whose blood he had drunk with the water. There was no rancour in either of them; no anger or spite; no blame. Only a shared acceptance of what had been done, and could not be undone. When Captain Sutton hauled him to his feet Jonathan blinked, and saw that the boy was dead.

In the coming weeks death was always with them. There were injuries, old and new; there was starvation; there was illness and disease; there were skirmishes, and there was the all-consuming cold. Then death, as if bored, began to find new and creative ways to take them. There was a strange reaction to some supplies of salt fish and rum that finally reached them – when consumed in quantity it blasted through the men's starving systems with devastating results. There was a swirling fog one day, so thick and white that the eye could not pick out what was ground and what was not. It hid the precipitous drop into a canyon, and more than one man stepped off the edge, all unawares. A pair of mules stumbled off as well, taking a cartload of wounded men with them. All were too weak to cry out as they fell – including the mules. Childbirth claimed one young girl, who remained seated in the snow in a crimson swathe of her own blood, cradling her baby as she waited to die. The child was born too soon; it moved weakly for only a minute or two before it died. Jonathan stopped beside the girl for a while. She sat mute and immobile, not struggling to rise; she looked very beautiful against the snowy ground, with her dark, dark hair and her silvery eyes. Jonathan stayed and waited with her, but he could think of nothing to say or do for her, and death seemed in no hurry to claim her. So he walked on, burrowing his face into his greatcoat.

The next time their path led them alongside a yawning nothingness, an empty drop in which the wind moaned and snow skirled, Jonathan saw a man step off the edge, quite deliberately. Horses collapsed underneath the men they carried and were butchered and eaten, if time on the march allowed. Dogs suffered the same fate. Otherwise, the men chewed the leather straps from their kit and uniforms for sustenance. By the middle of January 1809, as their path began to descend towards the fertile plains that would lead them to the sea, the retreat through the mountains had killed five thousand of them. Jonathan walked beside Suleiman with his arms around the horse's neck. He was too weak to walk unaided, but Suleiman was lame in both his front legs, and winced at every step, and Jonathan could not bear to mount him, however much Captain Sutton urged him to. So he half walked and was half dragged by his horse, and when he tried to check Suleiman's front feet to find out the problem, they were so hard-packed with ice he had no way of telling. The horse's coat was matted and bedraggled; it clung to his stark bones, hard with mud and frost. Jonathan tried to murmur encouragement as they went, but after a while his words became nonsense, and his lips cracked and bled when he moved them, so he only thought what he wanted to say. *Keep going, my brave friend, for I will perish here without you. I'm sorry. I'm so sorry. I'm sorry I brought you here, brave creature.*

When they reached the low plains the milder air was like a lover's kisses, soft on their faces and hands and in their lungs. There was winter grass for those horses and mules that had survived, but still nothing for the men. Starvation made them all a bit mad; it gave them a glint in their eyes like feral dogs. And Suleiman would not eat. He showed no interest at all in the brownish grass that was suddenly all around him; without the numbing ice in his feet he was in such pain that he trembled all over, all day long. It tore at Jonathan's heart to see him suffer so. There was no reproach in the horse's eyes, no blame, but there was also no fight, no spark. On a mild, damp day on which the men finally caught the tang of the sea, Suleiman's shuffling walk halted, his knees buckled and he lay down. The men trudging behind them parted around the fallen horse without a pause or a thought.

Jonathan knelt beside his horse's head. He tried to lift it onto his lap, but it was too heavy and his own arms were far too weak. For a while he was content to let the horse rest. He dribbled some water into Suleiman's mouth, but it ran back out again. Only after an hour had passed, and Captain Sutton came to find him, did Jonathan begin to see the danger.

'Major Alleyn, sir, we must move on. We'll make camp on top of the next rise, if we can reach it by sundown,' said the captain, rousing Jonathan with a hand on his shoulder. 'Come, sir, we will find you another horse from the lines.'

'What? I need no other horse. I have Suleiman,' he said, shaking his head.

'A valiant creature, indeed, Major Alleyn, but I fear he is spent. Come, let us end it for him the more swiftly, and be onwards.'

'You will do no such thing!' Jonathan struggled to his feet and staggered as a wave of woozy exhaustion swept over him. 'He will make it. He is not spent. Come, Suleiman, up! Up, my brave boy! We are nearly at camp!' He tugged on the reins, his voice growing louder and louder. He leaned with all his weight, but Suleiman did not even raise his head.

'Sir—'

'No! I will not hear of it! Up, Suleiman, up! Fetch me some brandy, Captain. That's all he needs, a little brandy for strength!'

Captain Sutton fetched a tot of brandy in a tin cup and dutifully handed it over, though his eyes said that he knew a lost cause when he saw one. Frantically, Jonathan lifted Suleiman's chin, peeled back his lips and dribbled the brandy onto his tongue. The horse's gums were greyish white, and the brandy had no effect.

'Come up, Suleiman! Up!'

'Leave off him, man, the poor beast is done for,' remarked another officer, walking past with the bandy-legged gait of a lifetime spent in the saddle. Frantically, Jonathan fetched his crop from behind the saddle and gave the horse a whack across the rump. It left a welt in his fur, but the muscles beneath the slack skin didn't even twitch. Jonathan could hardly see for the tears burning his eyes. He had never hated himself more. With a gasped breath he hit Suleiman again.

'You *must* get up!' he shouted. With slow surrender, Suleiman blinked his uppermost eye. Jonathan dropped the crop and collapsed beside him, weeping uncontrollably. He smoothed the thin coat around the horse's eyes and ears; a gentle stroking to make up for the blows he'd delivered. 'I'm so sorry, my friend. I'm so sorry,' he murmured, over and over again. He felt Captain Sutton's hands on his shoulders, coaxing him away.

'There's nothing more to be done, sir. There's nothing more you can do for him. Come away. Come away now.' Jonathan rose unsteadily and allowed himself to be led away. 'That's right, sir. Best leave him now. No more to be done, and it upsets the men to see you so distraught. Best to leave him; I'll make sure he's taken care of.' They'd gone only fifteen or twenty paces when a shot rang out, and Jonathan turned to see a man standing over his fallen friend with a smoking pistol in his hand.

'I made it down the mountain only because of him. My friend. And see now how he is rewarded for all his strength and bravery.' Jonathan loathed the tears on his face, and scrubbed at them angrily.

'There never was a better horse, Major Alleyn. But there was nothing more to be done.'

That night, Jonathan sat in his tent at his folding field desk, quill pen poised over a piece of blank paper. He'd been trying to write a letter to Alice, the first one in weeks, but there didn't seem to be anything he could write. To tell her anything was to invite her into the hell in which he found himself. To tell her anything was to tell her what he had become, and risk her loving him no longer. He was a man who watched newborn babies die in the snow; a man who drank the blood of dead comrades. He was a man who feared battle; a man without valour, who reviled the passionate violence that his country needed from him. He was a man who had left Suleiman lying on a grassy plain to die – that beautiful, powerful creature she had called *magnificent*, in the water meadow at Bathampton the summer before. He was a man who wanted to go home, and see nothing more of war, ever again.

Christmas had come and gone. Bathampton and everything in it seemed to belong to another world completely; a world in which things as sweet and pointless as Christmas could exist. The page stayed empty as the minutes crept past, and when Captain Sutton came in Jonathan was glad of the interruption. The captain carried a plate, and on it was a thick steak of roasted meat and a slice of bread; the smell of it made Jonathan's stomach twist in painful anticipation. But the captain didn't speak as he put the plate in front of Jonathan. He opened his mouth as if to, but then he said nothing, and would not meet Jonathan's eye. So Jonathan suddenly knew exactly where this meat had come from, and he stared at it with perfect horror. He was relieved when Captain Sutton left again at once, and didn't stay to watch him eat it. To watch him eat of his own horse. But eat he did, though it was with the sure knowledge that he would never be himself, would never be as he had been before, ever again.

'We reached Corunna the next day. That was how close Suleiman came to finishing the march. But part of me is glad he didn't make it – the lame horses . . . the lame and the weak were shot instead of being allowed to take up valuable space and supplies on the journey home. He would have been shot even if he had finished the journey. This is how men repay their loyal servants and companions.' Jonathan fell silent, and in the wake of his words the air felt colder, and harder to breathe.

'And you wrote to Alice from there. That day that you

reached Corunna, you wrote to her and told her of your shame.' Starling's voice was small and weak in the aftermath of his brutal speech.

'Yes. I wrote to her there. I dreamed of her. I thought of her as a man dying of thirst thinks of water. She was the only thing that drove me to survive.'

'And then she wrote to you in Brighton, and told you that you must for ever part.'

'They landed the boats at night, so that the people of England would not see our frightful condition. So that they would not be out in the streets to smell the stink of death and defeat on us,' Jonathan murmured.

'And you came at once to Bathampton. And you killed her,' Starling intoned.

'No!'

'But how do you know? You came at once, and I saw how deranged you were. You say you can't remember clearly from that time, that you have dark spaces from those days when she vanished, so how do you know? *How do you know you didn't?*' Starling's voice had risen to a shout but Jonathan didn't flinch. He stared up at her, wide-eyed.

'Because I would have cut my own heart out of my body first,' he said.

'You are *sure* of that? As sure as she loved you?' Starling trembled as she fixed her eyes on his, and did not look away. Jonathan's face was naked, somehow; without wine or opium he was wide open to her scrutiny, and though he said nothing Starling saw doubt in his eyes – unmistakable, rising like flames to consume him.

* * *

I know when my mother lies. Josephine Alleyn was sitting in the parlour when Rachel was ushered in. Jonathan's mother had no book in her hands, and no embroidery. Nothing to occupy her as she waited. A gilt clock on the mantelpiece ticked loudly, and Rachel noticed that the canary's gilded cage was empty. She decided not to ask what had become of the bird. Something about the older woman's absolute still- ness made her uneasy. Her blue eyes were clear and steady, and younger than her years, but Rachel could read nothing in them beyond an unusual intensity. No candles had been lit, and the wan light of day leached the colours from the room. The robin's-egg blue silk divan; the cerise drapes at the windows; the greens and golds of the carpet. All were rendered greyer, weaker. *My mother lies.* Rachel tried to smile as she came to stand in front of Mrs Alleyn, but the older woman did not ask her to sit.

'You walked out with my son, I believe, on your last visit.' She spoke without tone, without any particular emotion. Again, Rachel felt some warning. *It's only because of what Jonathan said, and he speaks from years of bitterness.*

'Yes, Mrs Alleyn. I thought it would be beneficial . . .'

'So it was your idea, and not Jonathan's?'

'Yes, madam.'

'I see. And do you think it was proper of you, to suggest such a thing? My son is an unmarried man . . .'

'But I am a married woman, Mrs Alleyn, and retained as companion to your son.'

'To read to him within this house, as I recall our arrange- ment.'

'Forgive me, Mrs Alleyn. I had not meant to cause offence. I only hoped to cheer your son with some fresh air, and a change of . . . vista. I understood that my role was to cheer him.'

'To cheer him, perhaps. Not to flirt with him, and expose him to public ridicule.'

'What ridicule have I exposed him to, Mrs Alleyn?' Rachel was at a loss. The accusation made her even more nervous.

'Cajoling him into leaving the house – for I cannot imagine he went willingly – when his appearance is so dishevelled, and his health so reduced. And on the arm of the wine man's wife! Not to mention in your current state of . . . injury.' She nodded to indicate the cut on Rachel's lip, still visible though the bruising had faded. 'I'm surprised at your boldness, going about so openly with your face thus disordered. And what if he had fallen, or taken a chill? Do you have any idea how disastrous that could be for my son?'

Rachel stood in stunned silence for a moment. Without raising her voice or changing her tone, Josephine Alleyn had thoroughly upbraided her, and cut her to the quick. *The wine man's wife*. Her cheeks burned in humiliation, but she felt a spark of defiance as well.

'Forgive me, Mrs Alleyn. If I . . . overstepped my role, I am truly sorry. But it seemed to me, in fact I am sure, that the walk did Mr Alleyn a power of good. We walked out of the city and onto the common, so as to suffer no unwanted scrutiny.'

'You walked the length of the crescent before you reached the common, however. Do you have any idea how the neighbours watch me? Watch *us*, my son and I? They are *always* watching, and wagging their tongues.'

'Such . . . rumours and falsehoods that are spread about your son can only have been undermined by seeing him in the flesh, and well enough to walk out, surely, Mrs Alleyn?'

'You were asked to read to him, Mrs Weekes. Nothing more.'

'Yes, Mrs Alleyn.' Josephine Alleyn watched her calmly for another long moment, then blinked slowly and turned her head away. At once, the tension in the room seemed to lessen, and Rachel breathed a little easier.

'If it is true, what you say, and my son was revitalised by this walk, then he will be encouraged to walk more often.

Properly attired, of course. But it is not for you to accompany him, Mrs Weekes,' said Josephine.

'I do not think he would like to walk by himself,' Rachel murmured. Josephine's gaze returned to her at once.

'Then I shall walk with him. Or I will invite one of his gentlemen friends to do so.'

'Yes, Mrs Alleyn.'

'I hear from your tone that you don't think he will go with them. Do you think you have special powers over him, Mrs Weekes?'

'No, Mrs Alleyn. No special powers; or powers of any kind. Only the . . . beginnings of trust, and friendship.'

'Trust? And he does not trust me, you mean to say? His own mother?'

'I am sure he does, madam,' said Rachel, hastily. *My mother lies.*

'And how does this trust show itself to you? Tell me. Does he confide in you? What does he speak to you about, if you have not been reading all these weeks, but making friends instead?'

'He speaks of his experiences in the war . . . Of their terrible nature. He speaks of growing up, and of his grandfather.' Rachel met Josephine Alleyn's cool gaze and hesitated before going on. 'He speaks of Alice Beckwith, and the loss of her.'

Josephine Alleyn reared backwards slightly, as though Rachel had struck her, but she quickly recovered herself.

'How could he not, when you look so much like the wretched girl?' she said tersely.

'Forgive me, Mrs Alleyn, but I had understood that it was my resemblance to Abi that led you to engage me here in the first place?'

'Abi? Who is this Abi?'

'Abi?' Rachel blinked, startled. 'Alice. I meant to say Alice.'

'And so it was. But I think now . . . I think now that perhaps that was a mistake.' She watched Rachel carefully for her reaction, and Rachel struggled to keep her face composed when fear sizzled through her, so quick and surprising that the hair on the back of her neck stood up.

'I think that it is partly not knowing exactly what . . . became of Alice that hinders his recovery, and keeps his mind trapped in . . . circles of questioning, and wondering,' she said.

'What do you mean, not knowing what became of her? She eloped. She disgraced herself and insulted my family. What more is there to know?' Josephine frowned in consternation.

'Miss Beckwith wrote to him before she disappeared. A letter that reached him in Brighton, just after he landed back from Spain—'

'A letter? Impossible!' For the first time, Josephine Alleyn's voice rose, and colour appeared in her cheeks. 'I beg your pardon, Mrs Weekes. It is . . . painful for me to speak of that girl. After what she did. And after we learned of her intentions towards Jonathan, she was forbidden to contact him. I had assumed that she would have enough respect for my father to comply with his wishes.'

'You knew, of course, of the profound affection that existed between your son and Miss Beckwith.'

'He was young. He . . . his head was turned by her. That was all. He could never have wed the girl, it would have made him a laughing stock.' Josephine twitched her skirts, though they were perfectly draped. 'Pray tell me, what did the girl say in this letter to Brighton?' The question was carefully spoken, her composure impenetrable once more.

'I do not know exactly, Mrs Alleyn, other than that she wrote to break off all connection with your son.'

'Well. Strange that she had the decency to do that, before acting so abominably.'

'Strange indeed,' said Rachel, attempting to emulate Josephine's tonelessness. She didn't altogether manage it. Mrs Alleyn watched her for a while, as if thinking something over. Then, to Rachel's surprise, the older woman smiled benignly.

'My dear Mrs Weekes, forgive me if this conversation has seemed . . . censorious in tone. But I take my son's well-being, and my family's good name, most seriously. It would be to the greater good if from this day you consulted with me beforehand on all matters regarding any extra . . . activities. Stick to reading, Mrs Weekes. I know what's best for my son. And perhaps it would be more . . . tactful of you not to encourage him to speak so openly about private, family matters.'

'Yes, Mrs Alleyn,' said Rachel, when it became clear that she would not be released without having agreed.

'You may go up to him now.' Mrs Alleyn waved her fingertips in an elegant gesture of dismissal. Rachel turned and left her, on legs that felt shaky after the encounter. She couldn't tell if what she felt was anger, fear, or embarrassment.

She climbed the stairs, through the column of old air that ran through the Alleyns' house like slow, dying blood. It caught in her chest, and she was gasping by the time she reached Jonathan's rooms. He was there to open the door for her, ready for her knock. He smiled, but then cocked his head quizzically at her breathlessness.

'I might come down next time, to meet with you. We needn't always stay in my rooms. Although, I do prefer to be away from . . . prying eyes,' he said, and Rachel shook her head. 'What's the matter?' he asked.

'Abi! I said Abi, instead of Alice . . . just now, to your mother . . .' Rachel spoke almost to herself, and shook her head again, in disbelief. She swallowed. There was a hard lump in her throat; her face felt hot and ugly.

'Abi? Who's Abi?' Something about hearing her sister's name on Jonathan's lips was so sweet that Rachel couldn't stand it. Her chest shook, and tears wet her face.

'Why do you weep? Come.' He took her hands and led her to the armchair by the window. 'Sit. Tell me what has happened.' Rachel sat down and pressed her eyes with her fingertips.

'Your mother . . .' she began, but couldn't decide what to say.

'My mother what?' said Jonathan, bleakly. Rachel looked down at his long-fingered hands, cradling hers, and tried to calm down. Outside, the wind tossed the trees and seethed through the cracks and corners of the city, sounding like a hungry ocean. The house creaked and shifted around them, as draughts nosed through doors and windows, down chimneys and under roof tiles.

'No . . . it's nothing. It's only . . . she questioned me just now, on the wisdom of our . . . recent walk . . .'

'And this questioning has left you in tears?' He spoke angrily, ever ready to flare up against his mother.

'No! No, it was not that . . . I made a mistake, that's all. We were talking about . . . about Alice. And I said my sister's name instead.'

'Your sister? I had no idea you had a sister – you've never mentioned her.'

'She . . . is lost. Drowned. It's thought by everyone – everyone but me – that she has been dead these twenty-six years . . .'

'Then she must have been a tiny child when she was lost.'

'Yes. Not yet three years old, and swept away by a river in spate.'

'But that is a bitter cruelty, to have lost a sister and a brother both. And her name was Abi?'

'Yes. Abigail. But don't you see?' Rachel stared into Jonathan's face, searching it, hoping that he would make the connection. *If he thinks it could be true, then it could be. It could be.* But Jonathan only looked puzzled. 'Abigail was my twin sister; identical to me. Nobody is quite sure of . . . the details of Alice's birth. She was delivered into Bridget's care as a child of around three years, *not* as a baby. Abi was carried away by the By Brook, which runs to join the Avon at Bathampton . . . And . . . and . . . our *faces*, Jonathan! We wear the same face!'

For a long moment neither one of them spoke. Rachel's tears went cold and stiff as they dried. She hardly dared to breathe, and then Jonathan stood and turned to the window, folding his arms. His shoulders were broad, sharp protuberances under the faded blue cloth of his coat; he'd tied his hair back with a thin black ribbon at the nape of his neck.

'I don't know . . .' he said at last, quietly. 'It is a strange thought, that Alice might have had a sister, and that you are she.' He turned to face her again. 'I can understand why you would want it to be so.'

'I have always felt that she was not gone . . . Throughout my life, I have always felt Abigail's presence in the back of my mind, and heard her voice, like a shadow, but one that comforts me . . .'

'Her shadow indeed, perhaps. Many people believe that our loved ones never truly leave us.'

'No, it is more than that . . . I can't explain it very well. There was a bond between us, something special and strange. And I never truly felt that bond break, though I can hardly remember having her with me; I can hardly remember those days. Yet I never truly *felt* her to be gone.' She gazed up at Jonathan imploringly, longing for him to believe it too. When she saw doubt in his eyes, her throat ached.

He sat beside her again, took up her hands and pressed her fingertips to his lips, and again his kiss made her feel both weak and strong, and quietened all her thoughts.

'You have Alice's kind heart. And you have the mirror of her face, but there are many differences between you. You are taller, and stronger in frame. You are stronger in other ways too . . . you have greater resolve. You are braver . . .' he said.

'All that could be the result of growing up, surely; of growing older?'

'And why would my grandfather take in and sponsor a foundling child, of unknown parentage? He was generous to his own, but he was no great philanthropist . . .'

'Abigail . . . Abigail was the sweeter of us two. My mother always said so. She was the sunnier, the more ready to laugh. Perhaps she charmed him, and he took pity on her . . .'

'If anybody could have charmed Grandfather, it was Alice,' Jonathan conceded. 'But it does not stand to reason, my dear Mrs Weekes. How would he have come by her?'

'By serendipity! By that same force that means I might find her now, after so many years, and after I thought myself cut off from family for the rest of my days. By *that* same force! For there must be some balance, some fairness, must there not? We can't always suffer only loss, and never also feel God's kindnesses, can we?'

'God's kindnesses?' Jonathan echoed, with a bitter smile. 'Dear girl, I don't believe in any such thing. Some balance? Some fairness? No. There is none to be had.' Rachel hung her head, but then felt his fingers lifting her chin towards him. His face was mere inches away, and in the light from the window she saw coppery flecks in his irises, hidden till then. 'Take this current unfairness, for example. For years I have punished myself for the things I have done. And how is this balanced? That you seek me out, and find me, and yet come to me already wed to the least worthy man I can think of. And you speak of God's kindnesses?'

Rachel opened her mouth to answer but it was empty of words. There was only the shine of light in his eyes and the feel of his skin against hers. All sensation, all awareness, seemed to crowd into the places where he touched her, so that nothing was missed, nothing not noticed. *He regrets that I am wed.* As simply as that, her mind cleared of all other hopes and fears, leaving a sudden, perfect clarity that, while it lasted, felt like the answer to everything. *If he kissed me now, I would be his.* Part of her yearned for him to do so, but behind that came relief when he did not. This relief clamoured to be heard; it grew into the perfect calm of the moment like threads of ice growing into water. It was fearful relief, it had doubts; it sent her the black, frightening thought that the hand now holding hers was the one that had taken her sister's life. *If that is true, I will know he is right – there are no kindnesses in this world. But I must know.*

The Pump Room was so warm that the flecks of sleet on Rachel's clothes melted at once, and soaked through. She was so distracted that she hardly noticed. The long, elegant room was crowded with people, walking and sitting and sipping at their beakers of hot water. It was the same water that filled the hot baths; steaming, raw from the earth and smelling faintly of eggs. There was a crush of wheeled chairs by the doors, as invalids were brought in for their dose. Rachel paced a circuit of the crowded room until she saw Harriet Sutton with a cup in her hand, talking to a group of middle-aged women. Rachel cut through the throng to reach her side.

'Ah, Mrs Weekes! How lovely that you could join us. Let me introduce you to our little circle of health-seekers.' Harriet took her hand, smiling as she introduced her friends. Rachel chafed with impatience as her manners kept her there, curtsying and exchanging pleasantries, until sufficient time had passed that she could draw Harriet to one side. The tiny woman took a sip of her water and grimaced. 'Do you know, I am quite convinced that drinking this must be truly beneficial, though I've never noticed any particular effects, one way or the other, for why else would we be counselled to drink something that tastes so peculiar?'

'I do not know, Mrs Sutton. I wanted to ask you, if I may, about . . . about the time Mr Alleyn left Brighton for Bathampton. When he received Alice's letter. You told me that your husband was with him, as he read it?'

'Yes, he was.' Harriet's face turned grave. 'Are you all right, Mrs Weekes? You seem . . . anxious.'

'Forgive me.' *There are dark spaces in his memory.* Of all the things Jonathan had said to her, it was these two words that troubled her the most. *Dark spaces.* 'I feel that I am . . . I'm perhaps close to finding out what became of Alice Beckwith. And I need to know . . . I *need* to know whether she is alive or dead.'

'Alive or dead?' Harriet breathed. 'But what is this? What are you suggesting?'

'I can't explain here . . . but I will soon, I promise. I—'

'You can't mean that Jonathan did her harm?'

'I know you think him incapable of it, but he has told me himself of the terrible things he saw and did in Spain and Portugal, and that his memories of the return to Brighton and then to Bathampton are . . . unreliable.' *Dark spaces, in which dark things might have happened.* Harriet was looking at her strangely, with something almost like fear, or a warning. 'Your husband was with him when he got the letter, and when he set off. I wanted to ask . . . was he violent? When he read the letter, did he fly into a rage?'

Harriet looked around uneasily, as if fearing to be overheard.

'When he read the letter, he wept,' she said. Rachel shut her eyes for a moment, as relief swept through her. 'But in a man grief and violence often go hand in hand.'

'Yes,' said Rachel, softly *And if he killed her, my sister? If he killed her I won't ever be able to forgive him.* 'He speaks of trying to make it right. Of atoning.'

'Listen to me, Mrs Weekes. Jonathan Alleyn is a good man. I live with the proof of it, every day. I'm sorry to make such a statement and not explain myself fully, but there are things that happened at war, with my husband and Mr Alleyn, that I have been sworn never to speak about. He is a good man, and there was nothing in that letter that should have made him attack the girl . . .'

'You saw the letter?' Rachel interrupted, confused.

'Yes, I—' Her friend broke off, and looked down at her hands. 'I have it still.'

'You have the last letter that Alice wrote to Jonathan? How is this?'

'He dropped it, after he read it. It was left on the floor as he rushed at once to catch the mail coach west. My husband was perplexed as to what could have caused such a reaction. He picked the letter up, meaning to return it to Mr Alleyn when he returned. But Mr Alleyn didn't re-join the regiment for a good long while, and what with everything that happened with the girl's elopement, my husband thought it better to . . .'

'To keep it from him?'

'He didn't wish to deepen a wound so fresh and painful. Jonathan Alleyn was ever one to brood and . . . lose himself in thought. My husband thought that if he had the letter to pore over, it might only serve to torment him. I said that if he didn't mean to return it, he ought to destroy it, but he said that the right time might come to return it to him.' Harriet frowned guiltily. 'There was nothing in it to make him violent . . .' she whispered. 'Only to make him grieve.'

'Will you give it to me, to take back to him?' said Rachel, gravely. *In a man grief and violence often go hand in hand . . . is that what hides in the dark spaces?* The thought made her stomach turn over, and for a second she thought she might be sick. She clamped her teeth together as Harriet nodded unhappily.

They walked back to the Suttons' apartment, and Harriet fetched the letter from a small drawer in her bureau. She hesitated as she held it out to Rachel, who felt a shiver of anticipation when she saw the small square of folded paper.

'You do understand, don't you? Why my husband never returned this note?' said Harriet. Her eyes were wide in a worried face.

'His intentions were good. But the time has come to lay the matter to rest,' said Rachel. Harriet nodded.

'Stay a while if you want. You must want to read it,' she said. Rachel looked up guiltily, and Harriet gave her a gently knowing look. 'I think that you, too, have the best of intentions. And far easier to read it here than out in the cold wind.' Rachel took the letter, sat down on the very edge of an armchair, and opened it.

When she left the Suttons' apartment minutes later, Rachel went straight to Duncan Weekes's rooms, but found them empty. The letter was in her pocket and her hand kept straying to touch the paper through the fabric, to check its safety. Her mind was clamouring as her rapid pace carried her through the city. Sleet fell from a collapsed sky, stinging in her eyes and forming small, wet drifts in the gutters. She felt as though she must hurry, must race to save Alice, though what had been done to her, or what she herself had done, was long past, and couldn't be changed. Her father-in-law's name was in the letter, and the suggestion that he knew more than he had ever said, so her path led, inevitably, to the Moor's Head. Rachel peered in through the window. The rippled glass deformed the faces of the inn's patrons, but since she saw no sign of her husband she steeled herself and went inside.

The transgression made her feel naked; eyes turned towards her, blatant and speculative. Keeping her face down, Rachel went to the bar where Sadie, whom she recognised from her wedding day, was leaning on her elbows, looking bored.

'I'm looking for Mr Duncan Weekes,' she said to the girl.

'He's over there.' Sadie hooked her thumb towards the far corner of the room. 'But I doubt you'll get much sense from him. He's proper swallowed a hare this afternoon.'

'He's what?'

'He's mauled. He's *drunk*. Been snoozing at his table these three hours gone,' said Sadie. Rachel followed her gesture to the back of the inn, where her father-in-law was resting his head on the table, a pewter beaker knocked over beside him and a puddle of spirits creeping close to his scalp. In spite of all the noise, Rachel heard the wet rattling in his chest as she sat down beside him. She shook his arm gently.

'Mr Weekes? Father? Wake up, please.' The old man mumbled something and slowly raised his head. His eyes were bloody and exhausted. When he saw her, he did not smile. If anything, his face turned even sadder. 'How are you, Mr Weekes?' Rachel asked, pointlessly.

'I cannot seem to find my feet today,' he croaked, and Rachel fought not to recoil from the stink of his breath. *That is not debauchery but the taint of decay. He must be seen by a doctor*. With a pang of anxiety she realised that he wasn't drunk at all, only weakened by illness, and unable to rise.

'I need to ask you something, sir. I have Alice Beckwith's last letter to Jonathan Alleyn. She says . . . she says you told her the truth about his family, and about Lord Faukes. She says that you told her what they feared to, and that she was an abomination. Mr Weekes? Are you listening?'

'They all have his blood,' Duncan mumbled. His expression was haunted.

'You mean that . . . Alice was Lord Faukes's child? Is that what you told her?'

'Not just his, not just his. Don't you see? I saw them. I . . . *saw* them.' Duncan wiped his mouth with a hand that trembled. He shook his head, bewildered. 'What letter have you, my dear? She wasn't to send any letters. I heard them say so. Any letter she wrote was to be intercepted, and not sent.'

'Intercepted by who?'

'Whoever she handed it to.' He shrugged, and shook his head again. 'That poor girl. That poor, poor girl. I should never have told her. It was the grog, my dear; the grog is the very devil.'

'So her other letters were delivered to Lord Faukes instead? She writes in this one . . .' Rachel drew the paper from her pocket. 'She writes that she has sent many letters, and is desperate to hear from him.'

'All went to Box. They can't have known of that one you have there, I'm sure of it.'

'Mr Weekes.' Rachel gripped both of his hands in hers; stared into his eyes. 'Please tell me what you told Alice. Tell me what you saw.'

Duncan Weekes picked up his fallen cup and peered into it, with little hope or expectation.

'I never told my boy. Perhaps that was a kindness, in all this rotten cruelty. He loved her, you see.'

'Richard? Loved who?'

'He loved Josephine Alleyn. With all the fire and fury with which a young man falls in love.' Rachel froze. She thought of the tremor that had run through Richard when he'd introduced her to Jonathan's mother, and his long, deep bow. *He loves her still.*

'But . . . she is twenty years his senior!'

'What matters that? She was beautiful, noble, refined. The most beautiful lady, and he was enslaved by her. He'd have done anything she asked of him. That's why he was so incensed when we were laid off. He had the blue devils for months after. So I never told him what went on in that house. That was a kindness, was it not?' Duncan gave her an imploring look but Rachel was too shocked to respond. She waited for what he would say next, and when all that came was silence, she swallowed.

'I . . . I must hear it, Mr Weekes,' she said.

Duncan Weekes tried to clear his throat but ended up coughing, and it made him wince.

'You must by now have heard something of Lord Faukes, from the Alleyns?' he said.

'Fine words from them, and . . . a differing account from Starling.'

'Who is Starling?'

'A servant in that house,' said Rachel. Duncan nodded.

'Aye, she'd have fewer fine words about him, I don't doubt it. Poor wench.' He spoke slowly, heavily. 'The serving girls at Faukes's house in Box all knew to keep out of his way. From his wife's lady's maid, while that lady yet lived, to the lowliest pot-washing scullion. If they were young, and comely, they knew their time would come. And the more comely they were – and the younger they were –

the more careful they had to be. But all the care in the world could not protect them at all times, for ever. If the master sent for them, or came down to their quarters, they could not deny him.' Duncan Weekes swallowed with an effort, and his face wore disgust. 'Indeed, denying him only seemed to increase his enjoyment of them. Some of them came to accept it, and stayed on. The master was generous with wages, and time off in the year; more generous than other lordly folk about. So the girls weighed it up, and some found that it was worth suffering his occasional assaults. Others had no such fortitude.'

Duncan's own sister urged him to put in a word with the house steward, and beg a place in the household for the daughter of a cousin of hers. Duncan put her off as long as he could, but his sister was a shrewish woman, with sharp eyes and a sharper tongue, and she would not be fobbed off for long. So Duncan tried to quash his misgivings, and spoke to the steward. The girl was taken on as second still-room maid, and the day she arrived Duncan's heart sank at the sight of her. She was a tiny thing, not more than thirteen, skinny and dark but with enormous green eyes that lit up her face; glassy, empty and afraid. *Oh, why were you not fat and hairy and sour of breath?* Duncan thought. He told the girl, whose name was Dolores – told her twice, three times – to keep herself out of the master's eye. But Lord Faukes came down to see what new gift had been brought for him, and smiled delightedly when he saw.

Duncan dogged the girl's steps as much as he could. He had vague ideas about protecting her, at least until she was a little older, but when the time came, of course, he could do nothing at all. Her terrified cries echoed through the lower halls of the house. Duncan could only sit and listen, and drink. So drink he did. So much, that night, that when Dolores stumbled out into the darkness, with bloodied lips and bruises on her neck, and wandered off towards her old home, he couldn't even get to his feet to follow her. He asked his sister, later, if the girl had made it back to her mother, but received only the hardest glare of her hard eye in answer. Dolores was not seen at the house in Box again.

One girl named Sue, pug-nosed and pugnacious, sussed the lie of the land immediately – she had the clever, calculating look of a girl who knew too much of the world. After Lord Faukes's first two tumbles with her she called herself his mistress, and sought to elevate herself to the upper serving positions. She went with him willingly, flipping her skirts and flirting like a doxy; calling him *Lord Gundiguts* to the other servants. The cook called her a buttock, but Sue was unrepentant. It availed her not at all, however, since Lord Faukes liked to take, not be given. She was dismissed when her belly began to swell, and Duncan saw her one last time, scowling on the back step with a screaming babe on her hip, as the steward handed over a few coins for the child. There were other bastards as well – born to tavern wenches, servants and farmers' daughters. People of no import. They were sent away with money, if they were lucky, and still comely; sent away with curses and warnings if they were not. Only one misbegotten child was lavished with all of Lord Faukes's love and care. Only one.

When the master's son-in-law died and his daughter Josephine returned to live in Box with her young son, Jonathan, Duncan Weekes and the whole household were pleased. Lord Faukes's appetite had worsened since Lady Faukes had died, and they hoped his daughter's presence would help to calm and moderate him. Duncan was standing next to his own son, Richard, when Josephine Alleyn arrived in a smart chariot drawn by a team of four grey horses. He heard his son's intake of breath as Josephine descended. Richard was still only a child, but Josephine Alleyn was as lovely to look at as any queen of hearts. She wore a long pelisse of umber-coloured velvet over a dark green dress, with a matching hat over her mahogany hair. Her eyes were a deeper, richer blue than any he'd seen. *No good will come of loving her*, Duncan silently warned his boy. So the household was cheered by Josephine Alleyn's arrival, though the lady herself was cool and reserved and, Duncan thought, sad to her very bones. But she was a widow, he reminded himself; that would surely account for it. And for a while Lord Faukes's visits below stairs, and his escapades in the cupboards and dark corners of the house, did lessen. Before long, Duncan found out why.

One fine May day, Lord Faukes and his daughter were to visit friends in Bowden Hill. Duncan waited on the box of the coach while Richard held the door. He was too young to be a footman, but Josephine Alleyn liked his face, and seemed to find some gentle amusement in the proud way he thrust out his chest to make up for his lack of height. Their route led them through the village of Lacock, and then across a series of narrow bridges that traversed a flat, boggy area of streams and reed beds. One of the bridges was blocked by milling sheep, and Duncan was forced to halt the coach.

'Clear the bridge!' he shouted to the elderly shepherd, who gave a nod and waved his crook unhurriedly at his animals. The horses snorted and fidgeted as the flock milled around their legs. The stink of their dung and their oily wool was ripe. 'Hop down, lad, and stand nearside of Santi's head. Keep her steady and the others will follow,' Duncan instructed his son. 'I'll stand by the coach to keep them clear.'

'Go wide, you wretched muttons,' Duncan muttered, as he climbed down and felt his boot slide in something soft and fresh on the road. He took up a position by the door of the coach and waved his arms to drive the sheep further from it. The curtains had been closed behind the windows, so he didn't knock to explain the delay in case Lord Faukes or his daughter were dozing. But as the last stragglers trotted past, and Duncan Weekes turned, movement caught his eye. The coach rocked slightly, as though something went on within, and the curtains crept open, just a crack. Without even meaning to, Duncan saw inside. It was only for a second, but that was long enough – the scene struck him with all the awful clarity of the night sky lit suddenly by lightning. Josephine Alleyn sat with her head tipped back, her lustrous eyes fixed on the ceiling. Her father's mouth was on her neck, questing hungrily, one hand squeezed her breast, his other reached under her skirts, between her thighs, out of sight. There was a straining of fabric in Lord Faukes's crotch, and an expression of perfect emptiness on Josephine's face; as though wherever her thoughts were, they were far, far away. It was a look of acceptance, disconnection; a look of numb oblivion. It was not a look of surprise.

The moment that Duncan stood there, immobilised by shock, felt like hours. He turned away as soon as he could; forced his stiff, unresponsive legs to climb, and flicked the horses on so sharply that they plunged in the harness, and the shepherd was forced to hop smartly out of the way.

'What's got into you?' said Richard, grabbing the box rail for safety. Duncan blinked at his son. He hadn't even checked that the boy was back aboard before he'd driven on. He glanced over his shoulder at the coach and knew that speed would carry him no further from what he'd seen, or from what he served. So he brought the horses back to a steadier pace, and reached under his seat for the bottle of brandy he kept there for cold, night-time journeys. He drank half of it down in one go, and lowered it with a cough to see disgust on his boy's face. 'You suck on that like at your mother's dug,' Richard chided, copying the language he heard in the stables. 'It'll get you kicked out one day, old man. You'd best hope I'm full trained as coachman the day that happens, or where will we be?' By the time they reached Bowden Hill Duncan had emptied the brandy bottle, but it had done nothing to expunge that lightning-bolt scene from his mind.

So Duncan had his suspicions already, when he learned about Alice Beckwith. A servant will learn the secrets of a household, however close-guarded they be – this he knew already, and could not forget no matter how drunk he got. He heard Lord Faukes talking to his grandson, when they came to the stables for their horses. He heard Faukes tell the boy that Miss Beckwith, who they would ride out to visit, was the love-begotten daughter of a good friend of his, and that he had agreed to care for the girl, but since she was a bastard born, Mrs Alleyn would not approve, and would stop their visits, and so Jonathan must not tell her. Duncan Weekes heard the little lad, who adored his grandpa, swear, in his piping voice, to keep the secret.

Other things overheard taught him that Alice Beckwith was kept at Bathampton, with a servant and a governess. He learnt that Faukes doted on the girl, and planned to marry her off as well as he could, eventually, when the time was right. When, twice a month or so, Lord Faukes came for his saddle horse and rode out alone, or with his grandson, for the afternoon, Duncan could guess where they were going. He knew of Alice Beckwith, and he had his suspicions; for no other man in the county was as likely to have sired a bastard as Lord Faukes. He had many other such children, and none of them were treated with anything like the same care and attention; why would he lavish it on the by-blow of a friend? A friend who was never named, or visited? Alice Beckwith was *special*, that much was plain. Duncan could not un-see what he had seen in the carriage; he could not un-hear Faukes forbidding his grandson to tell his mother about the girl. He could not undo the conclusions that he came to. He could only drink; and drink he did, knowing full well that he and at least one other in that house were going to hell.

So, when the young girl with the unusual face and the pale hair walked up to the main door of the house on a windy day in the autumn of 1808, and then came running back out again not ten minutes later, Duncan guessed who she was. It was past noon, and he had drunk enough brandy by then to knock most men out, but Lord Faukes was away from home, and if Josephine went anywhere she asked for Richard to take her, so he knew he wouldn't be called upon to drive that afternoon. He was making his weaving way from the stables towards the inn in the village when Alice Beckwith stumbled out of the door and down the steps, then hastened towards the gate and right into his arms. Her face was wet, and she shook like a little bird in shock.

'Steady there, my pretty maid,' Duncan slurred at her. 'And who might you be?'

'I'm A-Alice Beckwith.' After she spoke she fell into fresh sobs.

'There, there, child. Nothing is as bad as all that. Alice Beckwith – yes, I know you. The one kept at Bathampton – the special one. Why those gravy-eyes, when you have such noble parents? When you have such a cozened existence? You have turned your face quite red, child,' he said, taking her hand and trying to soothe her. He blinked owlishly, struggling to focus his sluggish mind, his blurred vision.

'Cozened? Noble? How can you . . . What do you know of me, sir? What do you know of my parents?'

'You came in search of your lord father, I don't doubt. And now you weep to find him not at home? Weep not, sweet girl. He will be home again 'ere long . . .' He paused after he said this, and frowned, befuddled. For a moment he couldn't imagine why any young woman would want to see Lord Faukes.

'My lord father?' she echoed, staring at him in shock. 'Is it *known*, then? Has the secret been kept only from me, and not from the rest of the world? What cruel joke is this?' she gasped, breathing so fast it hurried her words.

'Cruel — ah, yes! Cruel indeed. A cruel man, he is,' Duncan mumbled, still not quite finding the thread. Before him, the girl shook and wept. She raised trembling hands to her face, and seemed to think hard.

'You spoke of . . . my parents, sir,' she said at length. 'Do you know . . . something of my mother, then?'

'Your mother? Hmm? A fine lady, yes, and a great beauty, is she not? My son is deep in love with her, though he is less in age than you, I would say. But there are few that would not find her lovely.'

'You know who she is, my mother? How do you know, sir?' Alice grasped at his hands imploringly. 'Was her name Beckwith?'

'Beckwith? Beckwith — no, indeed. I do not know the source of that name — your wet nurse, perhaps.' Duncan shook his head and smiled at the girl because she seemed sweet, and in distress. He patted her hand. 'There, there. Dry those tears, young miss,' he said, having forgotten why she might be crying.

'I have so many more to shed, sir,' Alice whispered. 'I can scarce bear to think how many.'

'Oh come, now — why so? You are young and fair, and your parents are wealthy. And though you be a secret and a shame, see how bonny you are! You are not to blame, miss, no indeed.'

'I am a shame, sir? You know this? Am I a shame to my lady mother — is that why she knows me not?'

'Forsooth, how can you not be? For no woman in history

lay willingly with her own sire, and I declare that Mrs Alleyn is no different – for I *saw* them, miss – how I wish I had not! I saw him about his blasphemy, and I saw how verily disgusted she was.' Duncan shook his head, but it made the ground lurch and his stomach heave, so he stopped.

The girl had gone very quiet, very still.

'I . . . I don't understand,' she said, but from the way she gasped out the words, robbed of breath, it seemed that she'd begun to. Duncan had the vague and disquieting sense that he'd said too much.

'Hush and do not tell!' he said anxiously. 'Good girl, good girl. It is a very great secret. Even from the other servants, from which a house usually has none. Only I have found it out.' He tried to tap the side of his nose but missed; tried to smile but could not. 'But take heart, child. You've not yet grown into all of her beauty, but you may yet, and who could have guessed so fair a maiden could come from so foul a union? You have her blue eyes, and though her hair is dark and shines so well, still I have heard that a good many men prefer a fair head, such as yours. So weep not, dear girl, weep not.' He waved his arm magnanimously and threw himself off balance, staggering. Alice Beckwith was staring straight ahead, abject, her face a sketch of perfect horror. Duncan could not fathom her distress but he somehow felt he'd been the cause of it. 'May I help you at all, young lady?' he said tentatively.

'No, sir. You have helped me enough,' she said, in hushed and deadened tones.

Duncan Weekes was watching Rachel, bleary-eyed and hunched in on himself. Rachel's stomach was turning with nerves and disgust.

'You mean to say, you believe that Alice was Josephine Alleyn's child . . . sired by Lord Faukes, her own father?'

She swallowed, and tasted something bitter in the back of her throat.

'She was *special* to him. She was dear to him.'

'That is no proof,' Rachel said, her voice choked. *I am an abomination.* 'Josephine Alleyn speaks very highly of her father. She reveres his memory, and their good name.' *My mother has lied all her life.*

'I drove her to the church when he died, Mrs Weekes,' Duncan said gravely. 'She shed not a tear for him, and as I drove her home when he was safe in his grave she wore a smile behind her veil. She wore a smile, and was less sorrowful than I ever saw her previous.' *He took without asking. And this is Jonathan's family.*

'Oh, God. But . . . I cannot believe it – not of Mrs Alleyn! And you told Alice this?'

'You need believe nothing of Mrs Alleyn. She was innocent and helpless. You need only believe it of Faukes, and there'll be women a plenty that will vouch for his character; for what he wanted he took. And, God forgive me, I did – I told Miss Beckwith.' Duncan's chin sank to his chest, his mouth wrenched down at the corners by misery. *He's good now he's dead.* Rachel remembered Starling's words. *Alice would never have left me to Lord Faukes.* Duncan coughed painfully; wiped his mouth with a filthy handkerchief. 'I heard she ran off, not long afterwards. I heard she ran off to who knows what fate, and from the look on her face when I spoke to her . . . I ask you, who could blame her? That poor girl.'

For a long while, the pair of them sat in silence. Rachel could hardly believe all she'd been told, but a dark thought was growing in her mind, unbidden and irresistible. *Grief and violence often go hand in hand in a man. And if she told him this about his family – and hers – how strong must his grief have been?* It was hot and stuffy in the inn but Rachel shivered.

She would have been his aunt and his sister both, if it's true. But what proof is there, other than this old man's guess? There could be no proof, she realised then, other than to hear it from Josephine Alleyn herself. *No proof because it is all a mistake and supposition, and it is not so? No proof because Alice was a foundling? And I know, yes I know, who lost her.*

'Where was Alice before Faukes brought her to Bathampton? And how could Josephine have borne a child before she was wed, and it be kept a secret?' she said. Duncan raised his shoulders wearily.

'Who can say where the babe was? Somewhere else, with a wet nurse paid to keep her lip buttoned. The year before . . . the year before Josephine was wed, Faukes took her to Scotland for half a year. The retreat was to help them both recover from the continued grief of losing Lady Faukes, it was said. But there could have been another reason, too. The timing of it, from the age I took the Beckwith girl to be, would have been fitting. When they returned to Box she quickly wed and made her escape.'

'She told me . . .' Rachel swallowed. 'Mrs Alleyn said to me that those two years she was wed, and away from Box, were the happiest two years of her life entire.'

'Well might they have been, poor accursed lady.'

'But why would she return to her father, then, when she was widowed?'

'What he wanted, he took,' Duncan said softly. 'She was always in his power. Always.'

Just then, a voice behind her shocked Rachel even more than the story she was learning. It was loud, and incredulous.

'What the bloody hell is *this*?'

'Mr Weekes, I—' Rachel gasped. She struggled to her feet; the chair legs and her skirt and the table seemed to catch at her.

'You what?' Richard's eyes were flinty with anger.

'Now, my boy, you must not chastise . . .' Duncan Weekes began. He tried to rise but couldn't. Richard caught Rachel's arm in an iron grip and towed her towards the door.

'Let go!' said Rachel.

'Richard, you mustn't be sharp with her!' Duncan called after them, weakly. Richard swung back to point a trembling finger at his father.

'I'll deal with you later,' he said, and Duncan fell into fearful silence.

They burst from the inn onto the cold, grey street. There was no more sleet, but the fog that had barely lifted all day was like a wet, frigid blanket.

'What have you been doing?' Richard took both of Rachel's upper arms and hauled her close to him. 'I *forbade* you to know that man, and yet here I find you, fast friends!'

'He is my father now, too, Mr Weekes. And he is poor, and sick, and I am fond of him! We need to send a doctor to him, and soon. He is not a bad man,' said Rachel, indignation making her brave. She could feel Richard's grip bruising her arms, crushing the flesh down to the bone.

'What do you mean by that?' He gave her a shake, his lips curled back, snarling like a dog.

'He drinks, but then so do all men in Bath, it seems. But he does not go whoring, or lie, or beat his women!'

'*What?*' For a second, Richard seemed dumbstruck, and Rachel felt fear building, coming to smother her defiance.

'I know about Starling; about you and her. And I'm sure there have been others,' she said. Richard's eyes grew huge.

'By God, I'll kill that little slut!'

'It was your violence to her that led me to the truth about you!' Richard released her and ran his hands through his hair. Then he stood half turned from her, with one hand over his mouth, watching her askance. 'I know all about you. I know you loved another as well – Josephine Alleyn! No wonder she has been so helpful to you. Were you lovers, too? Tell me!' Richard raised his hand to slap her, and Rachel shut her eyes. The fog swirled around them. 'Do it then, sir. Why keep these things behind closed doors? Why not thrash me in the street, where all can see you do it?'

For a moment Richard stayed in that pose, arm pulled back to unleash a blow, his whole body harder than stone. Then he let the arm drop and turned to face her again, still angry but somehow defeated.

'Rachel. You were supposed to love me,' he said. 'You were supposed to make things better.'

'You give me nothing to love,' she said.

'Truly, no woman has ever loved me,' he said flatly. 'What strange fate is that – to be given this handsome face, and then let no woman love me?'

'I believe Starling did, at one time.'

'Starling?' Richard shook his head. 'She loves only Alice bloody Beckwith. And Jonathan Alleyn.'

'Jonathan? She *hates* Jonathan.'

'Hate, love. Aren't they oft-times the same thing?' He stared at her, and she could no longer read what was in his eyes. 'Perhaps in time I shall come to hate you, too.'

'What do you mean?' said Rachel, shaking so badly that she couldn't keep her voice steady.

'We've a long time together, Mrs Weekes. Our whole lives. If there's no love now then there's plenty of room for that other to grow.' His gaze was cold and unyielding, and Rachel felt his words weigh heavy on her; a burden of truth she had no choice but to carry. 'Go home and wait for me,' he said. The freezing mist chilled Rachel through her clothes. She shook her head. 'You *will* do as I tell you.'

'Where will you go?' she said.

'That's none of your concern.'

'You'll go inside and upbraid your poor father. Won't you?'

'That old cuff?' Richard shook his head. 'I have more important things to do. My father will die soon enough, by the looks of him. I shan't waste any effort on him.' Richard took a step closer to Rachel and smiled cruelly. 'I shall save that for you, dear wife.' He turned and walked away. The words were like a blow to the stomach, and Rachel felt her strength ebbing away. *He can, and he will. I am his.* She swayed, and felt despair stealing over her like a shadow.

* * *

Starling dreamt of horses with bullet wounds, their eyes bulging in agony as blood streamed from the black wounds in their skins. She woke clammy with sweat, weak and shaking. Jonathan's description of the war in Spain wouldn't leave her mind, though she told herself resolutely that it changed nothing. She couldn't help but think that to have lived through such horrors would make anybody numb to violence, and more prone to it, and that should – and did – make her more convinced than ever that Jonathan had killed Alice. But at the same time, inexplicably, she found some of her hatred of him leaching away. *It does not excuse what he did. It can't be forgiven.* She seemed to have the ghost of his stink in her nostrils. The metal and rot smell he'd had when he turned up in Bathampton in the ruins of his uniform, fresh from Corunna. She knew now that it was the smell of a person who has walked long miles with death riding on their shoulder like some malevolent imp, all needle teeth and poisoned claws. She blew her nose a dozen times, and sniffed deeply at pungent ingredients in the kitchen – cinnamon, cloves, pickled beets and peppermint oil.

'What are you, kitchen maid or truffle hog?' said Sol Bradbury, perplexed, but Starling only shrugged. *If he did it, and I finally know it for true, then what should I do?* She was swirling coffee beans in a skillet over the fire, waiting for them to roast, when she realised. *It makes no difference at all.* She froze, and stayed that way until the acrid smoke of the burning beans brought Sol over, cursing and flapping a cloth at the pan. *It makes no difference at all.*

Towards the middle of the afternoon she took to the streets, wrapping up against the fog with the vague but pervading urge to go home. She went down to the wharf but there was no sign of Dan Smithers, and no other boat moored up that planned to leave eastwards inside the next hour, so Starling set off along the towpath on foot. It was the longer route out of town but she didn't want to wait. She was at a dead end, after years of struggling through a maze of doubt and enquiry and conviction. Suddenly, she had no more energy; her anger had burnt itself out like the stub of a candle. *What's the point? It is as Mrs Weekes said – none of it will bring her back to me. None of it will change things for me.* When she reached the edge of Bathampton, with numb cheeks and clumsy feet, she paused. Her route had automatically been taking her to Bridget's cottage but now she stopped, and turned north, towards the house that was the first home she remembered.

Starling walked up to the yard gate and stood there, staring at the exact spot on the muddy ground where she'd first set eyes on Alice. *My saviour. My sister.* The trees had grown taller, naked but for a few ragged leaves remaining. Rooks had come to roost rather than starlings; they cawed and clattered down at her, their voices echoing peculiarly. Hunched in the fog, the house looked like the ghost of the place she knew. There was a yellow light glowing in the kitchen window, just as there had been then; and smoke rising silently from the chimney, a darker grey than the murk. Chickens still pecked and scratched the ground; there was the stink of pigs from the sty; a haystack in the open barn; a brown horse's head, drowsy-eyed, leaning over the stable door. Starling studied it all and made believe that she could walk right up and push open the front door, and that Bridget would be standing at the stove, ruddy-faced from the heat, and Alice would be by the fire with her feet tucked up underneath her, reading poems or a novel or one of Jonathan's letters. The thought put a lump in her throat that ached like a twisted joint, and she teetered, on the verge of stepping forwards as if it all was true. *I am no different now, after all of it, than I was that first time. I still have nothing. I still am nothing.*

She walked on past the George Inn, and then turned towards the toll bridge. She passed a few farmers and villagers along the way, none of whom she recognised, or who showed any interest in her. The mist and cold made people hunker into themselves; keeping their eyes low, their voices mute. Starling stopped on the bridge and leaned over, staring down at the smooth, grey water. She couldn't smell its dank perfume – the sodden air and the tang of wood smoke on it were pervasive. The stone of the parapet leached the last warmth from her flesh, but she let it. She could see the lovers' tree; a skeletal, drooping mass at the river's edge, almost obscured by the gloom, looking like a hunch-shouldered figure. There was frost on the broken meadow grasses; frost on the scarlet rosehips and hawthorn berries in the tangled hedges along the lane. In the slow eddies near the riverbank, a thin crust of ice rode the lapping water. Starling stared at the lovers' tree until her eyes ached and watered from it. And then she saw movement in the shadows underneath it.

Not daring to blink she waited to see it again, thinking she must have dreamed it. But there was movement again a moment later, and she was not mistaken. There was a figure standing beneath the branches. Starling gulped in a huge breath, and felt a desperate kind of hope. *If she did run away, if she lives . . . she would come back here. She would.* Without hesitation, Starling pushed a path through the hedge, scratching her arms and legs on blackthorn, and clambered down to the meadow. She hurried through the long grass with her skirts bunched up in her fists, breathing hard and sniffing at the drip on the end of her nose.

'Alice!' she called, as she drew near. The fog swallowed her voice. Behind the cascade of willow whips she could see the dark shape of a person. It made no response to her call; it made no move at all. Starling jumped down onto the hard mud at the water's edge, slipped and fought to keep her balance. 'Alice, is it you?' She hurried forwards again, but was suddenly uneasy. The prickle of a warning, at the back of her skull; just like she'd had many times before.

The shadowed shape was too big to be Alice. Too big to be a woman at all. Starling slowed to a halt just beyond the tree's embrace. 'Who's there?' she said, trying to keep her voice even, strong. *It will be hard to run on this ice. But I am smaller, lighter.* But whoever was waiting still ignored her. Starling took a deep breath; blood was pounding in her ears. She parted the branches with her hands and stepped into the deeper shadow. And finally the figure stood up from its seat on the protruding root; stood up and turned to face her, and Starling cried out in alarm. '*You!*' she said, as the air rushed from her lungs in astonishment.

* * *

Rachel paused by the front door of number one, Lansdown Crescent, her hand halfway to the bell pull. Dorcas would answer it, or the manservant Falmouth, and they would take her to Mrs Alleyn. *That's not who I wish to see.* She retraced her steps and went down the servants' stair instead, letting herself into the corridor outside the kitchen. She slipped past the kitchen door, checking in the still room and pantry before she reached Starling's room; all were empty. In the kitchen, Sol Bradbury was nodding in a wooden chair near the inglenook; a huge, half-peeled apple was going brown in her lap, cradled like a pet. There was no sign of Starling, and Rachel cursed silently, anxiously. *For months she's shadowed me around this house, now when I need her, when I have this letter to show her, she vanishes.*

'Mrs Weekes. How odd to find you here. Did you lose your way?' Rachel spun around to find Mrs Alleyn at the foot of the stairs, her hands linked calmly in front of her, her face a stony mask. At the sound of her voice, Sol Bradbury was wide awake and peeling industriously, blinking away her somnolence.

'I . . . I—' Rachel stammered.

'I saw you coming along the street and wondered where you'd got to. I wasn't aware that you had an appointment with my son today.'

'Indeed, I do not, madam. I only . . .'

'You only what?' said Josephine, in that level way of hers. Rachel's mind went blank, the silence rang. 'Perhaps you wanted to see me about something? I can't imagine there's anything you might need to discuss with my servants.'

'Yes, Mrs Alleyn. That is so,' said Rachel, still frantically trying to think what to say.

'Come, then. This is no fit place for a conversation, and I too have something I desire to tell you.' The older woman turned with an elegant sweep of her dress, and went back up the stairs. With dread stealing over her, Rachel followed.

Mrs Alleyn led her into the front parlour, and settled herself on the couch. 'Now, tell me what brought you here today?'

'I wanted to . . .' Rachel paused, and looked at Josephine's lovely face. *Whatever happened to Alice, you know all about it, don't you?* She summoned all her courage. 'I've been speaking a great deal of late to my father-in-law, about his time in your service.'

'Mr Duncan Weekes?' Josephine blinked, seeming to readjust herself minutely. 'He was a good coachman. He had a marvellous way with the horses. Such a shame his . . . affliction meant we had to let him go. My father was rather fond of him, in truth.'

'Yes. I have heard a great deal of your father's affection for his staff,' said Rachel. Josephine Alleyn's lips thinned into the smallest of smiles; her eyes glittered. 'He has also told me about the time Alice Beckwith came to visit Lord Faukes at Box.'

'Mrs Weekes, I can't for the life of me discern what possible interest you might have in Alice Beckwith, a common girl who made an outcast of herself twelve years ago.'

'*Did she?* Did she make an outcast of herself, or was she cast out?' *She will not have me back here again*, Rachel knew in that moment.

'I'm sure I don't understand what you mean.' Josephine Alleyn's voice was like ice. 'Now let us come to what I wished to say to you, Mrs Weekes. It's clear to me that your . . . employment with my son is leaving you tired and over-wrought. It's only to be expected, after so many weeks of close contact with an invalid—'

'Your son is no invalid, madam!'

'Please don't interrupt me. When I said that manners had abandoned us here, I did not expect to be taken quite so literally. The task is clearly too much for you, and I will not hear of you continuing, and risking your own health by doing so.'

'And that is your final word on it?' said Rachel, after a stricken pause.

'I never change my mind, Mrs Weekes.'

'May I . . .' Rachel took a breath. 'May I go and explain my coming absence to your son?'

'I have already informed him. Now.' Mrs Alleyn stood, her back immaculately straight.

'But . . . I'm *helping* him! He's been getting so much better.'

'You have my thanks, I'm sure. But to continue is quite out of the question. I was mistaken about your . . . suitability for the role. Do not let me detain you further.'

'It pleases you to keep him shut away, does it not? Far less trouble to you, less scandal. Far less chance of him learning the truth about Alice, and about your noble father!' said Rachel. Josephine's face went rigid with anger.

'Go no further, Mrs Weekes, into matters that are none of your concern. It would be a shame if your misconduct meant I could no longer support your husband in his business. You saw yourself in; now kindly see yourself out.' Rachel had no choice but to obey her. Falmouth opened the front door for her, a golem without the least flicker of an expression on his face. But Rachel hesitated on the threshold. *I will be allowed to see him no more.*

'I demand to be permitted to take my leave of Mr Alleyn,' she said, turning with her heart in her mouth. Josephine stood on the parlour threshold, her arms loose at her sides.

'I thought I had made it quite clear—'

'He would wish to see me. If you refuse me I will make it known to him that . . . that you have turned me away.'

'Oh? And how exactly—'

'I will make it known to him.' Rachel spoke with such quiet resolve that Josephine made no reply. For a moment they simply stared at one another, a silent war which Rachel won. Without another word, she started up the stairs.

She felt hunted; she felt Josephine's hard, angry eyes follow her every step. By the time she reached Jonathan's rooms she was almost running. She knocked and let herself in, closing the door fast behind her. The floorboards creaked under her feet like the deck of a ship. *And the storm beneath us is just now breaking.* Jonathan got up from his desk. There was ink on his fingers; his hair was clean and had been cut to skim his collar at the back. His face was clean-shaven. He looked so different that Rachel hesitated.

'Mrs Weekes, I didn't expect you today, though I am delighted you've come. See how I have tidied . . .' He trailed off, so she knew she must look desperate.

'Your mother has told me I must not come again. That I will no longer be admitted,' she said breathlessly. 'She said she'd already told you of this decision, but I wanted to . . . I wanted to be sure.'

'She lies. She said nothing to me,' said Jonathan.

'I had feared as much.'

'What has happened between you? You look as though she has hounded you up the stairs!'

'I feel as though she has!' Rachel almost smiled, but it would not come. She felt too desperate, too afraid. 'I came to speak to . . . to speak to you, but she found me first and I . . . said some things to her about . . . about Alice. And about your grandfather. I let it be known that I had begun to suspect . . . That I had developed a greater interest in Alice's disappearance than perhaps I should have.' She stopped, shook her head and tried to put her thoughts in order. *Will I accuse him outright, then?* 'But I fear that if we are to see each other henceforth, it will have to be in some other place.'

'What things about my grandfather?' Jonathan frowned.

'No – you must not let her prevent your coming, Mrs Weekes!'

'She is the mistress here, and if she tells the servants not to let me in . . . It would be impossible, to attend under such circumstances.'

'I own this house, and the servants – not my mother. I will *make* them let you in.' Jonathan's eyes were intent, his voice rose indignantly. Rachel shook her head.

'No. No, I could not. Not knowing that it angered her, that she had forbidden it. My husband . . . my husband would not permit it. She has some hold over him still – some powerful hold. He was in love with her, you see. Perhaps he still is.'

'Who? Richard Weekes in love with my mother? Who says so?'

'His father, Duncan Weekes. He's known it of old. Since Richard was a young boy, he says . . .' Rachel shook her head, still confounded by it. *Josephine Alleyn, and Starling, and others no doubt . . . all called him theirs before I did; some might call him theirs still. It is as well that I love him not.*

Jonathan thought for a while, and then gestured to the chairs by the window.

'Come. Sit,' he said, more gently. 'Let us discuss this, please.'

'It's hopeless, sir. I can come here no longer – you must see, it would be impossible? If my husband forbids me – and he will, should your mother decree it – then we could not hope to keep our appointments secret.'

'You must agree to still visit, however. You *must.*'

'How can I?' Rachel stared hopelessly at him. 'I am not the mistress of my own destiny – it is bound to his. To him. He has already found out that I see his father against his wishes . . . I have not yet discovered what the full consequences of that will be. And he would find out in an instant if I went against him with regard to you, and your mother. He might beat me, sir. He might indeed do something worse.'

'Mrs Weekes . . .' Jonathan paused uncomfortably. 'You must not let him. You must not abandon me so easily. I beg you. I . . . I cannot do without your friendship. That is, I would not want to.'

'You would not?' she breathed. They sat apart, not touching, but Jonathan did not look away from her, even for a second.

'Your visits are the only thing that makes life bearable, Mrs Weekes. In all the long years since the war, no one else has managed to . . . return a fragment of my former self to me. I have been so afraid, all these years, of the . . . lost, dark places in my mind. In my memory. Only you give me the strength to look into them. Please. Do not abandon me now, at the behest of two people who cannot understand. Not when you have shown me that forgiveness is possible.' After this he fell silent, and his face darkened, and Rachel thought of the letter in her pocket. It seemed to weigh more than a piece of paper should; her hands began to shake. *Why do I not hand it over to him? Do I fear him, still? Do I fear the effect it might have?* For a moment she wished she didn't have it; she wished she knew nothing, that her face was hers and hers alone, and no question of a vanished or murdered girl could come between them. To be with Jonathan, there in that room, and to hear him say such things, would be enough to make life happy. *Why couldn't it have been so?*

Rachel turned her face away. Outside, a man came with a taper on a long pole to light the streetlamp on the corner; the fog devoured its weak glow just a few feet from the flame. *I was going to show the letter to Starling, not to Jonathan.* Rachel wasn't sure whether the letter would bring Starling any joy. Combined with what Duncan Weekes had told her, she knew that Starling would be newly convinced of Jonathan's motive for killing Alice. *She could have ruined them with what Duncan told her. No wonder they tried to stop all her letters. Yet still my courage near failed me when I was told I could see him no more.* So she stayed silent a while longer, with the letter heavy in her pocket, and some other weight fettering her heart.

Jonathan cleared his throat softly.

'Mrs Weekes, I must tell you something,' he said. He was watching Rachel intently, and at once she sensed bad news.

'What is it?'

'I have been thinking a great deal about what you told me . . . about your sister, who was lost, and the possibility that she might have lived a second life, as Alice.'

'Yes?' Suddenly Rachel was alive with nerves; the blood seemed to swell in her veins.

'Something had been plaguing me over it. Mrs Weekes, how old are you?'

'I am twenty-nine, sir. I will be thirty next spring.'

'Then it is as I thought. I fear that . . . Alice was not your twin sister; she could not be. Alice was a year and a half older than me. If she lives, she is thirty-five now. You are too young.'

And as simply as that, Rachel's hopes were destroyed. There was silence after Jonathan spoke. The words fell dead from his lips, and landed at Rachel's feet like little bones, cold and hard. There was a writhing feeling in her chest, and she gasped at it. Tears burned her eyes. *Abi, no. Don't go.* But she couldn't bargain or riddle her way around this; she could not argue *it might not be so.* Even after everything she'd heard from Duncan Weekes, and Bridget, after everything she had come to believe of Lord Faukes and Josephine Alleyn, still her mind had clung to the idea that they might all be lying, or mistaken; that it was all talk and rumours and no proof; that the little girl Lord Faukes had put into Bridget's arms, and sponsored all her life, had indeed been Abigail. It had never occurred to her to check that most fundamental thing she and her twin had in common — their birthday. Rachel bowed her head and wept in utter disappointment; she felt so cold, and so tired.

Outside the window the world seemed to stretch away, endlessly grey and empty. *Say something to me*, she implored but the voice in her mind stayed silent. *Then I am alone*. She felt desolate then, as though she could never again move from the chair where she sat, because she would never have the strength to, would never have the cause. *This was why my heart was numb. To save me from ever feeling this way again.*

'Do not weep so, Mrs Weekes. Please. It would have been a wondrous happenstance, I know, but . . . wondrous things rarely prove to be true,' said Jonathan, gently.

'Wondrous? Perhaps.' Rachel shook her head. 'But it was the one thing I was hoping for. You break my heart, sir.'

'Losing your sister breaks your heart, and I am sorry for it. But I had to tell you, did I not?'

'Oh, why? Why could you not have just left me in ignorance, and with hope?' she cried.

'Because it was lies, Mrs Weekes,' he said grimly. 'Two girls were lost, not one.'

'But I had hoped that it was otherwise, Mr Alleyn. I had hoped so much,' said Rachel, brokenly. 'It was the one thing that could have given Alice a happy ending.'

'What do you mean?'

'If she was Abi, and not Lord Faukes's, then there was no cause for anyone to harm her. If she was Abi, the two of you could have defied them, and wed. And if she was Abi she might indeed have run away with another, and perhaps be alive somewhere. But I cannot believe any of that if she was Alice. I cannot imagine Alice a happy ending.'

'What are you saying? What do you mean, if she was not

Lord Faukes's?' Jonathan was frowning now, that darkening look that she had learnt so well, and learnt to avoid. But she was too sad and sorry to be cautious, then. She took out the letter and handed it to him. 'What is this?' He stared at it as if she offered him a live snake.

'It is Alice's last letter to you. The one that reached you in Brighton.'

Jonathan froze. Still held in mid-air, the letter began to tremble. Clenching his teeth, Jonathan snatched it from her, and Rachel saw a tremor pass right through him. He closed his hand, crumpling the paper tight inside.

'How came you by this?' he said, grinding the words out.

'I was given it, to return to you, by . . . by Harriet Sutton.'

'Sutton? Then he—' Jonathan swallowed, his throat constricting. 'He had it all the while, and kept it from me? My *friend* . . . why?'

'He . . . he didn't want you to dwell on her, I think – on Alice. Once you were back with the army, and preparing to fight again . . .'

'It wasn't for him to decide that.'

'No. No, it wasn't. But he could have left it where you discarded it, and it would have been lost . . .'

'*Damn* him!' Jonathan burst out. He stormed out of his chair and paced the floor beside her, his face contorted with anger. 'And you have read it, I take it?' he snapped. Rachel looked away in shame.

'I'd thought she was my sister—'

'Even if she was, you had no right!'

'No. I had none,' she said.

'But you made it your business, to enquire into mine. You and the rest of the world alongside you.' Jonathan stopped pacing and looked down at her with that blankness she had seen before. *Where is it he goes, when he is most angry or afraid?* Slowly, Jonathan flattened the letter out and slid it into his pocket.

'Aren't you going to read it?' said Rachel, wiping her face with her gloved fingers.

'Not here,' he said coldly. 'Not now.'

'She writes of the other man—'

'Say *nothing* more!'

Jonathan half turned away from her and covered his mouth with one hand, and Rachel was suddenly, horribly reminded of Richard, and the pose from which he'd raised his arm to strike her, just hours before. *When I first met this man he would have choked me to death, were it not for Starling.* 'How long have you had this letter? How could you keep this from me? I *trusted* you!' he said savagely. Rachel stood and moved away from him. She thought of the heavy glass jar, thrown down at her feet, and his blind empty eyes as he'd done it. *So much that is good, and so much that is bad, contained in this one room.* Suddenly, she couldn't bear to be enclosed by those four walls for a second longer. Jonathan's face was terrible; he took two steps towards her, and Rachel fled.

She quit the house on Lansdown Crescent, and knew it would be for the last time. She would visit no more; see Jonathan no more. *Who is he, in truth? The man I thought I knew, or the man Starling knows?* She hurried down the steps and turned west along the crescent, away from the city centre. She wanted to quit Bath too, she realised then. She wanted to quit Richard, and her home, and everything she had found out since her arrival. *I want none of it. I am alone; so let me be alone.* Rachel began to cry again; the ache in her chest was agonising, and made it hard to breathe. There was a shout behind her.

'Wait!' She turned to see Jonathan following her, shrugging on a black coat. He was a monochrome creature: pale skin, dark hair, dark clothes, as though life and pain had robbed him of colour. He limped more than ever in his haste; hunching his shoulders and turning his face away from passers-by.

'Leave me be!' Rachel called back to him. She turned and carried on walking, past all the mournful buildings with their streaked stone and watchful, empty windows. She was at the gate to the high common when Jonathan came up behind her.

He caught her arm as she unlatched the gate.

'Wait, Rachel. Where are you going?'

'Away from here! Away from—' Rachel coughed and sniffed; her face was wet, chilled.

'Away from me?' he said darkly. 'Do you think . . . do you honestly think I killed her?'

'Didn't you?' she cried. 'Wouldn't you have killed me, twice over, if Starling hadn't stopped you one time, and I hadn't dodged you the other?' She twisted her arm and he let it go. Rapid thoughts shifted behind his eyes.

'But I loved her,' he murmured, brokenly. 'I loved her. How, then, could I have harmed her?' Rachel's pulse was racing, it made her head feel bruised.

'Because of what she told you! Because of what she alludes to in that letter, and what she then told you when you saw her – when you came back to Bathampton all mad and undone!' she said. 'Can you claim to remember differently?'

'I . . . I . . .' He shook his head. Rachel felt the last pieces of hope crumbling down around her feet, till there was nothing left.

'I told Starling that she must have loved another, that that would be the only reason you might have to harm her, but I was wrong, wasn't I? She was innocent all along. She was innocent.' Jonathan said nothing, but he nodded. 'You said to me once that you had killed innocents,' Rachel said softly, full of dread. 'You said you had done things that would send me screaming from the room. You said you'd tried to make it right, but nothing would.' Still Jonathan only stared, and stayed silent. Rachel could hardly find the breath to speak; there seemed no air to breathe. 'You've killed innocents,' she said again.

'Yes!' he said.

'Do not flinch from the memory of it – what right have you to do that? Look at it, and tell me what you see!'

'I can't.'

'You *must*! It's there, in the . . . in the dark spaces in your thoughts – I know it. Did you kill her?' Rachel shouted. Jonathan would not look at her. His eyes were fixed on the shifting fog, searching. '*Did you kill her?*' Rachel said again. Gradually, a change came over Jonathan. His eyes grew wider and lost their focus, so flooded with guilt and horror it looked like it would drown him. He took a slow, shuddering breath. 'Did you?' Rachel demanded. '*Did you murder her?*' The words rang between them.

'Yes,' he breathed then, the word like a poison, killing all it touched. A sob punched through Rachel's chest and made her wail.

'Oh, God, how could you? I did not believe it! I believed she lived! I believed I . . . I *defended* you! When all this time Starling has denounced you, I argued against it, but she was *right*! It was all black lies, and you are the blackest of all! *How could you?*' She slapped his face; a feeble blow, puny compared to the pain she was feeling, but it seemed to rouse him. He grasped at her hands, and she fought him off.

'Wait, Rachel, I—'

'No! Let me go!' She wrenched herself free and fled through the gate, up onto the waiting white expanse of the common.

She slipped and struggled up the hill, wanting nothing but to be away from him, away from all of them and everything she knew. The grass was as icy and white as the air, sliding beneath her feet. Her breath came in uneven gulps, and she was half blinded by tears. *So I have nothing, only a husband who grows to hate me, as I hate him.* The grief she felt was like losing her father and mother again; like losing Christopher. She remembered the cool, unnatural feel of her little brother's cheek on her lips, as she'd kissed him in his casket. It was excruciating. *Abigail!* She reached out for the echo in her mind and it was there, weaker, fainter, but there. *Her shade then, only ever her shade. A memory, nothing more; or just my own mind seeking to comfort itself.* When she had no more breath to run she halted, bending forwards, body heaving.

'Rachel, wait!' She heard his shout, not far away, and it sent a jolt right through her. *He is coming after me.* She twisted around, unable to tell which direction his voice had come from. Nothing was visible in the mist but the uneven ground, and to her left, a stand of black, tangled hawthorn trees at the bottom of a steep dell in the hillside. Fighting for breath, Rachel gathered up her skirts and continued to climb the hill. Her head was throbbing. *There is indeed no fairness; no kindnesses. He did not lie about that.* 'Rachel, come back!' His voice sounded closer yet, as if he was hard on her heels, and Rachel sobbed in panic as she toiled onwards.

She had reached a point where the land seemed to flatten when she could go on no further. She sat down on the frosty grass, laid her head on her knees, and let her lungs fill and empty like bellows. Within minutes she felt the sweat on the back of her neck and along her spine begin to cool, and then chill; she felt damp creeping in through her skirts. For a long while, she felt nothing else. She thought she heard another shout, perhaps from Jonathan. But it was wordless, and seemed a long way away, so she paid it no mind. *What matter if he comes and kills me this time, anyway?* The only person who might care was Duncan Weekes. *Perhaps Starling would care? Perhaps not. She will never see Alice's letter, not now I have given it to Jonathan. And she's searched for it for so long.* Rachel shut her eyes and tried to think of nothing. Into the empty space came a memory of the By Brook, bright and glorious in summer light. Abi's small body bumping against hers, fighting for space at the carriage window; pale, pale hair, finer than spun silk; a lavender-blue dress; her mother's face, full of happiness for the last time. After that day there would always be a shadow behind Anne Crofton's eyes, all the deeper once Christopher also died. Rachel heard the frightened shout, saw the flash of distant blue in the lively water, rushing away, so quickly. She stopped herself, frowning. She pushed the thoughts back, concentrated hard on the memory of that small body next to hers; the blue dress, the pale hair. *Abi. How can I do without you, dearest?*

She drifted for a while, beset by sparkling glimpses of memory, and stinging shards of pain. When she opened her eyes it was because shivers were wracking her body, her every muscle cramping with cold. The light was failing, the grey all around deepening by the minute; she could see nothing around her, not even her own shadow, and a new fear gripped her. *What madness was on me, to run out here, away from help?* She stood up and spun in a circle, desperately searching for something familiar, some landmark or path to lead her back towards Bath. All she had were her own footprints, crushed into the frost; not easily visible but there for the following. She'd taken two steps with her eyes fixed upon them when she realised that Jonathan might also be following them, coming up behind her; slower on his lame leg, but still coming. *How long did I rest? Does he still follow?* On legs weak with fatigue, she turned to traverse the hill, the ground sloping treacherously under her feet. She meant to make her way down on a route parallel to that she'd previously taken, just in case Jonathan was still behind her. The darkness deepened with every second that passed; her eyes blurred with the strain of seeing. At one point her ankle crumpled sideways, twisting painfully and making her cry out. *I must get back to the city.* The thought of being lost on the common at night was terrifying. *He cannot see me, at least.* She felt a deeper chill at this thought. *And neither can anybody else.*

A pair of partridge erupted up from near her feet and she yelped in fright, pulling up short and holding her breath to listen. There was no other sound. The silence seemed to crowd in around her, amplifying the racket of her blood as it sang in her ears. Pointlessly, she turned about, gazing blindly into the gathering dark. *Downwards. It is the only option, the only way back to safety. The safety of my home*, she thought, bitterly. Then, with a jolt of relief, she saw the deep dell she'd skirted on the way up – that steep, rounded bowl in the earth with stunted, straggling trees knotted at the bottom. She was hurrying past it when something caught her eye. A colour, when all else was white or grey or black. Cautiously, she went closer to the edge, straining her eyes to see. And then she did see. A crumpled black shape, at the bottom by the hawthorn trees; twisted and lying at odd angles. *Jonathan.* He had fallen down the slope and lay with bright red droplets scattered around his head like the spent petals of some macabre flower; as still and silent as ice. Rachel fell to her knees; skeins of suffocating dread rose up and wrapped around her.

* * *

'What are you doing here?' said Starling, made stupid and slow by amazement. Her breath plumed in front of her face; there was a stink of unwashed skin and alcohol.

'What am I doing here? This is my place.' Dick Weekes swayed drunkenly as he took a messy swig from a bottle of brandy. Starling edged back until she felt the leathery touch of willow branches on her shoulders.

'Your place?' She shook her head. 'This is Alice's place; Alice's and Jonathan's.' She glanced at their initials on the tree and saw that the carving had been obliterated; gouged out by a mass of angry knife marks.

'I come here sometimes. Lately, a great deal. I come to visit her ghost, and see if she forgives me yet.' Dick smiled blearily, but there was no mirth in his eyes, only misery.

'Whose ghost? What are you *doing* here?' Starling couldn't make sense of the scene: Dick Weekes in Alice's secret place.

'Alice's of course, you bloody halfwit!' he snapped, sitting back down on the root. He sank his head into his hands, elbows on his knees, and Starling stared at him.

'You knew Alice? But you . . . you didn't know her! How could you know her? All this time I've known you, you've never said . . .'

'All this time.' He chuckled then, a nasty sound; looked up at her with savage eyes. 'All those times you straddled me, and slid yourself down my shaft to the baubles, you were doing the goat's jig with the man who killed your precious Alice Beckwith. Is that not a neat folly?' He waved the brandy bottle aloft as if to make a toast. Starling stared; mute, stunned. 'And she was meant to make it better. That other one, the one I married,' he mumbled. 'She was meant to love me and forgive me, and make it better.'

'It was you Bridget saw on the bridge, talking to Alice that time. It was you she went out to meet; who wrote her a note and left it here at the tree . . .'

'We were seen? I tried to avoid that. But by God, she was a stubborn wench! She would not love me.'

'What did . . . why . . .' Starling shook her head. She

clasped at her stomach, suddenly feeling like she would vomit.

'I was to woo her. I was to lure her away. I was to tempt her into loving me, and disgracing herself. I was to make Jonathan Alleyn discard her.'

'By who? By who were you sent to do these things?'

'By his lady mother, of course. By Josephine Alleyn, another one who did not love me.' He took another swig, his voice heavy with self-pity, slurring from his drink-thickened tongue. 'With my glorious face, she said, I could not fail. With my *glorious face*.'

With a bump, Starling sat down in the mud. Her muscles were unresponsive; she struggled to take in what Dick was saying.

'After Alice went to Box, after she went to Lord Faukes . . . When she recovered . . . she was quiet and secretive. She was sad . . . she wrote letters, but no letters came back.'

'Her letters were not sent. Not a one. All were intercepted and carried back to his lordship. I was to make her ruin herself and abandon Mr Alleyn before he returned from overseas. She was to tell him nothing, and do nothing to hasten his return.'

'One letter was sent,' Starling said woodenly.

It went on a February day not long before Alice's death, when the sky was a threatening mass of cloud, and there were tiny flecks of rain on the breeze. In those days Alice still went out alone, and at strange times, but rarely with Starling or Bridget. She was keeping a secret, Starling knew – possibly more than one; the kind of secret that gradually, inexorably, wore a person away. Her eyes looked bruised all the time, and she never smiled. Even at Christmas, which Alice loved, she'd been sombre and sad, picking at the roast goose on her plate and offering no opinion on the decorations.

'Won't you tell me, Alice? Won't you tell me why you can't marry Jonathan?' Starling whispered, lying nose to nose in bed one night. She pulled the blankets up over their heads, so that Alice would feel safe and Bridget would not hear.

'I cannot.'

'Then promise not to leave me!'

'I have already . . .'

'Promise it again!'

'I promise—' Alice broke off, and hesitated. 'I promise not to leave you, Starling,' she finished. But somehow this promise, extracted in darkness, did nothing to reassure Starling. She knew that change was coming, she just could not tell the shape of it.

Since the lovers' tree Starling was determined to prove steadfast and true to her sister, so she didn't keep cajoling her to speak, but only tried to cheer her. She fell back on that childish recourse of pretending all was well in hopes of making it so; begging Alice to read with her, to teach her poems, to go with her on walks and errands – all without success, until that cloudy day, when at last she agreed to go out. They went into the village, and Starling noticed Alice staring into the faces they saw, as if calculating, or searching for something. On the way back Starling waved and called out to a familiar barge travelling west, and Alice grabbed at her arm.

'Do you know that man?' she said, as they stepped back to allow the plodding horse to pass.

'Yes, that's Dan Smithers,' said Starling.

'Would he do a small favour, if you asked him? Is he an honest man?'

'I think he would. I think he is.'

'Then bid him take this letter for me, and send it on from Bath,' said Alice, urgently, pressing the folded paper into her hand.

Starling ran on a few paces, and called out.

'Mr Smithers! Will you carry this letter to Bath for us, and send it on?'

'What'll you pay me, bantling?' Dan called back, taking his pipe out from between his teeth.

'I have a farthing . . . and I can sing you a song, if you like?' At this the bargeman laughed and moved to the edge of the deck, reaching out to take the letter.

'Keep your farthing, girl. Only a goosecap would cast chink over water.' He tucked Alice's letter into his shirt and drifted on his steady way.

'Will he do it?' said Alice, watching the bargeman's retreating back with a strange, hungry look in her eyes. 'Will he send it?'

'Of course.' Starling shrugged. Alice sighed then, and the hand that held Starling's squeezed it tight, as if for courage.

'Then we shall soon see,' she said; words as desperate and hopeless as a faithless prayer.

'Jonathan Alleyn got that letter – it was that which brought him rushing back here, from Brighton,' said Starling. The frosty ground she sat on was eating into her flesh, but she could hardly feel it.

'Well, it made no difference,' said Dick.

'It did to him. It did to Mr Alleyn.'

'It made no difference to Miss Beckwith.'

'Why did you kill her? *Why?* She was good . . . only ever good! She was my sister.' Starling could hardly speak for the grief crushing her.

'I never meant to! Do you think I meant to?' Dick erupted to his feet. The brandy bottle flew from his hand and landed in front of Starling, the last drops splattering out. 'Do you think I *meant to*? I did not. I . . . she was kind, like you said.

I wanted her to love me.' He laughed again, high-pitched and strange.

'You're mad.'

'I was meant to make her love me, and the bitch made me *want* her to! How's that for a twist of fate.' He lurched to one side and retched violently, sending a spew of rancid brandy onto the riverbank. 'But by God, she was stubborn.' He coughed, spat, wiped his chin on his hand.

'She wouldn't betray him. She wouldn't betray Jonathan Alleyn.'

'Clung to thoughts of that Hopping Giles like a nun to Christ's bloody cross. She only agreed to meet me because I swore I would open my own veins if she refused. She tried to talk me out of it – out of all the devotion and unending love I professed, as ardently as any bleeding poet. She sat patiently and listened to me harp on, and then told me sweetly that it could not be; that her heart belonged to another for all of time, even if they could not marry. When I said I would drown myself in the river if she didn't consent to an elope- ment she just gave me a look, all grave and sedate, and said "Do not, sir, I beg you. Only try to forget me, and find another to love."' He strained his voice into a grotesque parody of Alice's.

'She was true to him,' Starling whispered. 'When she would not betray, did Mrs Alleyn bid you kill her?'

'No! Not . . . not baldly put, not like that. I knew she desired it, though. But I never meant to. I only . . . thought to frighten her. To scare her into obeying me, and accepting me . . .'

'To *scare* her into loving you? You're a pitiful fool, Dick Weekes.'

'And you were my whore, Starling,' he sneered at her.

'What did you do to her?'

'I only struck her. Just a blow, to that pretty face. I shook her a little first, and made threats . . . She said if I loved her I would let her be, so I gave her a blow across the chops, and she fell down, and . . . and . . . it wasn't enough to *kill* her! It wasn't enough for that! But she was pale as death itself, lying there on the ground, and she gasped like a landed fish. The only colour she had was the blood on her teeth. I thought she was playing me for a fool . . . I thought she was feigning injury. But then she . . . she stopped gasping.' He shook his head as if bewildered. 'Dear God but I've seen her gasping like that, and those red teeth, in a thousand dreams since then.' He shuddered. 'But it wasn't enough to kill her . . . it wasn't! I've hit enough women to know what force to use.'

'You dog.' Starling could hardly speak. Her body was shaking so hard her teeth rattled in her skull. 'You *dog*! Her heart was fragile . . . it could not stand a shock, or too much agitation.'

'It wasn't my fault. She wasn't supposed to die.'

'Where?' The word was a barely unintelligible moan. '*Where?*' Starling tried again.

'Here. Just here. She lay where you lie now, more or less,' he said woodenly. He shook his head again, and tears bloated his eyes. For some reason, the sight of them made Starling angrier than she'd ever been in her life.

'No, where is she *now*?'

Slowly, unsteadily, Starling got to her knees, and then to her feet. She curled her hands into fists, though it seemed to take every last bit of her strength. Dick ignored her, still staring at the spot on the ground where Starling had sat down. He tottered; staggered to keep his feet.

'At least, I thought, Mrs Alleyn would love me for it. What better way to get the girl out from under her feet? But none of it.' He stooped to pick up the brandy bottle, nearly pitching forwards as he did; peered into it and then cast it into the water with a feeble overarm throw when he found it empty. 'This is my place,' he mumbled. 'We were dismissed soon after. Father, and me along with him. I'd made myself a murderer at the age of eighteen, for her, but she didn't even want to see me after. Didn't even let me kiss her any more, or touch her breasts like before. She'd made me think . . . she'd made me think I could have *all of her*, if I did as she asked. She made me think that.'

'All this time . . . all this time . . . Where is she now, you bastardly gullion?' Starling shouted, finding a storm of rage to give her strength. With a snarl she flew at him, clawing at his eyes with their lying tears. Befuddled and slow, Dick fought her off, clumsily trying to grab at her hands and strike her at the same time.

'All this time you've been plaguing Jonathan Alleyn, and for *naught*, Starling! For *naught*! I can't say that hasn't cheered me, from time to time.' He grinned at her then, a cruel and sickly expression.

'*Bastard!*' Starling screamed, and with all her strength she shoved him in the chest, wanting nothing more than for him to vanish; to be no more. Dick reeled backwards, caught his heel on a root and launched full length into the river.

The splash was a huge white plume in the gathering dark; the sound seemed impossibly loud. Starling stood on the bank, chest heaving, and watched as Dick surfaced, coughing and spitting and shaking the water from his eyes. The water wasn't deep enough to drown him. *More's the pity. But I should run. I should run before he climbs out.* But Starling was rooted to the spot. Dick stood, and the black water was at his chest; he seemed to have trouble breathing.

'I'll choke the bloody life from you, you bitch!' he said, but his voice sounded thick and peculiar, and as he began to wade towards the bank his movements were jerky and slow; like it was deep snow he strode through instead of water.

'Where is she now? What did you do with her?' said

Starling. Dick didn't reply. His attention seemed to have turned inwards, to his own body. Spasms juddered through him; he scowled in confusion.

'Cold,' he muttered, through chattering teeth. 'It's too cold. My legs . . . cramp has my legs . . .' He stumbled then, and the water closed over his head again. 'Starling, help me!' he called when he surfaced, panic creeping into his voice. 'I haven't the strength!'

'Seems to me a man in the prime of life, who knows just how much force to use when he hits a woman, should have no trouble climbing a riverbank,' said Starling, icily. 'Unless he's drunk himself weaker than a kitten, of course.' She stared down at Dick, not moving, not blinking.

'Help me!'

'I will not.' Dick's face had gone as white as the fog; his breath came in snatches, hissing out between locked jaws. He made for the bank again and this time reached it, his fingers snapping the thin ice where water met earth. He scrabbled at the bank, found a root and curled his fingers around it, but when he pulled at it his grip slithered free. He stared at his hands as if he no longer owned them.

'Starling, help me. Please. Pull me up, for I cannot do it. I cannot.' His legs rose in the water behind him, floating of their own volition. He craned his head back to keep his face clear of the surface. His puffing breath made little scuffs on the water.

'Tell me where she rests.' Starling gazed down at him, feeling calm now, feeling safe.

'If you help me out, I will tell you. I swear it,' he said. The current had Dick's legs, pulling, turning his feet towards Bath. His eyes bulged in fear and he flapped at the root with hands that would no longer flex. 'Pull me out! Pull me out and I will show you the exact spot! Else you will never know, Starling! You will never know!'

'No, tell me now!' *There are only seconds*. The current had edged Dick away from the bank. He stared at the root that might save him, splashed and paddled to no effect.

'St-Starling, please,' he croaked. *In seconds he will be out of reach*. Starling glanced around for a fallen branch with which she might hook him, but saw none. She took a step closer to the edge, closer to him, and hesitated, frowning in indecision.

* * *

Captain and Harriet Sutton were at table when Rachel was let into the hall by their elderly servant. She could no longer feel her hands or feet, or her heart. Her head was ringing and she couldn't marshal her thoughts, or pick any one free of the tangled whole. Harriet came rushing out to her, alarmed, still swallowing a mouthful of food; her husband the captain was not far behind her, keeping a more tactful distance; and behind him Cassandra peeked out, keeping to the safety of her father's shadow.

'My dear, whatever has happened? You look terribly pale – come and sit by the fire, your hands are like ice,' said Harriet, as she took Rachel through to the parlour.

'Something terrible . . . I am so sorry.' Rachel sat down, unsure what to say now that she was given the chance. The earlier events on the common had an unreal caste in her memory, as if they could not really have unfurled that way. 'I am so sorry to intrude upon you like this, Mrs Sutton,' she managed to whisper. 'It's only that I . . . I wasn't sure where else to go.'

'But, has something happened at home, my dear? Has something happened to Mr Weekes?'

'At home? No.' Rachel shook her head. 'No, it is Mr Alleyn.'

'Jonathan Alleyn?' The captain broke in, brusquely. 'What has happened to him?'

'He is . . .' Rachel swallowed; her throat was dry and tight. 'He . . . I think he is dead.'

'*What?*' Harriet breathed. Rachel grasped at her friend's hands when it seemed she might pull them away.

'He killed Alice Beckwith! I never thought so . . . not truly . . .'

There was a hung moment; Captain Sutton was the first to break it.

'Cassie, you are for Bedfordshire. Maggie,' he called over his shoulder to their servant. 'Take this young lady up to bed, if you would.'

'But Papa, what about the butterscotch syllabub?' Cassandra protested gently. Rachel looked up at the sound of her voice, and found the little girl's dark, liquid eyes regarding her with curiosity and a touch of fear. *I must sound like a mad woman.*

'You may take a dish upstairs with you. Go on now, be gone.' Obediently, Cassandra turned and left them, her long hair swaying behind her. Captain Sutton came further into the room and closed the door behind him. 'He killed Miss Beckwith? Are you certain of this?' His tone was heavy with something like dread.

'He confessed it to me! He said . . . he said . . .' Rachel struggled to remember his exact words. 'We were speaking of Alice — I'd given him back her last letter, you see. And he was . . . most upset by it . . . He fell . . .' Rachel shut her eyes, because suddenly her head was lanced with pain. 'We were up on the high common and he . . . slipped, and fell into a deep hollow. I think he must have hit his head. Harriet . . . there was so much blood!'

'But you don't know if he lives? How is this? Did you not stay to find out?' Harriet was no longer holding Rachel's hands but gripping them, so tightly that Rachel felt her finger bones grind together.

'I . . . I'd been running from him. In the fog . . . Harriet, I . . . was frightened! He was so angry, and disordered . . . I thought he might do me harm, if I were to face him. After he fell, I found my way back down from the hill, and I sent the first men I encountered up to where Mr Alleyn was, to fetch him down. And . . . then I came here.'

Suddenly, Harriet Sutton released Rachel's hands and put her own to her mouth, her eyes stretching wide. Her husband took a step forward and put his hand on her shoulder to steady her.

'He was trying to fetch you back, on rough ground, in frozen weather and at sunset . . . you led him up there and left him struggling after you – a man made lame by battle? He will freeze, if nothing else!' said Captain Sutton, with quiet intensity.

'What? No . . . I . . . that wasn't the way of it, truly! I never meant for him to follow. I didn't even mean to go up onto the common. I only . . . fled, and did not think, until I was there. But . . . but, he is a killer! Don't you believe me?'

'I will send for news at once,' said the captain, leaving the room for a moment.

'Of course you did not mean to endanger him,' said Harriet, soothingly. When her husband returned, the two of them shared a long look. 'But he did say that he killed Alice Beckwith? Did he say those words?' Harriet asked, softly. She blinked, and tears streaked down her face; she turned to her husband again. 'Oh, my dear, what if he is dead? Poor Mr Alleyn!'

'I don't understand.' Rachel looked in bewilderment from her friend to the captain and back again. The Suttons seemed to communicate in silence for a moment, and then Harriet gave a tiny nod.

'We must tell her, my dear,' she whispered, and the captain looked down at his feet with a frown.

'Tell me what?' said Rachel. Captain Sutton let out a pent breath in a rush, his shoulders sagging in defeat.

'Mr Alleyn did kill a woman, Mrs Weekes. But it was not Alice Beckwith. It was Cassandra's mother.'

Rachel frowned, still not understanding.

'Cassandra? Your daughter, Cassandra? What can you mean, Mr Alleyn killed her mother?'

'Her real mother, Mrs Weekes,' said Harriet, softly. 'For it had become clear, a long time before he brought her to us, that my husband and I would not be blessed with children of our own.'

'Cassandra is another woman's child? But . . . whose? Who was she? Why would Jonathan kill her?'

'I will tell you,' said the captain. 'But I must beg you, Mrs Weekes. I must beg you to divulge none of this to anybody, not even to your husband, though I am loath to introduce secrets into a marriage.'

'Fear not.' Rachel's voice was leaden. 'We have many already.'

'Nobody but my wife and I and Jonathan Alleyn know this truth. Not even Mr Alleyn's good lady mother.'

'I will speak of it to no one.'

'Then you have my thanks, for that if for little else.' The captain sank into a chair opposite the two women; hands on his knees, suddenly like a small boy. 'It happened at Badajoz. After the siege, and the . . . madness that followed it.'

'Badajoz?' The name rang in Rachel's memory. 'I have heard of it. Jonathan . . . that is, Mr Alleyn, spoke of it once. Is that not where his leg was injured? The last battle he fought, before he was forced to come home?'

'Indeed. I'm surprised to hear he spoke of it. Most of us who were there would prefer to forget it, I think. It was a massacre. A massacre the likes of which I had never seen before, nor ever have since — for which I am profoundly grateful. I will not describe it in detail. Not to ladies.' The captain broke off and cleared his throat, though it sounded dry and clear. Rachel saw a measure of the same tension around the man's eyes as when she'd coaxed Jonathan to speak of the war. 'We paid most heavily for our entry to the city, and . . . when it was taken . . .' He paused, his jaw closing with an audible click of his teeth. 'When the city was taken, there was a mutiny of sorts. Looting and . . . violence, towards the defeated soldiers and the city's residents both. It was indiscriminate and it was . . . hellish. It was like hell.'

'My dear, enough. Do not speak on if it pains you,' said Harriet.

'Major Alleyn kept his head, though his leg was severely wounded by then, and he made me keep mine. We went into a church to . . .' He flicked a troubled glance at his wife. 'To prevent a desecration. There was a struggle, a fight. I left in pursuit of some of our own men, far the worse for wine. And then, some minutes later Major Alleyn came out, carrying a newborn infant.'

'Our Cassandra,' said Harriet, with a tiny smile. She looked at Rachel and took her hand again. 'He saved her. In the midst of all that.' Captain Sutton nodded.

'I never asked what had gone on within. Major Alleyn was doused in blood, not all his own. He was beside himself. He said, over and over, that he had killed her. He had killed her.'

Captain Sutton laced his fingers together, squeezing so hard that the skin blanched. 'I glanced in and wished I had not. But a woman who must have been the child's mother was inside, amongst the dead. Major Alleyn would not let go of the babe. He cradled her like she was his own. But of course a soldier can't keep a child at war. I suggested we find some Spanish woman to take her, but he would not hear of it. He told me that the country was cursed, and that if he left her there she would surely die. And he was probably right. Then he remembered my own dear wife, and our sad state of childlessness.'

'And he brought her back with him when he came. To give to you,' said Rachel. Her voice sounded strange to her own ears. *After Badajoz I did a kind thing . . . so Jonathan said, one time.*

'Yes.'

'He said to me . . . he said to me that he'd tried to make it right. That the last thing he'd done in the war had been a good thing, but that it could not make right what had gone before. He was speaking of this. Of the murder of one innocent, and the saving of another,' she said.

'Yes, he must have been,' said Harriet. The captain stood and paced the hearthrug.

'You cannot call it murder. Not with Major Alleyn. He was trying to restore *order* in the men! He was trying to prevent their bestial behaviour . . . If indeed he killed her, he surely cannot have intended to.'

'We have never asked him. And now I fear we never shall,' Harriet murmured.

'But . . . but we were speaking of *Alice*, when he told me he had killed her! We weren't speaking of the war, we were speaking of *Alice* . . .'

'Cassandra's mother haunts him constantly. That much I know. She and the war are with him always,' said Captain Sutton. 'But perhaps now he is at peace,' he added, in a hard voice that hit Rachel like a blow.

A long and steady silence fell. The fire seethed gently, and from upstairs came the muffled sound of footsteps – the light, rapid patter of Cassandra's feet; the more stately tread of the servant. Rachel tried to think back over everything Jonathan had said to her about Alice, and about the war; everything Starling had told her about him, and about her lost sister. She tried with little success to make order of it all, and with more success to maintain her belief in Jonathan's guilt. She *had* to still believe it, because the alternative was unthinkable. *Have I believed the worst of him? Have I caused the death of an innocent man?*

'But he is a killer,' she said, almost to herself. Harriet let go of her hand.

'He is a good man. He saved an innocent life when all around was chaos and death. He gave us the greatest gift a person could give,' she said passionately.

'And if he did kill Alice, what then? He does not remember that day,' said Rachel. 'Does saving Cassandra excuse him of that? Even he did not think so – he told me so himself!'

'If he harmed Miss Beckwith . . .' Harriet trailed off, and looked at her husband. 'If he did, then no. Nothing absolves him of that.'

'Except death, perhaps, for then the Lord will be his judge. By your actions we may never know the truth. I for one will not believe it. Not ever. But then, I have fought alongside him. He is my blade brother, and so I know him better than either of you.' Captain Sutton spoke in stony tones, then rose and left the room without looking at Rachel or excusing himself.

Harriet Sutton invited Rachel to stay longer, and take a bed for the night. She didn't ask why Rachel was reluctant to return to Abbeygate Street – she didn't seem to need to. But when Rachel refused the offer Harriet didn't press her, and Rachel saw relief in her eyes. She couldn't blame her friend, though it hurt nonetheless. She had broken into their family, and made a breach through which all they held dear might be threatened. *I will tell no one.* Slowly, she walked towards Abbeygate Street, along dark streets like tunnels through her caved-in world. She would have to confront Richard, and tell him what had happened that day; and he would beat her for her association with Starling, and for prying into the Alleyns' lives, and for accusing Jonathan and then leaving him lying on the frosty ground, surrounded by blood. *For doing anything to upset Josephine Alleyn, whom he loved dear. Loves dear?*

Was I mistaken? Didn't Jonathan tell me he killed Alice? She stopped on the cobbles of Abbey Green, where the fallen plane tree leaves had been rained and rotted into a slimy mulch in the gutters. Torch flares in the darkness flung dizzying lines across her vision, and suddenly the strain of thinking was utterly debilitating. She wanted nothing more than to lie down where she stood and let it all carry on without her. *Did I lead him to his death?* She stumbled on, and as she turned the corner into Abbeygate Street she saw a figure huddled on the steps of the wine shop.

Rachel paused, thinking from the way the figure hunched, leaning on the railings, that it was her husband or her father-in-law, far gone in drink. But the person was too small to be either of them, and as she approached she recognised Starling, curled with her arms around her knees, shivering under her shawl.

'Starling, what are you doing here? If my husband sees you he will thrash us both.' Rachel glanced up at the windows in alarm, and relaxed a little when she saw them unlit. Starling raised a pale face to her.

'Neither one of us needs worry about that any more,' she said.

'What do you mean? Wherever he is, he could be back any moment . . . it's late.' As she spoke, Rachel realised that she had no idea of the hour. The afternoon and evening had blurred nonsensically. She shook her head in confusion.

'I'm telling you, you don't need to worry about him any more,' said Starling, more firmly. She stared up at Rachel with her hard eyes, and Rachel's stomach lurched.

'Oh, mercy . . . what have you done?' she whispered.

'Me? Nothing at all. The fool fell into the river. He was drunk, as usual.'

'He fell? How do you know this?'

'I happened to be passing. It . . . it was at the lovers' tree.'

'At Bathampton? I don't understand . . . why was he at Bathampton? Why were you?' Starling stood up stiffly.

'Can we go inside? I will tell you everything, but I can't stand this cold any longer.'

'Mr Weekes might return, and find us—'

'He won't.'

Rachel opened the door and led her inside. Starling went straight to the stove, and the squeal of protesting metal as she opened the hatch was piercing. She reached for kindling and coals from the bucket, and blew on the old embers to relight them. Her hands knew exactly where to go for these things, and for the andirons, and Rachel realised that this wasn't the first time Starling had been in her home. In light of all that had happened she found she did not care one whit. She knelt down beside Starling as the coals began to glow, and the pair of them stayed that way, warming their hands in silence a while. When Rachel glanced across at the red-haired girl, she saw that her gaze was fixed, unfocused, far away.

'I . . . you were right,' said Rachel, shakily. 'You were right about Jonathan Alleyn. He killed Alice, and now . . . and now I think he is dead. He . . . What has really happened to my husband?' Slowly, Starling's face turned to her, and the coals glowed in her wide eyes with their peculiar, lost expression.

'It was your husband that killed Alice. I had it from his own lips,' she said.

Rachel could only stare at her, dumbly, as the full story of what had happened at the lovers' tree came out; she was glad she was on her knees already so she couldn't fall down.

'Josephine Alleyn said to me . . .' Rachel's voice was

small, shrunken in astonishment. 'She said to me that my husband had shown her great loyalty. It was this then. Don't you think? She meant this pretend wooing of Alice; this being rid of her.'

'Yes. I think so.' Starling still stared, and never blinked. 'Do you see, Mrs Weekes? Do you see what they've done to me? The very people I've served, and lived beside, and loved . . . these very people were the self-same that took her from me. My sister. Do you see?' she said, and Rachel knew she meant the cruelty of it, the injustice. She nodded. 'I have been tricked. I have been so wrong,' said Starling.

'We have both been wrong, about a great many things.' Rachel paused, swallowing hard. 'Jonathan Alleyn had nothing to do with it at all,' she said numbly. Behind the numbness a grief was building, swelling up like a black bubble.

'Nothing. He loved her and never harmed her, and these past nine years since he came back from Spain I have done all I could to torment him, and make him suffer! I have cursed him every way I know how!' Starling's chest shook so that her words were uneven. 'But he *said* it . . . I heard him say he'd killed her . . . he said her blood was on his hands . . .'

'But by her he did not mean Alice,' Rachel murmured. Starling's expression showed her confusion, but just then Rachel remembered something that hit her hard. 'Oh! When we met . . . when I met Richard Weekes for the first time, he reacted most viscerally. I . . . I thought it was *love*! He told me it was love, and I took his reaction as proof of it. But it was *recognition*. He saw Alice! Just as you did; just as Mrs Alleyn and Jonathan did.'

'Just so.' Starling nodded. 'I knew he started out in Lord Faukes's service; I had no idea he ever met Alice, or even knew of her existence. He said her face has haunted him – his guilt, is more like it. He said he hoped to make amends by . . .'

'By marrying me?' Rachel whispered. Starling nodded.

'But I don't understand . . . don't understand why Mrs Alleyn went to such lengths to be rid of her! Wasn't it enough to send her off knowing that they would never consent to the marriage?' Starling went on.

'No, it was not enough.' *Why didn't I see it? Why didn't I see that if Alice's origins gave Jonathan a cause to harm her, they gave his mother an even greater one?* 'She was his aunt, and his sister both. She was an abomination, through no fault of her own,' said Rachel, with a bitter feeling. Starling only stared, her mouth falling open, as Rachel took her turn and told her everything that had happened that day since she'd read the letter that the Suttons had long hidden.

Starling turned and stared into the burning coals again.

'Perhaps I should pity her then,' she said eventually. 'Perhaps I should pity Josephine Alleyn, to have had that monstrous buck fitch as her father, and suffered his attentions nonetheless . . . But I *can't* pity her. I can't, if she took it out on Alice when it was none of her fault. And if Alice was her own daughter . . . How could she?'

'For the honour of her family name,' Rachel said.

'Honour? What honour had she left?' Starling replied, bitterly.

'Precious little, indeed. Little enough to make the remainder all the more valuable, and to make her guard it like jewels, and do anything she could to keep word of what Alice had found out from ever reaching Jonathan's ears. Bad enough that Alice should tell him she was Lord Faukes's issue; worse beyond tolerance that she should learn the full truth from Duncan Weekes, and share that too.'

'Then that old man killed her, as surely as his son did.'

Starling's face clouded in thought. 'But Josephine can't have known, can she – what old Weekes told Alice that day?'

'Duncan Weekes meant her no harm,' said Rachel, firmly. 'Alice . . . Alice must have written of it. In all those letters that were intercepted, and carried to Box instead. If Lord Faukes read them, then to be sure, Josephine Alleyn would have learnt of their contents.'

'I have served her ever since Alice was lost. I have served that woman almost half my days.' Starling drew in a huge, shuddering breath, and Rachel glanced at her in alarm.

'What will you do?' she said.

'I will finish what you started.'

'What do you mean?'

'You have killed Jonathan Alleyn this day, you say—'

'Not killed. I—'

'And I have rid us of Mr Weekes. That only leaves the one who was behind it all. Because . . .' Suddenly her face crumpled in anguish. 'Because if Alice is dead, and Jonathan too; Dick Weekes . . . And Bridget lies dying . . . then I have nobody. I will not leave Josephine Alleyn in peace a second longer.'

'You cannot mean to attack Mrs Alleyn . . . or do her harm?' Rachel was shocked.

'Harm? I had not thought to harm her. But then, why should I not?'

'Because . . . your own life will be forfeit if you do!'

'I . . . I don't care.' Starling got to her feet, her hands clenched into fists, resolution on her face. Rachel scrambled up beside her.

'You must care! You must not attack her! Promise me!' Rachel cried.

'Why? Haven't you heard your own words this past hour? Why should you care for her?'

'I do not care for her! I care for *you*.' Rachel grabbed at

Starling's arm to stop her leaving. Starling glared at her suspiciously.

'What?'

'If . . . if you go and do this, if you harm her and go to the gallows for it, then . . . then I too will have no one. Do we not have each other? Am I not your friend?'

Rachel released Starling's arm and let her hand drop to her side. The cast-iron body of the stove clinked and popped as it heated. Then Starling broke off her gaze and turned again for the door.

'Perhaps you are. But I must go, even so,' she said.

'What should I do?' Rachel asked. Starling hesitated, looking back over her shoulder.

'You can only wait. Not everything that goes into the river is found. I think that's where Dick put Alice, once she was dead; like as not she was carried out to sea, all undetected. Food for fishes and . . . gulls.' She swallowed convulsively. 'If Dick is found, and recognised, they will come to tell you. You must seem surprised at the news, and grief-struck. Can you do that?' she said. Rachel nodded. 'It will be in the next few days, if it is at all. You can only wait.'

'And then what?'

'Your life is your own, Mrs Weekes.' Starling glanced around at the room. 'You have a home, and a business to run, or sell, or seek management for. I'm going now to Lansdown Crescent.' She gave Rachel one more look, steady and sad. 'I will send word.'

Starling closed the door behind her, and when the clatter of her footsteps had gone from the stairs, Rachel was left alone. She stood for a long time in the empty room. *My husband is dead. I am free again. I am nobody again. But then, he only married me because I reminded him of Alice; I never was anybody in the first place.* She stood until her legs felt wooden, as though the blood ran too slowly through them. Then, because there was little else she could do, she went to bed. She was exhausted, and sleep dragged her down before she'd even shut her eyes. Her last waking thought was laden with guilt and treachery and relief – it was knowing that her sleep would be undisturbed by Richard's late returning and un- wanted touch. But she dreamt of Jonathan, and the copper mouse. She dreamt that she was the copper mouse, that it was a figure of *her* that he'd made; her every tiny detail rendered in bright metal with meticulous care. She felt herself cradled in the palm of his hand, and there felt safe for the first time since her parents had died. She knew herself loved. Then she half woke to darkness, and remembered her last sight of Jonathan, crumpled and bloody on the frosty ground.

Starling had bade her wait, and wait was what Rachel did. She stayed indoors at first, and when there was a knock at the door she jumped to her feet, breathless with fear. But there was no news of Richard; the man who knocked was a client of his, trying the house when he'd found the shop floor empty and closed.

'I would have words with your husband, madam, pray send him out,' said the man. He was claret-faced and well heeled; all bluster and high dudgeon.

'Mr Weekes is . . . not at home, sir.'

'Then pray tell me where I may find him, for he has much to answer for. That last cask of sherry he delivered to me was supposed to be a mellow Lisbon, sweet and well aged – for that I tolerated his high prices. Instead it is new, and hot, and scarce drinkable – though I can taste the honey with which he's tried to improve it . . . And the hogshead of rum I had from him is so well baptised a *child* might drink it and find it mild!' The man raised a finger and pointed it steadily at Rachel's face. 'It will not *do*, madam – never let it be said that I, Cornelius Gibson, will stand to be bilked in this manner! I mean to call him to account, and you may tell him that, madam – he will be called to account, and word will spread that he is a pedlar of balderdash, and no honest man.' With that, Cornelius Gibson stalked away down the steps, rapping an ebony walking stick smartly at his side. Rachel shut the door and leaned against it to catch her breath. *When I am his widow will I be ruined all over again, by his debts and his frauds and dishonesty?*

In the afternoon she went out in search of Duncan Weekes, but found him not at home, nor at the Moor's Head, nor at any other inn she passed by. She went home again to her lonely vigil, but it was not for long. Moments after she closed the door there came a knocking at it, and something about its slow, ponderous rhythm gave her a shiver of prescience. *This is no angry customer. They have found him.* Nerves fluttered in her stomach as she opened the door to a tall, thin man in a brown coat and a greasy black hat. He had a hooked nose and pinched cheeks, and eyes like nuggets of coal.

'Mrs Weekes?' His voice was soft and oddly mellow. Rachel nodded. 'Madam, I am Roger Cadwaller, the wharf constable. It is my sad duty to report that a corpse was taken from the river this day, and that some amongst the river traders have named it Richard Weekes, your husband.' The thin man spoke without emotion, and paused as if expecting Rachel to comment or cry out. *Then he really is dead. I must seem surprised, and grief-struck.*

'He . . . he has not come home,' she managed, in a tiny voice.

'No, madam. And will not, I fear.'

'Where is he?'

'He is with an undertaker, behind Horse Street. Will you come?'

'Come? Why?' Rachel's heart lurched. *Do they think I killed him?*

'Aye, madam. You must look upon him, if you can, and name him your husband so that there can be no doubt it is he.' The man hadn't blinked since she opened the door. Rachel couldn't keep her eyes still.

'Very well,' she whispered.

She followed Roger Cadwaller for a few minutes, down Stall Street and into Horse Street, then off into a tiny alley. The day was dead and cold; a steady drizzle sifted down from low clouds. The constable stopped by a set of narrow steps and guided her down them, between tall flanking buildings, to a damp and shadowy courtyard. From there he led her to a door that hung off-kilter, its black paint peeling and flaking away. The constable knocked, and they were admitted at once. *I must seem surprised, and grief-struck.* Rachel put one hand to her mouth in sudden outrage at her own dispassion. Her steps faltered, and she threw out her other arm to the wall for support. Neither Roger Cadwaller nor the wizened old undertaker who inhabited the place spared more than a glance at such behaviour. *I am not surprised. I am not grief-struck. I am horrified.* Rachel's stomach and legs felt watery weak. She absolutely did not want to look at Richard's dead body, but the two men led her on inexorably. Down more steps was a vaulted cellar, cold, dimly lit by a single pane of smeared glass in a high slot of a window. There, on a wooden table, stripped down to his drawers, lay Richard Weekes. There was an odd ringing in Rachel's ears, and the room and everything in it seemed to recede from her. *No, it is I who am receding.* She moved unsteadily to stand beside him.

Richard's hair was matted with river mud and shreds of weed, but his skin was flawless and pale, unmarked by any injury. Yet even without a wound on him, there was no chance of making believe he was still alive. Something about his stillness, the way he seemed smaller than he once had, the marble smoothness of his face – all screamed of lifelessness. He had no more scent than the stone walls around him. Rachel knew that if she touched him he would be cool, and too solid; the flesh gone dense and leaden without the spirit to buoy it up. The hair on his chest and arms looked too dark, too wiry. His mouth was closed but his jaw had fallen slack, robbing him of the firm line his chin normally took; his eyelids were swollen and purplish. But even so, even lifeless, his face was beautiful. Rachel stared at it for a long time, and couldn't tell what she was feeling. *You did not love me, but you did love. You were violent, but you did not mean to kill. You never forgave your father for the loss of your mother, but he also did not mean to kill. Was there good in you, or only bad?* She came up with all these questions and more, but no answers; her heart was empty – she had no grief for him.

'It is him,' she said, long moments later when the undertaker had begun to fidget with impatience.

'My thanks, madam,' said the constable, in his smooth, unfeeling voice.

'How came he to . . . be in the river?'

'We shan't know, madam. He had no quarrel that any saw or knew of. The men who pulled him out pressed him well, to force the water from him in hopes of reviving him. The dregs that came out were ripe with the red tape.'

'The red tape?'

'Brandy, madam,' said the constable. Rachel blinked, and nodded to show she'd understood.

'The water's cold as a witch's kiss, missus,' said the undertaker. 'Like as not he stumbled in, beetle-headed and boozy, and was undone by the bite o' it before he even knew hisself drowned.' The constable winced at the man's rough speech.

'I see,' Rachel whispered.

'The river men that knew him said he was a man who was wont to . . . sample too much of his own wares,' said the constable.

'He was a borachio, just like his father before him,' Rachel said flatly. *I'll make no excuses for you, Richard.* 'It was rarer to see him sober than otherwise.' They stood a moment longer in silence, each one watching Richard's pale corpse as though it might sit up and nod ruefully in confirmation of its fate. *If they're waiting for me to kiss him farewell, they'll wait for ever.* 'Have you told his father of this ill fortune?'

'No, madam. Do you know his whereabouts?'

'Yes.' Rachel turned her back on her late husband. 'I will tell him all that's happened. And I will be back to make arrangements for the burial,' she said to the undertaker.

'As it please ye, missus.' The old man nodded. With that Rachel fled the room, hurrying out of the cellar, along the alley and up onto Horse Street, where she gasped in a huge lungful of mucky air to dispel the scentless, stony pall of death.

She walked slowly to Duncan Weekes's rooms, carrying with her the worst tidings a parent can ever be given. She thumped on the street door until her knuckles and the heels of her hands were stinging, and eventually a grey-haired woman in a filthy dress, red-eyed and white-lipped, let her in with a scowl. Rachel went downstairs and knocked at Duncan's door for some minutes; there was no sound of movement from within, so she tried the latch. The door was not locked; it swung open with a creak.

Inside it was as frigid as ever, and shadows lurked in all the corners. There was no fire in the hearth; no candles or lamps alight. A sour smell hit her, and by the overturned hearthside chair she saw a splatter of vomit on the floor. Rachel looked towards the bed with a mounting, stifling sense of the inevitable. Duncan Weekes lay there, huddled under his blankets so that only his face was showing. He was as still and lifeless as his son. Rachel crouched beside him.

'Mr Weekes? Father?' she said, though she knew it was futile. The old man's eyes were screwed tight shut, brows beetled and drawn together; his mouth was slightly open, lips blackened. The old woman who'd opened the door for Rachel appeared behind her, and peered over her shoulder at the corpse.

'The barrel fever, no doubt,' she said, with a sniff. 'Or mayhap the old man's friend. I've heard his churchyard cough, these past few nights.'

Absently, Rachel tucked the blankets tighter around Duncan's chin. *I knew he was sick, yet I did nothing, and let it slip from my mind.* 'I'm so sorry, Mr Weekes,' she whispered, stricken. *There are no kindnesses.*

'I've a boy you can send for the undertaker, if you've a penny for him,' said the old woman.

'Very well.' Rachel found a coin in her pocket. 'He is Duncan Weekes, and his son Richard Weekes lies with the undertaker behind Horse Street.'

'I know the one.'

'Fetch the same man, if you please. Father and son can lie together awhile. I'd always hoped to reunite them.'

'Fate will play these cruel japes on us,' said the woman, nodding. The coin vanished into the palm of her bony hand and Rachel left, walking away with a feeling that her head was swelling; it felt light, and strange. *How truly I spoke, when I said that I had no one.*

More than ever before, Rachel felt apart from everything and everyone else. She walked for a long time, and felt invisible; as though she was less real in the world than the people she passed. *I could vanish without trace; just like Abi. Just like Alice.* She felt like a boat with its line cut, and nothing to keep the current from tugging her away. She was laden and heavy with guilt and sorrow, so much that she could hardly feel anything. Just the ringing echo of it all in the big empty space inside her.

The city closed in on itself for the night. Lamps were lit and shutters closed; the doors of inns swung to against the weather, and people hurried towards their homes, not dallying in the street with the drizzle and the leaching cold. *These three days have been the longest I have ever lived*. Rachel tried to imagine what life would be like from that moment; with no husband, no family; no visits to Jonathan or causes to hope. *Will the Suttons still be my friends? I am a threat to them, and the captain blames me for Jonathan's fall*. It seemed impossible that she should be expected to continue, to bear it all. Weary and shivering, she reached Abbeygate Street and climbed the steps. Inside there would be no welcoming warmth or light for her; yet however sad a place it was, it was her only home. As Rachel pushed the door a scrap of pale paper caught her eye, fluttering across the boards like a tiny ghost. She bent and picked up the note, returning to the streetlamp outside for the light to read it by. She read it twice and then shut her eyes, sinking onto a nearby step as a storm of joy and relief took her balance. *Mr Alleyn asks for you. Come at once. Starling.*

* * *

The house at Lansdown Crescent was abuzz when Starling returned to it. It was only hours since she'd left to go to the lovers' tree, since she'd seen Dick there and learnt the truth, and then gone to share that burden with Rachel Weekes, yet it felt like weeks. In the sudden bustle and thrum of gossip her absence seemed to have gone unnoticed, and she slipped back into the stream without a ripple.

'There you are! You picked a ripe time to go off . . . pass

me that beef bone, and get grinding some salt, will you?' said Sol Bradbury when Starling appeared in the kitchen. Starling cocked her head curiously at the cook. She didn't sound troubled enough to have had news of Jonathan's death. Obediently, Starling picked up the heavy blade bone, still with some shreds of roast meat upon it, and took it to the cook. Sol dropped it into a huge pan of water on the stove, moving neatly aside of the splash.

'Why?' said Starling. 'What's going on?'

'What's going on! The master has cracked his head and lies abed all insensible, and the mistress is running half mad, and swears if she sees Mrs Weekes again she'll have her guts for garters. Dorcas keeps fainting at the sight of the blood . . . The doctor's with Mr Alleyn now, and I'm to brew up a beef broth for when he wakes . . .'

'He is not dead?' Starling's heart gave a jolt that left her breathless.

'Dead? Heavens, no! What, girl — is this not trouble enough that you go asking for more?'

'No. I only . . .' Unthinkingly, Starling turned for the stairs and went up.

She hardly spared a glance for a rotund man who was letting himself out of Jonathan's rooms; she recognised him vaguely as one of the many doctors who had come and gone over the years, having done nothing to help with the pains in Jonathan's head. Inside, the room was brighter than she'd ever seen it before — candles had been lit in every wall sconce, and along the hearth; on the desk and nightstand. The room was soaked in the golden glow of them all, the deep shadows banished; and as if a spell had been broken, the rooms that had frightened away a succession of housemaids were made commonplace. Untidy, cluttered with unusual things, but no longer threatening. *It is only secrets that scare us. It is not knowing; it is the things we cannot see.* Jonathan lay at the centre of this flood of light in the far chamber, pale skin and dark hair stark against his pillows, and a red stain seeping slowly through a bandage around his head. Starling went to stand at the foot of the bed, and then noticed Josephine, sitting in a low chair at the far side of it. Hatred scorched through her, and then her mistress spoke.

'He will not die, the doctor says. He has broken his wrist, but the blow to his head was not grave, only bloody. He will not die. He will wake.' Josephine spoke to nobody; she spoke to the room and the Gods, to all and none. She spoke to tell fate how things would go, and to dare it to deal otherwise. Starling looked at her for a long moment. Josephine's eyes were wide in an immobile face. She watched her son with steadfast intensity. *She loves him, and yet it was her doing – the thing that has grieved him most all his life. And she knows it.* Starling expected to feel angry, but did not. *She took Alice. She did it full knowing, and has hidden it ever since. She has let me serve her, and suffer her father's lusts as I waited for news of Alice. She has fed me lies.* All this she reminded herself, but still the anger would not come, and she was left to search for reasons why not. *Because that beast was her father, and he took from her as much as from me. Because she is Jonathan's mother, and right now she is as full of fear as a person can be.*

'I can pity you, but I do hate you also,' she murmured. Josephine Alleyn blinked and turned to look at her.

'What did you say?'

Starling was silent for a moment. She remembered Rachel Weekes's fear for her, and her own desire to come and wreak vengeance on this woman. But Jonathan was not dead, and so everything had changed. *I no longer have nobody. I have him.* She returned her gaze to the man in the bed and probed her heart to see what remained, now that her misplaced hatred had blown away like smoke. She remembered him laughing at her antics the day they swam in the river at

Bathampton, before he went to Spain and everything changed. A shard of grief cut through her then, for all they had lost since that day – both of them.

'I'm glad he will recover,' she said. Josephine Alleyn looked at her son again and seemed to forget what Starling had said before. She reached out and took his hand, tenderly, gently.

'He is all I have,' she murmured, and Starling understood then that Alice would be avenged, and all the grief of her death would be paid for at last. *Because I have much to tell him, when he wakes. And then you will lose your son, Mrs Alleyn.*

Jonathan showed no signs of waking. Josephine remained with him for a long time before retiring to bed, demanding to be fetched back if there was any change. Starling volunteered to stay with him then, as the long night crept by, one breath at a time. She sat vigil, and she waited, and she did not sleep. Faintly, she heard the long-case clock in the hallway strike two, and at that exact moment she remembered that Rachel Weekes had returned Alice's last letter to Jonathan. She got up so quickly that her chair tipped over and clattered to the floor, and she froze, ears straining for any sign that the noise had roused Josephine. None came. Jonathan's long black coat was hanging from the corner of the armoire, and she crept over to it, feeling for the stiffness of paper in the pockets. When she found it she returned to the bedside on soft feet, righted the chair and watched Jonathan's face for a long time. She couldn't shake the suspicion that he would guess what she was about, wake and snatch the letter from her or chase her from the room with curses; like all those times before when she'd searched for this exact piece of paper. *No. He is innocent. I must keep reminding myself of this.* With a slow inward breath to steady herself, she opened the letter.

My Dearest Jonathan

Oh, why do you not write? I have a suspicion about it. I have written so many times, these past weeks, and remain desperate to hear from you. You may be dead, injured, lost; or you may have had word from your mother, and shun me. I have no way of knowing, my love! It is cruel. Here is what I suspect — however it distresses me to write it. Since always we have handed our letters to the yardman here at the farm, to take up to the coaching inn and send on for us. Yesterday I walked along to the bridge and I saw our yardman hand what looked to be my letter to a scruffy lad, who made off with it. I am quite sure the boy was not in any way connected to the mail or the inn. Can it be that none of my letters have reached you, Jonathan? But this one will — I have a plan for it.

I went to Box and I met your mother. I know I ought not to have, I was not invited. I did not think to meet her, I sought only Lord Faukes, to find out if there was word of you. But it was your mother I met, Mrs Josephine Alleyn, so I confessed my reasons for going to her. She said such things, Jonathan! She was so angry, and so cruel. She hates me, and gave me news of my parentage that appalled me. And if this was not enough, soon afterwards I was given to understand why she might hate me even more — the coachman told me such things. Such dark, dark things. I will not relate them in this letter, in case it too goes astray. It was in my earlier letters to you — the ones which have gone unanswered. Forgive me for it, dearest Jonathan. In my distress, I did not stop to think. The words came pouring out of my pen, and now these tidings are out in the world somewhere, and could do you harm. Forgive me. The coachman was in his cups, and yet . . . and yet, he seemed so sure. He told me what even Mrs Alleyn feared to. Oh, I am an abomination! I am accursed. Do not come home to them, Jonathan — they are liars, and not what you think they are; and if you must come back, do not come to me. The pain of seeing you would be too great.

There is another thing. A man has appeared, with rough manners but a charming nature. He courts me as though his very life depended upon it. I know his face — I have seen it before, I'm sure of it. But I cannot think where; he is not from Bathampton. He begs to marry me, to take me away to Bristol or wherever I choose to live. I have done all I can to dissuade him but still he comes again and again to visit me, and says he will die without me. I thought — my darling, I must confess it — I thought for one moment, one dark day, that I should go with him — that I should vanish, and be sure you never had to set eyes on me again. For one moment, I thought it. Lord Faukes has not visited here since I went to Box. I feel some judgement coming, hanging over me like the sword of Damocles. So for one moment I thought I should go with this charming charlatan. For charlatan he is. But I could never do it, my love. I could never let you think I had forsaken you, for once I had gone they would surely tell you lies about me. Oh, how can I write such things about your family and about the man I have known and loved all my life as my benefactor? That seems a cruel joke now. My life has been a cruel joke, from the very beginning.

I am an abomination, my love. But I can call you that no more. Our love is an abomination. I feel my heart breaking, Jonathan. It is tearing in two, and I do not know if I will survive it. But you and I must remain apart, now and for ever. I will stay here and await my fate, once they have decided it. And if we never see each other again then let me swear it now — I loved you truly, and will love you ever.

One who is always, but can never be, yours.
Alice B

Starling read the letter right through twice; she held the paper to her lips, and breathed in any last lingering traces of her sister. *All these terrible things she knew, and never told me. All this she bore alone.* After the lovers' tree Alice had promised to keep no more secrets from her, but this one she had kept. *Did she think I would love her less? If she'd asked me to run away with her and live in a cave, I'd have done it.* Starling sat in her chair and wept quietly for a while. Then, as dawn seeped its grey light into the room, she felt a flicker of urgency. He had to wake, so that she could speak to him before Josephine returned. He had to hear what she would say without interruption, or denial. The house was silent; not even Dorcas was up yet, clonking the shutters or riddling cinders from the ashes. Starling leant over the bed, and reached out to touch Jonathan's uninjured arm.

'Sir,' she said, her voice a dry whisper. 'Mr Alleyn, you must wake.' She shook the limb gently. It was warm and limp. *What if they are wrong, and he will not wake?* She grabbed up his hand and shook harder, then leant forwards and slapped her fingers against his cheek, fear making her rough with him. 'Wake, Jonathan! Alice needs you! I need you!'

Jonathan's brows pinched together. Without opening his eyes, he spoke.

'Peace, Starling! Your voice is like a hammer to my skull.' He was groggy and hoarse, but he didn't sound confused; he knew her. Starling exhaled in sharp relief.

'You've hurt your head, Mr Alleyn,' she said, as softly as she could. 'And your wrist. You fell, up on the common.'

'On the common?' Jonathan's eyelids fluttered open, and he gazed up at the swags of the bed canopy in thought. 'Yes. I remember. I was trying to find Mrs Weekes. She . . . I said something, and only afterwards realised how it must sound to her. She ran off into the fog . . .'

'I know. She is quite well. That is – well, there is much to tell you.'

'You know? How do you know?' He turned his head to face her and winced at the pain of movement.

'We have become friends, she and I. I think. But listen now – can you listen? Are you awake? There are things I must tell you.' She stood and looked down at him, and Jonathan met her gaze with eyes full of apprehension.

'I am awake,' he said carefully.

So, in a quiet voice, Starling told him all of it. She told him about Dick Weekes and the lovers' tree; about Duncan Weekes and what he had seen and told to Alice the day she went to Box; about Rachel Weekes and why Dick had married her; and then everything Dick had said before he went into the river. Jonathan listened to it all without moving a muscle or making a sound; almost without any reaction at all, other than a look of pain that built like gathering clouds. When she finished she held her breath and waited.

'Am I to be happy at these tidings, Starling?' he said, at last.

'Who could be? I speak only as one who has mourned her, and yearned to know of her fate, as you too have mourned and yearned. But this is the truth; we have it now, however black and bitter it may be.'

'And the man who killed her. Rachel Weekes's husband. He is dead. You're sure of this?'

'He is dead. Worthless wretch that he was.'

'Worthless wretch perhaps, but one who also mourned her, it seems, in his own inadequate way. A puppet of my mother's. I should disbelieve you at once, and cast you out.'

'You know I speak the truth.'

'For years you accused me, and were wholly convinced of *my* guilt.'

'I know. I . . . am sorry for that.'

'And now you are convinced that my mother was behind it all instead.'

'Your mother, and your grandfather – who I *know* was a bad man, and not at all what he seemed from the outside; though you loved him, and Alice did too.'

'You know he was bad? How do you know?' Jonathan said angrily.

'Because . . . because he had knowledge of me, sir, against my will. The day he came to tell me I would see Alice no more, and times again after that, before he died. I swear to you by the air I breathe, this is the very truth.' Jonathan turned away as though he couldn't bear to look at her; Starling saw a tear streak from his eye and vanish into the pillow. 'You don't know the full story of how he died, do you, sir?'

'He died of apoplexy,' Jonathan intoned. 'A sudden fit, and painless.'

'He died on top of Lynette, the new upstairs maid. She put up a good fight, and his heart gave out in his chest. And, Lord love you, sir, you were the only person in that house to mourn him.' *If he does not believe me, I will go from here and never see him again.* 'And . . . we would have known it all far sooner – we would have known that Alice was Faukes's child, if Captain Sutton had only given you back this letter at once.' She handed Alice's letter to him, and when he took it there was a tremor in his hand. 'It confirms all we have learned.'

She waited while he read it, and watched the muscles of his jaw moving under his skin, alive, and playing out the fight of his feelings.

'My mother has lied all her life; this I already knew.' His voice was forced out through clenched teeth.

'Sir . . .' Starling whispered. 'Sir, might I have one of her others? One of her other letters?'

'What?'

'I should dearly love to have one of Alice's letters to keep.

Just to have something of hers, you understand – some keepsake, touched by her hand.'

'I have no other letters of hers.' Jonathan frowned at her. 'What letters do you think I have?'

'All of hers – those that you wrote to her, and that she wrote to you. Yours she kept in a rosewood box in her room, and it vanished after she did. I thought you took it? Did you not take it, sir?'

'No.' Jonathan shook his head. 'I did not take it. And hers to me I . . . I destroyed.' His voice failed him for a moment. He shut his eyes. 'All of them. When I returned and thought that she . . . when I believed, at first, what I was told of her conduct. I wish I had not. I . . . I wish I had not.'

'But if you do not have them, who does? And what of the letter I took from you – one that you wrote to her, your last from Spain, from Corunna, soon before she died?'

'I know not who took them. My grandfather, I daresay. And that letter from Corunna . . . I never sent it. She never saw it. It stayed in my pocket all the way back to Brighton, and then came with me to Bathampton after I received her letter. I never got the chance to send it. I have always had it.'

'Oh.' Starling felt even this small hope fade away. 'Then that letter, recently returned to you by the Suttons, is all that exists of her; all there is to prove she ever lived, except what we remember.'

'Yes. Between them, they did obliterate her.' Jonathan looked down as he spoke, his brows shadowing his eyes, his mouth a bitter line. 'Fetch my mother to me now.' Silently, Starling obeyed.

She knocked softly on Mrs Alleyn's door and was summoned inside at once. The older woman's face was hollowed out by fatigue but her eyes lit with hope and happiness when Starling said that her son asked for her. *Enjoy this, madam – your last moment without blame*. Starling trailed her back to

Jonathan's room, and at the door Mrs Alleyn turned and frowned at her.

'Why do you pester my steps like a tantony pig? Go now and bring up the beef broth, and some tea. And perhaps a little brandy.'

'No, madam. I am no longer your servant,' said Starling, and the words made her heart lurch with fear and elation both. A thrill that made her fingertips tingle. *There. I have cast myself off.*

'What? How do you say *no*? Go at once, and—' Something in the way Starling stood, resolute, with her face full of knowing, pulled Josephine up short. 'Well then,' she said instead, incredulous, but almost resigned. The first sparks of a terrible anger were in her eyes. 'Be gone, if that is so,' she said. Starling shook her head.

'I serve your son now, madam. Only he can send me away.' Josephine glared at her a moment longer, and turned a little paler. *She must wonder what gives me the strength to speak to her thus. She must wonder, and she must know.* It was not anger that blanched her, Starling saw then. It was fear. She pitied Josephine again, for what was to come, and for what she had suffered, the hand she'd been dealt. *But it was none of Alice's fault. The chickens will always come home to roost, Bridget used to say.* With a haughty expression that looked like a mask Josephine carried on to her son's bedside, and Starling went behind her like a vengeful shadow.

Jonathan had edged his way up the bed, to sit straighter. There was a glaze of sweat on his face and he was breathing deeply, flaring his nostrils.

'Jonathan! Dear boy, it gladdens my heart to see you woken, and well,' said Josephine.

'Does it?' His eyes were hard.

'Of course . . . why would you think to question?'

'Because you lie, Mother. You have lied to everyone all

your life. You lied to my father, and you lied to the world, and you lie to me. You killed Alice Beckwith with a lie.' There was a frozen moment, and then Josephine shot Starling a glare like the jab of a knife.

'What has this wretch been saying to you? What lies has she told? She is a mendacious rat, a muckworm . . . I only kept her because your grandfather instructed me to . . .'

'Grandfather told you to keep her?' said Jonathan. He looked at Starling, and she had no need to say anything more. 'And there, I thought you had done it to be kind. How foolish of me.'

'Jonathan, what is the matter? Why do you attack me – I who have only ever loved and cared for you—'

'I don't think you're capable of love,' said Jonathan. He continued before Josephine could reply. 'Richard Weekes has told me everything.'

'What?'

'I said Richard Weekes has told me everything. Your little puppet, that foolish boy who thought himself in love with you, all those years ago. He has told me you sent him to coax Alice away. To make her betray me in any way he could. To goad her into an elopement . . . and when that failed he killed her. On *your* instruction.'

'Lies.' Josephine's voice was almost lost; it was a breathy whisper, crushed by fear and anger. 'It is lies. How dare he . . . how *dare* he!'

'Do you deny it?'

'Yes, I deny it! It is base lies, every word!'

'Alice came to visit you one day, to ask for news of me. You told her . . . you told her that she was my grandfather's bastard. Didn't you? You told her that and then sent her away. You thought that would end our connection to one another for ever. But Duncan Weekes met her that day too, and he told her something else. Do you know what else he told her?' said Jonathan. Josephine only watched him now, her face as still as stone. 'Do you know what your coachman saw, peeping through the curtains one day?'

'Enough! I will hear no more!' Josephine exploded. She threw up her hands as if to cover her ears; turned away from the bed and made for the door.

'Stay!' Jonathan shouted. 'Mother you will *stay*!' The command was like a whip crack which nobody might disobey. Starling shrank back from the bedside, seeking a friendly shadow in which to hide. There were none to be had. *This might break him.*

Josephine turned to face her son but came no nearer to the bed this time.

'Do you deny it?' said Jonathan. 'I knew you for a liar. I've always known. But I never knew what you lied about, until now. And I can forgive you for it . . . of course I can. Such evil . . . such a sinful blight on our family, on all my memories, it turns my stomach to even think it! But it was not your doing. Not that part.'

'I beg you, continue no further with this,' Josephine whispered.

'It's too late for that. I *know*. Do you deny it?' he demanded. In response, Josephine only stared at him, her eyes filling with tears. She took a long, shuddering breath.

'You were never meant to know about your grandfather! My whole life I have guarded against your *ever* knowing!' Her face distorted with horror.

'I understand. I understand that you sought to . . . protect me. From such ugliness. But now I must have the truth. Because I have tortured myself, Mother. Do you understand? I have tortured myself for the loss of Alice for twelve long years, trying to think what happened to make her leave me. I even thought, in dark moments . . . I even thought I'd killed her! When I came back after Corunna, and my mind was disordered . . . I have lain here and thought myself a murderer, and a madman, and all the time you knew! You *knew*!'

'She was an *abomination*.' This was more like a growl than speech; low and brutal, vicious with hatred. Starling's heart stirred at the sound of it. 'When she came to Box and asked for my father, I knew at once she was some issue of his. But the more I looked at her, the more I thought . . .' She trailed off, shaking her head. 'I knew. I knew who she was, then, though I thought that child had been dispatched at her birth, into the far north. I confronted my father. I made him tell me . . . Oh, Jonathan! It stilled my very blood that she still walked the earth! She was an *abomination*!'

'She was *innocent*! And I will have the truth, for her sake and for mine, because this house – all our fortune – is mine, and if I think you are lying to me, *ever* again, I swear I shall put you out and you will end your days a washerwoman, or begging in the hedges.'

'You would not! The *shame* of it!'

'I have no shame left, Mother; I'm surprised to hear that you do. So speak truly now, and let us have it all. Am I my father's son?'

'Yes. You are . . . perfect. You are my salvation—'

'Alice was your daughter. Yours . . . and my grand-father's.' To this, Josephine gave only more silence, as if she could not bear to say it.

Tears swelled in Jonathan's eyes and dropped onto his cheeks. 'But I loved her, Mother. I loved her so dearly. You knew that.'

'She wasn't meant to exist! I was . . . I was so young when she was born. She was taken away at once; it made me sick to even look on her, to hear her wail. Oh, I wanted to drown her right then! But my father told me she'd be adopted away and would never know of her parents. He told me this, and I believed him, like a fool. Then I married your father, and moved away from *him*, and . . . it was like waking from an evil dream. It was like life had started anew, and all the old tyranny could be forgotten. But my father, he . . . he *kept* her instead; he raised her up in comfort, close at hand. He *loved* her.' As she said *loved* Josephine's lips curled back from her teeth; she turned it into a curse word.

'You didn't know she was nearby, all those years? At Bathampton? You didn't know Grandfather saw her regularly – that he took me to meet her?'

'Of course I never knew! I would *never* have allowed it to continue – never! And he knew it . . . I was kept ignorant for that very reason. But when she . . . when she turned up at Box, asking after you, and after her *benefactor*, Lord Faukes . . . I knew then. I knew. My aunt Margaret had that milky pale hair, just the same as hers.' Josephine's eyes widened. 'Only look at the miniature downstairs in the parlour and you will see.'

'My grandfather was not at home when Alice called. You were cruel to her. Vicious to her.'

'She asked me for news of you, her beloved . . . that's what she called you. *He is my beloved, and this silence is more than I can bear.* When I realised what my father had done . . . that he'd let you *know* her . . . that he'd let that *creature* fall in love with you . . .' Josephine stopped and put her hands to her midriff, clamping her jaws tight shut. She looked like she might vomit; spitting up these truths that revolted her so. 'There was no quicker way to be rid of her, and to ensure she would renounce you, than to tell her. Half of the truth, if not all of it.'

'But why did you not stop there? She wrote to me to say we could never wed, she wrote to me of her broken heart. Why was that not the end of it? Why send Richard Weekes after her, why kill her?' Tears ran freely down Jonathan's face; he didn't seem to notice them.

'I didn't think . . . I didn't *think*, when I told her. Your grandfather was furious with me . . . because, of course, she would tell you. She would tell *you*. We could not allow it. I wanted her sent away – far away. I wanted her reduced to a hedge whore, where no one would listen to her!'

'She was *innocent*!' Jonathan's voice was raw.

'She was an *abomination*! But your grandfather . . .' Josephine shook her head incredulously. 'He loved her too well. What fools and devils are men! He loved her, and would hear of no harm coming to her. But he made sure she could send no letters to you, while he thought on what to do about her. But he must have known, right away, that there was no solution. None but mine. And from her letters, we learned what Duncan Weekes had told her – that treacherous old fool. And we learned that she would tell it all to you, the first chance she got.'

'So you sent Richard Weekes to ruin her.'

'And if she would not be ruined willingly, then he would take her against her will, carry her away somewhere and stain her for ever. But he did better than that, wastrel that he is. He did better than that.'

'*He did better*.' Starling echoed the words in the silence that followed, unaware at first that she'd spoken out loud. Jonathan and his mother turned to her abruptly, as though both had forgotten she was present. 'Even Dick Weekes wanted to please her, by the end. Did you know that? What he did to her tormented him, and I don't think he could forgive himself. That's the kind of person she was. Bridget always used to say that two wrongs never made a right, but that's what happened with Alice. You and Lord Faukes so wrong, and Alice coming out so right. God must have taken pity on such a cursed birth and decided to bless her in every other way. By the time he killed her, even Dick Weekes wanted her heart,' she said.

'I care not whether he loved or hated her. What he did that day was the only good and useful thing he ever did,' said Josephine.

'A good thing?' Jonathan whispered. 'You say he did a good thing?'

'It was for the best! Jonathan, my dearest boy – what life could you have had with her, knowing that you were so close related? Knowing that whatever feelings you had were a sin?'

'Whatever feelings? Let me tell you what they were, Mother, though you have ever refused to hear it: *I loved her*. I loved her like part of my own soul. Or perhaps its whole . . . perhaps she was my whole soul, for it felt as though she took it with her, when she went.'

'You must not say such things – the very words appal me! She was an *abomination*. She should never have lived, and did nothing better than to die!'

'We could have lived on in this knowledge, grievous as it was! We could have called each other cousin, and quashed all thought of passion, and been content to know that the other was safe. Even now, even having seen my anguish all these years, even after I have pulled my mind apart to guess her fate, even now you exult in her death?' Jonathan's eyes bored into his mother's, but Josephine never flinched.

'She should never have been born. She did nothing better in her life than to die.'

'Then I will see you no more. You are the abomination, Mother, and it is a symptom of your affliction that you cannot see it. Go away from me.'

'What do you mean? Jonathan, my son, I—'

'*Go away from me!*' His roar split the air like a thunder-clap. A tremor ran through Josephine; she tottered slightly, and raised one arm for balance. Then, with the immaculate care of one at a cliff edge, she turned and walked to the door.

'We will speak again,' she said, barely audibly, on the threshold. Then she left.

For a long time Starling didn't dare move or make a sound. She had never seen such anger. She stayed where she was, in the corner of the bedroom with her back to the wall, and listened to the blood thumping in her ears. Behind it, the quiet sounds of the house awakening could be heard; the opening and closing of doors, the scrape of an iron in a fireplace. From outside came the keening of seagulls as they laid claim to the city's rubbish. Their voices were high and woebegone. Gradually, the heaving of Jonathan's chest decreased; he grew calmer, and sat under a pall of such deep sadness that it was almost tangible. *If Alice was here she would cradle your head, and stroke your hair, and murmur of better things until your heart was less sore.* But Starling didn't dare. After ten minutes or so, Jonathan put his fingertips to his eyes and rubbed them hard.

'Starling,' he said quietly.

'Yes, sir?' She suddenly felt almost shy of him, ashamed of everything that had gone on between them since Alice disappeared. Jonathan looked at her with red-rimmed eyes.

'I feel as though my head might explode,' he muttered.

'You are injured, sir,' she said.

'Yes. But it's not that. Will you . . .' He paused, and for a moment seemed almost as shy as she. 'If you sent word that I wished it, do you think Rachel Weekes would come to see me?'

'I am certain of it, sir,' Starling replied.

* * *

There was no answer to her ring at the front door of the Alleyns' house, so Rachel let herself in through the servant's entrance, bold as brass, and went all the way up the back stairs to the second floor. She felt like a thief, a trespasser intruding where she didn't belong, but she had Starling's note clenched tight in her palm. She carried it like a talisman from which hope and courage flowed. As she came through the door in the panelling and onto the landing, she froze. Mrs Alleyn was standing in front of the naked window at the end of the corridor, as still as a carving, with her back to Rachel and her face to the black glass. She must have heard Rachel's approach, but gave no sign of it, and Rachel's exclamation of surprise died on her lips. It was still dark enough outside that Josephine could have seen little but her own reflection, staring back at her. Rachel saw the ghostly echo of herself in the glass. *My own image*, she thought, sadly, *nothing more*. Suddenly, her heart tumbled into the pit of her stomach. Jonathan's mother stood too still, was too removed. *Has he died after all?*

'Mrs Alleyn!' she cried out, before she could stop herself. Josephine turned slowly. Her face was empty of expression; she didn't seem surprised to see Rachel, and she said nothing to her. After this moment of dispassionate study, she turned away again. Rachel went a few steps closer and stopped right outside Jonathan's rooms. 'Your son has asked for me, Mrs Alleyn,' she said. 'Is he within? Mrs Alleyn?'

'If he sent for you then go to him, and leave me be.' Josephine's voice was as cold and raw as a winter wind. With a shiver, Rachel knocked on Jonathan's door and slipped through it at once.

The shutters in Jonathan's rooms were closed, the fire was burning merrily and candles lit all the walls. Rachel was temporarily bewildered by the abundance of light and warmth where there had only ever been darkness and a stony cool before. There was a smell of beeswax, smoke and spiced wine.

'Starling? Is that you? Is there still no word?' Jonathan's voice came from the bedroom. Rachel tried to answer him but joy stole the words. She walked in silence to the doorway where she saw him, sitting up in bed in a crumpled white shirt, one arm bound up with a splint. There was a long, stitched cut on his forehead, couched in bruises. He looked up and saw her, and for a long time he did not speak. He took a slow breath, and his eyes shone.

'Mrs Weekes,' he said, at last. 'You have come.'

'Could you doubt that I would?' she said.

'When last I saw you, you were running from me.'

'I . . . I was upset. Everything you'd said . . . my sister, and Alice. I thought . . . I thought . . .'

'I know what you thought.'

'And do you know what I now know?'

'Yes. Starling has told me all.'

'Then you two are reconciled. I am glad.' Rachel swallowed painfully.

'Reconciled? I suppose we are. She and I should have been united in all of this, through all these years. It was only mistakes and suspicions; only lies and silence that drove a wedge between us. But to Alice she was a sister. So to me, perhaps, she should have been the same. In my own grief and disorder I never considered Starling's plight, but she needed my protection. It was wrong of me. Selfish.'

'In times of ordeal, such omissions can be forgiven. She will forgive you, I know. That you loved and never harmed Alice will be enough for her.'

'And what of you, Mrs Weekes? Can you forgive?'

'I have nothing to forgive you for. I accused you, wrongly. I led you into danger, and injury. I should ask rather that you forgive me.'

'But I am a killer. You were right about that.' Jonathan

sounded grim, sickened. Rachel walked closer to his bedside, and he didn't take his eyes from her.

'How are you? The wound on your head looks quite . . . bad,' she said. Jonathan grimaced.

'It is not grave. It should be bandaged still, but the heat and pressure of it were too much, and I tore it off. In truth, my head thuds like cannon fire.'

'I should go, and let you rest. Sleep and make yourself well.'

'Seeing you makes me well,' said Jonathan. 'Don't go yet.' Rachel smiled, but then it faltered.

'My husband is the one. All this time, he is the one who killed your Alice,' said Rachel. Jonathan looked down at his hands.

'I know. But he was not the only one. I . . . her heart. Did you know that Alice could not see colour? At least, not all colours. She tried to hide it from me, but I knew. As if a flaw like that could have made me think less of her. She was colour blind, and her heart was weak. She often used to grow faint if she got overexcited, or was shocked by something. Starling said . . . Starling said that was what killed her, in the end. Dick Weekes only hit her, and her heart could not cope with the fear.' Anger made his voice shake.

'Yes. She says Mr Weekes claimed not to have intended to take her life.'

'Yet take it he did, but he was not solely to blame. You have seen the books on my shelves, Mrs Weekes. I told you that at one time I studied medicine, and anatomy, in order to . . . understand how human beings work. What drives us – where the soul resides, and if it can be lost.'

'Yes, I remember.'

'I have read that in unions where people are . . . too closely related, their offspring will often miscarry before birth, or be born weak, and flawed. And die young. It is the same in animal husbandry. Stock books are kept carefully, to ensure such consanguinity does not occur.' He stopped with a gentle shake of his head.

'You mean to say that . . . that Alice's constitution was a result of her . . . unusual birth?'

'It is just as I once said to you, Mrs Weekes. We are merely animals, after all, subject to the same rules that govern all of God's creatures.'

'Then you know of your grandfather's . . . relationship to Alice?' She gazed at him searchingly. He looked up, his face stricken.

'His, and my mother's. And so mine too. Starling has told me everything.' Jonathan's brows pulled together, which made him wince.

'*Everything?* That was no kindness on her part!' Rachel cried. 'She need not have—'

'Yes, there was need. It is better that I know,' Jonathan interrupted.

'What will you do?' Rachel whispered.

'Do? About this crime against Alice? I see precious little that I can do. The only one who could have declared my mother's part in it is dead, Starling says. Drowned in the river.'

He hesitated then, and seemed to remember that it was Rachel's husband he spoke so heedlessly about. 'Forgive my callousness,' he said.

'There is nothing to forgive. He is dead. I . . . I have seen him with my own eyes.'

'My condolences, Mrs Weekes,' Jonathan said cautiously. Rachel thought for a moment.

'I . . . I do not grieve,' she confessed, in a small voice. *I am set free.*

'His father, Duncan Weekes, might speak against my mother, if I asked him to. If a case against her was to be made. He knows things about . . . my family . . . that nobody else knew, until these last few days. You are grown quite close to him, are you not? Do you think he would . . .' Jonathan frowned. 'But then, who would take his word, poor and drunk as he is, over my mother's?'

'Duncan Weekes lies next to his son. Sickness and poverty have taken him.' As Rachel spoke, guilty tears crowded her vision.

'And for him you do mourn. Poor creature,' Jonathan murmured.

'He was a good man, beneath his weaknesses and sins. A poor creature indeed.'

'Then,' said Jonathan, pausing to think, 'then there is nothing to be done. I will see my mother no more. That will have to be punishment enough for her.'

'She waits outside. She haunts your door like a sentry.'

'I will not see her.'

'What she did . . . what she did, she did to protect you.'

'And to protect herself. To hide her sins. You cannot ask me to forgive her.'

'I ask nothing. I only say . . . I only say that to have family is a blessing, and one not to be sloughed off without due thought.'

'A mixed blessing at best, Mrs Weekes. And this day mine feels more like a curse. You have a deeply forgiving nature, Mrs Weekes, this I have come to learn. But you should not forgive indiscriminately. People must pay for their crimes.'

'Indeed.' Rachel studied him for a moment. 'You have paid for yours, Mr Alleyn. I have met Cassandra Sutton.'

Jonathan shut his eyes for a moment, and looked ill.

'Starling . . . Starling said as much,' he said. 'But you cannot forgive me. You do not know what I did.'

'I know the outcome! A live, healthy child—'

'The child of a murdered woman! A child robbed of her mother.'

'Cassandra Sutton has a mother, and a father. No — you must listen. She has a mother and father who love her very much. She is bright, and sweet, well cared for. She has been robbed of *nothing*. Her current happiness is all your doing, and you should be proud.'

'*Proud?*' Jonathan laughed then, a taut and empty sound. 'There is nothing from that time, from that war, of which I can be proud.'

'I know how you came to rescue Cassandra. Captain Sutton said—'

'Captain Sutton does not know. Captain Sutton was not there, in that church. What occurred was between the child's mother, and me. And you cannot forgive me, because you *cannot* know.'

'Then . . . tell me, Mr Allcyn. Tell me.' Jonathan stared at her, and for a while she thought he would not speak. *He must. This is the only way.* She suddenly knew that this was the final step in a long and wearing climb; that by taking this last step, the path would go easier from there on. *Let it be so.* She sat down in the chair at his bedside and leaned forward, reaching for his hand. 'You must tell me about Badajoz,' she said.

'Badajoz.' The air left Jonathan's chest, streaming out like surrender. He shut his eyes again, and then he spoke.

He spoke of the three years of war after his return from Bathampton, leaden-hearted because Alice had gone. Three years in which he lived by rote, and fought with silent, grim distraction. After the flight from Corunna the French had flooded back in to retake Portugal, but in April 1809 Sir Arthur Wellesley returned to Lisbon to take command, and the French were driven back towards the Spanish border once more. Jonathan and his fellow officers struggled to keep order in the ranks; the men were restless, and disobedient.

After battle they turned thuggish and cruel. Jonathan noticed the empty look in their eyes and knew he had it too; the self-same brutishness. Wellesley called the men scum, and rabble. He hanged them for plundering, but it did no good. Jonathan was popular with the rank and file of his company; he understood their anger and their fear, the way they were losing themselves. He did not reprimand them for acting like animals, when the war required them to be animals.

And yet the heart of him looked on, and recoiled in horror from the bloodshed and the pain and the wanton destruction. At Talavera, after they'd pursued the French through a burnt and ruined landscape into Spain, he was with the light dragoons as they charged headlong into a hidden ditch. He was catapulted from his horse as it fell, and heard the crunch as the beast's two forelegs snapped. He had not named the animal – he hadn't named any of his horses since Suleiman – but still its screams cut through his battle fog like knives. He didn't blink as he put his pistol to the horse's head and pulled the trigger. The British and Portuguese were outnumbered by almost two to one at Talavera, but they won what would be proclaimed as a glorious victory on the sides of mail coaches at home. The battlefield was almost four miles long, and two miles deep. Towards the end of it a grass fire started, racing across the parched ground and burning many of the wounded alive. Scores of those that did not burn died of thirst instead, under the merciless Spanish sun. Jonathan searched through fields of crack-mouthed, black-tongued corpses to find Captain Sutton, who'd been knocked insensible by a clod of earth thrown up by artillery fire. Jonathan took him into the shade of a cork tree, and sat with him there until his wits returned. A wounded French rifleman dragged himself over to share the shade; he shared his water and his tobacco tin with Jonathan as well, and made remarks about the heat and the search for food, as they sat with their eyes stinging with the smoke of their burning comrades.

After that great battle, Wellesley was made Lord Wellington. French troops arrived in Spain in ever increasing numbers, but Spanish guerrillas and Portuguese partisans were everywhere, slitting the throats of sentries and harrying smaller troop movements. Back and forth the advantage went, an ebb and flow of men across the Spanish border like the sea around a mid-tide mark. By the end of the year the men were more afraid for their next meal than they were of battle. The looting and pillaging continued, as did the hangings. As the autumn grew old, starvation circled them like carrion crows. Jonathan punched new holes in his belt with the tip of his sabre when it would no longer fasten tight around his shrinking middle. The two warring sides sent out foraging parties to look for food. These men met frequently, and greeted each other courteously, sharing tips and insights into the terrain, into water supplies and edible plants. Jonathan wondered what would happen if they all, on both sides, just declared peace and refused to fight any more. The thought was so bittersweet that Captain Sutton found him crying like a child one day, sitting cross-legged on the muddy ground with autumn rain soaking him.

'Up, and be doing, Major Alleyn,' the captain told him kindly. 'You're that sodden, the men might think that you weep. It will do them no good to think it.' He put an arm around Jonathan's bony ribs and half carried him out of sight of the men, who were carousing – dancing to a fiddle and pipe with a kind of desperate levity. It was the tenth of October, 1810; King George III's birthday in the fiftieth year of his reign. They'd butchered a donkey that the retreating French had hamstrung and left to die. Jonathan ate the roasted meat alone in his tent, and thought of Alice, and of Suleiman.

At the battle of Fuentes de Oñoro, in spring the following year, a truce had to be called at the end of the day so that both sides could clear the bodies from the ruined village. There were so many that the narrow streets were near impassable. Jonathan stepped on an outflung hand by mistake, looked down and saw that it was tiny, no bigger than a woman's or a child's. The arm it belonged to, and the rest of the body, was buried beneath others, five or six deep, so he never had to see who had owned the hand – the delicate finger bones he'd ground beneath his boot heel.

They moved on to Badajoz, a fortified town in a strategically important location near the Portuguese border. Betrayed by its own governor, Badajoz had fallen into French hands, and been heavily garrisoned. The allies laid siege, digging in as winter approached. There was heavy, relentless rain. Jonathan had seen wounded soldiers burn to death after battle, now he saw them drown in waterlogged mud. The men, hard-bitten and proven, grew idle and restless over that winter of 1811. They occupied themselves with scorpion baiting, cock fighting and horse racing; with picking the fleas out of their clothes and bedding and hair; with whoring and wrestling and hunting for game; with watching friends sicken and die from festering wounds and outbreaks of a plague-like sickness.

Jonathan came down with a bout of fever, and lay listless and sweating in his tent for five days. Captain Sutton visited often, wet his lips with wine, and tried to cheer him with funny stories about the tomfoolery of the men, but Jonathan could not raise a smile for him. In their japes and their games and their contests he saw the lust for violence, coiled inside each one of them like madness; like embers that might burst into flames in a second, and consume the last of the man's humanity. These were the men who were invested to retake Badajoz on the twelfth of March, 1812. These men made brutal by all the fear and pain, hunger and violence; made brave and savage by their own suffering, and half mad by all they had seen. Jonathan looked over them as they approached the city, and he feared them. Lord Wellington might see a rabble, but he saw a pack of wolves, liable to turn on each other, on their officers, on him. Captain Sutton kept close to him as the siege was set and the barrage began. Jonathan felt his friend's eyes upon him, measuring. He wondered what madness the captain saw in him; whether he saw the fear and sorrow and the yearning to hide away from it all, or whether he saw the urge to kill and destroy, to vent his rage on all around him. Both were in him, and when he pictured Alice's face it fed both sides of him equally – the surrender, and the fury.

The artillery barrage succeeded in making three narrow breaches in the town's crenellated walls. The French waited inside in their thousands; any attempt to storm the breaches would result in a slaughter. Wellington could see it; Jonathan could see it; the lowliest foot soldier could see it. Nevertheless, the command came for the attack to begin at ten in the evening, under cover of darkness and with the French unprepared. But some sound was heard; some inadvertent tip-off betrayed them. The French set fire to the body of a British soldier and hurled it out from the walls to cast light on the advancing men, and as easily as that the element of surprise was lost. The British charged, right into a series of traps the French had set for them. They were blown up by mines, drowned in flooded ditches. They were impaled on iron spikes, and on makeshift barriers of sword blades; the momentum of men behind ensuring the death of the vanguard. Those that reached the breaches were slain in their hundreds, and all the while the French inside hurled out insults and taunts; goading them, laughing.

'*You must not laugh at us!*' Jonathan roared as he came

close enough to the walls to hear it. He was standing on the bodies of the fallen; he was sprayed with flying blood, drenched in sweat. He knew that the beast in them all was awake, and that the laughter of their enemies ran like fire in their blood; a red frenzy that turned them from men into something both more and less. It kept the attack alive; it stormed the walls, and pressed into the city; it opened the breaches to the onrushing men; and after two hours in which nearly five thousand of the allied besiegers were slaughtered, it sealed the fate of the city of Badajoz.

The wolves were unleashed, and nothing could rein them in. They were the sum total of all they had seen and suffered, all they had been required to do and to bear. They were a vision of mankind stripped of all decency and pity, and they were hell-bent on revenge. Women were raped, and raped again. Children, even crawling infants, were kicked around for sport, stuck with bayonets. Men were tortured, killed, torn to pieces, be they French invader or Spanish resident. Men looted, men desecrated, men ravaged and pillaged; men turned on one another and fought to the death over spoils as trifling as a piece of food or a bottle of wine. Over the right to rape a woman before she died, or afterwards. Their officers could not hope to control them. Their officers dared not try, for fear of being torn apart themselves; the men were blind drunk on brandy and wine and blood.

Jonathan wandered through it all without seeing it, for the first twelve hours or so. He found a dark cellar, entirely empty; lay down on the dirt floor and slept a while. He did not feel as though he possessed his own body; he felt like a ghost, drifting unseen amongst it all. Only when he awoke and rose did he notice the pain in his leg, and the way it would not take his weight. He looked down and found a chunk of wood thrust straight through his calf. The exit wound was a chaos of black clotted blood and shards of grey bone. The sight caused no emotion in him at all. He stumbled out into the violated streets. A cloudy day had dawned, but the light brought no respite to the degradation of Badajoz. The men went about in packs, under no command. Jonathan did not speak to any, nor interfere with the things he saw. He did not dare, since to interfere was to see it, to take it in; and to see it was to run the risk of losing himself for ever.

But Captain Sutton found him, and brought him to a group of five men, the sparse remnants of his company, who had banded together for safety from the pillage.

'Thank God you're alive, Major! I had feared the worst. If anyone can restore some order here, it's you, sir.' Captain Sutton splinted up Jonathan's shattered leg, tearing strips from his own uniform to bind it. 'But I should get you to the surgeons first. Come,' he said.

'No!' Jonathan cried. He remembered the surgeons: the stink of rum and bile and open bowels; the mound of severed limbs that piled up outside the window of a Talavera convent where they'd set up their tables. Huge black moths, circling the field lamps. The pain in his leg was coming in waves now, a rising beat of agony, but he would not submit to the surgeons. 'No! I can stand. I can walk. Let us bring a halt to this madness.'

'Are you sure, sir?' Sutton wasn't convinced, but Jonathan stood, using an abandoned musket as a crutch.

Talking had returned Jonathan to himself, however reluctantly. Nausea bubbled in his gut as they moved cautiously through the ruins of the town; smoke skirled around them from a hundred different fires. They broke up fights and issued orders that were sometimes heeded; more often ignored. They hastened the passing of soldiers and citizens who had been left in dreadful agony, deliberately, and with no hope of survival. They pulled a man from a barrel of brandy only to find that he had drowned himself in it, and was beyond reprimand. They fired their guns to scatter a group of men squabbling like magpies over the gilded treasure from a plundered church. And as the hours passed, Jonathan's heart grew sicker and sicker with it all. He knew, with complete certainty, that not one man of them would ever feel himself possessed of his whole soul again. They must lose a part of it, or risk the corruption spreading to every corner. All too often, it was clear that this had already happened.

It was the woman's screams that drew them. Many women wept noisily, or prayed, or were mute or unconscious as they were violated. This woman screamed with such anger and outrage that Jonathan flinched away from the sound. He did not want to witness what would cause her to make such sounds. Grim-faced, his small band of men rushed towards the church from which her voice came echoing. She was at the far end of the aisle, near the dais where the altar sat. It was a small church with a pretty rose window high in the wall, its glass miraculously intact, lighting the scene of torment playing out below in shades of blue and gold. A group of ten or so British soldiers surrounded her, and had been with her for some time by the looks of it. She had been stripped naked, and struggled to rise even though her lower body was awash in blood. Each time she got to her knees she was kicked back down, and as Jonathan approached a man climbed on top of her, and began his work again. She screeched with that wild rage, and the hair stood up on Jonathan's arms.

'*Enough!*' he bellowed. He levelled his pistol at the man with his breeches down. 'You will desist, there. That is an order!'

For a startled moment the men all turned to look at him and were silent; and Jonathan's heart, which was speeding so fast that he couldn't feel its separate beats, filled with the hope that they would obey him. But then the one who appeared to be their leader, a big man with close-cropped hair and a pocked face, snarled.

'You can buss the blind cheeks, *sir*. We've paid with our blood, and now we'll have our sport.' Behind him, the woman's face, which for a moment had mirrored Jonathan's hope, crumpled into desperation again.

'I order you to leave her be,' said Jonathan, but the hand that held the pistol had begun to shake, and even though Captain Sutton and their few loyal men stood to either side of him, he felt the shreds of his authority evaporate. He put a bullet in the lead man, but his aim was off; the wound was in the shoulder, and did not fell him. And then the two groups fell upon each other like bitter enemies, not like the comrades they'd so recently been. Jonathan and Captain Sutton were outnumbered, but their small band fought with right on their side, and for once that seemed to count for something. Nevertheless, most of the woman's rescuers fell to her tormentors before it was done. One of them, a lad no more than seventeen, was driven off down the aisle with his foe hard behind him, a hunting knife gripped in his hand. Moments later Captain Sutton went the same way, pursuing two others who fled before him. Jonathan was left alone to fight the lead man, the man he had shot, with his bare hands.

They fought gracelessly, grappling at one another, Jonathan's crippled leg offset by the bullet wound in the other man, which spattered blood onto both of them. His opponent was bigger and stronger, but he was also drunk, and Jonathan's slim frame belied the wiry hardness of his muscles. The lead man got his hands around Jonathan's neck and would have crushed his windpipe if Jonathan hadn't gouged a thumb into the bullet hole in his shoulder, pushing until he found where the bullet had lodged against the bone, still burning hot. The man roared and thrust him away, so violently that Jonathan staggered and went to his knees. In front of him was another man's musket, spent, the bayonet stained with blood. As he stood, Jonathan grabbed it by the muzzle and spun about, swinging it as hard as he could. The butt caught the pock-faced man across the side of his head with a hollow knock and a splintering sound; he dropped like an empty sack, and didn't move. The sudden silence roared in Jonathan's ears. He felt as though his blood was simmering in his veins, poisoned. As he turned to leave, a scuffle of movement behind him jolted him into action again. Hands closed on his arm, and he wheeled around, thrusting blindly with the bayonet. He felt it meet resistance; felt that resistance part around the sharp steel. Then he looked down into the Spanish woman's face, and knew himself a murderer.

She made a strange gulping sound, as if trying to swallow the air instead of breathing it. Jonathan knelt and tried to hold her up as she sank forwards, to stop her pushing herself further onto the blade. He didn't dare pull it free; he'd seen that done too many times, and knew the spurt of blood and rapid death it would bring. In his horror and shame he tried desperately to think of a way to save her, a way to undo it, when he knew there was none. He turned her carefully onto her back, and knelt with his arms around her, cradling her naked body. There was blood on her breasts; bruising on her neck. Her face was long and hard-boned, but her mouth was beautiful, sensuous and full. She tried to speak, but could not. She gulped at the air some more, staring at him with such intensity that he knew she was desperate to tell him something.

'I'm sorry,' he murmured, wretchedly, over and over. '*Lo siento, lo siento* . . . forgive me, I beg you.' He rocked her gently but it made her whimper in pain, so he stopped. Still she gave him that piercing look, her black eyes shining in the jewel-coloured light from the window. She raised one hand

and reached it towards the wooden pews flanking the aisle; her fingers grasped at nothing. Her hands were slender, and elegant; there was blood underneath her fingernails, and the smell of her sweat and her skin was in Jonathan's nostrils. In that moment, the only thing he was aware of, in all of existence, was the woman dying in his arms. She turned her face to her outstretched hand, murmuring in her throat, a sound too weak to be words. Then she stared back up at Jonathan for a moment, and he was looking into her eyes at the exact moment life left them. A tiny, cataclysmic shift; as simple and irreversible as the passing of time.

Her reaching arm dropped, her head lolled to the side, and Jonathan felt that he was living through the worst and blackest moment of his life. And when he followed her gaze and her gesture to the pews, and found her baby hidden there, he understood why she had bled so much, and why she had been so outraged at the thought of her own death. The child was no more than a few days old, tiny and unaware, wrapped in a grubby blanket and unharmed, untouched. Its eyes were closed, edged with black lashes; a peaceful face below a mass of dark hair. The woman had refused to accept her fate for the sake of this child but Jonathan had robbed her of everything, anyway. He lifted the baby into his arms and ran his stained finger gently down its cheek. Its skin was so soft he couldn't tell if he was touching it or not. He knew at once that any chance of saving himself lay in saving this one tiny life, pure and miraculous amidst all the corruption.

* * *

Neither Mrs Weekes nor Jonathan Alleyn seemed to notice that Starling had returned to the room. She carried a jug of bishop — warm, watered wine in which a roasted orange bobbed — and stood quietly in the doorway between the two chambers, where she heard the latter part of Jonathan's tale and all the anguish with which he told it. Mrs Weekes lifted his hand when he fell silent; she held it to her cheek, and the gesture struck Starling violently. Rachel Weekes looked so like Alice in that moment, with her face bowed and her pale hair shining, that it gave her a wrenching feeling inside. *It's because she loves him. That's what makes her look like Alice.* With this realisation came a flash of jealous fire, which lasted only an instant and was followed by a strange emptiness, like loss.

'She would forgive you. You must see that,' said Mrs Weekes.

'Would she? I think not. She wanted so much to live, for her child. She was *determined* to live, and she survived the brutal treatment she was given only to die by my hand,' said Jonathan.

'She wanted her *child* to live. That's what she wanted more than anything. The battle had nothing to do with her, but that woman gave birth to her baby amidst it all, and somehow keep her safe until that moment. And you did what she wanted – you kept Cassandra safe. I think she would forgive you.' The pair of them stared at one another for a moment, and Starling saw that Jonathan hardly dared to believe it.

'Mrs Weekes is right – what happened was an accident. You didn't rape her, you meant to save her – and you saved the babe. This was no crime,' said Starling, and at once felt that she'd intruded into their intimacy. She stiffened, and colour came into her cheeks. She deposited the jug of bishop on the side table to cover her discomfort.

'Everything that happened there was a crime,' said Jonathan.

'But not one you are responsible for,' Rachel Weekes insisted.

'Then, this story does not make you despise me?' he said. Rachel Weekes watched him steadily.

'Nothing could,' she said.

Starling saw how easily their hands stayed clasped; how unabashed they were. Their touch seemed at once casual and essential, to both of them, and Starling was excluded. Their feelings put up a barrier to her, just as the feelings between Alice and Jonathan had done, years before. She was powerless to do anything about it; she felt herself diminishing, becoming less substantial because of it. She could only watch, and try to find a voice with which to reach them.

'What will you do now, Mrs Weekes?' she said, and was surprised to hear how hard her voice sounded. Rachel Weekes looked from Jonathan to Starling and then back again, and it was her turn to show confusion.

'I must . . . I must bury my husband, and my father-in-law. I must sell the business, or find a manager. I must . . .' She frowned, letting go of Jonathan's hand and smoothing the skirts in her lap. 'I must find a situation, I suppose,' she concluded, then looked up at Jonathan Alleyn with questions writ large on her face. *She doubts him, but she dares to hope.*

'Mrs Weekes. You have some onerous tasks ahead of you. If I may be of any assistance, during any of it, you must please tell me,' said Jonathan. Rachel Weekes said nothing, but gave a tiny nod. 'I plan to leave Bath,' Jonathan went on. 'I've stayed here too long. This house has been my gaol and I would be free of it. Let my mother stay here, and reflect on all that has passed. I could go . . . I could go to the house at Box. There are tenants in it, but they may be given notice . . .' Here Jonathan paused, and glanced at Starling. 'Then again, no. Perhaps that place has as many unhappy memories as this one,' he murmured. 'I may even sell it. There are plenty of other places I could go.'

'I think a change of situation and surroundings would be most advantageous to your continued recovery, Mr Alleyn,' said Rachel Weekes, in a constricted voice that shook slightly. He studied her for a second, perplexed.

'But, Mrs Weekes . . . Rachel,' he said. 'I will go nowhere unless you will accompany me.' For a heartbeat Rachel Weekes did not react, then her smile broke over her face like the sunrise.

Starling's throat squeezed tight, aching, as she watched this exchange and felt herself sliding away from them, quite alone. Her eyes burned and she turned, stumbling blindly for the door and the corridor outside, where Mrs Alleyn waited – another invisible person, another unwanted remnant of the past, with no place in the now.

'Starling, wait!' The voice that called her back was Rachel Weekes's. Starling pivoted clumsily on her wooden feet.

'What will you do?' Rachel asked.

'I know not,' Starling replied. 'It matters not.'

'You cannot mean to serve Mrs Alleyn from now on, surely?'

'No. I shan't serve her.'

'Then . . . will you come with us instead?' *Us. Already they are become 'us'.* But they were too new an entity; it was too soon, and Mrs Weekes seemed to flounder after using the word. 'That is, will you come with me?' she corrected herself. Starling gave her as hard a look as she could find; a glare as weighty as she could make it.

'You'll have need of a servant, no doubt. Perhaps I might prove too costly for you, though,' she said. Rachel Weekes blinked, and looked hurt.

'No, I . . . have little need of a servant, in truth,' she said. 'But I have great need of a friend.' The two of them watched one another, and then Rachel Weekes smiled; a fleeting, transient expression. *She doesn't know if I will accept her or spurn her. She gives me that power.* Starling swallowed. *You cannot replace Alice.* She'd meant to say it out loud, but couldn't bring herself to. How could she, when this tall, pale creature had fought for Alice alongside her, as if she had known her, as if she too had loved her? Starling's face was frozen; she was afraid that if she moved a muscle, all would fly out of her control. 'Will you then? Come with me?' Rachel Weekes asked again. And this time Starling managed to nod.

'I will,' she said.

1807

After the fair in Corsham Jonathan dropped them off on the Batheaston side of the miller's bridge, holding Alice's hand as he helped her down. Then he flicked the reins and Starling and Alice watched him vanish into the gloaming; the haze of day's end wrapping itself gently around him, and muffling the metal ring of the pony's hooves. Alice put her arm around Starling's shoulders and they set off towards home with the slow, tired, contented feeling of a perfect day spent. The sun's remembered warmth was in the stones of the bridge; Starling put her hand on the parapet and felt it. The river was low and sluggish, easing sleepily between its banks and glowing faintly with borrowed light from a fat, baleful moon that had risen.

Alice was still humming the tune that the Irish girl had sung at the fair, and Starling picked it up.

'How did it go?' said Alice, smiling.

'*Then she made her way homeward, with one star awake, as the swan in the evening moved over the lake,*' Starling sang. 'Only this is a river, not a lake, and I can't see any swans.'

'Oh, we need not be so literal, I think.' Alice laughed.

'No, but it would have been perfect if there had been swans on the river just now.'

'Your singing voice is so lovely, little sister. Far lovelier than an actual starling's.' Starling glowed at the praise. She tipped her face up to the blue-black sky.

'There's more than one star out, too. I count . . . seven – no, eight,' she said.

'Sing some more.'

'*She laid her hand on me and this she did say, it will not be long, love, till our wedding day . . .*'

'I felt as though she was singing just for me, when I heard that song today,' said Alice, dreamily. 'I felt she was singing it just for Jonathan and me. Did you see how he blushed?'

'Yes. But don't say that – the girl in the song died, remember?'

'Oh, so literal again! Well, perhaps not that part. But the first verse, and the refrain.' Alice sighed, and then threw her arms wide, laughed again. She turned to Starling, taking both her hands and spinning her around until both were giddy and giggling. 'He loves me well, does he not?' she asked, breathlessly.

'You know he does,' said Starling, embarrassed. Alice grew calmer, her face softer, still wreathed in smiles.

' "If it were now to die, 'Twere now to be most happy . . ." Oh, I feel just like Othello, Starling! I'm so happy, I could die,' she said. 'So perhaps every word of the song *was* for me, after all.'

Starling walked on again, pulling Alice along by her hand. She couldn't place the warning she felt just then. She looked back over her shoulder but there was no one else on the bridge; no one in the lane ahead of them.

'Perhaps I'll sing the song to Bridget, when she comes home,' she said.

'You must, dearest. You know how she loves your singing, even if she won't say so. Only don't forget to say you heard it from a pedlar in the village.'

'I'll say I heard it from Dan Smithers, the bargeman. He's always warbling old tunes.'

'Good idea.' Their voices made a bird clap its wings in the leaves overhead. 'You know, Starling, when I marry Jonathan, he will be your brother.'

'He will?'

'Of course. You're my sister, so he will be your brother. Do you know what that means?' Alice glanced down at Starling, swinging her arm in time with their languorous strides. 'It means no harm can ever come to you. It means you will always be looked after, and kept safe.'

'But having you for my sister means that already, doesn't it?'

'I wish it did, dearest.' Alice turned her face to the moon; she was grey and silver, bathed in its light. 'But women alone are never safe. Not truly. It is the men who rule us that decide it all.'

'Are we not safe at Bathampton, then? You and me and Bridget?' Starling was troubled by this news.

'We are safe. But only because of Lord Faukes, and his good grace. Do you see? But when I am wed to Jonathan, then he will be our *family*. And that is the safest thing of all,' said Alice. Starling thought about this for a moment.

'A brother like him would be a good thing,' she decided. 'When will you marry him?'

Alice chuckled. 'Just as soon as I can.'

In the distance a dog barked, and they heard the clatter of a gate latch closing. Alice sighed. 'As soon as he is free, and it can be no secret, and be celebrated instead. People like him are rare, I think – people in whom the goodness runs right through. People like that should be cherished,' she said. Starling felt a little guilty as she considered this.

'*I'm* not like that,' she confessed, sombrely.

'Nor I. But we that aren't can always strive to be. And you and I can cherish each other regardless, can't we?' said Alice, putting her arm around Starling's shoulders again. They reached the George Inn, and turned along the towpath to take them back to the farmhouse. The more that Starling thought about it, the more she wanted it. She pictured life after Alice was wed, and it looked like a wide, open space in which there was freedom, and peace, and no more warnings in the back of her head. A place full of Alice's smiles, and Jonathan's pleasing laughter. 'I shall very much like having Mr Alleyn for my brother,' she said quietly, as they carried on towards home through the warm, unhurried night.

1822

By February, the three of them were ready to leave Bath. The weather had set fair, though the air was still freezing; the sun was richer, softer, seemed finally to hold the promise of a spring not too far away. With the furniture sold from the house on Abbeygate Street, Rachel watched her trunk loaded onto a cart that creaked and clattered away, just five months after it had arrived. *But how much longer it seems. A lifetime.* The cart would go on ahead of them to the new house near Shaftesbury, a market town snug in the rolling, wooded hills of Dorset. It had taken time to find a house to rent, and for Rachel to settle her husband's affairs. There was little of the business left to sell once the main part had been set against Richard's debts, left here and there all over Bath. At inns and gambling halls; with his tailor; with their landlord. The remainder of his stock, and his account books, were sold to a rival. Duncan and Richard Weekes lay side by side in the dank little cemetery on the southern edge of the city. Rachel had been there a few times over the winter, to say a prayer and lay flowers on their graves. *Would I come to the son if the father did not lie beside him?* Perhaps she would, she decided, compelled by the guilty heart of a wife who did not grieve, if nothing else.

Once the cart was out of sight Rachel went upstairs to the kitchen-cum-parlour and listened for a while. Through the walls and ceilings came all the usual muffled sounds, of voices and footsteps, scrapes and thuds, snatches of song. The shutters were closed, but a shaft of sunshine eased between them and cut across the floor. Rachel stood in the light and felt its feeble warmth. *Soon there will be nothing of either of us here but the dust we leave.* She was glad of it, she could not wait to go; and yet she felt the need to observe the moment, and not let it pass unheeded. She shut her eyes and imagined how different everything would have been if she had not, by pure chance, resembled Alice Beckwith. *I would have stayed at Hartford, unwed all my life. Or I would have lived here, married to a man made miserable by his own guilt and failings. And he would have beaten me for it, and ruined us with bad debt. I would never have known Jonathan, or Starling. Or happiness.* And the city of Bath would go on just as it ever had, and the troubles and laughter of the lives all around would carry on seeping through the walls, and she would have no part in any of it, from that day. Her boot heels were loud on the wooden boards as she left the house at last, locking it behind her and handing the key to the landlord's clerk.

At number one, Lansdown Crescent, the carriage and four was waiting in the side alley, and Falmouth was overseeing a pair of boys as they loaded and secured an array of boxes and trunks.

'I'll have that one inside with me,' Starling told Falmouth, as Rachel approached. 'Oh, never mind. I'll put it in myself,' she muttered, taking her own dowdy bag from the frigid butler and climbing up into the carriage.

'You should let them do it, Starling. You're not a servant any more,' said Rachel, smiling. Starling rolled her eyes.

'I am as I ever was – pitched halfway between gutter and gentry, and owned by neither one,' she said, climbing down again, putting her hands on her hips. She wore her plain servant's dress, but the work apron that normally covered it was gone. Her coppery hair was hidden beneath the only good hat she owned, a straw bonnet with a lilac ribbon that had previously been saved for church. 'Your things have gone on ahead?' she said.

'They have. And Mr Alleyn?'

'Around here somewhere.' As Starling spoke, Jonathan appeared in the doorway, narrowing his eyes against the light. The cut on his head, from his fall on the common, was a faint red line. *A reminder I'll always have, of how wrong it is possible to be.*

'Mrs Weekes,' he said, coming carefully down the steps. His lame leg had grown stronger, as he used it more, but stairs were still hazardous. He gripped the railings tightly, but refused to use a cane. He did not smile; there were still shadows under his eyes, and he was as pale as ever. *Come the summer that will change.*

'Mr Alleyn, are you well?'

'Tolerably.' He took her hand and kissed it.

'You have not slept,' she said.

'No. But tonight I will, I think. In a strange and blameless room.' He smiled briefly; kept hold of her hand. 'Are you ready, my dear Mrs Weekes?' he said quietly.

'I am, sir. I have been to see Captain and Mrs Sutton, to take my leave.' At mention of them, Jonathan's face darkened. Rachel squeezed his arm. 'I told them we would write to them soon. And I . . . I would speak with your mother, if I may. Just a word of farewell.'

'You will not find it a fond one.'

'No. I do not expect to.'

Rachel found Josephine Alleyn in the grand front parlour, in the exact place she'd been when Rachel first saw her — standing in the window by the now empty canary cage. *Why does she not remove it, or get another bird?* She was wearing a severe dress of midnight blue, long-sleeved and high at her neck; a swaddling of darkness to show her displeasure.

'Mrs Alleyn,' said Rachel, determined not to be cowed by her composure, or the chill that radiated from her.

'Oh, leave me be, can you not? You come to gloat, I assume.' The older lady kept her face to the window, as if determined to turn her back to everything that went on that day.

'No, madam.'

'No? And how long was your husband in the ground before you became engaged to my son?' She spoke savagely.

'Scant weeks indeed, Mrs Alleyn,' said Rachel, evenly. 'But I need not answer for it to you, I think, who'd kept Richard Weekes in thrall all his life.' At this Josephine turned at last, with a wintery smile.

'Yes. It was I that had his heart, not you. It was never you.'

'And you are welcome to it, madam.' Rachel heard her voice shake; she took a slow breath to steady it. 'To the memory of it, anyway.'

'What do you *want*, Mrs Weekes? Haven't you done enough? Haven't you stolen my son from me — and isn't that enough?'

'Can you not be happy, that he wishes to move on? That he starts to forget his pain, and has a chance of happiness now?'

'I shall never be happy to be separated from him. If that is all you came in to say, then leave me in peace and get you gone. It pleases me no end to know I will never see your face again. *That* face.'

'I pray you might,' Rachel said quietly, and Josephine frowned. 'What I came to say is this: I know the pain of losing family. I know the loneliness of believing yourself separated from them for ever. I know how you must . . . suffer, now.'

'And you delight in it?' Josephine whispered, shaking with feeling in spite of herself.

'I do not. Jonathan . . . your son knows loss and suffering too. You told me he hadn't the strength for it, and that was why he did not heal, but you were wrong. He only needed some way to set it down, and break from it. He will always remember it, but his anger will burn itself out. I believe he will forgive you, in the end; and I will try my best on your behalf. I will try to remind him of how greatly you have suffered, and how greatly you suffer still.'

For a long time Josephine only stared at her. A tremor passed through her, a shiver of pain, or revulsion, Rachel couldn't tell.

'Leave me be,' Josephine whispered.

'It will take time — he needs time. But I will not forget, I promise you. Family is too precious a thing to set aside.'

'I wish you had never come here. I wish that wretch Starling had never convinced me to let you in!' Josephine spat.

'But she did, and now all can move on. I hope . . . I hope one day your anger will also burn itself out, Mrs Alleyn. Or you risk that it consume you utterly. I . . . I will write to you, if you wish it.'

'Mrs Weekes, I have never once got any of the things I wished for.' With that, Josephine turned back to the window, her shoulders rigid above her straight spine, draped in inky darkness. She was a silhouette against the sunlight; a single still figure, like the drawing of a woman, all hollow inside.

'Farewell, Mrs Alleyn,' Rachel murmured, dropping into a curtsy that nobody saw.

Outside, Jonathan handed her up into the carriage. He frowned at her serious expression but did not ask what had passed between his betrothed and his mother. Starling sat perched on the edge of the leather bench inside, looking desperately uncomfortable, as though she ought not to have been there at all. When Sol Bradbury appeared on the servants' stair, she swore and climbed out again, rushing over to the cook and hugging her. Once she was back and seated the coachman stirred up the horses, and Starling turned to look back at the house, craning her head out of the window. Jonathan did not look back, and neither did Rachel. He gripped her hand so tightly it was almost uncomfortable, and kept his eyes set straight ahead. Rachel felt Josephine's sorrowful scrutiny like a cold shadow behind them.

'We must stop in Bathampton,' said Starling, as Lansdown Crescent passed out of view behind them. 'I must see Bridget.'

The carriage waited at the side of the Batheaston road. Jonathan and Rachel stood on the miller's bridge, against the parapet; looking west, downstream along the river. The sunlight on the water was blinding, the sky too bright to make out the edge of Bath. Below, along the riverbank, the lovers' tree stood where it ever had; a little older, a little more gnarled. It trailed its long fingers in the water, and didn't feel the chill. Rachel had imagined it as a more graceful tree, and further from the road, out of sight of passers-by. Perhaps in some secret dell somewhere. She looped her arm through Jonathan's, and waited for him to speak.

'I scratched out our initials. I wish I had not,' he said, shielding his eyes with one hand. 'I remember it now.'

'Your initials?'

'Mine and Alice's. An A and a J. We made them when we were ten years old – painstakingly, I might add. It took me hours to do. When I found the note there, after she vanished . . . I took out my knife there and then and destroyed the carving.'

'Richard Weekes's note, it must have been,' Rachel said softly. Jonathan glanced at her.

'Would it upset you to see it?'

'You have it? I thought it lost?'

'So it was. I found it as I emptied my rooms. It had fallen through a split in one of the drawers of my desk, and was caught beneath it all this time.' He handed it to her; a small square of paper, yellowed with age. She knew the writing at once, and thought of the letters Richard had written her when they were courting, all full of love and promises. That crabbed hand with each letter drawn separately, laboriously. She'd burnt them all, in one bundle and without feeling, as she'd packed up her own few things. 'Is it his hand?' Jonathan asked.

'Yes.' Rachel nodded. 'Of course it is.' He took the note back and looked down at it, frowning; it fluttered in his fingers.

'One day, only,' he said softly. 'She went to meet him for the last time the morning before my return. I missed her by just a single day.'

He read the note once more and then let the breeze take it. The paper vanished into the sunlight; they glimpsed it further downstream – a yellow fragment, hurrying away. The breeze rattled the winter trees beside the bridge; the river made a quiet slithering sound. Behind them the sluice gates were closed, the race dry, and the mill wheel sat silent and still.

'Your eyes are sad, love. Tell me your thoughts,' said Jonathan. 'Are you sorry to leave Bath behind?'

'No. How could I be?' Rachel smiled, tightening her arm around his. 'I was thinking again, as I have before, how strange it was God gave me this face. Gave it to Abi and me, and also to Alice.'

'But it is not the same face. Similar, but not the same. When I first set eyes on you, I saw Alice, but I was mad and addled then. I saw what I wanted to see. Now when I look at you, I see only Rachel.' He reached up, brushed his thumb across her cheek. 'It is this woman that I love, and she is very different to the girl I loved before. And I like to think it was fate, besides.'

'Fate?'

'Your face is the only reason we met in the first place, so it cannot be chance. It cannot be, when you are the one person who could make me . . . who could help me to be whole again.'

'I like that idea.' Rachel smiled, wryly. 'Then my first marriage was not a catastrophe, but a means to a better end,' she said. Jonathan grimaced.

'Speak not of that. Speak not of him,' he said.

'Very well,' Rachel agreed. 'No more, from this day.' She stared down in to the brilliant water, until its rushing made her dizzy. 'We have all three of us lost a sister to this river,' she murmured.

'What?'

'You, and I, and Starling. This river took Alice and Abi both, and vanished them without trace; yet it spat up Richard Weekes within hours of him entering it. Perhaps the river has a spirit that only welcomes the good of heart, and rejects the others.' She saw Jonathan's face darken, as it did at any mention of his blood relationship to Alice, or when Richard Weekes was named. 'Forgive me,' she said hurriedly. 'I thought out loud, and should guard my words better.'

'No, never do that,' said Jonathan. 'Never guard your words – promise me. There has already been far too much of that in my life. Always say what you think, and what you feel, and I will do the same. Even if you think I would rather not hear it. Promise me.'

'Very well. I promise it,' said Rachel. She looked up at Jonathan's serious expression; saw the cares that still crowded him. 'My heart had been half dead since my family died. For years, that part of me slept . . . but you woke it, Jonathan,' she murmured. She put her fingertips to his mouth and felt his breath catch; he pulled her hand away and kissed her lips. A soft and silent kiss that made the sky widen and the ground seem deeper; that pushed the world away from them, because only they could know the elation it caused. When they broke apart it was not far. Jonathan curled his hand around the back of Rachel's neck and leant his forehead to hers, with his eyes closed, serene.

When she heard footsteps, Rachel looked up reluctantly. 'Look, here she comes,' she said. Starling was coming along the lane from Bathampton, carrying her hat in one hand, its lilac ribbons trailing out behind her. The sun shone in her red hair, and made her squint. Suddenly, for the first time, Rachel could see how young she still was. Without her anger she seemed less certain, more tentative and anxious. Her diffidence around Jonathan bordered on shyness. *She knew how to act when she could hate him. Now, she doesn't know.*

'Did you see her? Was she well?' Rachel asked her. Starling nodded, and took a position next to Rachel, leaning over the bridge.

'Yes. She . . . wept when I told her of Alice's fate but she thanked me also. For giving her the truth of it, once and for all. She even . . . she even said sorry. For not believing me all these years when I said Alice was slain.' Starling cast a guilty glance at Jonathan.

'Will she be all right, do you think?' said Rachel.

'She will grieve, of course. Her health is not improved, but spring is coming. I told her I would send word when we arrive; I told her I would send money.'

'She does not wish to travel into Dorsetshire with us? Some lodgings could be found, I am sure . . .' said Jonathan, but Starling shook her head.

'Too old to travel, she claims. Bathampton is her home. She—' Starling cut herself off, frowning and examining the stonework. She gouged a strip of lichen from a crevice with her thumbnail, so Rachel knew that she didn't like what she had to say next. 'It was Bridget that took Alice's letters. Her rosewood box . . . On Faukes's order, after I let slip to him that you and Alice wrote to each other, sir. She took the box and gave it to him, soon after Alice vanished. He did not give her a reason. I suppose they wanted to destroy all evidence of the bond between them. Between you and Alice, sir.'

'But . . . she knew all this while you were searching for them!' said Rachel.

'She said she feared to tell me,' said Starling, sounding puzzled. Rachel smiled at her.

'Yes. In her place, I think I would have feared to tell you too.'

'I am not so very fierce,' said Starling.

'You are.' Rachel and Jonathan spoke near in unison. Rachel put a hand on Starling's arm, apologetically. 'That is, you were.'

For a while they watched the water, each lost in their own thoughts. Then Starling asked, tentatively:

'Mr Alleyn, did Alice ever tell you anything about where I came from? I often asked if she'd ever found anything out, or if anybody had come looking for me, but she always denied it. I thought, perhaps, she had found out something she did not want me to know . . .'

'No.' Jonathan shook his head. 'No, she did not. As far as I know, she never tried to find out. She was too afraid that she would uncover some reason to have to give you up.'

'Then I will never know,' said Starling.

'I'm sorry, Starling,' said Rachel.

'No, do not be. I . . . I am quite happy not to know. It was something Alice and I used to share – the mystery of our undisclosed beginnings. Look what sorrow finding hers out brought her. I would rather my story started when she picked me up out of the mud at the farmhouse that day. That is the only history I need; the only family.'

'There's wisdom there,' said Jonathan.

'And look – look what Bridget gave me.' Starling took a small, cloth-bound book from her pocket. 'One of Alice's poetry books – one that she often read from. Bridget hid it about her when we were removed and the house cleared out. She also wanted a keepsake. When she told me about Alice's letters, and I said I had so longed to have something of hers . . . She felt bad about it and gave me this book.' She handed it to Rachel with due reverence. 'Look inside the cover.'

'*This book belongs to Alice Beckwith, and it is her favourite – pray do not leave it out in the rain, Starling,*' Rachel read, and smiled. The handwriting was small and precise, slanting forwards elegantly.

'I did the very thing with another one of hers – a novel she'd been teaching me to read from. It was quite ruined,' said Starling.

'So there – you have a letter of hers, of sorts, and one addressed to you,' said Rachel.

'And this proves that she lived. This means she can never be forgot.'

'She never would have been,' Jonathan said quietly. 'So, then, I can let this one go. You do not mind?' He took Alice's last letter from his coat pocket. 'I . . . I do not want to keep it. Her last words to me should not be ones of such sadness and pain.' Starling stared hungrily at the letter for a moment, but then she shook her head.

'You are right. It should not be kept to remind us,' she said. Jonathan smoothed the paper between his fingertips for a moment, as if to remember the feel of it. Then he let it go into the water, without another word. They watched it spin away in silence.

When it was out of sight, Starling hung her arms over the parapet and stared down at the lovers' tree. Jonathan and Rachel had already taken their leave of the place, and so they waited for some sign that she was ready, and did not hurry her. It went unspoken between them that they would never return to that same spot; that it must stay in the past, and not haunt the future. So they waited, and the breeze fluttered Starling's lilac ribbons, and the red strands of her hair; and in distant treetops rooks clattered and muttered to one another. Then, with a whistling rush of air, a pair of swans flew low over the bridge and skated down onto the water, sending up dazzling waves from their feet. They were incandescent with light. Calmly, the birds folded back their wings, crooked their necks and moved into the gentler current near the bank. Starling gasped and watched them intently; then she turned to Rachel and Jonathan, smiling unguardedly.

'Come, let's not linger here any more,' she said. Jonathan nodded, and they moved away towards where the carriage waited, and did not look back.

Acknowledgements

As ever, my profound thanks go to the whole team at Orion for all their expertise, support and hard work, and especially to Eleanor Dryden and Genevieve Pegg for their enthusiastic, insightful and exacting treatment of the manuscript. Many, many thanks to my agent Nicola Barr for being so talented, skilful and patient.

A big thank you to my friends and family, who are always behind me all the way, handing out books and only ever feeding back the good comments; and this time especially to Sarah Green, for her infectious enthusiasm about Bath and her guided walks – even with that knee.

The Misbegotten

Reading Group Notes

About the Author

Katherine Webb was born in 1977 and grew up in rural Hampshire before reading History at Durham University. She has since spent time living in London and Venice, and now lives in Wiltshire. Having worked as a waitress, au pair, personal assistant, book binder, library assistant, seller of fairy costumes and housekeeper, she now writes full time. Her first novel, *The Legacy*, was a Channel 4 TV Book Club pick for 2010 and won the popular vote for Best Summer Read.

The Story Behind The Misbegotten

In the summer of 2011 I moved to a stone cottage, built in around 1820, in a village near Bath. I love old buildings, and as I set about redecorating and getting to know the place, my imagination tried to conjure up all the people who had lived here before me; what their lives might have been like, and how different it would have looked. I also spent a lot of time wandering around Bath and getting to know it better — I'd visited several times before, and read books set there. It's a place rich in history, full of unspoilt Georgian architecture. As I enjoyed my new surroundings, I suddenly had the mental image of a man and a woman, meeting on a frosty morning at around the time my cottage was built. Their meeting was charged with unsaid things, and secret anguish. This pair became Rachel Weekes and Jonathan Alleyn, and they were the seeds of a story that was beginning to grow.

It's impossible to miss Bath's connection with Jane Austen, especially if one has read those novels of hers that she set in the city. There are museums and festivals dedicated to her, and you sometimes see fans wandering about in Regency costume, just for the fun of it. There is a frisson to be felt, walking the streets that Austen and her characters walked, and seeing views of the city which, despite terrible bombing during World War II, are largely unchanged since that time. But I also feel that our modern obsession with Austen's stories has become a bit rose-tinted. I knew at once that the story I wanted to write was one firmly rooted in its era (actually a little after Austen's time) — that is to say, one in which the highly precarious position of women was made plain. Women had little choice, except in rare cases, but to rely wholly upon men for their position in society, their security and well-being. As a modern, independent woman, this really hit home to me as I began my research. I knew that this hard truth, and the ways in which my characters would deal with it, would be central to the story.

Starling appeared to me exactly as she does in the book — a starving, barefoot child wandering into the story with no past and no name. In a story about sisterhood, and loyalty in the face of persecution, Starling is the fiercest embodiment of both. Since she has nothing but a history of abuse until Alice takes her in, their relationship is an unusual and very intense one. They are not related, and yet Starling sees Alice as her big sister. In some ways Alice is also the mother figure in her life, the one to whom she owes whatever sense of security she has about the world. So, when Alice is taken from her, her reaction is every bit as intense. She absolutely cannot, and will not, accept what she is told when it runs contrary to what she believes about Alice. She is also a very knowing character — in some ways, she is both older and more worldly than her 'big sister'. She has good instincts about people, particularly people in positions of power, and the terrible things they are capable of doing. But in spite of Starling's strength, intelligence and grim determination, losing Alice leaves her very alone, very vulnerable.

I wanted Rachel to have lived a wholly different life to Starling, right up until the day they meet. Her situation is one that must have been very commonplace at the time: she has been raised in comfort by a good family that has since fallen on hard times, so she has been forced into employment as a governess. Without family or fortune, her marriage prospects would have been very bleak, so she 'marries down', accepting a proposal from a lower-class man whom she hopes is honest and industrious and 'on the up'. But things get worse after she marries, not better. I wanted to try and understand how it must have felt, in a time when you relied on your husband for everything, and divorce was practically unheard of, to realise that you have married the wrong man. That you have married a violent man, and that you're stuck with him for the rest of your life. I (who am rather averse to commitment!), could well imagine that the feeling of being trapped must have been all but unbearable.

Starling and Rachel have taken the only options available to them, as women without independent fortune: marriage, or service (they could also, of course, have fallen into beggary or prostitution…). They are both grieving for lost loved ones, they both long for family, for security; to feel that they are not alone in the world, that someone else is on their side. Two such different women were never going to become friends immediately, but given time, would they find the solution to some of their problems in each other?

I wanted Jonathan Alleyn to remind these two women that there are good men in the world as well as bad! The damage that war inflicts on men is a theme I have touched upon before in my fiction, and I think it's one of the major ways, historically speaking, that men were also trapped and had little choice. True to say, Jonathan didn't have to join the army, but, coming from a distinguished military family, he would certainly have felt pressure to. It is manly, after all, to show valour in battle. We have well-documented evidence of the terrible treatment meted out to men who didn't want to fight at the time of World War I, and a hundred years earlier the charge of cowardice would have been an even graver stain on a man's honour. And, in those days, there was certainly no understanding of post-traumatic stress, or shell shock. Once he's in the army, Jonathan must fight, even if he discovers that he abhors it. Even if it damages him dreadfully. A lot of historical military campaigns also seem to have been blighted by a lack of food and supplies, and of course medical care was not what it is now, which left men at the mercy of disease, the enemy and the elements — facing death from all sides in a foreign land. I struggle to comprehend just how terrifying battle must be, both then and now, and my heart breaks at the thought of all those gentle young people who must have been shattered by the experience.

So, *The Misbegotten* is a mystery about the disappearance of a young girl, and the lengths a noble family will go to keep their secrets safe; but at its heart it is a story about loyalty, loss, and three people who are all, in their own ways, dealing with the consequences of society's constraints upon them. It is, perhaps by necessity, the darkest story I have written to date; but ultimately, I hope readers will be uplifted. For a lot of poor or unwell people in 1820, there would have been no happy ending, but I grew so fond of my characters that I had to give at least some of them a brighter future than that!

Katherine Webb, 2013

For Discussion

- How does the author use the weather and landscape to set the scene at the beginning of *The Misbegotten*?

- 'How strange and limited a kind of freedom marriage might be.' To what extent is *The Misbegotten* about the plight of women in 19th-century England?

- 'A thing that is born wild, stays wild, and can never be entirely trusted.' Is this true of Starling, do you think?

- 'There must be some joy in life, must there not? You must allow some happiness, or 'tis all for naught.' To what extent is the novel about the search for happiness?

- How has the author demonstrated the difference between Lansdown Crescent and Abbeygate Street to us?

- How does the author use betrayal as a theme in *The Misbegotten*?

- 'The older one gets, the more power memory has to enthral, I find. To enthral, and sometimes to overpower.' What does this tell us of Mrs Alleyn?

- 'The truth will set us free.' Will it?

- 'We are just machines.' What does this tell us of Jonathan and his experience of life?

- To what extent is *The Misbegotten* a novel about family?

- 'Hate, love. Aren't they oft-times the same thing?' What does this tell us of Richard?

- 'But you should not forgive indiscriminately. People must pay for their crimes.' Does this say more about Jonathan than Rachel? Or is she too ready to forgive?

In Conversation with Katherine Webb

Q Are you Rachel or Starling or both?

A I'm probably more Rachel than Starling. Starling is so tough, and so unconcerned about other people's opinions of her. She's been through some terrible things in the early years of her life, and they've left her understandably angry and unforgiving. She has a far bleaker view of the world and the people in it than I do. Rachel was born into a comfortable family and raised by loving parents, and even though she has since then been forced to change her life completely, she still relies on the manners and social conventions she was brought up with to inform her own behaviour. I'm a bit like that! Far too polite sometimes; far too ready to compromise, to swallow emotion and maintain a stiff upper lip...

Q Silence or music while you write? If music – who do you listen to?

A Always silence when I'm actually writing; any music is just a distraction. But with this book, I got completely obsessed with Joby Talbot's haunting original soundtrack to the film *Franklyn*. For some reason, it exactly embodied the mood I was trying to create at certain points in the book. I would listen to it to get into the right frame of mind if, for example, I'd woken up in a bright and sunny mood, but needed to write a dark or unsettling part of the story.

Q 'To lie is a terrible thing.' Is it always?

A No. Little white lies are harmless and necessary, I find, in a hundred everyday interactions. They smooth out arguments, save people's feelings, and generally help things tick along. But big lies – those are quite a different matter. Lies about things that actually matter – things that other people might base an important decision or opinion on, that might affect the way they think or feel about a person or a situation . . . those are a big no-no. And they always come back to bite you, sooner or later; even if they seem to make life easier at the time.

Q Which authors do you admire and why?

A I find something to admire in pretty much every book I read – and I read a lot. I know how difficult writing a novel is, so I appreciate the hard work of others! The writers I really enjoy are the ones whose books hold me completely captivated, so that I forget that I'm reading and feel like I am actually inside the story; who make me care so deeply about their characters that I develop genuine feelings for them, be they positive or negative. Some favourites include Ian McEwan, Jim Crace, Margaret Atwood, Helen Dunmore, Kate Atkinson, Sir Terry Pratchett, Pat Barker, Rose Tremain and Andrea Levy. Justin Cronin thoroughly creeped me out with *The Passage* recently; and I was riveted to Gillian Flynn's

Gone Girl. I also loved *Pure* by Andrew Miller – it just blew me away. I'm always so impressed when an author, apparently effortlessly and with such lightness of touch, can recreate a historical setting like that. I was very envious after reading it!

Q 'She only needs an excuse, sometimes, to let out what's inside her. She only needs a reason to release it, and reset the balance.' How did you set about creating Alice?

A What I wanted to convey about Alice is that here is a sweet, cheerful soul, very loving and giving, who is only just realising the true nature of her situation . . . As children, we don't question what we're told, or the way we're taught to live. Alice has been raised in comfort, and educated to the normal degree of young ladies at the time; she has a mother figure in Bridget, a father figure in her lofty, beloved benefactor, Lord Faukes; she has village life in Bathampton to give her a sense of community.

But at the time Starling comes into her life, when she is in her late teens, Alice is finally starting to question those things she doesn't have – answers about her real parents, her prospects; her lack of freedom to go beyond the bounds of Bathampton, to have close friends, marry, or really take part in society. She has begun to realise that her life is controlled, that she has no freedom, and no rights. Her anger and her frustration at this are at odds with her naturally buoyant personality. She keeps these negative emotions hidden, for the most part, and distracts herself with poetry and projects (like adopting Starling!), but they're always there, inside her, increasing all the time. I wanted to communicate her troubled state – that here is a gentle person trying to be good, ill-equipped to deal with a growing inner turmoil.

Q What comes first for you – plot or character?

A It's very hard to separate the two, but I think the answer is character. The very first spark that became *The Misbegotten* was the mental image of a man and a woman meeting beneath frost-covered trees, having terribly important things to say to each other but not being able to say them. Starling came next, walking into the story as a barefoot child . . . From these sketchy beginnings the plot developed, as these skeleton characters come to life, and I come to understand what they mean to each other, and how their lives intersect. Interestingly, the season in which a story will be set always comes to me at that very earliest of stages; and once it's made itself known, it never changes.

Q Does misery long for company?

A Sometimes! It's such a personal thing. When I'm feeling really down and despairing, I'm best left alone to work my way through it. People trying to 'cheer me up' only makes me feel worse, because I can see them trying and failing, so I feel guilty to boot . . . But humans are social animals, after all, and I think if I had a well-defined problem, one that actually needed a solution – like Starling has with her quest for the truth about Alice – my impulse would be to find somebody to help me with it, and share it.

Q How did you physically write *The Misbegotten*?

A I write directly into my laptop. I have a workbook full of scribbled notes which I have to have open beside me, even if it's no help at all – it gives the illusion of planning and forethought when, to a large degree, I'm never quite sure exactly what I will write until I write it! I work from a good outline of the plot, but from scene to scene the books evolve very organically. It's better that I type – my handwriting is atrocious. Half the time I can't read my own notes.

Q Do you believe in signs, portents?

A No, not really. It's so tempting to . . . but ultimately I believe our lives are lived by chance and coincidence, not by fate or destiny. The habit is easy to get into, though. I've only just stopped saluting magpies, having caught the habit from a school friend twenty-five years ago! I told myself for years that I only did it 'just in case', but I've finally forced myself to stop. They're just birds . . . they're just birds . . . I do believe in gut feelings though – I believe they're the subconscious picking up clues from other people and situations and reacting to them, even when we can't logically process the information in thought.

Q How did you go about creating such a strong sense of time and place?

A I've read historical novels where the author has been so caught up in their research and in bringing a historical scene to life that the period details become conspicuous, laboured. And I have read historical novels that wear their research so lightly that you hardly even notice it, and yet are utterly convinced . . . I was aiming for the latter. It would be easy to describe every little thing in a room, or about a character's dress or views, with the kind of obsessive wonder of a time traveller, dropped into that scene and seeing it through modern eyes; but I think that rather gives the game away – it makes both the author and the reader just such wide-eyed observers – voyeurs on the characters of a story, rather than living it with them, if that makes sense.

I wanted to describe the minutiae of life in the 1820s no more than I would if I was writing a contemporary setting, but make sure that those details I did include were completely right for the era. It's also crucial that characters speak and behave in historically appropriate ways, although, obviously, it can only ever be my interpretation of two-hundred-year-old speech and behaviour – it's likely that Starling and Richard would have talked to each other in a slang that would be hard for modern readers to follow. There's a fine line to be trodden! I hope that readers will be immersed in the historical settings without feeling that I've hit them over the head with them. I hope that they will be as emotionally engaged with and understanding of these characters as they would contemporary ones. I hope they will feel transported into the past, rather than that they've been told what it might have looked like.

Q 'It is only secrets that scare us. It is not knowing; it is the things we cannot see.' To what extent is *The Misbegotten* about truth?

A It seems to be a characteristic of human beings that we can't bear not knowing things, especially if we think other people around us do know! I don't mean the esoteric secrets of the cosmos etc. – I'm quite content not knowing about them. But if someone said they knew an incredible thing about my sister . . . and then wouldn't tell me? Torture! And frightening, too. So we feel a nagging urge to hear about what our favourite media personalities have been up to, and to keep up to date with the lives of fictional television characters; and if something does occur to our nearest and dearest, then the need to know about it can and does become all-consuming. Even if we're told it doesn't matter . . . it still does. It's this urge, this need, that I wrote about in *The Misbegotten*.

Starling knows she's been lied to about the fate of the one person she cared more about than anyone else on earth – how can she be expected to accept that? And Rachel, too, has this need to know – hers is more deeply buried, more distant at first; but gets stronger the more she comes to care about Jonathan, and the more she learns about Alice. Their shared need for truth is what drives the story, and what drives them to act. So, yes, truth and the pursuit of it are central to the book.

Q 'Women alone are never safe. Not truly. It is the men who rule us that decide it all.' What made you want to explore the life of women in early 19th-century England?
A There are certain things about any historical era that you, as a citizen of the 21st century, will notice at once – the things that have changed the most between then and now. As a writer, it's hard to ignore those things. For example,

it's almost impossible to write about Victorian or Edwardian England without writing about class structures in some way. With the early 19th century, what struck me most were the lives of women, and how different they were — subject to such comprehensive restrictions on their behaviour, their rights, their independence. Women could be and often were horribly abused, and had little or no recourse to law, and precious few ways to remove themselves from the situation. Of course, class was in the mix as well — if a lower-class woman was abused by a rich and powerful man, she was even more helpless.

I suppose I really wanted to highlight this because the injustice of it is so glaring, so galling to me with all my rights and freedoms. And I also feel that this era is often misrepresented. We (particularly women) have generally seen a good few gorgeous adaptations of Jane Austen's novels, where the focus is on the romance, the manners and scandal, the beautiful costumes . . . I'm sure a good many of us have at one time or another secretly wished to be Lizzy Bennet, but in truth it would have been an awful era in which to be a woman.

Q Any clues about your next book — any snippets for us?
A It's set in Puglia, southern Italy, in the 1920s — a time when the area was restless and poverty-stricken, and fascism was closing its fist around the whole country. It concerns a rich widow with a secret; a powerful landowning family at war with the underclasses; an English architect and his impressionable young wife, and a careless love affair that will all but destroy them all.

Suggested Further Reading

Jane Eyre by Charlotte Brontë

North and South by Elizabeth Gaskell

Les Misérables by Victor Hugo

Pride and Prejudice by Jane Austen

A Tale of Two Cities by Charles Dickens